HIS ARMS TIGHTENED. BIG STRONG A   LIT twitched with delight. I gritted my teeth   to ignore it. I do have a brain in my head and I'm not about to let my nether parts tell me whom to sleep with.

Against my will, my left hand left the confines of my right armpit where I stuck it for protection. It slid sensuously up over his chest and shoulder before it slowly wrapped itself around his neck.

To my complete surprise and mortification, I buried my hand in his hair and brought my head closer to his.

"Why can't I stop myself?" I asked just before I pressed my lips against his.

"You find me irresistible," he growled against my mouth. His voice was compelling. The low timber crawled through my body like a living thing. It made me want to do all sorts of interesting things with this man. His tongue dueled with mine, both of us wanted to win a war of dominance.

When our lips met, I felt much as I did with Brock, but with Micah, I felt...more. I wanted to kiss him, to fondle him. To know I gave satisfaction as much as I was receiving it.

With Brock, it had been different. I had wanted nothing more than to feel his huge cock as it pounded inside me.

"Stop thinking of other men," Micah said, against my mouth, then playfully nipped at my lips.

I looked around and noticed, for the first time, that I was lying on my bed. Either I hadn't paid attention while he searched the upstairs for my room or he had a great sense of direction. I'm pretty sure it was the former.

I pulled away and fought for my next breath. I needed space. I needed to get away from him to think. I couldn't concentrate when he was so close, when I could feel the heat from his body as it seeped into mine. It sent little licks of flame through my blood.

It wasn't normal that he could read my mind. Sure, I've heard of telepathy, but I've never met anyone with it. The whole idea was absurd. If I believe that, the next thing he'll tell me is that we can communicate without talking. It was all I could do, not to snort.

He ran his hand through my hair and pushed my bangs back from my face to look into my eyes.

"You must rid yourself of your virginity. It is a weakness—a weapon that can be held against you."

The Chosen
Copyright © 2008Tianna Xander
ISBN: 978-1-55487-116-2
Cover art and design by Martine Jardin

Published by eXtasy Books
Look for us online at:
www.Extasybooks.com

Library and Archives Canada Cataloguing in Publication

Xander, Tianna, 1963-
    The chosen / Tianna Xander.

ISBN 978-1-55487-116-2

    I. Title.

PS3624.A54C48 2008   813'.6   C2008-905606-X

THE CHOSEN

VIRGIN's BLOOD

BY

TIANNA XANDER

Dedication
To my husband, Kevin, my real life hero.

Chapter One

NEVER TAKE SIX THOUSAND DOLLARS WITH YOU TO A DRUG DEALER. He *will* kill you for it. I filed this little bit of information away in my mind as I hurried to cram stacks of money into my book bag.

I searched the place for possible evidence. I didn't want anyone to be able to place me here and was glad we brought Trina's car instead of mine. At least it would be harder for the police to put me at the scene of the crime.

I stuffed the cash in my bag. In my hurry, it was hard to tell just how much of it was ours, since Marco stacked it all together.

Besides, I figured since I'd have to run for the rest of my life, I might as well get off to a good start. Several thousand dollars in cash should get me somewhere.

I reached over to the filthy counter, stretched my arm over a barstool and picked up a used napkin with some sort of red sauce smudged on it. It was probably pizza sauce. Several flat, square boxes littered the filthy floor and table.

"It's a good thing Marco always used linen," I mumbled to myself, while I wiped the place clean of my fingerprints.

My gaze dropped to the still warm body draped over that of my recently deceased friend. I rubbed my eyes. The scene of him raping her as she died replayed in my mind.

"He got what he deserved."

It was a poor attempt to rationalize what I'd done. I looked down at Trina and wiped my hand over my face.

"Bye, Trina. I love you, Sis."

I turned my gaze to Marco, scowled down at him and drew my foot back. The urge to kick him was almost overpowering. I stared down at my bag, searching for a reason to curb my desire.

Does cocaine get stale? I frowned at the inane thought. Well, it isn't like anyone will be eating it. So what does it matter? I toyed with the idea of taking

1

some, then decided against it. It was a temptation, but I didn't sit through ten days of withdrawal for nothing.

Stepping over the two bodies entangled together like lovers, I smiled and gave in to the urge to kick Marco's filthy carcass away from Trina. He landed on his back beside her.

I couldn't bear the sight of his naked ass across her body any longer. The vision it inspired was cheap. Like she'd been in such a hurry to have him inside her, she wouldn't even let him take off his clothes. His black designer jeans were bunched around his ankles and caught on his expensive Italian boots.

That's how I found them, Marco grunting over Trina's body as she died. His shirt unbuttoned and pants still on, sweating cocaine as he rammed himself into her.

Trina's head fell to the side and she stared at me through nearly lifeless eyes. When I saw the ring of bruises around her neck, I lost it.

I grabbed Marco's gun, a .45, I think. It was big, heavy and already equipped with a silencer. I aimed it at his head and closed my eyes as I squeezed the trigger. It jerked in my hand, making a strange spitting noise. Stunned, I dropped the gun to the floor.

The sound of Trina's gasp brought my eyes to her face. It was nearly purple from lack of oxygen. The bastard must have crushed her windpipe. Her chest heaved with the effort to draw in one lifesaving breath.

"I love you, Tash," Trina mouthed before she closed her eyes for the last time.

I didn't feel much when I finally looked down. Marco stared at the floor, his chin propped on Trina's shoulder. There was just the immense satisfaction of knowing I killed the asshole that just murdered my best friend.

My only friend.

Now, I'm alone. The thought filled me with dread. How can I go on alone again?

I gathered my thoughts together, turned my head and lowered my eyes to my bag. I grabbed it, slung it up over my back with one arm through the strap and hitched it up onto my shoulder. Then I turned to give Marco one last glance.

"It didn't have to end like this, you prick. You would have gotten most of the money anyway."

Marco didn't answer me, of course. He'd landed on his back when I kicked him and his eyes were blank as he stared at the smoke stained ceiling. I shuddered with distaste. He was my first and, with any luck, my last kill.

I never asked for this. When Marco found out how much money Trina had on her, he probably figured it would be an easy stash to steal. He hadn't planned on me. Since I wanted to kick the expensive habit, I usually stayed home, but something told me to come this time.

When my father disappeared, his lawyer had sent me a quarterly check for twelve-thousand dollars. Half of which, I gave to Trina to clean herself up and get her off the streets. She didn't want to quit. Instead, she brought the whole six-grand with her tonight.

If all Marco wanted was the money, I know Trina would have given it to him. Her sense of self-preservation was as strong as anyone's. But she would have drawn the line at rape and murder. She was a druggy, not a masochist.

I finally gave in to the urge for just one more taste. I picked a pinch of coke from the table and snorted it. Why not? It's good stuff and it definitely wasn't going to do Marco any good in Hell.

I took one more glance around the place, drew a deep breath to steady my nerves and wrinkled my nose. The metallic odor of blood hung in the air and an aura of death surrounded the bodies. Gooseflesh rose on my arms.

The coffee table, which had escaped my notice before, had two plastic bags on it. Obviously ripped open during Trina's struggle with Marco, they lay open on the tabletop and cocaine dusted the room. It was everywhere, with the exception of where I wiped it clean of my prints.

Little paw prints made their way across a table and a few thin skid marks crisscrossed the counter. I picked the gun back up from where I'd dropped it and wiped it clean, sure to remove all of my prints from the weapon I borrowed.

I may be blonde, but I'm definitely not stupid. Okay, so maybe I'm dumb for doing drugs, but I have tried to quit. Besides I'm not crazy enough to leave any of my fingerprints at the scene of what the authorities are bound to call a double homicide.

Gingerly stepping back over their bodies, and mindful of the puddle of blood around Marco's head, I didn't see the blur of orange until it was too late. I nearly tripped over his damn cat. It arched its back, hissed at me and spit its opinion of my failure to see him when I stepped on his tail. It looked at me through eyes it could barely hold open. The left eye danced around inside of its head, bouncing around like a pinball on crack.

"Getting a little high, Kitty?" I giggled. The little bit of coke I'd snorted from the table started to take effect. It made me a bit giddy. But just a bit, I'd only snorted enough to make a newbie high.

Or just enough to make me have my withdrawal symptoms start all over, I thought with a sigh. When will I ever learn to think things through?

"Whew, Toots! Now I know where you got your name." I gasped as I waved my hand in front of my face.

The tabby staggered off. It slipped haphazardly through the blood and cocaine, leaving little red footprints behind him. The smell got stronger and I plugged my nose. I turned, shook my head and picked my way through the garbage on the floor. The last thing I needed was to slip on this filth and break something.

Then where would I be?

Jail, that's where.

"I have to get out of here," I mumbled and tripped over the damned cat again as I headed for the back. "Oh, God, Toots. Go put a cork in it or something!"

Apparently cocaine gives cats gas. Who knew?

When I finally reached the backdoor, I flipped up the hood of my sweat jacket to cover my gold-blonde hair that tends to shine like neon in the glow of the streetlights. I used the soiled napkin, still in my hand, to turn the knob and stepped out into the rain.

THREE HOURS LATER, BEFORE the withdrawal symptoms began, I was smart enough to realize if I didn't quit cold turkey, I would never manage to quit at all. I knew from experience that the pain would be even worse in a few hours. I decided to hide my keys. Later, I'd be tempted to drive back to Marco's and try to break in for another hit.

I promptly stashed my keys and hoped I'd be too far gone by that time to look in my mother's old sewing desk for them.

On my way back to the living room, someone rang the bell. I didn't think and opened the door before I looked through the little peephole.

Imagine my surprise to see a cop standing on my stoop. My knees went weak as I wondered how they found out about me so soon.

Oh, shit!

Visions of international orange jumpsuits with County Jail emblazoned on the back, in big black letters, danced through my head and I promptly fainted.

"Miss, can you hear me?"

The muffled question swam through my mind, as I sifted through a nightmare of darkness, snakes and bugs. My skin itched as the sensation of swarming insects crawling over me heightened. I screamed within my nightmare and searched for a way out.

I spied a sliver of light and reached for it. Even death was preferable to this torment. But it wasn't death that awaited me as I opened one burning eye.

At least I wasn't in Hell, unless, of course, Hell is comprised of an eighteen-hundred-square-foot house in the suburbs of Grand Rapids. But I didn't think so. Turing my head, I wondered absently how I ended up on the couch and got another glimpse of the cop.

Oh.

He sat perched on the edge of my coffee table.

If I'm not in Hell, he's sure to think he is if he doesn't get his ass off my grandma's glass-topped table.

"Get off of that!" I glared at him. "I don't even put my feet on it."

Of course I don't. Grandpa made it for Gram. I'd be damned if I'd see it ruined by some cop's ass. No matter how cute an ass it may be.

He was hot. I tried to ignore how incredibly delicious he looked in his uniform and resisted the urge to fan myself.

His thick, blond hair made my fingers itch to see if it was as soft as it looked and ice-blue eyes gazed at me from an open, boy-next-door face. Well over six feet tall—a pre-requisite for dating, since I'm five ten—he was the epitome of handsome. I closed my eyes and gave a mental shrug.

He probably just appeared taller as I keeled over earlier. People do tend to appear a bit bigger while you're peering up at them from the floor at their feet.

His silver-blue eyes gleamed, even twinkled at me for a bit, as he watched me. Then his mouth drew down at the corners. How can a person frown and still have their eyes twinkle at the same time?

I damn sure wasn't going to ask him.

"How long has it been?" he asked, as he inspected me with an interest that was somewhat more than professional.

He kind of gave me the creeps looking at me like that. I squirmed under his scrutiny.

Hey, I was attracted to him and all. Hell. Who wouldn't be? The man resembled a Greek God, but there was something scary about him I couldn't put my finger on. I stared up at him and blinked.

"Since what?" Heat rushed to my cheeks. If he mentioned sex, my troubles would be over because I'd die of mortification right here on the spot.

"How long has it been since your last fix?"

He reached up, took his hat off and pushed long fingers through that glorious thatch of blond hair. He looked frustrated about something.

I avoided his stare because I don't lie well. I never have. I could only hope he would attribute my inability to hold his gaze to my withdrawal symptoms. Otherwise, I'd be in some really deep doo doo.

If I don't count that little snack after offing Marco...

"Well?" He raised his brow.

"About forty-eight hours. Why?" I tilted my head to the side, pushed my hair back over my shoulder and peered up at him, curious.

He stood up and paced the room and my gaze followed his tall, lean frame. I couldn't help but admire the way he moved. I loved to watch as his thick muscles rippled under his uniform.

His pure, sensual grace as he crossed the room was enough to make me drool. The rise and fall of his nicely rounded cheeks under his slacks made me squirm in my seat.

What in the hell has gotten into me? I shifted my gaze away with a frown. A nymphomaniac, I am not!

"Sit down, will you? You're making me dizzy." I shook my head as he started to walk toward me. "So help me, God, if you park your butt on my coffee table again, I'll bean you. It's disrespectful for you to sit down on that table. You should know better."

I surprised myself. I'm not usually so mouthy. I guess the knowledge that he most likely had orders to arrest me no matter what I said, gave me a bravado I normally wouldn't have had.

He made a detour to the wing chair in the corner and lowered himself slowly into the seat. His gaze burned a trail over my flesh as it traveled slowly and deliberately up and down my body.

I shivered as I imagined what it would be like to have his hands and mouth on my skin instead of just that heated gaze. I sat up and gave him my best *come hither* look. It must have lost something in the translation because he just sat there, his face blank.

A drop of perspiration ran down my temple and I wiped it away. I was so covered in sweat, I could have been in a sauna instead of my living room. To top it all off, I shook more than San Francisco during a seven-pointer. Not that I know much about it since I've never been there. So that may or may not be an apt analogy.

"Are you going to tell me why you're here? If you planned to bust me for possession," I coughed out what passed for a laugh, "you're obviously too late."

He didn't even crack a smile, he just stood and stared at me as he waited for my answer.

I took a deep breath, let the air out on a rush and blew the bangs out of my face. At that moment, I just wanted to curl up into a little ball and die. My life, having never been great, was suddenly in the toilet and circling the drain. I might have let Marco kill me last night, if it wouldn't have included the defilement of my dead body. A shudder of distaste traveled through me. Marco was a pig.

"I'm trying to quit. My last hit made me sick." That wasn't a total lie. I did throw up two miles or so down the road from Marco's, before I called the cab. But I'm pretty sure it was more from having to run those two miles, or nerves, than the drugs.

My drug-deprived mind played tricks on me. The officer stood up, raised his hands to his waist and began to remove his clothes. His uniform top and t-shirt came off first.

I marveled at the site of his well-honed abdominal muscles. I never realized a six-pack could be so sexy. Then his gun belt hit the hardwood floor with a loud thunk. It drew my gaze further down and I watched as his pants followed the path of the rest of his clothing. I swallowed thickly. He didn't have any underwear on!

I licked my lips with anticipation. I've never seen a naked man up close and personal. Girls like me just don't get strip shows like this, very often.

"Um..." Should I say something or just enjoy the show?

Oh, I was interested, to be sure. Another of my late friends, Darla, always preached that a good screw was never amiss. I never put that thought into practice, of course. I'd never been tempted to, before. Now all I could think of was what it would be like to have this huge hunk of testosterone lodged inside me.

"Ma'am, why are you staring at me like that?"

Apparently, I came to my senses when he spoke. His clothes magically reappeared and covered every delectable inch of his yummy, butterscotch colored skin.

Isn't that just a damned disappointment? I frowned. I certainly wanted to see more. Oh well, it was just my imagination anyway.

This sure is a strange way for the withdrawal to affect me.

The officer stood before me, now completely dressed in his form fitting uniform, I shook my head to clear it.

"Looking at you, like what?"

I gazed up at him, attempted to appear as though I hadn't just imagined him naked and resisted the urge to fan myself. Is it getting warm in here?

He took a deep breath and cleared his throat. "You're looking at me like you're a starving woman and I'm a bacon cheeseburger—with fries on the side."

He tucked a finger behind his collar and tugged. His badge winked at me, shining into my face. It blinked like a neon sign that read, guilty, you're guilty!

I peered up at him and stiffened my spine with mock self-righteousness. "I have absolutely no idea what you mean." I crossed my arms in front of my chest to cover my hardened nipples. "It must be the withdrawal that has made me look at you funny." Yeah. That's it. Blame it on the withdrawal symptoms.

I forced myself to look just over his shoulder and focused my gaze past his right ear, to the portrait of my newly deceased dog, Tavi. Even I, in my state, couldn't stay horny while I sat and stared at a dog. Not the four-legged variety, at any rate.

I've never been able to look anyone in the eye and lie. Gram always said it would keep me honest. I closed my eyes and willed myself not to cry. I wish she'd been right. If Gram had been correct in that assumption, I wouldn't be in this predicament now.

Maybe I'd be married to some nice dull guy, right now, with a tedious job and a little dreary house. We'd be Mr. and Mrs. A. B. Normal as we commuted down the highway to Hell.

Chapter Two

I SHOOK MY HEAD AND PULLED MYSELF OUT OF MY WITHDRAWAL-induced funk. "You never did tell me why you're here," I said as my eyelids drooped in a sensual perusal of his perfect physique.

He sat across the room from me. Uniform or not, this guy was fine, with a capital F.

I decided to get comfortable and took my shoes off, then tucked my feet up under me on the sofa. My gaze slid around the room, darting from one thing to another as the withdrawal symptoms returned with a vengeance. The horrible itch was back, too, and I knew that no matter how much I scratched, it wouldn't go away.

God, I hate this.

Experience told me it wouldn't take long to deal with it. In the meantime I had to put up with the sensation of a thousand tiny bugs crawling over my skin. It was only a matter of time before I started to dig the flesh from my bones as I tried to rid myself of the sensation.

If my unexpected guest noticed me squirm, he was polite enough not to comment on it. He stood up and began to pace again. He seemed nervous.

I assumed his agitation was because of all of the hot looks I threw his way. I scowled and attempted to turn down my libido's thermostat, but it wouldn't budge.

A cold shower looks good right about now. Or, better yet, a date with my battery-operated buddy.

"Your pacing makes me nervous. Why don't you light on something?" I snarled and glowered at him.

I waited for him to arrest me and wondered why he didn't. I did kill a man, after all, even though it was to protect myself. Nothing could make me believe Marco would have let me live after what I witnessed. I can't stress *that* enough.

"There was a double homicide across town last night. I was sent to bring

9

you in for questioning."

He stopped pacing and pinned me with a stare. I fidgeted a bit and my left eye twitched. It was a nervous reaction I hoped he missed.

"Why me?" I asked, managing—through my fright, no doubt—to appear properly stunned. I didn't quite trust myself to say much more.

I glanced down at myself. Was all of this shakiness really from the withdrawal or was I scared to death that he'd see through my act and figure out I'm the one who pulled the trigger on that scumbag Marco?

I stood up and strode toward the other room. I needed to move and work off some of my nervous energy.

"I need a drink. You're welcome to come with." I indicated the door that led into my outdated kitchen.

"Make yourself strong coffee," he said as he fell into step behind me.

His footsteps against the hardwood floor were loud compared to the soft slap of my bare feet as he followed me into the next room. Each hard clomp of his boots reminded me of the guards as they made their rounds in a prison movie I'd seen recently. I could understand how the inmates in that movie felt. That short distance seemed like a mile.

"I hear caffeine helps." He shrugged at the unspoken question in my glance. "It's a stimulant."

"Well, you're right about that." I shoveled eight scoops of ground vanilla-flavored coffee beans into the filter and set the pot to brew. "In the meantime," I mumbled and headed to the fridge.

I opened the door, reached in and pulled out a half-full, twenty-ounce bottle of Mountain Dew. It belonged to Trina and I figured that since she wouldn't need it anymore, it was fair game. I chugged it down with the hope that he was right about the caffeine. I could use all of the help I could get.

I grimaced at the over-sweet taste. I don't like my drinks really sweet and I'd never liked regular Mountain Dew, but to get rid of the sensation of bugs eating my skin off, I'd do just about anything.

I tried not to think too much about Trina. If I did, I'd lose it. I knew I needed to be strong. I knew that if I gave in to the hurt and the anger I felt over her senseless death, I just might go crazy. I looked up and braced myself for his questions.

"Who was killed and why does anyone need to talk to me about it?" To avoid his scrutiny, I buried my head in the refrigerator again, under the pretense of searching for another bottle of pop. "Shit! There isn't any more.

Now I have to wait for the fuckin' coffee."

The cop chuckled, "My, my, you do have a potty mouth, don't you?" He shook his head. The grin on his handsome face was too big to make me believe he really disapproved of my strong language.

I don't know what it was about this guy, even though he scared me half to death, he made me think of sex every time I looked at him. That's saying something, when it comes from a twenty-eight-year-old virgin. Well, almost virgin.

"What's your name?" I refused to entertain another fantasy about the guy without at least knowing what to call him.

I scowled and slammed a lid on my runaway libido. I quashed the desire to strip him and have my wicked way with his delectable body. Then I shot him another sidelong glance and shivered. Okay, maybe I'll have my wicked way later.

"Carson, Brock Carson."

"Mind if I call you Brock or do I have to call you Officer Carson?" I asked when I really wanted to call him lover.

"Brock is fine," he said as he leaned against the counter and stretched those mile-long legs out in front of him. He crossed his arms over his chest.

Damn, if he didn't look absolutely edible.

My gaze dropped back down the massive bulge in his pants and I wondered absently, if it was all him or if he was prone to stuffing a pair of socks down there. A roll of ring bologna, maybe?

I bit my cheek, deep in thought. *Wouldn't it be fun to find out if what you've imagined is really under those clothes?*

Frowning, I wondered what in the world had come over me. I've never been so horny in my life. I was practically drooling over this guy in spite the withdrawal symptoms I've had. And he seemed so...so untouched by it all, as if I didn't appeal to him in the slightest.

What did I expect? I'm a drug addict. And he's a cop. Why would he even want to associate with me? Let alone have glorious, mind blowing, multi-orgasmic sex. I bit my lip, frowned, then blinked slowly, trying to dispel the urge to walk over to him and grab a certain bulging appendage.

It didn't work.

"I can't tell you much about our investigation. Although, I can say I radioed headquarters while you were unconscious. After explaining the condition you were in when I arrived to the chief investigator, he instructed

11

me to make sure you were okay, then report back to the precinct. He doesn't want me to waste any more time here."

"Why the change of heart?"

I pulled a coffee cup from the cupboard above the dishwasher. Before I closed the door, I reached in to straighten the handle of a cup that was out of alignment with the others. I turned around just in time to see him make a face at my action.

"Yes, I'm an anal-retentive bitch. It's scary to imagine someone like me on coke, isn't it?" I said, to his raised eyebrows.

The coffeepot finished its cycle. I walked over, poured myself a cup, then took a sip and gagged.

Did I mention I hate coffee?

"It tastes like shit, but if it will help, I'll drink it by the friggin' gallon." I looked at him over the rim of my cup. I'd avoided it for a while since his clothing was gone again. And I was too damned horny to keep my mind from imagining what he would do if we were both naked.

I marveled at the way he filled my kitchen. My mind insisted I saunter over to him and let my fingers do some walking over all of that beautifully tanned flesh. Instead, I tried to keep my eyes focused above his neck. I really did, but I couldn't help it. My unruly gaze drifted down to his extremely large erection. If the man had any deficiencies, it definitely wasn't below the waist.

"Why the change of heart?" I still needed to know. I didn't want to get false hopes.

Finally, I gave up the battle, glued my gaze to his crotch and leaned against the opposite counter to enjoy the sight of him in all of his naked glory. Imagination or not, the guy was definitely hot.

"One of the victims was a known area hooker, and an acquaintance of yours, Trina Devereau. The other was Marco Fargo, a known drug dealer."

I forced my gaze to return to his face, it was all I could do to keep from shouting out that Trina was more than an acquaintance of mine. She was my best friend. Roommate. Partner in crime. Sister.

"The perp stole all of Marco's money and most of his stash. The Chief figures you haven't had a fix in some time, considering the condition you were in, when I arrived."

I realized where he was headed. Somehow, I managed to keep myself on my feet when my body wanted to crumple with relief.

"And, if I'd just killed a drug dealer and stole all of his smack, I'd either be high as a kite or as dead as a three day old fish, if I had it," I finished for him. I immediately took a drink of the nasty coffee. I wanted to keep the smile that tugged at the corners of my mouth from crawling up my face.

I gazed down into the depths of my café au tar and made an effort to control myself. Whoever took those drugs was a mystery I hope never got solved. I certainly didn't care to meet any of Marco's business associates.

To think, if I would have taken those drugs last night, I'd be on my way to jail. The authorities would have said I'd murdered that dickhead son-of-a-bitch. Not that I believe for a second that it was really murder, but I wasn't about to argue semantics with the police.

Brock nodded. "You get the picture. Good."

He left the kitchen and I followed his ass—I mean him—back into the living room. He was still naked, but hey, you won't hear me complain.

When Brock put on his hat, he was suddenly dressed again. Damn, another disappointment! I had admired the tremendous size of his flaccid penis. And imagination or not, it was spectacular.

I shook my head. I really need to go take a nap. My mind is playing tricks on me.

"Would you like me to take you to a hospital, or something?"

The expression on his face clearly stated he thought I should seek professional help.

I took another sip of coffee, then wiped the drool from my mouth. God, he's hot. I shook my head when he threw a questioning look my way. "No, thank you. I think I'll be fine." Are these hallucinations part of my withdrawal or am I just extremely attracted to this guy?

He reached up and tipped his hat back. "It was nice to meet you, Ma'am."

I frowned. Ma'am? How the hell old do I look, anyway?

"Call me Tasha, please." I didn't just gush, did I? Cause if I did...yeech!

He took my smaller hand in his and smiled. "Tasha, such a beautiful name."

To hell with it. If I make a fool of myself, I always have the withdrawal to blame.

I reached up with my free hand, stood on my toes and pulled his head toward mine. "I don't have the slightest idea why I'm saying this," I said. "But stay."

I put my hands on his shoulders and kissed him. My tongue darted out to run along his bottom lip and demanded entrance to his mouth.

He remained straight for a moment and mortification began to set in before he raised his arms and pulled me tight against him. He groaned into my mouth and his tongue finally rushed out to play with mine. My arms snaked around his neck and my cup of mud fell to the floor, forgotten.

He ground his lower body against mine. It made my pussy clench. Warmth flooded my middle and moisture dripped from my nether lips and onto my panties.

Brock was the first to regain his senses. He reached up, took my hands in his and unwrapped my arms from around his neck where I attached myself to him like a leech. I fought the urge to whine and wrap my legs around his waist. I had to keep at least a little dignity.

"I can't," he panted, his lips still wet and glistening from our kiss. "You're not yourself and I'm on duty." He looked like he was in pain. "If I stay, we may regret it."

He pressed my trembling hand against his crotch. I squeezed his erection ruthlessly and ran my fingers up and down the massive blood-engorged shaft. I reached down with my other hand, cupped his sac through his slacks, squeezed and used my nails to heighten the sensation.

Trina taught me a few useful tricks one day when I made my first and only attempt at prostitution to support my drug habit. I couldn't bring myself to do it, but it wasn't because I didn't know how.

To me, sex was supposed to be between two people who cared about each other. At least that's what I thought before I met Mr. Universe here. That was the main reason I'd stopped using cocaine. I didn't have the money for it and I couldn't bring myself to sell my body to get it. If my Johns had been like this stud, there wouldn't have been a problem.

"I want you to stay, Brock. I need you to stay." I peered up at him through my lashes and smiled. "I don't ask this of just anyone, believe me. Stay, fuck me."

"I can't," he groaned. "I know you're not yourself. You can't be. You must be yourself before I can—" He cut himself off, then pulled a business card and pen from his shirt pocket. He scribbled a number on the back with his strong, tapered fingers.

"If you still feel this way in two weeks, give me a call." Then he turned and walked out of the house.

It was all I could do to keep myself inside. I refused to follow him through the door and beg him to come back. I never wanted to kill someone so much in my entire life as I wanted to kill him for leaving me so damned horny. And apparently that's saying something these days.

"Damn it!"

TWO WEEKS LATER:

"YOU don't want to go out to dinner first?" Brock asked, chuckling when I started to undress him at the door.

Buttons flew in all directions as I pulled on his shirt and it flew open. I jerked to a stop for a minute and giggled, my mouth already pressed against his chest.

"I guess I don't know my own strength," I breathed against his breastbone. My tongue reveled in the salty taste of his sun-kissed skin. Slowly, I worked my way lower to the treasure under his belt.

"Are you...ah, sure you don't want to have dinner first?" He ground the words out. He sounded like his mouth was full of marbles.

Brock pushed the front door shut with a laugh when I shouted, "Hell, no! You are dinner."

I've never wanted anyone so much in my life. It's a wonder I didn't meet him at the door naked. I had contemplated wearing nothing but a big red bow. I didn't give much thought to why I was so attracted to him. After years of men turning me down because I wasn't attractive, I was too relieved to realize I was normal after all.

"I hope I'm not getting some sort of weird fetish for guys in uniform," I said before I ruthlessly sucked his tongue into my mouth as I held him by the hair.

"I should certainly hope not."

The strange, cultured, male voice came from behind me. The rich baritone flowed through me like warm honey and made me shiver.

The voice was magic, pushing thoughts of Brock right out of my head. It brought me to my senses and I wondered, if however briefly, what the hell I'd been about to do.

Brock stiffened and pulled away. He turned us around and put himself between the newcomer and me. He took up a protective stance as he shielded my body with his.

"Who are you? Take whatever you want, just don't harm the girl," he said, in his cop-like tone.

I peeked out around Brock's shoulder. This new man had even more in the looks department than my companion did. In fact, he was drop dead gorgeous! I swallowed thickly as my mind went through sensual overload with so much testosterone flying around the room.

A little voice in my head urged me to leave Brock to saunter over to this new man. I ignored it. Instead, I sidled closer to Brock to show my support.

I wasn't about to get fickle. This new guy may be scrumptious, but Brock was still mine. I glanced up at him and worried my lower lip. He was mine, wasn't he?

The newcomer turned his dark gaze on me. I couldn't help but notice that his hair was perfectly groomed, with not one ebony strand out of place.

His eyes were almost black, hard, a complete contrast to Brock's open, silver-blue eyes. He was very tall, over six and a half feet. I knew that because his head stood higher than the bottom of the landscape over my mantle.

I shivered again, my arms suddenly covered with goosebumps. I fought the ridiculous urge to come out from where I hid behind Brock and walk toward him.

The man had some sort of weird pull over me. Like magic. My skin prickled and I felt hot and cold all over. I could feel his gaze on me like a caress. Each sweep of those dark, dark eyes was like a touch. A stroke of his fingers. Just a look from him made me burn.

You can't possibly know this man, my mind raged as I fought to understand why he seemed so familiar to me. I shifted to peer out and Brock grabbed me around the waist.

"Stay behind me, darling. I don't want you to get hurt."

I sighed, thankful that he obviously didn't plan to give me up too easily.

The new man bowed gracefully, and visions, like memories, flashed through my mind. Mental pictures of this man as he sat in this room on the sofa. He held a photo-album on his lap, a glass of iced tea in his hand and laughed with my grandmother.

Could they be memories? I shook my head as I tried to deny the things, buried deep within my subconscious mind. The man sat at the dining room table with my father, looking over a stack of papers after dinner.

These weren't memories. They couldn't be.

In another vision, I was a child and I sat on his lap. My hands were on his face as I looked into those beautiful espresso eyes. It couldn't the same man. He wasn't old enough to be the person in my visions. Could he be that man's son?

The newcomer wore black, designer silk slacks, expensive black leather boots and a black turtleneck sweater. He reeked of old-world elegance. Wore it like a second skin.

Only, I knew from personal experience, that elegance didn't necessarily make a man good. More often than not, it was used as a cover by someone intrinsically evil. Like Marco.

Suddenly, I remembered. The man held a beautifully carved cane. He handed it to my father. Pulling on the handle, he showed my father a sword inside. Daddy had carried that cane everywhere he went.

I watched with growing suspicion as he bowed gracefully, before he introduced himself. "I am Micah. You need not fear me. I have been sent to protect you." His dark eyes bored into mine and I had the ridiculous thought he could see straight into my mind.

Brock turned to face him and stiffened as he stood taller. He still held me behind him. He blocked my view of the new man as he kept himself between us.

"I can protect her, even from the likes of you. She needs no one else to see to her needs."

The new man, Micah, smiled. He bared his even white teeth and held his arms out to his sides. I felt, more than saw, the immense power that emanated from him.

"And who, pray tell, shall protect her from the likes of you, Incubus?"

This, of course, was a bit too much for my newly straight state. I collapsed to the floor and welcomed the approaching darkness as it claimed me.

CHAPTER THREE

MICAH STOOD OVER ME AND RUBBED MY HANDS AND WRISTS TOGETHER AS I woke. He wore a worried expression.

"It is a good thing I was able to find you before he separated you from your innocence."

"Huh?" I couldn't form a more lucid question in my befuddled state. I hurriedly sat up and scurried away from him, my crab-like movements, no doubt, looked ridiculous.

Then I latched onto the most vacuous thought.

"I hope you don't think I faint like this all of the time." I looked up into his fathomless eyes. "I'm not a fainter. Really," I explained, not sure why I cared what he thought of me. My legs wobbled as I stood and made my way to the couch to lie down.

I was too weak for anything else, and if he planned to kill me... Well, I wouldn't be able to put up much of a fight. And right now, especially after all I've been through, I'm not sure I would have.

Micah sat down next to me and his leg brushed mine. I moved away with impotent dismay. What else could I do? Absolutely nothing.

If he'd overpowered Brock, I knew it was very likely he could do whatever he wanted to do with me. That said, I decided to sit and listen. For now, anyway.

"That was no man you were with, Tasha. He is an incubus," Micah stated. "He is not of this world. His job, if you will, is to search out pure individuals, such as you, to have sex with. When this poor woman has sex with him, her life is forfeit along with any psychic powers she might possess."

I must have given away the fact that I thought him nuts. Certifiable. One itty-bitty step away from being dragged off by the men in white coats. Not to mention a whole basket short of a picnic.

"You must believe me. One such as he can eat away your will to live. If you are untouched, it can make him even more powerful. Power he can turn on others to claim their innocence." He turned bleak eyes my way. "Power enough to kill even those who have the strength to stop him."

I sat back and rested my head against the pillows on my sofa. What could it hurt to listen? And if, during the course of our conversation, a vase should fall on his head, could he sue? He did break into my house after all.

He turned those intense eyes on me and I shivered with dread as the gleaming onyx bored right through my mental defenses. Somehow, he knew what I'd been thinking.

"Do not try it, little one. You do not have the strength to overcome someone like me."

How does he know what I'm thinking?

He sat down and stared at me through those cold, empty eyes. A part of me wanted to scream for Brock. He clamped a hand over my mouth.

"You will not call out to him." It was a decree—one he expected me to obey. "I will gag you, if I must, but you must never call out to him. It will bring him to you."

Oh, what a deterrent.

My inner voice screamed for help as those warm fingers mashed my lips against my teeth. My vision grew blurry as my frustration gave way to tears.

"He must be near then," I said with a sniff when he finally removed his warm hand from my mouth. I ignored the tingles and itchy sensation between my legs as I determined not to be attracted to him.

"I don't understand. Bro—" He gave me a severe look so I decided to humor him. For now.

"The...incubus," I almost choked on the ridiculous word. "Could have made love to me two weeks ago, but he told me he wouldn't until I was myself again." The familiar heat of a blush stole up my cheeks. "I was going through withdrawal."

I fisted my hands in my lap and stared down at them. I didn't care to see the disgust on his face when I admitted that I was an addict.

Micah leaned against the back of the couch and crossed his legs. He rested his hand on the doily-covered arm and drummed his fingers impatiently against the rough material.

"An incubus cannot draw power from their victim if the victim is not able to make a conscious choice to participate in the act. You were not yourself while you experienced the withdrawal symptoms and not able to make the conscious choice to lie with him." He shifted in his seat. "So one could say your addiction may have been a good thing. It may have saved your life."

"Oh." I tried not to breathe. Every inhalation brought me closer to trusting him. It made me want to act on the desire I felt as it pulsed inside me. He wore the same cologne my father always wore. How could I not begin to feel comfortable in his presence? His scent alone could put me at ease.

I wondered how much the man knew about me and whether or not he wore the scent because he knew it would keep me off guard.

That's just stupid, Tasha. It's a coincidence, nothing more. When had I become so paranoid? After all, he did say he was here to protect me.

"I wear this scent because it is my favorite. It also brands me as a Cartuotey. It is made by us and solely for us. We protect humans from the evil entities bound to this Earth and from others, like the incubus, who are not." He shrugged his broad shoulders. "The scent helps guides identify a Cartuotey if a Rogue or other creature should attempt to impersonate one of us with a glamour."

I tried very hard to ignore the fact that he'd said they protect humans, as if he wasn't human.

"Car-too-oh-tie?" I repeated. "What in the world is that?" I decided to leave the human and evil entities remarks alone since I already passed my quota for impossible things today.

"It is a word from the ancient language which means, Defender of the Gates. Essentially, it means that I am a paranormal police officer, of sorts. We are helpers, partners to the Guide."

Police officer? What the hell is it, with me and cops lately? Well, I suppose it's not too unusual. I did kill a man two weeks ago. I guess it's lucky that I haven't seen more of them. I bit my lip and changed the subject. I didn't want to hear him spout any more of his crazy paranormal-cop, incubus and power stealing crap.

"How can you read my mind?" Oh, yeah, Tasha, that's a safe, normal subject. I frowned, then told myself to shut up.

It's not like the idea of reading minds was new to me. Darla's mother tried to teach me how to keep mental blocks up. She used to tell me that I may find it to be a useful tool one day.

"It is a gift. I'm sure you have heard of mental telepathy." Micah raised one perfectly arched, ebony eyebrow and he looked sexier than any man had a right to. "If not, you should think of getting out a bit more."

He bent, reached down, grabbed me by my upper arms and straightened me in my seat. I contemplated running, but I wasn't sure if my legs would work right or not. Even if they did, something told me I'd never outrun the guy, even if I'd been in the best shape of my life. Which, of course, wasn't the case. A runner, I am not.

It took me a while to digest his last statement. He's not normal! My mind raged. Normal people couldn't read minds. They could be empaths. They knew when you were hurt, mad or happy. Even I could do that to a certain extent.

That's why Darla's mom had trained me to use the mental blocks. She found me bent over her toilet as I cried and puked my guts up over her sick baby. At the time, it never occurred to me that she knew I could feel the baby's distress.

Another thing Micah said sank in. "Wait a minute. Did you say that my father was some sort of weird cop? Explain."

Maybe this guy knew something that would shed some light on my father's disappearance.

Micah lifted my legs and brought them over the side of the couch, then lifted me into his arms and straightened. If I hadn't been impressed by the man before, I certainly was by then.

I'm not a skinny miss at five feet ten inches. I'm a size fourteen, with an over-abundance of womanly curves—as my grandmother always put it. And he just picked me up like I weighed nothing.

"Um. Just what the hell do you think you're you doing?"

"Your father was a friend of mine." He looked away for a moment. "My best friend," he added almost as an afterthought. "He was a member of my group. Humans are discouraged to use this scent when they sometimes inadvertently find it hidden amongst our belongings. He alone was allowed to wear it, for his own safety." He turned from the couch and walked toward the hall. "It identified him as being under our protection."

"Aren't all Guides under your protection? I thought you said you protected all humans?" I was confused. I looked at him through narrow eyes, not sure I wanted to believe anything he said. But a part of me, the part I thought needed its head examined, wanted to keep him in my life.

Not only was he carrying me, but the muscles in his neck didn't even bulge. That had to count for something. Yet I still sat stiffly in his arms. I refused to surrender to him in any fashion.

"I don't understand what you're talking about. Maybe you should explain it to me."

My mind still raged, telling me to run for my life. I chose to ignore it, for now. I attempted to blank the screams of protest in my mind before he could read my thoughts again and hold them against me. I am human, after all and the things he told me stretched the bounds of my limited, human, imagination. Impossible things. Too many impossible things.

"First things first," he said, starting for the stairs. "Where is your bedroom?" He was taking the steps two at a time and I barely had the time to wonder just how strong the man was that he could do that while he carried me. Not to mention the fact that he wasn't even breathing hard.

"Why are you taking me to my bedroom?"

Micah looked down at my upturned face with a mask of patience that told me he thought of me as some recalcitrant child.

"We must divest you of the burden of maidenhood, of course." He said it so calmly, so nonchalant.

"Excuse me?" I sputtered. I screwed my face into what I hoped was a mask of disbelief. I've never been so shocked or insulted in my life! "Look, mister, I may be horny as hell, but I'm not about to have sex with a man I don't know!"

He quirked a glossy black brow.

"Well, okay, I didn't really know Br—"

He gave me another sharp look. Those eyes of his did weird things to me. Sometimes, like now, they scared the crap out of me. Other times, I wanted nothing more than to drown in the dark-chocolate of his heated gaze. Warmth pooled in my middle as I felt the rush of moisture between my legs. I did my best to ignore each of my reactions and looked away.

"Okay, okay." I rolled my eyes. "I didn't really know the *incubus*," I stressed the unfamiliar word. "But I certainly knew him better than I know you."

I stubbornly crossed my arms in front of me. It wasn't an easy thing to do while being held close against his chest.

"At least he didn't insist that we have sex the day we met."

I purposely left out the part where I attempted to jump Brock's bones that first day. What Micah didn't know certainly wouldn't hurt him.

His arms tightened. Big strong arms, too, I might add. My clit twitched with delight. I gritted my teeth and tried to ignore it. I do have a brain in my head and I'm not about to let my nether parts tell me whom to sleep with.

Against my will, my left hand left the confines of my right armpit where I stuck it for protection. It slid sensuously up over his chest and shoulder before it slowly wrapped itself around his neck.

To my complete surprise and mortification, I buried my hand in his hair and brought my head closer to his.

"Why can't I stop myself?" I asked just before I pressed my lips against his.

"You find me irresistible," he growled against my mouth. His voice was compelling. The low timber crawled through my body like a living thing. It made me want to do all sorts of interesting things with this man. His tongue dueled with mine, both of us wanted to win a war of dominance.

When our lips met, I felt much as I did with Brock, but with Micah, I felt...more. I wanted to kiss him, to fondle him. To know I gave satisfaction as much as I was receiving it.

With Brock, it had been different. I had wanted nothing more than to feel his huge cock as it pounded inside me.

"Stop thinking of other men," Micah said, against my mouth, then playfully nipped at my lips.

I looked around and noticed, for the first time, that I was lying on my bed. Either I hadn't paid attention while he searched the upstairs for my room or he had a great sense of direction. I'm pretty sure it was the former.

I pulled away and fought for my next breath. I needed space. I needed to get away from him to think. I couldn't concentrate when he was so close, when I could feel the heat from his body as it seeped into mine. It sent little licks of flame through my blood.

It wasn't normal that he could read my mind. Sure, I've heard of telepathy, but I've never met anyone with it. The whole idea was absurd. If I believe that, the next thing he'll tell me is that we can communicate without talking. It was all I could do, not to snort.

He ran his hand through my hair and pushed my bangs back from my face to look into my eyes.

"You must rid yourself of your virginity. It is a weakness—a weapon that can be held against you."

"Now I've heard it all," I laughed derisively and pushed at his chest. "All of my life, my father, my grandmother and the church have told me to abstain. Then suddenly you come along and tell me that I have to have sex to save my life? Puhleeze!"

This is too much!

I slid out from under him and tried to avoid his roaming hands. Then I stood up, walked to the window and looked out through the darkness. I wrapped my arms around my churning middle and wondered how many more impossible things I was expected to face in one day.

"Do you have any idea how crazy this all sounds?" I resisted the urge to rest my forehead against the cool glass.

He sighed and stepped up behind me. "Of course I realize how it sounds." He ran his fingers through his hair and it stood up in adorable spikes.

I watched his reflection in the window and refused to smile. I couldn't afford to be weak now, no matter how cute and approachable those little spikes made him seem.

"I blame your father for this. I told him your innocence would make you an easy target. Still, he wouldn't listen to me. I could feel your power, even as a child. He should have prepared you for this."

I could feel the anger as it radiated from him and it scared me.

"You need never fear me, little one."

"Will you stop that?" I snarled and turned to face him. "Can't you at least give me the illusion that you can't read my every thought?"

I stomped from the bedroom and headed back downstairs where it was safe. Where I would be safe.

Why didn't he just kill me and get it over with? Isn't that what crazy people like him do?

He sighed behind me as if he wanted to say something, but thought better of it. "You can refuse me, if you wish, but I cannot leave you unprotected. If you don't want me, surely someone as beautiful as you shouldn't have a difficult time if you tried to find someone else to have sex with. If you refuse to allow me to divest you of your maidenhead, I must stay here with you until you're no longer in danger of succumbing to the incubus as a virgin."

I turned and searched his eyes. "Oh, my God. You can't mean to stay here with me indefinitely."

He nodded and raised his brow. "Yes, that's exactly what I mean. If you continue to refuse me, I must stay here with you until you submit to someone else."

"Shit."

He inhaled deeply. "I wish you would refrain from speaking like that. It is unseemly."

"Maidenhead? Unseemly? Where in the hell do you come from anyway?" I asked. Then I shook my head and held my hand up. "Never mind. I don't think I want to know that much about you."

He sighed, crossed his arms over his chest and leaned against the wall, his face devoid of expression.

I paced between the kitchen and the downstairs bathroom. I needed to regain control of my traitorous body. How could I fear this man, yet still want him with a need that bordered on obsession?

"Are you trying to tell me you're not going to leave until I have sex with you?" Something else he said earlier finally sank in. "What powers? What did you mean earlier when you said you could feel my powers?"

I bit my bottom lip and thought, impossible things, impossible things. My overwrought mind chanted the words like a mantra.

Grandma must be laughing her head off in the afterlife. I frowned and wondered if this was the very thing her constantly repeated speeches about impossible things had been preparing me to accept.

Micah pushed away from the wall, strode into the dining room, sat down at the head of the table and indicated I should join him.

If I could get my libido to stop singing and dancing for a minute, I might be able to pay attention to what he said. I stopped to give my nether parts a short lecture on abstinence before I prodded Micah to explain.

"Well?"

"You do not have to have sex with me, but you must have sex with someone or you will remain at risk. As to the powers you wield, you are a Guide to the Portes en Cristal of the L'autre Monde."

"Huh?" There I go, being so articulate again.

Micah sighed deeply. He looked more than a bit irritated. "You are a guide to the Crystal Gates. They are the ethereal doorways to the other worlds." He stood and took a step toward me.

"What in the hell is that?" I snorted, then raised my fist in the air. "I swear to God, if you touch me again, mister, I'll be your guide to the Pearly Gates!"

He just smiled, backed up and lowered himself back into the chair. "You have such a lovely way with words, my dear." He tilted his head. "And you have a lot of spirit. Your powers as a Guide must be immense."

Now he was patronizing me and it pissed me off. I bared my teeth in what, I hoped, passed for a grin.

"Ya think?"

I made my way over to the chair in front of my Gram's old secretary desk and sat down. I didn't trust myself to sit very close to him and his wandering hands. I bent over, put my head between my knees and took several deep breaths. I could feel another faint nudge the edge of my consciousness.

"The phrase means you are a..." he paused as if searching for a relative term. "A sorceress, of sorts."

I inhaled sharply and sucked spit down my windpipe. I choked and tried to clear the moisture from my lungs. "What did you say?" I gasped. I didn't dare to believe what I just heard. A sorceress? *The guy's a loon. He's beautiful, but he's a loon.*

Micah straightened in his seat. His eyes blazed with anger. "I am not crazy," he bit out between clenched teeth.

"Yeah, right, and I'm the great, great granddaughter of Abraham Lincoln."

"What makes you think you are not?"

Those dark, dark eyes bored into mine again in an attempt to make me believe so many impossible things.

"I'm not touching that remark with a ten foot cattle prod," I mumbled.

"You shouldn't mumble. It doesn't become you."

"Oh, shut up. Who asked you, anyway?" I'd never be able to put up with this crap on a daily basis. He'd drive me nuts! I frowned and resisted the urge to tell my subconscious mind to go take a hike.

I began to wonder if I shouldn't go ahead and have sex with the man just to get him out of my hair. It's not like I hadn't been thinking about getting laid lately. Hell, lately, it was just about all I thought about. I let my gaze travel up and down his very fine form and tried not to drool.

Micah shook his head. He looked disgusted. I had the sneaking suspicion he eavesdropped on my thoughts again. I really wish he'd stop that. It gave me the creeps.

I stood, approached him slowly and eyed him with no small degree of trepidation. I stuck my tongue out to let it slowly trail over my upper lip. I watched as Micah's Adam's apple bobbed in his throat. He may want to look unaffected, but his body told me a story of its own.

When I stepped a bit closer, he just sat there, unmoving. He stared at me with his intense, obsidian gaze while he remained conspicuously still. And waited.

I gradually closed the distance and suddenly felt like a wild thing that slowly, foolishly, trusted the hunter.

He lifted his hand and I took it. He pulled me between his knees. I rested my hands lightly on his shoulders and leaned down, pressing my mouth to his. I wanted to experiment a little.

I suppose, if I really wanted to divest myself of my virginity, Micah was as good a candidate as any. I frowned against his skillful lips. When did I become such a slut?

I tried to pull away from him, but he held me close, his mouth burned a trail down to my collarbone. He suckled on it for a minute before his tongue danced back up to my ear. "Oh, my," I breathed, when the velvet of his mouth made contact with the outer shell.

He drew the lobe into his mouth and suckled. How could anything feel so good? Heat pooled low in my middle and I felt a rush of warmth between my legs. I barely realized it when he lowered me to the sky blue comforter on my bed.

I gave little thought to the fact we were back in my room and didn't even question how we'd gotten there.

Micah took both of my wrists in one hand and raised them over my head. He brushed his other hand up my waist. His talented fingers played over my sensitized breasts. It was an agonizing torture, even through my shirt and bra. Ruthlessly, he squeezed and plucked at the now hardened tips. Then he quickly removed my tee shirt and made short work of my front-clasp bra and jeans.

I almost shot off the bed when his mouth closed over my extended nipple. I'd never felt anything like that before in my life. I fisted my hands in the comforter, grabbed at anything I could. I tried valiantly to fight my growing desire toward this man, torn between wanting him and wanting to be rid of him. I knew if I grabbed onto his head and pulled him closer to me, it would be a sign of surrender. It was one thing I still wasn't certain I wanted to do.

To surrender to him, to a stranger, was little better than prostituting myself on the street.

Chapter Four

YOU DIDN'T KNOW BROCK. A LITTLE VOICE REMINDED ME.
What if what this man says is true? The stimulation became too much then, and I could barely think, let alone argue with myself. Micah reached down between my legs, thrust his hand under the waistband of my embarrassing, cotton, granny panties and thrummed my clit.

"Oh, God, Micah," I mewled against his neck as he brought me closer to the edge of some previously unknown precipice. "I've never felt anything like this before in my life." If I hadn't been a virgin, I don't think there would have been any fight in me after that.

Micah released my breast and blew across the turgid peak. My nipple grew tighter against the cool air. It jutted toward the ceiling and begged for the return of his warm, wet-velvet mouth.

Heat rushed to my face as I realized, with growing horror, that my body, the brazen hussy it had become, changed sides on me. The traitor had warmed toward Micah. It waited, practically begging, for his touch.

"Dammit, you bastard, stop teasing me!"

He chuckled as his kisses delved lower, then even lower, until his head was poised above my newly assaulted pussy. He pulled my panties down over my legs, threw them over his shoulder and looked up with a lopsided grin.

"I hope this changes your mind if nothing else has," he said, then lowered his head to my quivering flesh. His tongue pushed apart the folds of skin between my legs and I whimpered.

My face blazed with embarrassment, even as my legs drew further apart and made room for him, inviting him to impale me. He threw my legs over his shoulders and easily lifted my hips from the bed.

He took my clit into his mouth and sucked, hard. My head thrashed on the pillow as I reached my limit and screamed. I fisted my hands in his hair and squeezed my thighs around him, holding his head to me until I climaxed.

After that, I lay on the bed, spent. I was nothing more than a writhing,

28

quivering, ball of sensitive flesh that still hadn't had enough.

Micah knew he had me at that moment. He knew there would be no going back. Still, he asked, "Would you like me to stop?"

"Stop?" Oh, god, if he stopped now, I'd die. I had to know. What was next? What followed something so earth-shatteringly wonderful? "If you stop now, I'll kill you," I panted as he chuckled and crawled up my inert form, licking his way back up my quivering body. I was too weak to protest the feel of his bare skin sliding against mine.

When did he undress? I pushed the thought aside and deemed it unimportant. The length of his erection pressed between my legs and I reached down to grasp him in my hand.

"Oh, my God," I gasped. "It's huge, it will never fit!"

Even Brock's hadn't been that big. I tried to censor the thought. Somehow, Micah seemed to be able to read my mind. I don't know why I didn't find that as strange as I did before. I gave a mental shrug. Maybe I'd just gotten used to the idea.

He dipped his head and lapped at my nipples again, first one, then the other, he gave each one equal attention. My mind swirled down into the dark sensual abyss it had just left, and my legs drew even further apart as my body prepared for his entry.

"Would you like me to stop?" he asked again. His breath brushed my sensitive flesh and raised goosebumps. He kissed me behind the ear and his lips did wonderful things to my neck and collarbone.

"N-no. I want you to fuck me, Micah. I want your cock buried so deep within me we'll never get it out." I closed my eyes with shame. How could I want this man more than I have ever wanted anything in my life? He was a complete stranger.

"No more a stranger than the incubus," he reminded.

"That wasn't nice," I bit out, then pushed ruthlessly at his chest. I started to sit up. "I have enough problems without taking your abuse." I slapped at his hand on my breast and glared at him. "Leave that alone!"

"I'm sorry, Tasha." He moved back to my ear and suckled on the lobe. It didn't take long to have me crazy with need once again.

"That feels so good," I sighed, totally forgetting my anger. "Don't stop."

I swallowed thickly as he placed his body between my thighs. His hips nestled between my legs and his huge cock pressed against me.

"It's not going to fit." I moaned.

Every fiber of my being wanted to feel him inside me. But the little spear of doubt that crept inside my head made me want to sob with fear.

His hand caressed my face, brushed the sweat-dampened hair off my forehead. "It will only hurt for a moment, little one." He whispered in my ear. "I would never tell you so if I did not believe it to be true."

I nodded and screwing my eyes shut tight, I said, "Okay, go ahead."

He chuckled. "I will, but only when you are ready, when you are aroused beyond reason. I will enter you only then. Then you will scream, but not with pain. You will scream with ecstasy." His mouth began to work its magic on me again. My little niggle of doubt slowly eased as the fire began to blaze anew.

His hands followed the path his mouth had taken before. They burned a trail down to the golden curls nestled between my thighs. His fingers eased inside. They stretched and prepared me for the entry of his enormous erection. All the while, his thumb expertly thrummed my clit and worked me into a frenzy of mindless lust.

I barely realized when he stopped massaging the little bud, which I would never view as merely functional ever again. I barely even felt it when he slowly slid inside of my virginal pussy. Until he hit the barrier that proclaimed me still untouched. That thing I should be proud to possess, but was wont for nearly a year to be rid of.

This is it.

His eyes met mine before he dropped his head. He kissed me as he surged forward to the hilt and caught my scream in his mouth. It was a scream of pain mixed with one of triumph.

Never again, would I sit with a group of women on the sidelines as they joked about sex and not know what they meant. So many things came to me then. So much understanding of the things I'd heard over the years. Now I knew.

"Oh, my," I breathed with awe as he eased in and out, slowly, gently. His cock filled me to capacity and then some. Yet it didn't hurt. It just gave me the sensation of fullness as my inner walls stretched to accommodate him. "I didn't know it could be like this. If I had known, I may not have waited so long," I said, yet realized I still didn't know everything.

Micah gave me a strained smile. His lips were clamped together, his muscles tense. I could tell it was an effort for him to continue his slow, even strokes let alone speak. He looked down at me and grimaced, or was that a smile?

Something near the tip of his penis rubbed the inner wall of my pussy in such a way I thought I would explode. "Does it hurt?" I didn't think it was supposed to hurt the guy. But he was so big. "Am I too tight?" I moaned. I felt bad that it could feel so wonderful for me and obviously so bad for him.

He shook his head, his blue-black hair falling over his forehead. It covered his eyes and I gave into the urge to reach up and push it back. He kissed my hand as it brushed over his cheek.

"No, it doesn't hurt. It feels good, too good, and I want to be sure to bring you pleasure." He ground the words out between his teeth as he eased himself in and out of me. The veins in his neck bulged with the effort he used to hold back.

I ran my fingers down his smooth muscular back to his ass and lightly ran my nails along the firm muscles beneath my hands. He took me to the edge of another orgasm. Something I didn't think possible my first time out of the gate, so to speak.

Micah lowered his head to my neck and kissed me. He suckled my neck just above my clavicle and nibbled lightly on my skin. The sharpness of his teeth added to the pleasure. He suckled harder and the pleasure bordered on pain.

"Micah, yes. Please," I panted and held his head to me as he took me over the edge and I came for the second time.

He reached down, grabbed my legs and wrapped them around his waist. It gave him better access to pound into me.

"Tasha," he groaned, "you feel wonderful, so wet, so tight. I can't tell you what it feels like to have your little cunt clasped so tightly around me."

I screamed his name again as he drove his massive cock into me. All pretext of being gentle gone. He no longer held back. He lowered his head and kissed my chest. His mouth traveled up to my neck, to the point where he suckled earlier. Then his tongue lapped at my collarbone, moving lower to glide over my still hard nipple.

Micah bucked inside me, the muscles of his neck stood out as he drove himself deeper into my womb. I could tell when he neared his climax. He held himself over me, his entire body stiff. My own third orgasm of the night crept closer. Micah looked into my eyes. In that moment, I believed he could look into my soul.

"Now," he urged. "Come for me now, Tasha. Let me feel that little cunt spasm around me. Come for me again, baby," he whispered the words in my ear as he somehow grew larger within me. He stretched me even more, the extra sensation of fullness added to the wonderful feeling of his hard shaft as it moved inside me.

"I'm coming!" I cried as he took me over the edge again before he came deep inside me. His cock bucked, surging as it released the warmth of his seed into the depths of my womb.

I came down from the apex a bit and tried to catch my breath. I realized absently that we didn't use any protection and I wasn't on the pill. I gave a mental shrug. I didn't really give a damn. There were worse things in life than being a single parent, like not having anyone at all.

I came back to my senses when Micah rolled me over and tucked me under the covers next to him. He lay behind me, spoon fashion and, exhausted, I surrendered myself to sleep.

I woke a little while later, stayed within the comfort of his arms and listened to his light snores as I contemplated my strange day. I shook my head. *I really am a slut.*

I'm more of a loose woman than Trina ever thought of being and she used to turn tricks for her drug money. At least she'd been honest about it.

Me? For years I've hidden behind my so-called morals, flaunted my virginity until it was no longer useful. No longer useful? When was it ever useful? I brushed the tears away from my eyes. Silent sobs wracked my body as I came to terms with what I had done.

Micah stirred behind me and wrapped an arm around me protectively. He drew me closer to the warmth and protection of his body and somehow knowing, even in his sleep, that I needed comfort.

I thought back to before he arrived. Would I have been able to finish what I started with Brock? I had no idea. I only knew Brock wasn't as handsome, as strong, or as compelling as Micah.

I turned my head and attempted to get a better look at Micah as he slept. His ebony hair fell over his eyes and my fingers itched to push it back. I loved the feel of his soft hair in my hands as it sifted through my fingers, like black silken threads.

I attempted to remember the exact color of his eyes, but could only remember the dark, chocolate of his aroused state. I rolled over and took the opportunity to look my fill while he slept.

Dark, coffee-colored lashes fanned out over his high cheekbones and the shadowy crescents gave him a vulnerable look. I smiled. He looked so cute while he was asleep. My fingers reached out of their own accord and smoothed the frown that formed on his lips, my fingers traced the fine lines on his face.

Micah's hand snaked up from under the blanket and grabbed my wrist. "I am not cute," he said with the frown back on his face. "Don't you know that when a woman calls a man my age cute, it is the kiss of death?" He shot me a dirty look and his expression made me giggle.

"No, I like you and don't want to ruin our friendship is the kiss of death."

He laced his long fingers through mine and absently caressed the back of my hand with his thumb. "You've heard that one before?" Micah asked. He lifted my hand, pulled it up to his mouth and brushed my knuckles with his lips. He turned my hand over and pressed a kiss into the center of my palm.

I nodded. "Yes, many times." I gave him a rueful smile. "How do you think I remained a virgin to the ripe old age of twenty-eight? Every man I ever contemplated having a serious relationship with had been attracted to either Trina or Darla. Every one of them only wanted to be my friend."

Micah just looked at me with his expressive dark chocolate eyes and said the most beautiful thing I could imagine. "I'm glad I was the first." He kissed my knuckles again and smiled. "That way, I have ruined you for all others and you will not feel the need to cleave unto any other man."

Yeah, like he plans to be around after tomorrow. And what's with that weird speech?

"I will be around, until you tell me to leave, even then, I shall stay to protect you." He frowned after a moment, obviously deep in thought. "I will have to leave from time to time, but I shall always return. I promised your father I would protect you."

I deliberately ignored the fact he could read my mind. The need to find out how he did it wasn't worth my sanity. I've met my daily quota. Gram told me I had to believe one impossible thing per day. Well, that was the incubus. I at least believed Micah believed Brock was some other-dimensional being who wanted to steal some latent psychic power I supposedly possessed. The telepathy bit was another matter entirely.

"My life has been filled with too many impossible things already." I wanted to believe he would stick around, but knew he would leave. He would leave on his own or someone would kill him. Either way, he would be gone. Everyone I have ever cared about died. I think I was meant to live my life alone.

He wrapped his arms around me. "I know," he sighed onto my neck and his breath fanned my ear, causing gooseflesh to rise on my skin.

I watched his face get closer to me as he lowered his mouth to claim my lips. My eyes closed as his lips met mine. The maelstrom of desire that accompanied his kiss washed away all of my thoughts. My arms circled his neck and I drew him closer, lost in a whirlpool of sensuality.

Would Brock have been better? I doubt it. Did I want to find out?

Not on your life!

CHAPTER FIVE

W E SLEPT MOST OF THE DAY AWAY. SOMETIME AROUND DAWN, MICAH got out of bed, closed the blinds and the curtains and went down to the kitchen nude.

He brought up a veritable feast of fresh fruit, juice and coffee. He sat beside me on the bed and watched me eat, totally at ease with his bare body.

"Are you sure you don't want some?" I asked and offered him a particularly juicy bite of cantaloupe after I sat up on the bed. My only garment, the flowered sheet tucked modestly around my breasts and under my arms.

Micah shook his head and smiled. "No, thank you. I ate while I was downstairs to get yours." He patted his flat stomach. "I'm stuffed."

He tilted his head to the side and stared at me in an odd manner. It reminded me of a bird of prey.

"I didn't see any meat in your refrigerator. Don't you eat meat?"

"Why didn't you just pick the information out of my head? It's not as if you haven't done it before."

"I've been trying to afford you some privacy since you expressed a certain revulsion to my ability to read your mind."

"Hmmm...so you're not going to do that anymore?"

"I am attempting to refrain, yes." He tilted his head to the side and eyed the way I popped the fruit into my mouth. "Now, will you answer my question? Do you eat meat?"

I laughed, relieved that he'd finally stopped poking around in my head. "Me, eat meat?" I pushed my hair back with sticky fingers. What the hell, I need a shower anyway. "Of course I eat meat. Give me a nice thick steak any day." Yeah, a nice thick, well-done steak. Blood just creeps me out.

He smiled, and for some reason, looked relieved. He must be a big meat and potato man, or something.

Micah waited for me to finish, took my plate and pounced on me. He pushed the sheet away from my chest, his head moved directly to the tip of my breast. He captured my nipple in his mouth and suckled. His teeth scraped erotically over the sensitized tip as his hand fondled the other and he rolled the nipple in between his thumb and forefinger.

I moaned, unsure if I could live through another bout of lovemaking. I was exhausted.

"Mmm," Micah hummed onto my nipple and I squirmed beneath him.

"Micah," I panted. "I don't think I can—"

His hand delved lower, his slender fingers curled into the short, crisp hairs of my pussy and probed deep into my sensitive flesh. Micah plunged his fingers deep within my dripping vagina. Then he shocked me by pulling his fingers from my sex and bringing them to his face. He inhaled deeply and seemed to delight in our mixed scents.

Hmm...Maybe I could survive another bout. And if not, well...what a way to go.

I raised my arms, wrapped them around his neck, tunneled my fingers through his silky, black hair and tugged his head down to mine.

A part of me was ashamed that I could be so free, so wanton, with a complete stranger. Another, more slutty, part that I never knew existed, reveled in all of the new sensations I experienced. That part of me enjoyed each and every sensuous act Micah introduced me to.

Can a person die like this? It's a valid question. The French do call it La petite mort.

"Aiiee!" It was the only sound I managed to get passed my lips as Micah flexed his hips and drove his cock deep into me.

He looked down on me with those expressive eyes and smiled. A smile so filled with happiness, I felt it all of the way down to my toes.

I looked into those dark chocolate pools and wondered absently how he managed to make them look as if they glowed from within. He blinked slowly, his sooty lashes brushing his cheekbones. When he opened them again, the strange, inner glow was gone.

I chalked it all up to a residual hallucination left over from my inexperienced detoxification. I closed my eyes, attempted to bar other distractions and concentrated on reaching the elusive, orgasm that hung on the outer edge of my consciousness. It hovered just out of reach as Micah plunged his huge cock into me.

I wrapped my legs around his waist as his tempo increased. I was on fire, the slow burn started in my toes, working its way up to my stomach and blossoming out into a fiery conflagration as I finally climaxed.

"Micah," I screamed, his name forever emblazoned on my mind, in my heart. "I'm coming!"

Again, Micah lowered his head to the crook of my neck and suckled fiercely. The pleasure-pain became so intense that the sensation was too much for my exhausted body and I lost consciousness.

I woke to the feel of Micah's lips on my forehead, blinked my eyes open and attempted to look through the growing darkness.

He leaned over and flipped on the light, which was set on the table next to the bed. He relaxed back into a sitting position and smiled sadly. Dressed in the same black turtleneck, black slacks and shiny, black shoes he'd arrived in, he looked good enough to eat.

It's funny how comfortable I'd become watching him move so gracefully around my house without a stitch on. Now the sight of his clothes made me nervous.

"I must go now." He gazed down at me with sad eyes. "If the incubus returns, he will no longer have the ability to steal your untapped power. He will only be able to drain small amounts of it while you are," he paused for a minute. He looked uncomfortable. "While you are engaged in the act," he finished, after swallowing visibly.

I looked up at him, my eyes wide with disbelief. "You're leaving?"

Isn't that what you wanted?

I ignored the annoying inner voice that reminded me that was why I'd slept with him in the first place. I couldn't admit to myself that I didn't want him to leave. What about the promise he said he'd made to my father to protect me? Was it all just a line to get into my pants?

I dropped my gaze and looked everywhere but his eyes. I stupidly waved my arm toward the empty half of the bed that had, until just a few minutes ago, held his warm, sexy body close to mine.

His warm, virile, sexy body. I closed my eyes and took a deep breath. Shut up, just shut up. My mind raged at the thought that I fell for his trick.

"After, after..." I sputtered. My face blazed red with shame. The last thing I'd expected to feel was remorse. "You said you weren't going to leave. You said planned to stay and protect me."

I clamped my lips tight, determined to keep myself from begging him to stay. Tears burned the backs of my eyelids. I blinked furiously. The last thing I wanted was to have the tears spill over onto my cheeks. I'd never been the weepy sort and I refused to cry in front of him. I swallowed hard, trying to dislodge the growing lump in my throat.

The edge of the mattress dipped as he sat down beside me and I scurried to the other side of the bed.

It was a mistake.

His scent, and the unmistakable smell of sex, surrounded me. I squeezed my eyes closed against the onslaught. The stubborn tears wouldn't be held back. They slipped silently from the corners of my eyes. They slid down my cheeks unchecked.

I reached down, grabbed the sheet and ruthlessly tugged it up to cover my bare breasts. I held it against me, my fingers curled around it. My knuckles white as I held it in a death grip against my chest.

"What have I done?" I whispered to myself. I squeezed my eyes tighter and turned my head away as I felt his fingers slide under my jaw. He pulled on my chin, turned and lifted my face and forced me to meet his gaze.

"You have done what you must to keep the incubus from gaining the power to wreak havoc on mankind." He leaned down, placed a soft kiss on my lips, then stood. "As I have always done what I must. I have to go now. There are others. I will be here to protect you, but I must help the others as well."

I looked up at him and thinned my lips. "Others who need your kind of help?" I asked sarcastically. "Oh, you must really love your job!" I stood, grabbed the sheet from the bed and wrapped it around me like a toga.

"I wonder. How many guys get to bed virgins for a living, claiming it is all for the better good? No fucking wonder you were so patient." I looked at him scathingly and ignored his wince at my profanity. "Hell, I should feel honored. I've just been deflowered by a professional! How many women have you been with?" I held my hand up. "Never mind. Don't answer that." My voice broke. "I really don't think I want to know."

He looked at me through bleak eyes before he turned his back to me. He tilted his head back and looked toward the ceiling. "It never gets easier, Tasha. Yet it must be done to keep the incubi from overrunning the earth."

"How do they get here?" I asked, disgusted with myself for even giving a damn.

I sat back down on the bed with my back against the headboard, drew my legs up to my chest and wiggled my toes in the wrinkled bottom sheet. Micah sat on the other side of the bed. He made no move to touch me.

"They come through portals opened by the inexperienced or those who would sell their talents for profit. Portals, which can only be closed by one such as you."

"One such as me, huh?" I asked, as I slid from the bed. My feet missed the braided rag rug and made contact with the cold, hardwood floor. I danced back onto the rug and I alternately rubbed my bare feet up and down my legs for warmth.

"If one of them should manage to steal the untapped power from an untouched Guide, he would be able to seal an inter-dimensional door open, thus enabling a multitude of creatures to pass into this world from their own dimension, unchecked."

I dropped the sheet, grabbed my jeans and pulled them on. I walked across the room to my dresser and pulled out a tee shirt and yanked it furiously over my head. I'd worry about underwear later.

"So, let me see if I have this straight. You're a guy who just happens to be some sort of weird superhero-type gigolo sent to defile virgins who have some previously undiscovered abilities to close portals to other dimensions?"

The tone of my voice rose higher and higher with every unbelievable word until it ended in a near squeak. I was sure that either I had suddenly gone mad, or he had.

Micah nodded. A half smile on his too handsome face. "You understand. Good. If you wish, I could return to you between assignments."

By this time, my head pounded so bad, part of me was afraid I was suffering an aneurysm. I reached up and slapped his face, startling myself with the force of the blow. I stood, mouth agape, and watched as the imprint of my hand bloomed red on his cheek.

"Get out," I said softly. I needed to be alone to think. And I wanted him to leave before I started to bawl like an infant. I should have known better. I've known for some time that I was destined to be alone. "Get the hell out," I repeated louder when he didn't move.

He inclined his head. "As you wish."

I watched as he turned to walk out of my life. I held my arms at my sides and clenched my fingers closed. My hands, balled into fists, rested on my thighs. I refused to rescind my order even though I wanted to do nothing more than beg him to stay. I heard a creak and the muffled thud of the front door as he pulled it closed behind him.

I stumbled down the stairs and into the kitchen in darkness and only turned on the light when I reached my destination. Then I made myself a pot of coffee. The dark, bitter brew had always been Trina's drink, but I'd been addicted to the foul tasting stuff ever since I went through withdrawal. I was afraid to quit. I feared I would return to the unyielding grip of a harsher stimulant.

I sat down and placed my hands flat on the table. Only the tips of my thumbs and forefingers touched. I wanted to test a theory.

What if Micah had told me the truth? If he was, maybe I could forgive him given enough time. Like a million years or so.

Darla's mother, a Wiccan, and another one of my hordes of dead friends and family, once told me I was the direct descendant of a powerful Mage. She also said it was my destiny to save the world from an all-powerful evil. At the time, I was positive she smoked a bit too much of her smudging stick. Now I wasn't so sure.

I closed my eyes in an attempt to remember what it was she'd tried to teach me all of those years ago. The lessons, still buried deep in my mind, were precious to me, memories of friends who were gone, but would never be forgotten.

I took a deep breath and opened my mind to all of the possibilities governed by the laws of the Earth as I searched for the open portal. It must be near my home to allow an incubus to visit me. That is, of course, if Micah was telling the truth and Brock really was an incubus.

An unsettling thought hit me. Micah could be the incubus and Brock was what he seemed. After all I was just as attracted to him as I was to Brock, more so.

My eyes flew open at the disturbing thought and I had to work hard to empty my mind again. I relived Linda's lessons and strained to picture my normally quiet neighborhood as it should be. Suddenly, I felt light, almost airy, as if I left the tight constraints of my body behind to float effortlessly down the street.

A low, unearthly vibration caught my attention and I turned toward it. The sound was grating, like nails on a chalkboard. I floated smoothly into a backyard, three houses down from my own and passed a window. Mrs. Cooper was in her kitchen cooking. How can she not know this gaping hole was in her back yard? My ethereal mouth fell slack when I saw it. All of this was hard to believe, even as I stood and stared at the proof.

The open portal was just down the street from my house! Strange creatures slipped through, one every few seconds or so. Some of them looked liked the demons of legend. They were short, squat and a fiery, red orange with small, pointed horns on the tops of their heads.

Others were half man, half goat-like creatures. Their four legged frames sported two sets of genitals. One set for the animal and another, similarly sized set, for the man. One of them looked directly at me, then grinned and grasped himself suggestively.

Instinct told me this was the true form of an incubus. The body Brock used was nothing more than a borrowed shell. The sight shocked me so much I lost my concentration. My soul, consciousness, whatever, was sucked back into my body. I found myself still at my kitchen table and had to work even harder to clear my mind again.

"At the rate you're going, a million of those damn things are bound to pour out of that gate," I snarled at myself.

This time I tried to relax. I didn't try as hard and the trip down the block was easier. My return to the portal took almost no time at all. I drew on my memories of Linda's lessons and imagined a thick steel door that I closed over the portal.

Immense heat welded it shut, forever blocking the doorway. After a few minutes, all I could see in the yard, where the portal had been, was a door-sized patch of dry, brown grass.

I breathed a sigh of relief and mentally thanked Linda for the things she taught me before she died. I may have been a surly, smartass brat of a teenager, but at least I paid attention.

The gateway was closed and my powers as a Guide were no longer untapped. I frowned, thinking, as I sat in the chair at my table with my hands still splayed in front of me.

"Why can't they teach all of the virgin Guides to use their powers instead of sending someone to screw their brains out and leave them feeling like a cheap tramp?" I chewed on my lip for a minute as I thought that one over. "I bet it was a guy who came up with that solution." I shook my head. It really wouldn't surprise me a bit.

I stomped upstairs to put on some underwear and fetch my bag. I still had all of that money I took from Marco's. The least I could do was use some of the cash to help my fellow Guides.

CHAPTER SIX

I'D BEEN ON THE ROAD FOR THREE DAYS BEFORE I WOULD FINALLY ADMIT TO myself that I was completely, if not irrevocably, lost.

I pulled into a rest area somewhere in southeast Georgia to get a look at a map. I decided to get out of the car to stretch and use the facilities since they were available. Who knows when I'll see another place to stop on this lonely stretch of highway? Besides, I've found that apparently my bladder and kidneys work much harder while I'm on the road. Who knew?

"Face it, Tasha, you have no idea where in the hell you are," I groused as I stomped out of the restroom and looked for the usual sign with the big map of the state.

I frowned. Did Micah have some sort of sixth sense that told him where all of the virgin Guides were? Or did he just remember about me?

"Shit! If life were a cartoon, there'd be a friggin' light on over my head, right now," I said as the answer popped into my mind.

I hurried over to the nearest picnic table and placed my palms flat on the top, my fingers splayed wide, with the tips of my thumbs and forefingers touching.

I closed my eyes and attempted to zero in on the nearest portal. There was one, but it wasn't very close. I could feel its presence, but I was nowhere near enough to close it, especially alone, and using nothing but my newly discovered mental powers. I concentrated harder and tried to get a direction. Northeast, the portal was somewhere near Pennsylvania.

"Pennsylvania, huh?" I shook my head. "What a hotspot of other-dimensional activity."

"My, my, what have we here, a Guide? Lucky me."

I jumped at the sound of the sinister voice that came from behind me and caused my skin to crawl.

A tremor of fear shot up my spine as I stiffened in my seat. I slowly moved my hands to the edge of the table and began to stand.

Strong, cruel hands pushed down on my shoulders and forced me to sit back down on the bench. Pain shot up my spine as my butt made contact with the hard wooden surface.

I clamped my lips shut, since I've always been prone to being a smartass. I didn't want to have to fight my way out of this. My self-defense classes were very few, and far between, enough to make them almost nonexistent.

"What do you want?" I ground the question out between my clenched teeth. I turned my head. I wanted to keep an eye on him as I sat praying for an opening to escape.

"What do you think I want?" He bent low and breathed the answer in my ear. "Your blood, darling. I want your blood." His hot breath brushed the side of my neck and I almost jumped with fright. Okay, I was in big trouble now. My gaze darted around the small rest area as I looked for something I could use as a weapon.

I turned and threw first one, then the other of my legs over the bench. I needed to face my enemy. Seated, I was at enough of a disadvantage. Besides, this way, it would be easier to run when, and if, the opportunity presented itself.

I blinked, stunned, when I got my first, good look at my aggressor. Why would such a gorgeous guy feel the need to accost women in rest areas? But, from what I understand, it was all about control with guys like him.

"Look, handsome," I said with a tremulous smile. "You don't have to force me." I stood slowly and began to unbutton my blouse. Rapists liked the illusion of power. Take that away and most of them lost interest. I hoped so, anyway. I loosened another button and struck, what I hoped was a seductive pose.

Will I forever be cursed to jump to the wrong conclusion?

The man shook his head and smiled. "Wrong answer, sweetness." His smile grew broader and I almost fainted at my first glimpse of his lengthening incisors.

"Oh, my God," I gasped. How many impossible things would I be forced to believe? Had Gram drummed that into my head because she knew something like this would happen someday? By this point, I was sure she had.

I stumbled back against the bench I'd just vacated. I sat down hard and winced at the pain that shot up my spine as it made contact with the sharp edge of the tabletop.

The man stood still for a moment and stared at me. Then he laughed.

"Your God can't help you now."

He moved closer and his eyes glowed red. It made him look demonic. He grabbed me roughly by the arms and jerked me up from my seat, his fetid breath hot on my face.

"Expose your neck to me, mortal, that I may take sustenance."

My first thought had been that I was about to be murdered by some insignificant little snot with delusions of vampdom and great special effects. That is, until I felt myself expose my neck as he'd ordered.

At the same moment that I decided he was real, I remembered what Micah told me earlier about Brock, the incubus.

Call him and he will come.

I grimaced and hoped I wasn't about to make a huge mistake. The last thing I needed was to have to fight the two of them off. The vampire leaned closer, sniffing my neck. "Too bad you aren't still a virgin. Virgin's blood is so sweet. So addictive."

I took a deep breath.

"Brock!" I screamed his name as loud as I could. About two seconds passed and he appeared before me, minus the cop uniform. Brock looked mighty handsome in worn blue jeans, pointy toed cowboy boots and a blue and brown plaid shirt. He looked like I just pulled him from a square dance or something.

Brock growled at the vampire that had just begun to sink his sharp fangs into my exposed neck as he held me a foot or so from the ground.

"Get your hands off my woman, scum."

It appeared as though any woman belonged to an incubus when he was near, or so he thought. It was a good thing there wasn't a busload of tanning models here or I may have been in real trouble. Then again, the vamp may have considered them an all-you-can-eat buffet. Me? I'm just cheese and crackers.

The vampire tilted his head back and laughed. "Such thoughts you have, ma petite."

I fought the urge to tell him that I wasn't his little anything. Instead, I breathed a sigh of relief. At least his teeth were away from my neck at the moment.

He turned toward Brock and scowled. "The woman is mine, incubus. Leave us while you still have your head upon your shoulders." The deranged vampire answered as he set me on my feet and placed me beside him. He held my wrist in a painful, inescapable grip.

Since I didn't want to draw either of their attention, I fought the urge to raise my hand and clamp it to my neck where the vampire's teeth punctured my skin. I felt the blood ooze down the front of my chest, inching toward the collar of my favorite silk blouse, threatening to ruin it.

Brock looked at the vamp and laughed. "She called for me, did she not?" He asked the agitated vamp as he paced back and forth.

"Tell me your real name, incubus, so I may see to it that your remains are disposed of properly," the vampire bellowed.

He was so preoccupied with Brock that I don't think he realized when he released my arm. I waited a few seconds and inched sideways, away from him. I moved slowly so I wouldn't draw attention to myself.

"I'm an other-dimensional magical being, I don't have remains, dickhead," Brock scoffed. "I don't even have a corporeal body on this plain of existence." He grinned and held his arms out to his sides. "Sorry to disappoint you, but this is all just an illusion, Rogue."

By this time, both of them had forgotten all about little old me. I took the advantage I'd gained by calling Brock and slipped away while they practiced their male posturing. I made it to my car just before the blows started.

I didn't stick around to see who won me.

I DROVE IN THE general direction of Pennsylvania and the open portal. Since I had managed to get a tentative lock on it before ole-toothy arrived, I was pretty sure I was headed in the right direction. I stopped once for gas and two other times for a pit stop. Both times I chose well-lit, very populated areas.

"What is it about being on the road that makes you have to pee so much?" I asked myself in the fourth ladies' room in less than seven hours.

Finally, exhausted, I rented a small room on the outskirts of some small town in Ohio that I can't remember the name of. The motel I remember, it was The Nineteenth Hole. It was a hole, all right, but it had a shower and a bed, and that's all that really mattered.

I'd just stepped out from a nice long shower when there was a knock on the door. This is the time that, in a perfect world, I would grab my Glock from my bag, check its load and sneak toward the door to look out through the little peephole.

Instead, I grabbed two towels from the holder on the wall, wrapped one around my head and the other around my body, then crept toward the door. I expected certain doom in the form of one very pissed-off vampire.

"Oh God," I whispered as I looked through the tiny peephole on the door. My hands trembled as I reached for the deadbolt, all the while wondering how he'd found me.

I hadn't expected Micah, but there he was, in all his masculine glory, and he was infinitely better than ole-toothy. Certain parts of my traitorous anatomy began to cheer.

"What do you want?" I asked and crossed my arms. I feigned nonchalance when all I wanted to do was jump his miserable, wonderful, bones.

He stood and stared at me from the sidewalk just outside the door. "You, of course," he said with a smile.

That smile was devastating. He was devastating. I fought the urge to fan myself. Goodness! He looked good enough to eat in those navy blue slacks and cream silk shirt. I licked my lips.

"Aren't you going to invite me in?"

"Why?" I joked, "Are you some sort of vampire and you can't come in unless I invite you?" After what happened earlier, I may have given that some serious thought if he hadn't entered my home uninvited a few nights ago.

Micah smiled and shrugged. "Invite me in and find out. Maybe I'm just a gentleman." He leaned against the doorjamb, looking sexier than anyone than anyone had a right to.

My nether parts twitched out a reminder of what this man could do with that muscular body and I capitulated.

"Come in already and shut the door behind you."

Micah did exactly as I instructed, then leaned back against the door, his hands in his pockets.

His heated stare blazed a trail up and down my almost bare torso. He took a deep breath and I wondered, a bit madly, if he could smell my arousal. I pulled the towel from my head, combed my hair with my fingers and watched him through the mirror over the dresser. I picked up my brush and he was behind me in a blink, removing it from my hand.

Micah gently pushed me into the chair next to the dresser. Then, standing between my legs, he combed the tangles from my long hair. He was so gentle it almost brought tears to my eyes.

"Why are you here?" he asked. His deep voice caused little ripples of desire to dance through my body. I shivered even as my blood began to heat.

"I've had an idea to help the others," I answered breathlessly. The slow strokes of the brush were turning me inside out. My body burned, already preparing itself for his possession. "I figured that if someone can teach other Guides to use their powers, they won't be at the mercy of the incubus." Or at the mercy of the Cartuotey.

By the time he finished brushing my hair, I was a quivering mass of goose-pimpled flesh. He helped me stand on wobbly legs, then kissed me until my legs gave out completely.

Micah scooped me up in his arms and carried me to the king sized bed. His mouth doing magical things to me as it traveled from my mouth to my neck, down to the edge of the towel covering my breasts, then back to my kiss starved lips.

Oh, yes. Micah's mouth was a drug that I was definitely addicted to.

He smiled against my lips and I opened my eyes. It was a slow, satisfied smile. One that told me he'd been eavesdropping on my thoughts again. I pulled away from him.

"You said you wouldn't do that." I frowned. Besides, I wanted to know how he did it. I scooted away from him, slapping at his wandering hands and put my back against the headboard.

"Do what?"

I shook my head. "Don't give me that innocent look. You know exactly what I'm talking about." I glared at him, drawing my knees up against my chest in an attempt to hinder his view of my exposed body, since my towel had gone missing. I shot a look over the side of the bed, briefly wondering where in the heck it went. "How do you read my mind?"

Micah looked at me, obviously uncomfortable with his gifts, and sighed. "If you must know, I am Vampyr," he said with a strange accent. He sat up next to me, his arm brushing mine.

I felt my eyes widen and my hand flew to my neck, feeling for the place where he'd suckled it the last time we were together. He'd drawn so hard at the spot just above my collarbone, I was sure I'd have a mark there the next day, but there had been none.

I had to invite him into the room.

"Oh, God!" I jumped off of the bed and whirled around, trying to keep my distance. "Why didn't I have to invite you into my house?" I nervously cast my gaze about, searching for a weapon.

Micah smiled softly, "You already had. You once told me I would be welcome there anytime, as long as I had orange slices." He dug into his pocket and pulled out two individually wrapped pieces of my favorite childhood treat.

My mind filled to overflowing with memories, memories of my father and his group of friends. One man in particular I once called ... "Meeka?" I asked. My gaze met his in recognition as I spoke that beloved name. I hopped back onto the bed, no longer able to fear him. I wrapped my arms around his neck, resting my head on his shoulder. "Where have you been? I haven't seen you since..."

"Since you realized I wasn't aging," Micah finished for me, gently stroking my hair. "You sat on my lap one day, tracing my features with your chubby little hand," he picked up my hand and kissed my fingers one by one. "You said, *Why don't you get lines like Daddy, Meeka?* That was when I knew I must stop making my visits to you." He turned suddenly sad eyes my way. "Your father had forbidden anyone to tell you of us. I was forced to leave, no matter how much the separation would hurt you."

I hugged him to me, tears running freely down my face. I remembered his earlier comment about feeling my power when I was a child. I thought he'd been lying, trying to get me to trust him.

I laid my hand against his cheek. "I missed you. Daddy told me you went away and couldn't come back. I assumed you died."

Micah nodded. "As you were meant to. I vowed to your father to keep you safe, no matter the cost." He ran his fingers through my still damp hair, whispering nonsensical things to me as I cried happy tears against his chest.

I pulled back a bit, needing to look into his eyes. "Also meaning, if you had to take my virginity, you had his blessing?"

His hand stilled at my question and I had my answer. I took a deep breath. "Look. I'm over being angry about that, Micah," I rested my hand on his chest. "I just have this problem with sharing, that's all."

"I know. You never did play well with others, even as a child," he said with a chuckle.

I chuckled for a minute before turning back to him, serious. "I mean it, Micah. I can get over the fact you'll never age. I can even deal with the fact that you are, technically, *way* too old for me." I winked up at him and grinned. "By the way, you've got to be the sexiest geriatric I've ever laid eyes on," I said, giggling at his outraged expression.

"Ow! That hurt," I gasped when he pinched my ass.

He smiled and waggled his brows at me. "Want me to kiss it and make it better?"

I smiled sadly. "This thing about sharing," I reminded him.

"You won't have to worry about it."

I sat up and scowled at him. "Of course I have to worry about it. If you think, for even a nano-second, that I'll just stand by while you go off and screw every magically inactive Guide in the world, you're out of your fucking mind!"

I started to pull away, but Micah took my hand and pulled me toward him. He smiled and held my trembling hand in his.

"Such language, Tasha. What would your grandmother think?" he deliberately reminded me of her hatred of profanity.

"This may sound crude, but every Cartuotey knows when he has met the woman he wants to spend his life with. It's usually a Guide. We don't know who he or she is, until we have been close to them for some time or have been intimate. That is the main reason we do what we do. We don't do it for our egos or because we want a—a piece of ass." He said the last softly, as if he felt uncomfortable saying it. Perhaps it did make him uncomfortable. He never pretended to like my use of foul language. Maybe I'd humor him and try to clean it up.

"My mother was a vampire?" I asked incredulous. As usual, I concentrated on the most irrelevant thought that popped into my mind.

He shook his head. "No, a Guide can find love anywhere. They are born mortal and find love where they will. With one of my kind, it is different. We must find a person we are completely compatible with—a mate—to find the unconditional love we crave. It seems that only our mates are mentally strong enough to overcome the shock of knowing the truth of what we are."

"Let me see if I understand this." I pulled my hand free and sat up to better look at him. "All Cartuoteys are vampires, and all Guides are mortals?"

He nodded. "Then there is a Guardian of the Gate, this is the child of two Guides. They have more power than that of a regular Guide, but less power than that of a vampire."

I tried to absorb all of this and it took me a minute to catch up.

"If I wanted to, I could go out and find any man to love, marry and have a life with?"

He nodded.

But if I do that...what?" I asked. "What does it do to the vampire? To—to you?"

49

"It leaves them alone until another is born who is compatible. For some that never happens. But, to be honest, for most it is usually a few hundred years before we are given a second chance. Otherwise he or she can relieve the sexual tensions of their body, but they will never find unconditional love and they will never be able to procreate." He shrugged. "Unless they turn humans, but that isn't true procreation."

"So you've been dancing around the globe having sex with as many women as you can?" I bit my lip, deep in thought, still not sure how to take all of this. My head was ready to spin from my shoulders after all of the crap I'd learned over the last few days.

"Pretty much," Micah agreed with my assessment.

I looked up at him. For the first time, I wondered about his age. He obviously wasn't the thirty-five or so years I'd originally believed him to be. He still looked the same as I remembered him and he'd been gone from my life for at least twenty years.

"Eleven-hundred and thirty-six," he answered before I could ask.

"Yep, you're way too old for me," I said with a grin.

Another thought barely formed in my head when he said, "I was born in the year eight-hundred and seventy. And yes, I have seen much."

"Oh, my God." Once again, my mind latched onto the most irrelevant fact. "And you and your...your libido have been globetrotting since...when? The year eight-hundred and ninety, or so?"

CHAPTER SEVEN

I HIT THE ROAD AGAIN EARLY THE NEXT MORNING. MICAH LEFT ME TO my own devices, after a night of mind-blowing sex, with the promise to find me later that night. He said he had some sort of business to attend to and I wasn't inclined to argue. I enjoy a bit of solitude, to a certain extent. I am used to being alone, after all.

Besides, I understood his motives. I just didn't agree with them. He, in his infinite stupidity, thought it was better for the two of us to remain separated as much as possible until one or the other of us—namely me—needed backup. My argument was I wouldn't need backup if he was with me.

He promised to leave the deflowering of virgins to the other vamps who hadn't found their mates from now on. It wasn't hard to wring the promise out of him, especially after I threatened to call Brock and have sex with him while Micah watched. I wouldn't have, of course, but a girl has to do what a girl—well, I'll just leave it at that.

I drove down the interstate with a newly marked map. Micah didn't want me to get lost again. Especially after I told him about the grander-than-thou vamp I'd run into. He'd highlighted the route with a bright pink pen and even told me what hotel to go to.

I started to get a little peeved at his bossiness. But I tried to make allowances. He had been raised when women were to be protected and all. And besides, I think I'm beginning to like it.

I followed his directions and ensconced myself into the motel of his choice before nightfall. Apparently vamps can come out in the daylight, but they're weak and without power until sundown. That's why most of them chose to sleep during the day. I can't say I blame them. I'm more of a night person myself. I still wondered where Micah went when the sun was up though. It wasn't as if he could do much, apparently.

I showered and ordered a pizza while I waited. I wasn't about to miss dinner again. If I have to keep feeding Micah, I need to keep up my strength. A small pizza ought to do the trick.

51

I checked the peephole when someone knocked on the door later. It was my small pepperoni and onion pizza. I paid the guy, tipped him a five and apologetically closed the door in his acne-covered face.

An hour later, I finished my dinner and started to pace the floor. It was long since dark and I needed to know where Micah was.

"Good grief, I hope I haven't turned into one of those clingy women who can't be without their man for a day."

I shuddered at the thought. Daddy always taught me to be independent. I wondered, a bit briefly, why he never thought to teach me to use my powers as well.

I never really knew Daddy as well as I should have. He always left me at Gram's and went off with his friends. He remained almost as much of a stranger as they were. Micah was the only one of his friends who ever came around a lot. Then, suddenly, he'd stopped his frequent visits. At least now I know why.

It felt good to know that there was still someone around who had a connection with my youth. I haven't lost everyone after all.

It was a wonderful thought.

I have to assume that Gram had known what Micah was. She was Daddy's mother after all, even if she was a...mortal. God, using that word in that context sticks in my throat. And she had been a Guide.

Gram died just after I turned eighteen. She held on just long enough so I could inherit her house and live there by myself without fear of the authorities sticking me in a foster home.

Daddy still visited me infrequently over the next few years. Until one day, about five years ago, he left and never came back. I always assumed he died on the road somewhere. I wonder if Micah knows what happened.

Maybe I should ask him.

I finally worked off most, if not all, of my nervous energy and sat down on the bed to wait. I turned on the TV and wondered where in the hell Micah could be.

BANG. BANG. BANG.

"WHAT the hell?" I sat up abruptly and pushed my fingers through my sleep-tousled hair. I glanced at the clock on the bedside table. The large digital display blinked three forty-five a.m. at me in bright green numbers. I reached over to the nightstand and switched on the lamp.

"This better be good," I grumbled as I crawled out of the bed and stumbled to the door. Since I knew it could only be one person, I decided to forgo the peephole so I could immediately commence with some serious bitching. I unlocked it and slung the door wide.

"It's about damn time you showed up," I snarled. "I've been worried sick. Get your ass..." My voice trailed off as I stared with horror at the very pissed off vamp in the doorway.

I quickly stepped back with a squeal before he could reach in and grab me. So, I was safe for the moment. But the door still hung wide open and he glared in at me, a very hungry expression on his face.

Leave it to me to find myself in a situation where I was stuck in a hotel room with a vicious vampire just outside the door. One who could trick me into inviting him in at any minute.

"Why me?" I shook my head. "Go away." I made a shooing motion with my hands while I wiggled my fingers, hoping he'd get the idea. But he didn't budge. "I don't want any. I'm quite happy with my own vamp."

He just stood there and stared at me, a terrifying smile on his face. One that said he knew something that I didn't.

"Your friend is not coming," he lisped past his lengthened incisors.

My mouth fell open as I watched them grow and I stepped back a few more feet when his eyes did that funny glowing thing I've seen Micah's do on occasion. It scared me when this guy did it. He wasn't horny. Well, at least I was pretty sure he wasn't horny, not that I would have accommodated him if he had been.

I looked around the room for an object I could use as a weapon. The desk held a pad of paper, three envelopes and a pen. The table next to the bed wielded the more substantial weapon. A four-inch thick phone book and the telephone. I shook my head. I just didn't think it would do much good against an assailant of his caliber.

"Invite me in."

I pinched my lips together between my teeth to keep my mouth shut. The voice attempted a compulsion and I chalked my resistance up to my being a Guide. I closed my eyes, trying to shake off the absurdity of my previous thought. Am I really going to buy into all of this?

"Invite me in. Now."

I ignored him and continued with my inventory of the room. The dresser held my bag of money, suitcase and purse. All of which were totally useless at the moment.

Behind me on the vanity, which was set just outside the bathroom, were my mousse, brush and blow dryer. No weapon there, unless I could style him to death. Then my eyes lit on the bathroom door.

"Invite me in," he repeated. The voice held a heavy compulsion that I found nearly impossible to resist.

My body turned leaden as I moved to face him. My mouth actually opened to utter the words he needed to hear to be able to enter the room, which was mine for the evening.

I clamped my hand over my mouth, bolted into the bathroom, and locked the door behind me. I turned the water on in the tub to block the dreadful sound of his beautiful voice as he attempted to compel me to invite him in. I didn't mind being Micah's dinner once in a while, but I drew the line at becoming an all night, all-you-can-eat buffet.

Where was Micah? I needed him and he was nowhere to be found. He knew there was a possibility this could happen. How could he leave me? I sat down on the floor, drew my knees up to my chest and prayed. I prayed that whatever magic bound the vampire from this room, without invitation, would hold, at least, until Micah finally arrived.

That was how Micah found me. Huddled in the corner, tears staining my cheeks and my arms wrapped around my knees. I jumped when he touched me, screaming hysterically, until I realized who it was. I cried on his shoulder when he lifted me in his arms and carried me to the bed.

"I'm sorry, sweetheart," he whispered against my temple. "I had to prove to the others that Camen had turned Rogue. It had to appear as though you were alone, without protection, so he would act." Micah wrapped his arms around me and cradled me against the warmth of his chest.

"I'm so cold." My teeth chattered as he took my frozen hands in his and rubbed them together.

"He can't harm you now. The others have taken him for punishment."

I shuddered at the word knowing what he meant. But I rationalized, if anyone deserved a death sentence it was the vamp who attempted to kill me twice. He was no better than Marco had been.

I finally relaxed in Micah's arms and wrapped my own around him. I let him hold me and absorbed his heat. I snuggled closer to his warmth, inhaling his scent as if I could never get enough. I ignored the little voice in my head that proclaimed I would never get enough of him and buried my face in his neck.

After I calmed down, I pulled back a bit and looked up at him. "Why didn't I have to invite you in?" I worried my lower lip. What if the other vamp had found that he could just waltz in here uninvited? My eyes widened. Would I ever be safe anywhere?

Micah smiled. "I made the reservation, remember?"

"Oh, yes, now that you mention it," I nodded. I'm sure my relief showed in my sagging shoulders. He had insisted on it, now that I recall. It was a good thing, too. Otherwise I'd still be huddled on the bathroom floor in a heap.

At least now I knew why he'd been so adamant about why he should make the reservation. I rested my head on his shoulder, and thought about how nice it felt to snuggle up to him on the bed. I couldn't remember the last time I was able to just revel in the sense of being close to someone. I had the sneaking suspicion it had been with Micah, though.

I turned my head a bit and buried my nose in the vee of his shirt. Goodness, he smelled good enough to eat.

Micah's hand stilled where he'd been smoothing my hair and I felt a bulge in the general vicinity of his crotch.

I cleared my throat, "Well, either you've taken to packing lead, or you're really happy to see me." I half joked, not caring that he'd read my mind. All I cared about was that I was still alive and he was with me.

He clenched his teeth together, fisted his hand in my hair and tugged. My head tipped back and I looked directly into his fathomless, ebony eyes.

"I'm extremely happy to see you," he growled, just before his lips lowered to mine.

I thought of reprimanding him for bullying me around, for a split second. But I gave a mental shrug and decided I liked it.

Micah's hands were all over me. His fingers bunched in my hair, feathered down my back and over my bottom. My arms wound around his neck and I pulled his head to me as his tongue traced a fiery trail down between my breasts.

My nightshirt was no longer on my body, even though I had no memory of removing it. We were skin-to-skin, chest-to-chest. Micah cradled me in his arms as his mouth moved sensuously over my breasts. The feel of his unshaven jaw added to the decadent sensations as the short hairs prickled my skin. It made me tingle and burn as he scraped his cheek over my hardened nipples.

"Ooh, yessss. I like that," I moaned.

He lifted me easily, effortlessly, and lowered me to the comforter. I placed my hands on his smooth chest, then let them wander lower, across his flat stomach, to the part of his anatomy that was so happy to see me.

"Ah, Tasha," he hissed between clenched teeth. "You'll be the death of me."

I looked up at him and grinned. "Maybe, but what a way to go," I said before I lowered my head to wrap my lips around the tip of his cock.

Micah groaned. He buried his fingers in my hair and held my head in place as he moved his hips and drove his thick length into my mouth.

I never would have believed I would like this. But somehow, as his mind filled mine with the pleasure I gave him, I knew I could never imagine doing this for another living soul. But with Micah, it felt right.

I ran my tongue down around the base of his engorged shaft while I squeezed his sac and ran my nails over his upper thighs. His hips bucked, driving him deeper. I fisted my hand around the base of his cock and squeezed. My hand milked his hard shaft as I drove him closer to the edge.

I pulled my head back, ran my tongue around the head and felt the ridge around the crown. Then I plunged my mouth down over his length, using my teeth to scrape lightly over his cock. It nearly drove him wild.

Micah cupped my cheeks and lifted my head before I could give him the ultimate pleasure. His cock bucked wildly, impatient for its moment of ecstasy.

I felt him shudder beneath my hands as he fought to regain control of the need to come. He closed his eyes, breathing heavily, and held me against him with a strength no mortal could possibly possess.

He pulled me to a sitting position, cupped the cheeks of my ass in his hands, raised me up over his engorged erection and lowered me slowly onto him.

I cried out with my first orgasm as soon as his thumb thrummed the engorged nub at the apex of my thighs. I bounced up and down on his lap wildly until he rolled us over to regain control.

I had none. My control had vanished the moment he lowered me onto his massive staff.

"Fuck me, dammit!" I bit his lower lip, drawing it into my mouth.

He grinned. "I like that kind of language in the bedroom. It shows me what a hellcat you are." He raised himself up and pulled his cock out of me.

He flipped me over onto my stomach, wrapped his fist around his bucking member and caressed its length as I stared back at him, impatient.

"Raise your ass into the air."

I groaned when he gave my rear a playful slap. I never knew how erotic something like that could be. The light sting added to the fire Micah built within me. He positioned himself behind me and rammed his cock into my me.

"Ah, that feels so good, you prick."

I needed this. After everything I'd been through earlier, I needed this with everything in me. More than anything, tonight, I needed to feel alive.

Micah answered the urgency within me. He drove deep inside my tight channel, he pistoned his cock into the moist warmth of my body. He thrust hard, moving his blood-engorged length in and out, faster and faster. He pulled out and rolled me back over.

"I want to see you when you come," he said, his breathing rough. Reaching down, he pulled my legs up and wrapped them around his waist before he plunged into me again.

I knew when he neared the edge. I felt it, even as he brought me to another climax. I saw the burning need in his eyes and the familiar glow that accompanied both his lust and bloodlust. I reached up, wrapped my arms around his neck and drew his head down to me. He buried his face in my neck when I turned my head and opened myself up to his need.

A moment of pain gave way to a pleasure so intense I climaxed again. The warm, wet velvet of my channel milked his engorged shaft as it plunged in and out of me.

He pulled his mouth from my skin and called my name in a hoarse growl, a sound so primitive it barely sounded human.

I retained my consciousness, this time. I stayed within the circle of his arms, beside him, my fingers threading through the sable silk of his hair. I held his head to me and drifted to sleep.

THE MORNING SUN BEAT through the windows. It cast a golden glow through the open curtains onto the empty side of the bed. Micah was gone. He'd written a note on the hotel stationary and left it on the desk.

Dearest Tasha,

The room is paid through another night. The portal is near.
Please forgive my absence, I shall return tonight.

Yours,
Micah

"Now what in the hell do I do?" I asked my reflection as I crumpled his note and threw it into the trash. I looked in the mirror and shrugged.

Well, with my gold-blonde hair I wasn't beautiful, but I haven't seen anyone throw up when they look at me yet. So I suppose that's a plus.

Trina always said my eyes were too blue and too big for my face. I frowned at my reflection critically. Maybe she'd been right. I examined my neck where Micah bit me. There was still no mark. I wondered if he had some sort of healing power. It was just as well if he did. The last thing I want was to run around looking like some demented pincushion.

I turned back to survey the room and did a mental inventory. I had a few options. I could hung around in the hotel room twiddling my thumbs while I wait for Micah to have all of the fun. Or I could try to find the open portal and close it myself. I am supposed to be some sort of sorceress, after all, aren't I?

A hot shower and an hour and a half later, I was in the diner down the street eating breakfast. I have my priorities and the first one is staying well fed and hydrated. I never know when Micah is going to show up and want a snack.

I sat in a booth near the window and slurped down my fourth cup of coffee while I read the local paper. The front-page story told of a serial killer at large who had slit the throats of eligible young misses. The murderer had also drained their blood into some type of container. At least that's what the authorities thought since there was never any blood left at the scene. I, of course, had my own theory. But I couldn't tell that to the police, not without getting locked in the loony bin anyway.

My breakfast passed in silence, the only noise was the chink of my silverware against the cheap, china plate as I ate a western omelet and a side of hash browns. I informed my waitress of my addiction to coffee upon my arrival and she frequently passed by to top off my cup with a smile. I stayed for a while and happily slurped my coffee in between her visits.

An hour later, I stepped out into the bright sunshine and wondered where Micah was and, what it was, exactly, he did in daylight hours. He'd already informed me that he didn't necessarily have to hide from the sunlight. He wasn't the kind of vampire from legends. Those vampires, the ones like Camen, had turned Rogue and would kill anyone, where and when the mood struck. Even one of their own kind. Micah informed me that type of vampire was very rare. Thank God!

I stepped from the sidewalk, crossed the street and peeked in the window of the nearest dress shop. I looked down at my worn jeans and grubby sneakers.

"I want new clothes."

Five years of addiction had me wearing nearly worn out everything. I looked down at my slovenly appearance and wondered exactly what it was Micah saw in me. I puffed out my cheeks and blew a stray lock of hair out of my eyes with a sigh.

I definitely needed to do some shopping. A homeless person I am not and it was time I stopped dressing like one. The virgin Guides and murderous Rogues would just have to be patient and wait another day.

Two hours and a thousand dollars later, I stepped from the shop dressed to the nines. I held four bags and a business card for the hair salon down the street. The note the manager wrote on the back read—Help her, please!

I wasn't sure whether I should feel insulted or flattered. I opted for blind ignorance and limped down the street in my newly acquired three-inch pumps.

When I finally arrived at the salon—after three rest stops at various points in between—where I removed my shoes to rub my aching feet—I found that there had been a hidden message in that short note. The hidden message being, give her the works, spare no expense and wax her everywhere she has the hair of an Australian bushman.

It was a lot to fit on the back of a card, so, apparently they'd worked out this little code...

I was snipped, waxed, manicured and given a pedicure before they gooped up my face and stuck me under a hairdryer. I looked at myself in the mirror behind the chair across from me and nearly screamed with fright.

Who was that creature that stared back at me with bits of tin foil stuck in her hair and green goop on her face? I shook my head. That couldn't possibly be me. I looked like an advertisement for a UFO buff convention.

I sat back in the chair with my magazine. I might as well relax and enjoy it. My plans to save the world from creatures that come through open portals to other dimensions would just have to wait another day.

Chapter Eight

EVERY BIT OF THE TORTURE I WENT THROUGH EARLIER WAS WORTH IT. JUST for that one moment when Micah got his first glimpse of my newly-styled self.

He knocked on the door before he walked in. He used the key I'd given him the night before. His first glimpse of me as I lay on the bed in my new sheer emerald-green negligee had obviously been a surprise. His mouth fell open with shock.

Imagine mine, when he'd finally managed to unglue his tongue from the roof of his mouth to tell me I had to get dressed so we could go apprehend an incubus and close the open portal.

"Damn it," I snarled, stumbling a bit as I stuck my legs into my almost worn out jeans. "The one time I try to look nice for you, you want me to dress like a slob to close a damned portal."

"I did not say you should dress like a slob. I merely suggested that a silk dress and high heels were not necessarily the best choice for incubus hunting," Micah said with a smile. He sat on the bed and watched me dress with no small degree of interest.

I wiggled into my jeans, then noticed the path of Micah's stare. "Get your eyes off my ass. We have work to do," I growled. "And it's not fair. Stop looking at me like that. You're going to make me horny."

He continued to watch me and raised his sculpted brow. His dark chocolate eyes took in every move I made.

"I'd say, by the way you're acting, it's too late already."

"Oh shut up, you, you vampire," I snapped when I couldn't think of a more scathing retort. I stalked into the bathroom to put the rest of my clothes on. I *so* didn't want to see the smug male look of satisfaction he kept throwing my way.

"NICE CAR," I WHISTLED, when he led me to a sleek black limo parked down the street from the hotel. "Why didn't you just have him pick us up?" I asked before I got a glimpse of the driver. "Oh. Why didn't you have her pick us up?"

He probably doesn't want his hottie of a driver to know he's been hopping in the sack with you. Can't say that I blame him. She's gorgeous.

We settled ourselves into the backseat. Micah grabbed my hand and brought it to his lips.

"You are beautiful. If I have not told you this before, I apologize." He kissed each and every one of my fingers slowly, reverently, before he pressed another opened-mouth kiss onto my palm.

My mouth went dry as I went all girly inside at his blatant show of affection in front of his gorgeous female driver. I looked up into his eyes and curled my fingers around my palm in an attempt to hold the sensation of his kiss against my flesh.

I leaned my head against his shoulder and relaxed as the driver eased the car out onto the road.

"Thank you," I whispered into his neck. I didn't trust myself to say much more without saying something sappy and, therefore, embarrassing.

"For what?" he asked aloud. He gently probed my mind when I clamped my lips tight. I slammed my mind's door closed, barring his intrusion. I think the move shocked him. I remembered the exercise from when I was younger and stayed over at Darla's house a lot. It was another lesson Linda insisted I sit through. She said it was to bar psychic vampires from sapping my energy. She'd never mentioned the blood drinking type. I wonder if she'd known about them.

What happens to a guy when you tell him he's perfect? I was afraid it would go to his head, so I opted for silence.

Micah gently withdrew his mind from mine and gave me a small smile. He wrapped his arm around me and we settled back into the comfortable seat. I reveled in our closeness and enjoyed the warmth of his body seeping into mine as we sped toward the open portal.

The car drew to a smooth stop in the parking lot of a Catholic Church. I gaped through the window for a moment before I turned my stunned gaze to Micah.

"This is where the open portal is?"

Micah shook his head. "No, but it is easier to open them near areas of great spiritual power. The stronger the energy, the longer the portal can draw from it, allowing it to stay open."

He looked through the window, out into the darkness. He was obviously able to see much more than I could, with my very human, very limited night vision.

I squeezed my eyes shut. "Are you telling me a portal opened near a church can stay open indefinitely?" Isn't that just great news? The one I'd closed down the street from my house released six other-dimensional creatures before I'd closed it and those were just the ones I'd actually seen. There was no way to be sure how many creatures had made it through before I found it.

"Correct." Micah nodded. He looked out into the darkness and drummed his fingers on his knee impatiently. I wondered what he was waiting for.

"How do they keep people from seeing them?" I asked with a frown. "I mean, I think I'd remember seeing a green and orange spotted half man, half goat-like animal roaming the streets of *my* city."

"Only the gifted can see them."

"The gifted?"

"People like you," he answered absently while he looked out into the darkness.

"People like me?" I scowled. "Listen, bubba, I don't want to be the one who rains on your parade, but this is a curse, not a gift."

"As you wish," he shrugged. "According to my calculations, this portal has been open for nearly two months."

"Two months? What are we waiting for then? Shouldn't we close it?"

The words had barely left my mouth when I saw something move in the shadows. Micah leapt from the car and pounced into the inky blackness before I could even blink.

I scrambled through the door to join him.

"Bro—"

"Do not!"

I fisted my hands on my hips and scowled at Micah. "What was that for?" I asked and waved my hand toward the seemingly humanoid creature Micah held in a chokehold. "He's already here."

The creature sneered at me and sniffed the air around us as if we smelled bad. I fought the ridiculous urge to sniff at my armpits even though I'd had a shower less than two hours ago.

"I am not Brock, you weak, sniveling mortal." He spat the last as if mortal was a dirty word.

Micah slammed him up against the brick wall at his back. The incubus grunted in pain as a network of spider-webbed cracks formed on the wall behind him.

Micah's eyes glowed red. They were the same strange, iridescent-orange as when he'd come to save me from the incubus at my home.

"Quit while you are ahead, incubus. Do not think to insult my mate," he growled in a voice that wasn't quite human. "You will not survive it." Micah enunciated each word carefully.

I put my hand on Micah's arm. "Why have you captured this poor, ignorant—not to mention ugly—creature? What possible use can it serve?" I flicked it a glance. "It's not like he's important or anything." Unless, of course, Micah wanted the pleasure of sending the thing back to whatever dimension it came from. What do I know?

I was under the impression it would automatically happen when the portal closed. I refused to think of all of the creatures there could be roaming the Earth if they weren't returned when the portal was sealed.

"Don't you think our first priority should be to close the big gaping hole to whatever dimension has spewed forth these demonic looking creatures? In other words," I waved my hand in the Brock lookalike's general direction. "Hideous Hank's home?"

The incubus snarled at the insult. He looked at Micah, then smirked with his superior knowledge. "She knows nothing of her own world. Do you see? Human. Pathetic. The words are synonymous." The last of his sentence was garbled as Micah's temper peaked and he tightened his grip.

"Do not!" Micah's teeth lengthened and his eyes glowed blood red. He turned toward me. He still held it a foot or so from the ground by its neck.

"We need a magical being to close the portal. There is a ritual we must perform." He closed his eyes and shook his head. "Your father should have taught you this years ago. So you could protect yourself. I told him, but he would not listen. He felt if you were ignorant, you would be safe."

He turned his attention back to the creature as it began to struggle again. "There is a banishing ritual we must perform. It will send all those that have used this portal back and will close the gate forever."

I looked at Micah, completely confused. "Why can't I just close it the way I closed the other one?"

"What other one?" Micah asked. He turned to look at me, his eyes wide.

"The one Br-the other incubus came through. It was only a few houses down from my home."

Micah looked at me through narrowed eyes. "You closed it? How?"

"It was easy," I shrugged. "I just imagined this big steel door closing over the big, shaft to..." I waved my hand. "Whatever dimension it is, Hank comes from," I said and indicated the incubus. "And it closed."

"Try it again." Micah's eyes were wide with disbelief.

"Okaaaay." I don't know why he thought I couldn't close the friggin' thing. He was the one who told me I was some sort of witch to begin with. I shook my head. "Men!"

I walked to the nearest bench, knelt down on the cool, damp grass in front of it and placed my palms flat. The tips of my thumbs and forefingers touched on the seat. What had Darla's mother called it? Oh, Yes. The pyramid. How could I have forgotten that?

I closed my eyes and followed the psychic link that I discovered I had with these harbingers of evil and found the open portal.

It was three blocks away in the parking lot of a Chinese restaurant. I didn't see any other-dimensional creatures about. They were all probably inside the restaurant, I know I would be. I love Chinese.

I imagined the steel door closing over the hole. Again, the heat from the other side sealed the door shut. I sagged to the ground, barely able to hold my head up.

Closing this portal had taken a bit more out of me than the first. Either that or I was weaker this time than I was before. I had been giving a lot of blood lately.

I wondered if I should start taking multivitamins since becoming anemic was a real possibility with me feeding him every time we had sex.

By the time I gathered enough energy to pry myself off the ground, Micah was on his knees before me and the incubus was nowhere in sight.

"You are the Chosen One." He stared at me through eyes filled with awe. "I never dreamt the legends could be true. They must be."

"What?" I gaped at Micah who was still on his knees in supplication before me. I stepped closer, reached down and, as weak as I was, dragged him to his feet.

"The legend tells of a unique Guide. One who can seal the portals with the power of his or her mind alone, one who will lead all vampires from darkness. This guide will save us from the destruction of our race. Only death awaits those being led by the Rogues."

"Huh?" I asked stupidly. I should be used to this weird shit happening by now. Can I help it if crap like prophecies and legends still shake me up a bit?

I stumbled over to the bench and sat down hard. I missed the seat and landed with a thump on the ground. I looked around for a minute and wondered how in the world I'd ended up on my ass on the pavement.

Micah strode over and helped me up. "The Rogues are doing something that will endanger us all. You are the one who stops them. And in so doing, you save our race."

My thoughts tripped wildly through my head as I stood in his arms. I thought back to what I'd read earlier that morning.

Of course.

"The Rogues are the serial killers," I whispered. My mind filled with the horror of what their victims must have gone through.

"Serial killers?" Micah asked. He supported my weight since I couldn't seem to stand on my own. He sat down on the bench, holding me on his lap.

"I read about them in the paper. They're killing people here in this town, leaving their drained bodies to be found by the authorities."

"You read about this in the paper?"

I nodded. "Yes. I read about it over breakfast. Alone, I might add."

Micah ran an agitated hand through his hair. "I can't believe they are going out of their way to draw so much attention to themselves. The council was bound to find them."

I darted an accusing glare his way. "You could stick around one of these days and learn these things on your own, you know. I'm getting tired of you showing up at night, screwing my brains out and then disappearing for the day. After all, if the sun won't harm you..." I let my words trail off to see what he would say.

Micah put his hands on my shoulders, I tipped my head back and looked into the dark chocolate of his eyes.

"I never said the sun wouldn't harm me. It harms you every time you're out in it. Why wouldn't it harm me?"

Okay, so I'd misunderstood. I decided to ask him straight out to avoid any future misunderstandings. "Can you or can't you go out in the daylight?" I asked him with narrowed my eyes.

He inclined his head. "I can, but I must take certain precautions."

"What kind of precautions?"

He shrugged. "The same kinds of precautions you should take. I wear long sleeves, SPF thirty or better sunscreen and dark glasses with UV protection."

"Can you eat real food?" If he kept answering, I was damn sure going to keep asking until he answered every one of my questions. Or until he clammed up again.

Micah nodded. "Yes, I can eat real food." He grinned. "It just that most of us choose not to, it has...inconvenient side effects. I can even drink coffee. Although caffeine has its own set of side effects as well."

"What do you mean by that?"

"If I drink more than half of a cup, the caffeine acts as an aphrodisiac." He waggled his eyebrows at me suggestively.

That was an interesting tidbit. I pushed the thought aside. Maybe one day when I felt a bit adventurous... "Will you eat breakfast with me?"

"When?"

I shrugged. "Oh, I don't know. Sometime in the very near future." I leaned into him and looked up into his eyes. "Will you spend the day with me tomorrow?"

"Tomorrow?" He looked a bit taken aback. "Why tomorrow?"

"Why not?" Now it was my turn to look surprised. Why didn't he want to spend the day with me? I shrugged and tried to make it appear as though it didn't matter. But it did. It mattered a lot.

"If you don't want to..." I trailed off, hurt that he avoided me during the day.

"It's not you, little one." He cupped my chin and attempted to compel me to look up at him.

I kept my head down, slammed a door shut in my mind and refused his compulsion. "Stop calling me that," I snapped. "I'm almost as tall as you are. I haven't been little since I was twelve. If you would have stuck around, you'd know that." It was a low blow and I knew it but I didn't give a crap.

He moved his hand to cup my cheek, tucked a stray lock of hair behind my ear and offered me his arm. "Come," he said softly, resigned. "We will go back to the hotel and I shall spend the day with you tomorrow."

I jerked away. "Don't inconvenience yourself. I'll manage to get along fine all by myself. Just take me back to my room." I said my room, not our room, and he got the message.

I cried myself to sleep in my empty bed. I knew we couldn't go on as a couple if we both kept secrets. I'd killed a man and, for some reason, Micah hadn't plucked that information from my head. I was too damned scared of what he'd think of me, to tell him. Not to mention the fact it seemed Micah had a few secrets of his own.

I checked out of the hotel the next morning and drove west. I'd never taken a real vacation and I figured it was about damn time I did. I needed to get away and I needed to think. I knew if Micah showed up on my doorstep, I'd take him in again. In a heartbeat. I also knew I wouldn't be able to forgive myself for it. So I ran.

Yes, I'm a coward. It's what's kept me alive so far.

I knew he would look for me to head for the closest portal. That had been to the east. I headed west, instead, hoping to avoid him for a few days at least.

Besides, I figured California had more than its fair share of gateways and someone had to close them. Why not me?

Part of me felt guilty about not sticking around to nail the people responsible for murdering the locals in that small community. Something told me Micah would take care of that before he started to search for me again. I sensed a deep-seated moral code within him. It was at the courtesy of my newfound abilities, no doubt.

I stopped for breakfast at a big truck stop along the highway. Breakfast was good. The price was even better. And the fact that I could take a shower without renting a room was awesome.

I showered after breakfast, using a towel and washcloth I swiped from the hotel at a weak moment. Then I shopped around the attached convenience store and bought two new CD's before I was on my way again.

I could sleep here and there in my car. The backseat folded down so I slept in a reclined position with my feet in the trunk.

I could live like this indefinitely. From now on, I would sleep in my car and shower in full service truck stops. I needed time to myself and I knew if I stayed in one place for too long, Micah would find me. I just hoped a vamp couldn't enter my car uninvited if I used it as my dwelling.

I took my time as I drove through states I'd never been to before. I even went out of my way a few times just to see certain landmarks and wonders of the world. I passed up the opportunity to get a look at the world's largest ball of string and opted for The Grand Canyon instead since it was number-one on my list.

Chapter Nine

I'D BEEN AWAY FROM MICAH FOR NEARLY A WEEK WHEN I FOUND MYSELF in Colorado staring out at a particularly beautiful scenic overlook. Strong hands landed heavily on my shoulders. I jumped and screamed.

"Have you been enjoying yourself while you've avoided me, this last week?" Micah asked when I turned to glare at him for scaring me half to death.

"Yes, as a matter of fact, I have been," I spat. "Do you enjoy sneaking up on people? You scared the crap out of me, you know." I smacked him on the arm for good measure and tried to ignore the fact that, as usual, he looked good enough to eat.

Dressed in black leather pants, which hugged his long legs like a second skin, he exuded masculinity. The pants framed his toned muscles like they were made for him. I wanted to reach out, cup those magnificent cheeks and squeeze for all I was worth.

"We need to talk."

"No shit, Sherlock," I commented in my ever so eloquent manner. "You first. Where do you go during the day?" I had to know. Did he spend his days with another woman, a vamp woman?

Micah chuckled and shook his head. "If it were only that simple."

I ignored the obvious fact that he'd been poking around inside my head again. "Well, what is it, then?" I couldn't help sounding snide. His whole manner was uppity as if I had no business knowing what he was up to everyday. Well, damn it. If he wanted a relationship, he'd just better learn to deal with my *petty jealousies*. I'd picked that thought out of his head. How, I'm not quite sure.

"Come, let's sit in the car. We can talk and travel, can we not?"

I conceded the point and allowed him to escort me to the driver's seat. I fastened my seatbelt and waited for him to settle in beside me and fasten his. When he buckled his seatbelt, I started the car and headed farther west.

"You must go home."

"Why?" I asked and made a little moue with my lips. "I'm on vacation." I failed to add that it was the first vacation I'd been on since Gram died. I didn't want, nor need, his pity.

I refused to look at him and used the excuse of having to keep my eyes on the road. I didn't trust myself to even glance his way. The man had a way about him. He could get me to agree to almost anything.

"The police are investigating the death of your roommate and a drug dealer. Since you can't be found, you are their primary suspect."

My grip tightened on the wheel and my knuckles turned white. I knew they would eventually draw that conclusion. So why was I so surprised?

Here goes nothing, I thought as I pulled off the road and into the grass, then I put the car in park and turned to look at him. "I did it. I killed him." I felt unwanted tears stream down my face. Tears I wouldn't allow myself before. "He'd already killed Trina. She was dying. He'd crushed her windpipe and I found him grunting over her nearly lifeless body like some insane, sex-starved pig."

I turned to look him in the eyes. "I killed the bastard and I'd do it again." More tears ran down my face, fell from my chin and hit my shirt like raindrops. "What was I supposed to do, let him kill me, too?" I choked the last out, barely able to speak around my sobs.

Micah got out of the car, walked around to pull me from behind the wheel and held me in his arms.

"I know." He rubbed my back soothingly. "I was waiting, hoping you would come to trust me enough to tell me."

I pulled away to look into his eyes. "What do I do now, go back and confess?" I didn't have to tell him I was frightened. He read it in my eyes and my trembling body.

His arms tightened around me. "No." He raised his hands, cupped my face and thumbed my tears away. "We will continue on to Las Vegas where we will be married." He bent to kiss me lightly. "We will then return to Grand Rapids, with all haste, to inform the authorities we had no previous knowledge of Trina's murder."

I gaped at him. "We can't get married! Never mind the fact that you're suggesting we falsify a police report." I frowned. "Can't you get into big trouble for that?" Hell, I'd already killed a man. I was in enough trouble as it was.

"Why shouldn't we marry?" he ignored my previous question. "We are two consenting adults who are very much in love. It is the next most logical step."

Aside from the fact that it was exactly what I'd dreamed of... "I barely know you." I refused to dwell on the fact that I couldn't deny I loved him.

Micah's eyes widened with shock. "You have known me a good portion of your life, Tasha. There is no one on this Earth who knows you better than I." He stepped away and appeared hurt. "Are you saying jail is preferable to marriage to me?"

I grabbed his arm and thumped his chest as he turned toward me. "You know damn well that's not what I meant. I'm not sure I even want to marry anyone. Ever."

He just stood and stared at me with those emotionless eyes of his. "Then I hope you have a good story for leaving a paper trail all of the way to the last motel you registered at. I've already suggested the only one I have. And yes, we both can get into a lot of trouble for falsifying a police report." He said, then grinned. "If we get caught, that is." He turned away from me and strode back to the car.

He'd left it up to me. Did we drive further west to Reno and marriage, or back east to the police and jail?

What a choice.

"I CAN'T BELIEVE IT," I whispered. "In less than an hour, I'll be married to a vampire."

A very handsome, virile, well-endowed vampire, but a vampire, just the same.

I shot a glowering glance toward Micah. Why did he always seem so cool and collected? I thinned my lips. And what was that smile about? I frowned. Good grief, what if he'd read my mind again" That well-endowed thought would put a smile on any man's face.

We stood in front of the podium of the Golden Hearts Chapel of Love and Adult Bookstore and waited for our witnesses to arrive so we could say our vows.

I scowled at Micah. "I'm sure we could have found a more suitable and romantic place had we tried."

He grinned at me and winked. The ceremony was short, sweet and to the point. Our rented witnesses signed the papers and took their payment next door to the casino. To feed the slot machines no doubt.

I didn't feel any different as Micah led me back up the aisle as he held my hand in his larger, warmer one. We stepped from the seedy chapel and he lifted my hand to his mouth, kissing the back of my fingers. He looked into my eyes.

"What next, my beloved?"

I yanked my hand back and wiped the sweat from my palm onto the leg of my worn jeans. This wasn't a real wedding and I refused to dress for it. Especially since it had taken place in such a rundown, ramshackle chapel as that.

"I am not your beloved," I snapped. More because I wanted to be, and knew I wasn't, than for any other reason.

He'd only done what he'd promised my father he would do. He was only protecting me. If he really loved me, he would have at least insisted on a real wedding, or at the very least, a real chapel.

Micah winked at me and grinned again. He gripped our copy of the marriage certificate in his hands. He read over the print and a perverse pleasure filled his face. He folded the paper carefully and stuck it into the inside pocket of his jacket.

"As long as you bear my name, you are my beloved. My love, mi amore..." He'd laid his hand over his heart and tried for a sappy lovesick look.

"Oh, stop with the beloved, life-mate, we were meant to be together forever crap, will ya?" I snarled.

I started to walk back to the hotel we'd agreed to stay at with Micah close at my heels. I looked up at the bright lights of the busy city, barely able to tell it was dark.

I still hadn't forgotten that Micah never revealed what he did in the daytime. I planned to find that out as soon as we got back to the hotel. I smiled grimly as a plan formulated in my mind.

Micah stepped up beside me and recaptured my hand. "Slow down. It's a beautiful night. You should enjoy it."

His grip wasn't painful, but it was unyielding. He tugged on my arm and urged me to slow down. We strolled toward the hotel at a more leisurely pace. I'm sure we looked like the happy newlyweds we were supposed to be.

He carried me over the threshold and promised to do the same with every new dwelling we entered. How could I not think that was romantic? He carried me into the room. His lips never left mine. I let myself enjoy it for a moment while I buried my fingers in his coal black hair and wound my arms around his neck. My breath caught in my throat when I realized this was my wedding night. My clit twitched with anticipation.

He settled me on the bed and lowered himself over my body. I reveled in his attention, loved the feel of his lips trailing over my eyelids, cheeks and the sensitive places on my neck. It didn't take long to have me panting with need beneath him.

He wasn't in much better shape. I reached down between his legs and fondled his growing member through his slacks. It leaped eagerly to my ministrations and I smiled. I pulled my hand away and pushed him from me.

Micah groaned. "Are you trying to kill me, woman?"

He dipped his head and pulled the hardened peak of my breast into the warmth of his mouth. I clutched his head to me for a moment while he suckled me through my shirt and bra before I determinedly pushed him away again.

"Oh, no, you don't," I panted and rolled out from under him. "If you want any semblance of a wedding night, you'd damn well better tell me where you go during the day. Like you promised."

Micah sat up, straightened his clothes and gave me a puzzled glance. "I don't remember making a promise."

I stood, crossed my arms over my chest and scowled. My foot tapped impatiently against the black-veined marble floor.

"Oh, all right," Micah said and looked resigned. He gave me a pleading look. "I didn't want to frighten you, but if you insist, I have no choice."

"I insist. I can handle something frightening better than not knowing." *Or imagining him doing horrible things.*

At first, I thought he'd lied about his ability to go out in the sunlight. However, the last couple of days had proven him no liar about that. I still needed to know what it was he did during the hours he spent away from me.

I'm not the clingy, I-have-to-know-where-you-are-every-moment type. But I did need to know I was the only woman in his life, or at the very least, the only one in his bed.

"There are some among us who believe they can turn humans anytime they wish. For fun or profit."

I gave him a blank look. *That can't possibly mean what I think it means. Can it?*

Micah nodded. "Yes, it means exactly that." He continued a bit faster at my sharply drawn breath. "You don't have to die to become one of us," he laughed nervously, fidgeting.

That worried me. It wasn't like him.

"We are not the undead. That is just an old wives tale."

He ran a hand through his hair and looked so tired that I almost wanted to let him stop. I made him continue because I needed to know.

"When a person is changed, they must learn to feed. They must learn to control the bloodlust and their teeth. It's hard to blend with humans when your teeth lengthen at the least provocation." He stared at me, his expression grim. "Those who aren't taught…kill. They know no other way. They are like wild animals. If they kill enough, they don't want to change. Or they can't, I'm not sure which. The adrenaline in the blood of their victims is like a drug habit, one that cannot be broken."

Well, if anyone could understand that analogy, I could. "They become like the one who tried to kill me?"

Micah nodded. "They have to be put down like the rabid animals they have become. They aren't really evil. It's similar to a drug addict who needs a fix."

"So, you hunt these…others who kill when it's light out?" I guessed.

"No. Well, yes, but not in the daytime. During the light of day, I help train those who were turned and abandoned by their makers. I help them learn to control themselves when they first experience the blood lust. We care for them and help them learn to feed without acquiring a taste for the tainted adrenaline laced blood."

"Oh."

If I thought him nothing short of a hero before, he was definitely one in my eyes with that declaration. I hoped I deserved him. Everything in me wished our marriage had been a real one instead of what it really was. It was little more than a marriage of convenience.

I bent down and kissed him then and hoped to pick up where we'd left off earlier. I knew in my heart it was lust on his part. But with my burgeoning affection for him, I would take whatever I could get. I knew it was stupid to fall in love with a vampire. I just didn't know how to stop myself. And to be honest, I wasn't sure I wanted to.

Chapter Ten

I GROANED WHEN HE WRAPPED HIS ARMS AROUND ME. HIS TONGUE waltzed into my mouth and invited mine to play. He pulled me to him with such force that we slammed together and the bed quivered beneath us.

I wrapped myself around him like a warm, human blanket. If I could, I would have happily crawled inside him. I wanted to be closer to this man than I ever wanted to be with any other person. I craved him. I hungered for him, just as certainly as he hungered for my blood.

My body burned everywhere he touched me. His hands skimmed lightly over my skin and I shivered. Gooseflesh rose on my arms and warmth pooled between my legs.

Our tongues danced together as I rode him, my legs wrapped around his waist. The pleasure was intense even through the layers of clothing we both still wore.

I wished we were naked with our bare skin sliding together sensuously. Soon we were both skin to skin and I wondered, however briefly, where my clothes had gone. Micah rolled over, pinned me beneath him and kissed his way down my quivering body.

"Micah, please," I begged. "Fuck me, now!"

But he had ideas of his own. He shook his head and grinned. "Tonight you are finally my mate." He dipped his tongue into my belly button and I squirmed. "Tonight you will know what it is like to truly be mine."

He said the last with so much possession that I reveled in the knowledge that he wanted me so much. At least for now.

Forever. You are mine, forever.

The words shimmered in my mind for a split second. It made me wonder if it was something I'd picked up from his mind or if it was just my imagination.

He dipped his head between my legs and his lips caressed the warm folds of my nether lips. He drew my clit into his mouth and I screamed out a release so

75

strong, I'm not entirely sure it was real.

Again, Micah brought me to a fevered pitch. The warm, slightly rough pad of his tongue slid over my engorged bud and I sobbed out my ecstasy. "Yes. Oh, God, Micah, yes!"

His tongue drove inside me, lapped at the warm cream that ran from my clenching vagina. He suckled my hardened nub once more and I nearly flew off of the bed. Over and over I climaxed until I lay beneath him like a limp, wet rag.

"Now, you are mine," he said, his face an implacable mask.

He crawled up my body and kissed me and I tasted the essence of my own arousal on his lips. He rolled me over onto my stomach and, using his massive strength, wrapped one arm around my waist, lifted me into the air and placed one of the thick pillows beneath my hips.

Apprehension rushed through me at the thought that he may want anal sex, but I was still too weak to move. To protest.

"Please," I whimpered. I was too inexperienced and was afraid he would enter me there.

"You are mine," he growled.

Micah positioned his body behind me as he repeated the words. I felt the heat from his body against my butt and the tip of his cock brushed my cheeks.

My rear was in the air and my legs spread wide. I felt the cool air in the room as it caressed my most private parts. I scrunched my eyes closed, expecting pain when he placed his hands on my ass, massaging my cheeks. Sliding his hands around my hips, he lifted me and positioned me for his entrance. A tear slipped from my eye as I waited for his possession.

Then without warning, he pushed himself inside me. Up to the hilt and I cried out. Not with the tearing pain I had expected, but with ecstasy. Micah drove inside my hungry channel. My vaginal walls clasped around his huge organ as he moved within its tight confines. He moved into me so deep, I was sure he touched my womb.

At that moment, I opened myself up to him. He hadn't abused my trust and I let my newfound love for him flow from my heart and mind.

"Yes!" I sobbed.

Micah groaned and increased his tempo. He pulled me back toward him with such force our bodies slapped together with a strange sucking sound.

"Yes, please." It was all I could manage to say between my screams of pleasure. I found the strength to push back, wanting to heighten our pleasure.

I needed to feel him drive into me harder, faster.

He bent forward and blanketed my body with his. I felt him nuzzling the crook of my neck and turned my head to the side to give him better access.

When he growled in my ear, he sounded more like an animal than the gentle man I knew him to be.

"Now you are mine," he vowed, right before he sank his teeth deep into the crook of my shoulder. His mind filled mine with the ecstasy he felt as he sated himself with my body and my blood.

An intense pleasure flooded through me as he shared his mind. I screamed his name as I came again. His thickness pulsed inside me as he emptied his seed deep within my womb. For one moment, I had the wonderful thought of what it would be like to have his child growing safe within my body and to live beside him always and I felt at peace.

"Oh, baby," he groaned and rested his forehead on my heaving back as I panted and tried to catch my breath. "You don't know what you've just done." He pulled his now flaccid member from my body and rolled me onto my side and held me in his arms.

I rested my head on his shoulder. My fingers lazily traced random patterns on his chest as I listened contentedly to his even breathing. I've never been so relaxed, so content, in my life.

That's when I decided that I was going to enjoy every minute of my faux marriage to this man. I snuggled closer to him and knew if I ever chose to marry for real, I could never choose a better man than the one asleep beside me. I drifted off with the knowledge that in that moment in time, I was truly happy.

I woke to the incessant buzzing of the alarm. I rolled over, slapped the snooze and buried my head under the downy pillow and froze. I reached my arm over to the other side of the bed. It was empty.

"Damn it!"

I sat up, let the sheet fall to my waist and pushed the hair out of my eyes. "He promised," I whined.

My gaze fell on the bathroom door across the room. It was closed. I wondered if I should go look, even though I knew he wouldn't be in there. It's not as if he ever needed to use it.

"The hell with it," I said and stood up. "I need to go anyway."

I padded across the cold marble floor, pushed the door open and was greeted by puffs of steam spiraling up from the tub. Micah, his back to me, had just added bath salts to the steaming water.

My eyes filled as I watched him test the water and I deliberately rattled the knob.

He turned toward me and his gaze devoured my bare body. I fought the urge to cover myself. I'd thought I was alone, so didn't bother to drag the sheet with me.

"I thought you'd gone."

"I'm sorry." He straightened and strode my way. "It certainly wasn't my intention to make you think so. I'd planned to wake you with a surprise." He smiled softly and gave me a look so hot I was afraid the hotel would spontaneously combust. "I knew exactly how to wake you, too."

"How do you get so tan?" I asked, deliberately changing the subject. "I never would have imagined a vampire could get tan."

"It doesn't take long." He flashed his white teeth at me again and my nipples tightened at the memory of his use of them to heighten our ecstasy.

I glanced over at the toilet. "Do you mind? I really need to...you know," I asked, waving my hand in its general direction.

"Oh, yes, of course," he said and turned to leave. Then, as an afterthought, he went to the tub and turned off the water. "Let me know when you're ready."

Micah must have heard the water splash when I climbed into the tub. He knocked on the door and waited for my permission to enter.

I lowered myself into the soothing water. I didn't want to reveal any more of my body than I had to. But that didn't stop me from enjoying the view as Micah approached, dressed in nothing but a smile. He was obviously a lot more comfortable in his skin than I was in mine. But then again, he'd had centuries to get there, too.

My gaze darted down and I admired his already hard cock. I licked my lips. I couldn't wait to wrap them around the thick length of his engorged shaft again.

He stepped into the tub and I inspected the smooth, high arch of his feet. I reached out and ran my hand up his leg. I loved the feel of the soft hair that dusted his calf and thigh. I frowned. The man even had gorgeous knees! Micah was, in a word, perfect.

He slowly lowered himself into the tub and pulled me between his legs. "Lay back."

I relaxed and let him lower me into the warm, scented water. He wet my hair, sat me back up and I leaned my back against his chest. He reached for the bottle of shampoo, squirted some in his hand and began to massage my scalp.

"Mmm. That feels so good, Micah," I said on a sigh. After the workout he'd given me last night, his pampering felt wonderful. He lowered me back into the water with gentle hands.

"Let me rinse the soap from your hair."

"Mmm hmm," I nodded.

He set me from him after rinsing the lather from my hair. He waggled his brows and leered at me. "Now, for the fun part," he said and reached for the body wash.

AN HOUR AND A half later, we both collapsed on the bed exhausted. Sated to within an inch of my life, I could do nothing but lie on the comforter like a quivering heap of flesh colored gelatin.

Micah rolled me onto my stomach and I groaned, cursing his vampire strength and stamina. I couldn't possibly move any of my tired aching muscles.

So much for feeling adventurous and giving him a couple of cups of coffee. Uh, uh, no way. He'd kill me!

I didn't complain though. I asked for this after all. An entire day of Micah's undivided attention, I must have been crazy! I only hoped I could live through it.

I moaned softly when I felt his long lean fingers mold the sore muscles of my neck and shoulders.

"Not again, Micah. I'll never survive it."

He chuckled and kissed the back of my neck tenderly. My eyelids flickered. There wasn't even a hint of sensuality in that kiss. His hands moved down my arms and back and he splayed his fingers on the twin globes of my behind. By the time he'd gotten to my feet, I was in heaven.

Micah's talented hands worked magic on my tired, aching muscles. He rejuvenated me so quickly, I felt like I could do nearly anything.

"More vampire magic?"

I rolled over, looked into his eyes and smiled. I reached up to brush a lock of hair from his forehead.

Micah shrugged. "You learn much when you have lived as long as I have."

I snorted. "I'll say. And quit reminding me of your age. Do you think I want to remember the part about you being so much older than I am when we're having sex or something?" I rolled my eyes. "You know, you *are* a serious geriatric."

Micah smiled. His mouth was a white slash in the tanned lower half of his face. He looked over his shoulder to the window.

"Would you care to go for a walk, dear wife?" He stood and held out his hand.

I sat up and giggled. "If we go out like this, we'll get arrested."

Micah looked down at himself. "So we shall."

He pulled me from the bed and held me against him. The few coarse hairs on his chest teased my sensitive nipples. I stood within his embrace, enjoying the feel of my body pressed so intimately against his.

He released me long enough to get dressed. We left the confines of our room hand in hand, enjoying each other, like true newlyweds.

Thirty minutes later, I scowled and darted another surreptitious glance Micah's way.

He grinned and lifted one perfectly arched, glossy, black brow. "I won't turn to dust, you know." His gaze bored into mine. "Why do I detect a hint of disappointment?" He straightened and looked away. I wasn't sure, but I could have sworn he'd looked hurt there for a minute.

No matter how long we spent in the sun over the last few days, the only thing that ever happened to him was that he got a tan—all over—despite the SPF 30 sunscreen. I'd hoped to find a weakness and all I got was a tanned vampire.

I looked away and shrugged. I felt a bit guilty. Even though it wasn't him I wanted to have turned to dust in the sunlight. I bit my lip, feeling bad anyway.

"I was looking for a weakness." I hurried to add, "Not because I want anything to happen to you." I looked away, unable to meet his hurt stare. "I was hoping to..."

"Find a weakness in me that could be exploited in another?"

I nodded and bit my lip. Why lie about it? "Yes, I wanted to know how to protect myself if I'm confronted by another of your counterparts. I never want to go through that again."

Even if they are what they considered weak during the day, they were still just as strong as a mortal man. I needed to know how to protect myself the next time he left me alone.

Micah held my hand in a loose grip as we passed a crowd of cheering people. I heard the sound of bells ringing in the distance. Apparently, someone had just won a sizable jackpot. The cheering crowd washed around us as I felt a heavy hand on my arm.

"Ow!"

I tried to shrug the hand off, but it wouldn't budge. The fingers dug deep into my shoulder, the long nails biting painfully into my tender flesh.

"Lemme go!"

Micah's hand shot out, grabbed the offending appendage and squeezed. I grimaced at the sickening sound of bones cracking beneath his iron grip.

The humanoid creature squealed. It sounded more like an animal than anything else. It resembled a man. It had two arms and two legs. It even looked like it had once been human, but was now something else, something entirely different.

Sunglasses blocked the sight of the two black pits where its eyes should have been until Micah knocked them off with a strong right hook to its jaw. And that was definitely a jaw. As evidenced by the hinging motion it made as it opened the big gaping maw that I assumed was its mouth.

Micah's punch caused its head to jerk back. I heard the gruesome sound of the bones snapping in its neck.

I swallowed convulsively in an attempt to hold down the bitter bile that rose to the back of my throat. My body attempted to empty itself of the breakfast I'd eaten.

People screamed and ran from us. They hurried back into the casino and scurried down the street.

"Run." Micah thrust our marriage license into my hands and gave me a push before he rushed one of them and knocked it down. "Run, Tasha, it is you they are after!"

I stared at him stupidly for a second. It was the first time he'd ever raised his voice to me. Then his words sank in and I looked around. Four more of the creatures headed our way. All of them, dressed in black suits, wore cheap, black sunglasses. Like some sort of weird retro rock group.

They all plodded toward me slowly, one step after another. Slowly, surely. With one purpose on their one-track minds. Getting to me.

That knowledge put wings on my feet and I ran as far and as fast as I could. I never once looked back, at least until I couldn't run anymore. When I finally turned to look behind me, I realized I was alone. Micah had stayed behind to buy me time. I hoped the brave action hadn't cost him his life.

"No." The sound came out just a whisper. A mere thread of nearly, inaudible sound muttered through my trembling lips. I was alone again as I most certainly was destined to be.

I trudged back to the hotel, constantly looking over my shoulder, torn between staying another night to wait for Micah and moving on so those...things, couldn't find me.

What were they and what in the hell did they want with me? There was only one person whom I would trust to answer that question honestly and I was afraid I would never see him again. No matter how much I wanted to.

Self-preservation won out. I knew Micah could find me if he needed to. If he was alive. God, it was hard to believe how much I needed Micah.

I packed my bags and left a twenty for the maid and another twenty for the pillow I filched. I couldn't bear to leave it behind. It still bore Micah's scent.

I hoped he survived his encounter with those creatures. It was hell not to know what happened to him and I scarcely dared to hope he was okay. I could only need and want.

I drove on autopilot. My subconscious mind seemed to know the way home. I tried to keep my thoughts from dwelling on my recent losses. Trina's death had been such a blow. But there was a place deep inside me that feared Micah's loss would kill me. Or if it didn't, I would want to be dead.

I drove four hundred miles and stopped, hoping it would be far enough that those things would at least leave me alone for the night.

What were they? The questions plagued me. What did they want with me? I paced the confines of the small, square room. I hoped Micah was okay and would knock on the door any minute. His knock never came and I feared the worst.

I filled the tub with hot water and bubble bath, then stripped. I needed a good, hot soak. What the hell, if I fell asleep from exhaustion and drowned, who's to say I wouldn't be better off?

I sat down in the warm water, brought my knees to my chest and cried. I cried for Trina. Tears I should have spent weeks ago flowed freely as I finally allowed myself to grieve for my best friend.

Funny how so much time had passed and I'd somehow avoided thinking about her, of how much she'd meant to me. We had been sisters of the heart. We weren't related by blood, but we had been sisters just the same. We had laughed, cried and lived together. Sometimes I wondered if we should have died together as well.

Part of me wished it had been me who had died that night. It was so difficult to be the one left behind. Why was I the one who must learn to cope, to live with the loss and the consuming guilt that accompanies outliving a loved one? I couldn't help but think it should have been me that Marco had raped and killed. And another part of me was selfishly glad it wasn't.

I felt the sensation of a hand in my hair and jumped. I whirled around in the tub, splashing water everywhere. I was alone, yet the touch had felt so real. Then I heard Micah's voice.

It is always more difficult for those of us left behind. We find it hard to deal with the passing of loved ones. Yet we must continue. To realize that, without the pain, there can be no real joy. And that those who dwell within our hearts will remain with us forever.

"Micah," I cried.

My tears flowed unchecked down my cheeks. I realized then how much I'd grown to care for him. I rocked in the tub, the water sloshing around me. I made a huge mess, but I just didn't give a damn.

Much later, after a good cry, I came to my senses. I pulled myself from the now cold water and went to bed. I hugged my stolen pillow close, inhaled deeply, taking in Micah's scent, and cried myself to sleep.

I woke before dawn the next morning, determined to stay on the run. Micah had sacrificed himself for me and I wasn't about to let him down by letting those things catch up with me again. I thought briefly about going home to confess to the police. I wanted to tell them what really happened. The coward in me, however, wouldn't allow it.

I didn't want to go to jail. Nothing would convince me I wouldn't go to prison for shooting an unarmed man. The man had been raping and strangling my best friend. If I wouldn't have shot him, she would have died and he would have continued to violate her corpse.

Instead, I decided to stick to the plan Micah formulated. I sat locked in my car and clutched our marriage certificate to my chest. I wished I'd told Micah, just once, that I loved him.

How could I have? I hadn't even known myself. Why is it that most of us never see what's right in front of our faces before it's too late?

I closed my eyes. "I do love you, Micah. Please come back to me. I don't think I can survive your death."

"It's nice to see you've finally figured that out."

I jumped, turned at the sound of Micah's whiskey smooth voice and gaped at him as he finished solidifying on the seat next to me.

I tried to speak, but nothing would come out. My mouth flapped like a fish

gasping for water.
   Holy shit!

Chapter Eleven

"I MEAN IT, MICAH, SPILL. I WANT TO KNOW HOW YOU DID THAT," I grumbled as he made good on his earlier promise and carried me into our new room.

I ignored the tingling sensation in my breasts and the way my vagina clenched at the sight of the bed. He was in big trouble and I wasn't about to succumb to my base needs. Well, not until he gave in and told me just what he and his kind were capable of anyway.

My shock and happiness at seeing him alive and well had prevented me from interrogating him until we checked into the hotel. Now I wanted answers and I wasn't above using sex as a tool or a weapon.

All's fair in love and all that jazz. Like it or not. Tease or not. The only way I could think of to get information from him was with sex. Or to be more specific, the threat of no sex. I'd done a good job of it, too, until we'd gotten into the damned room.

I set my bag on the floor at the foot of the king-sized bed. I tried not to look at it—the bed—not my bag. I turned away from the large piece of furniture when my gaze fell on it with longing.

I swallowed convulsively, my body had already began to hum with desire. And he hadn't even touched me yet! I tried not to think of how wonderful Micah would make me feel later on that huge bed.

Much later.

After he explained what it was he'd done earlier and what else he could do. And what the hell were those things that were coming after me last night? He knew. I steeled myself against the sexual hunger rising within me until he answered my questions.

I turned away from the bed, paced to the window and looked out through the darkness. Micah stepped behind me, put his hands on my shoulders and kissed the back of my neck.

"Come to bed, Tasha," he whispered in my ear.

My traitorous nipples pebbled at the brush of his breath against the back of my ear. They jutted against the emerald green silk of my shirt, obviously uncaring that they were about to surrender a battle I was determined to win. My hands clenched and unclenched at my sides.

If we were to have any type of a relationship, Micah needed to give more of himself than just his body.

That's when I realized I knew nearly nothing about the man I'd just married. I was upset that he didn't trust me. I turned to him with tears in my eyes.

"I can't do this anymore, Micah. A relationship is give and take. You never give." I pushed past him and snatched my bag up off the floor. "You want me to trust you. And I do. I have trusted you, with my life. Yet you still do nothing to earn that trust."

He saved your life in Nevada, don't forget that, my conscience reminded me.

"And what in the hell were those things back there?" I asked, waving my hand toward the west. "I know you know what they were so don't even try to deny it," I said when he started to shake his head.

My shoulders slumped with defeat when I realized why he didn't want to tell me things. I could never be a permanent part of his world. He was so different. So magical, and wonderful, and I'm just plain old...me.

Micah grabbed my shoulders in a painful grip and I winced. His grip loosened immediately and I looked up into his eyes, which had darkened to a near black.

"What do you know of trust?" he spat. "You accept my help, accept my body and do nothing to make our union a real one."

My eyes widened at his words. He wanted a real union, a real marriage? Then why wouldn't he trust me with the knowledge I'd asked him for?

"Because if you were truly committed to this union, you would be able to sift through my mind. You could search my memories and retrieve those answers for yourself." He scowled at me. "We do have a mental bond, you know. You have the ability to read me, just as I can read you." He released me and I stepped back rubbing my arms.

"How?" I wondered aloud. I know I love him. At least I'm willing to admit that to myself now. So why couldn't I read him? "Maybe I'm not the soul-mate you've been waiting for. I may be a Guide and you a Cartuotey, but that doesn't mean that we were fated to be together, does it?"

My voice hitched as I thought of that possibility. What if he belonged to someone else?

His eyes began to glow and his teeth exploded in his mouth and forced his lips to bulge out a bit.

"You are mine. And no one will take you from me. Anyone one who tries will have to go through me. And they will die."

He paced away from me and I had the sense that he wanted to regain control of his temper.

"Those who tried to take you yesterday were revenants."

"Revenants?"

"Yes, they are humans who are partially turned by the Rogues to do their bidding. The Rogues do not bother to tell the humans that they cannot become one of us by drinking our blood." He grimaced. "When they drink our blood, they become nothing more than zombies driven to carrying out the commands of their makers. I will find out who sent them for you," he growled. The sound came from deep within him and made him sound almost animalistic.

I stepped back slowly, scared of him for the first time. I swallowed around the lump in my throat and my mind searched frantically for a way to run. To leave this thing that I didn't know existed within him. I chewed on my lip thoughtfully as I danced from foot to foot. I needed to run, yet wanted to stay. I bit down a bit too hard and a drop of blood beaded on my lip. Micah was on me in a second, growling in triumph. I screamed and tried to fight him off, afraid he was out of control.

His arms locked around me like iron bands and I could barely move. His lips lowered to mine and his tongue darted out to savor the drop of blood on my lower lip. He sucked my lip into his mouth and I was lost.

Micah's mind filled me with such a maelstrom of lust I could barely stand, let alone think. I wouldn't have known my own name at that point had he asked. My arms snaked around his neck, pulling him closer, as I lost myself in his kiss.

Flames licked at my skin and I could almost feel my blood moving slowly through my veins like lava. I burned for him as surely as his body burned for my blood.

Micah's hands were all over me, he tore the clothes from my body as he inflamed my skin. He took me to a place I'd never been before. Oh, yes, Micah was out of control, but in a way that only endangered the clothes I wore.

Our clothes disappeared and I picked the information from his brain that he'd simply wished them away and they were gone.

He lifted me in his arms. "Wrap your legs around me," he growled into my ear as he lowered me onto his massive erection.

"Aiieee!" I screamed my first orgasm when he filled me and shared the sensation of the wet velvet walls of my channel clutching and milking him. "I think I can feel you hitting my tonsils," I groaned when he rammed himself deep inside me. "Yesss. Don't stop." I mewled into his shoulder and nipped at his neck.

"You are mine," he said as he drove into me. His hands on my hips, he lifted me and dropped me back down on his member as it pulsed in and out of my drenched pussy.

"Yes," I gasped. "I'm yours." I meant it, too. I realized that I didn't want to live my life without him in it. I couldn't bear the thought of losing him.

I felt it then. Something stirred deep within me and I felt a painful wrench in the vicinity of my heart. Micah was in my mind as a slightly younger man dressed in glossy, black knee-high boots, tight tan breeches and white shirt. He wore black leather gloves and carried a riding crop as he walked purposely through an ancient castle.

Then the vision was gone, replaced with Micah in a British Army uniform. He stormed through enemy lines, draining people as he went. I couldn't fault the use of his unique talents to help his country. I heard the whine of a bullet just before it slammed into him and I gasped. The sharp pain overwhelmed me.

"Enough," Micah said while he stood, still holding me in his arms, his hard cock buried deep within me. "I will share my mind, but you will only feel what I feel now." His eyes bored into mine and I felt the push of compulsion.

I let him compel me because I knew that I could revisit his memories later. I just wanted the other torment of waiting to come to an end. I had been on the verge of another orgasm when his memories assaulted me.

I opened myself to him, reveling in the sensation of his body invading mine. He picked up the tempo, surging deeper, until he finally shouted his release as I tumbled over yet another precipice.

I cried out his name, screamed my love to him and the heavens as he poured his seed into my womb. I collapsed and my legs dropped from around his waist. I hung from his arms like a limp rag-doll as he carried me to the bed and placed me under the covers.

I smiled with my eyes closed and ran my fingers through his silky hair. I felt him kiss my forehead before he climbed into bed behind me and pulled me back into his comforting embrace.

TWO DAYS LATER, I was ready to hit the road again, before I started to walk funny.

"I mean it, Micah. I can't stay here another day." I opened the trunk of my car and dumped my bag in it. "Besides, you're the one who said I needed to get my butt back to Grand Rapids before I get arrested." I felt silly using the word butt, but Micah didn't like me to swear unless we were in bed so I made an attempt to tone down my language. "Isn't it better that I go to them and—and turn myself in, instead of them finding me?"

Micah nodded, put his arm around me and gave me another toe curling kiss. "Yes, but it doesn't mean I have to like it. I do have a plan but there is still a small chance that it won't work."

He put me down slowly. I was back on my feet before I even realized I'd been off of them. I shook my head. The man can kiss, that's for sure.

I had to concede his point. I really didn't want to turn myself in either. But what else could we do?

Nada.

I made an abrupt about face to walk to the driver's side of the car. Micah stepped in front of me and held his hand out.

"My turn." He wiggled his fingers.

I looked up and tried to figure out if he was serious, but his eyes were covered with dark sunglasses and the lower half of his face was a blank mask.

"Huh?" I put my hands behind my back, pretending not to know what he wanted.

"Hand me the keys, Natasha. It's my turn to drive."

"You are *so* not driving my car, mister. And no one calls me Natasha anymore." Only Gram and he had. It brought back bittersweet childhood memories I refused to dwell on.

I tried to walk around him, but no matter what I did, he was there blocking the way.

"The keys, Tasha." He wiggled his fingers again.

"Why?" I asked as I fisted the keys in my hand and crossed my arms over my chest. "Does Mr. Big, Bad Vampire get nervous when I drive?"

"Well, now that you mention it," he said, then rubbed the back of his neck.

"Don't even go there, bud. I'm not about to let you drive my baby." My hands made their way to my hips as I glared up at him.

Micah sighed and shook his head.

"This is not a baby, Tasha," he said, then rested his hand on the roof of my car. "A baby," he leaned closer to whisper in my ear as he placed his hand on my stomach, "is what you have growing inside of you, right here."

I dropped my keys.

Micah scooped them up from the pavement so quickly it barely registered what I'd done.

"Hey! That wasn't fair," I groused as I fought him for my keys. "And I don't have a baby in me."

"As you wish." He bowed slightly and then climbed behind the wheel.

I hurried to the other side of the car. "Do you even have a driver's license?" I snapped the seatbelt securely around me. "Probably not, he probably would rather ride horses and be stuck in the dark ages where women were chattel," I mumbled, pissed because I let him trick me like that.

Me pregnant? Yeah, right. Like he would know anyway.

Micah turned toward me and gave me a look that could melt pavement.

"You are pregnant, little one, never doubt that." He gave me a blinding smile. "And it is my pleasure to be the one to give you this wonderful, yet surprising news."

My hand covered my stomach and I frowned. Could I be? I bit my lip and wondered. I had to admit that I could be, that is of course, if vampires can get a girl pregnant.

"My God, Tasha. It's not as if we are a different species. Think of us more like a different breed. A German Shepherd can breed with a wolf, can it not?"

I glared at him. "You had better not be calling me a dog, buddy." I crossed my arms over my chest and turned to look out the window.

He shook his head and started the car. "How many miles would you like to cover today?"

I shrugged. "I don't know. At least a couple of hundred, I guess. Why?"

He shrugged. "Just asking."

Three hours later I had to admit he was a damn good driver. It was either that or pee my pants because he wouldn't stop unless I did.

"You're a damn good driver, you're a damn good driver," I chanted it like a mantra. "Now stop the goddamn car!"

When he finally pulled off the road into a gas station, I climbed out of the car and rushed to the bathroom. Only to find, much to my consternation, the damn thing was out of order.

"What have I done to deserve this?" I whined and stomped back to my Stratus, which was really a feat since my bladder was about to burst.

I glared at Micah like it was his fault.

"Use some of your magic and fix the toilet. The damn thing is out of order."

He just looked at me and shook his head.

"Then use the men's room. I'm a vampire, not a plumber."

"Look, *Dr. McCoy*, I have to take a piss." I was deliberately crude because I knew he didn't like it. "And if I don't go soon, I'm going to spring a fucking leak!"

"The things I do for you," Micah sighed and shook his head. He got out of the car, stalked to the ladies room and pushed the door open so forcefully it banged against the wall.

The noise was so loud it drew the attention of the two old women at the gas pumps filling an old, baby blue Cadillac. They both watched him enter the women's restroom and giggled behind their hands.

I fought the urge to glare at them and wondered if one of them was responsible for the condition of the toilet.

When I heard the sound of the toilet flushing, I hurried to the open door. Micah stepped out and walked toward the car. He did his best to look like a big, bad dude as he walked toward my Stratus. His dark sunglasses hid his eyes and his black leather pants hugged his rear. The man was six-foot-six of total male perfection. I had to admit he did look cool. I gave him a slow once over and grinned.

"Hey, honey?" I called after him.

He turned toward me all tall, dark, good looks and testosterone. "Yes?" He bit the word out, clearly peeved I made him use his powers for something so nasty.

"Could you fill the car up while I'm in here?" I asked as I slowly backed away from him. I was in the restroom now with the door almost closed.

He nodded once. "I intended to." He turned and started to walk toward the car again.

"One other thing, honey," I said to draw his attention once again. When he turned, I was glad those dark glasses prevented me from seeing his eyes. Otherwise, I might not have had the nerve to go on.

"Yes?" He bit the word out from between clenched teeth.

91

I coughed. "You have toilet paper stuck to your shoe." I slammed the door just as he looked down to discover the little rider he had attached to his boot and shook it off. His expression was priceless.

My amusement was short lived, however. When I returned to the car, Micah gave me the silent treatment for the next hour. He pulled off of the highway at four to gas up and I noticed a restaurant and hotel across the street.

"Why don't we stay there for the night?" The hotel looked good and appeared to be relatively new and clean. "I bet they have real nice, comfy rooms and we can even eat at the restaurant." I said when I climbed out of the car to stretch.

I got a horrible pain in my stomach as soon as I stood. "I don't feel too good. Maybe that strawberry ice cream was bad." I wrapped my arms around my middle.

Micah snorted, shook his head and looked disgusted. "It's probably a mixture of the ice cream, the bag of chips, two hot dogs and four bottles of cola you drank."

"I mean it," I said as I leaned against the front fender. Sweat beaded my brow and upper lip. "I really don't feel good." I got another horrible pain just then and it doubled me over.

Micah was at my side in a heartbeat. He removed the dark glasses and his eyes were filled with concern. "Tell me what it feels like."

"It hurts," I groaned. Tears ran down my face. I've never felt a pain so intense in my life. Withdrawal had been a picnic compared to this. "It feels like someone is stabbing me and cooking my insides with a blow torch."

"Open your mind, little one. Let me in."

I tried to relax. I imagined the door in my mind—the one I recently locked to the outside world—open just a crack to let him past the barrier.

He could have stormed past that barrier of course. But he apparently respected my privacy enough to stay out of my mind. I wondered absently how long that would last.

"A large portal has just been opened. Since you have been using your mental powers more, your susceptibility has been increased and you feel it more intensely. Before, when a portal was opened, you probably just thought you had gas."

"Great." I muttered through clenched teeth. At least that explains most of those cramps I'd been worried about. "How long is this going to last?" I leaned over as another cramp stabbed through me and made me groan.

"Not long. I will continue to attempt to block the pain for you while we wait for it to settle and become a constant. At that time, your brain will ignore the warning as it has already been received."

I marveled that he could do that for me even as I felt him stir within my mind. He took most of the pain and shouldered it himself. It slowly receded in waves, almost like a tide and I began to relax, relieved.

"We must stay here tonight." He turned to look at me, his eyes unreadable. "We must close this portal quickly. It was not opened by demons, but by those who worship the Dark Lord."

"The Dark Lord?" I looked up at Micah's knowing stare and gasped. "Not the devil? You mean these people are Sa—"

"Do not!" Micah grabbed my arm in an unyielding grip and put his warm hand over my mouth.

"Names have power. For an innocent with power to say his name, out loud, so close to a portal could draw him from his home. He is not the fallen angel that so many of your people believe, but he does exist."

"So this portal is opened to a different dimension than the one Bro— er... Hideous Hank and his cohorts are from?"

"Yes," he nodded as he led me back to the car and tucked me back into the passenger seat. He slid behind the wheel and gave me a grave look. "We must close this portal tonight. There is no time to waste."

"Why, what's so different about this portal?" I had to know. Just because devil worshippers opened it didn't mean it was more powerful, did it?

"The people who opened it are planning a sacrifice to the Dark Lord, tonight. The sacrifice will allow him to walk the earth in human form. They must be stopped, of course."

I barely even noticed he'd put the car in gear so I was rather surprised to see that we were already just outside of the hotel lobby.

"Excuse me?" I said my eyes wide. "Did you just say that they're going to sacrifice someone?"

Micah turned to me, his eyes did that strange, glowing thing again. "Yes. They plan to sacrifice a Guide. Who better to house the dark one's spirit than one who can open or close the gates at will?"

"A Guide?" I fought the ridiculous urge to look around and search my surroundings for another person like me. "There's another Guide in this area?"

Micah peered into my eyes. His own were a blood red and lit from within.

93

"No." His fangs extended again and made me afraid to hear the rest of his answer. "The Guide they plan to sacrifice is you. These are the people who sent the revenants for you. They have included a Rogue within their ranks. He is making more revenants as we speak."

"Oh, he—shit."

I don't want to say the H-word if another stupid portal is open. That word could have a power all its own and I sure as he—dang it! Anyway, I didn't want to find out what kind of power it wielded.

I shook my head in denial. "There is no way I am going to become anyone's sacrifice." I put my seatbelt back on and looked over at him. "What are you waiting for? Let's get our asses out of here."

Micah shook his head. The expression on his face was scary. Almost as if I was already dead, my body tied to the slab, or altar, or whatever they intended to do to me for this thing.

"We cannot leave this portal open. Even if they cannot release him, they can release other, stronger beings than the incubus, or succubus."

Shit!

"So we have to close it and I may get sacrificed while we're at it?"

Didn't this just sound like a blast?

Not!

He shook his head. "It will not come to that, little one. I will not allow it." He smiled a cold evil smile that I did not want aimed at me. Ever. "They do not know I am your mate. I will be a complete surprise to them. They cannot kill you without killing me first. And they cannot kill me. They do not know how."

I shuddered and turned away from the terrifying smile that promised death to anyone who laid a finger on me. I almost pitied those poor people, duped into thinking that the guy downstairs was some sort of trapped god who needed to be released.

Almost.

I turned to him and smiled and tried to keep the overwhelming fear at bay. I said I trusted Micah with my life. This was my chance to prove it.

"Okay. What's the plan?"

Chapter Twelve

WE SAT AT THE BEST TABLE IN THE RESTAURANT, AN EXCEPTIONALLY NICE table for two overlooking the river that was the boon of the economy.

The locals boasted the river was the best around to fish, canoe and tube down. Further down the wide fast moving stream, were rapids they claimed to be one of the best to raft down. I took their word for it. I had no aspirations for whitewater rafting. Not in this lifetime, anyway.

I picked at my dinner. I knew we were about to embark on a quest that may end my existence. I never dreamed I would ever be involved in the kind of crap I found myself involved in lately.

Sometimes I wondered if I'd made a mistake when I killed Marco. Perhaps I should have just turned the gun on myself and done the world a favor.

Micah glared at me. "Stop feeling sorry for yourself and eat. Were you feeling sorry for yourself when you pulled the trigger?" he asked, his voice low.

"No," I scowled. "I only felt overwhelming rage and self-righteousness that I'd killed the asshole who was capable of doing such a thing." Then I smiled. "It was my distinct pleasure to wipe his contemptible presence from the face of the Earth."

"Then you should feel the same about this." Micah leaned across the table and covered my hand with his. "It should be your distinct pleasure to free these people from this world as well. They are wholly evil and nothing you can say or do will change them."

I took a deep breath, unsure if I could kill anyone else. Once was more than enough for me.

"You won't have to kill anyone, baby." Micah picked up on my thoughts. His eyes gleamed. "It will, most assuredly, be my distinct pleasure to do so."

"Yeah, like that's supposed to make me want to eat," I remarked as I played with my food. I mentally checked my mind's barrier and wondered how in the world he was still able to read my mind, but was too pre-occupied to really care.

"The weaker you are, the more susceptible you will be to their power. And the more ineffective your own powers will be. You must not engage them in a weakened state. Yet you will engage them tonight. They are on their way here as we speak."

I started to shovel my salad into my mouth.

"God, I hope I don't get sick."

"You may wish to pray more often, and better than that, my dear. You must believe He can help you. Or at least believe someone can."

"I believe you will help me, Micah," I said around a mouthful of buttered bread. I crammed a bite of steak in with it and chewed. "I stopped asking God for favors when my grandmother died and my dad disappeared."

The candle-flame flickered and I noticed a commotion behind us. An ominous breeze brushed over me as a large group of people entered. The hostess escorted them to the banquet room on the other side of the restaurant. I turned and caught the eye of one in the group who grinned evilly at me.

"They have arrived." Micah set his fork down and covered my trembling hand with his once more. "Do not fear them, my love. They may have powers, but they do not realize who I am."

"You mean what you are," I corrected absently as I watched them steadily file through the room. Every one of them looked our way.

Micah shook his head. "No, Tasha. I meant exactly what I said. They know of my kind, and they know of me. If they knew you were my mate, they never would have begun this foolish quest."

He turned his gaze from the group and looked at me with confidence.

I peered into his eyes. I wanted to know what he meant. The information zinged into my mind. I had the distinct impression that this was how information passed between computers as I had the sensation of downloading Micah's memories into my brain.

"You aren't like the others."

He shook his head. "No, I am not. My kind was marooned here years ago, destined to remain for all eternity. Or until inter-galactic space travel develops enough to take us back to our home. We can survive here, but our technology fails in this atmosphere. We cannot even signal our own kind."

"You're an alien?" I almost swallowed my fork. I pulled it out of my mouth and gulped down my mashed potatoes before I choked on them. "Oh, my God! I'm married to an alien?"

"Can you say that a little louder? I don't think they heard you in Canada," he groused and looked around to see if anyone overheard.

"I'm sorry," I said. My voice pitched lower now that the initial shock had passed. "Vampires are aliens?"

I couldn't seem to grasp it. In the last few weeks, I'd lost my friend and killed her murderer in the same day. I quit using drugs. I was almost screwed senseless by an incubus, if his boasting was anything to go by.

Then, of course, there's everything else that's happened since then. Not the least of which being that I was and hopefully would continue to be screwed senseless by one gorgeous alien vampire.

I giggled hysterically. "I don't think I can handle anymore," I said. Then promptly fainted.

IT WAS DARK WHEN I woke up. At least it was dark where I was. Stuffed in the trunk of someone's car headed to who knew where.

Geeze. For someone who never fainted before the age of twenty-eight, I sure was making up for lost time. And where in the world was Micah?

I felt around the close confines of the musty trunk. He wasn't with me, that's for sure.

"Shit!"

I quickly covered my mouth, thinking it may be to my advantage to let my kidnappers believe I was still unconscious.

At least they hadn't tied me. Although what good that was to me I hadn't figured out yet. I was still stuck in the dank, smelly trunk of someone's car and it wasn't mine.

I felt around the small compartment and searched for something I could use as a weapon. The people who kidnapped me may be psychotic, but they weren't stupid. There wasn't any form of weapon anywhere in the trunk. Not even a screwdriver.

Well, hell. I covered my mouth at the thought and almost giggled. At least I hadn't drawn the attention of the denizens of that place by my thoughts. It was bad enough I'd been kidnapped by people who—if Micah had his way—would soon be residents of that nether world.

If it even existed.

If Satan wasn't really a fallen angel, then was hell really hell? I needed to stop trying to figure that stuff out. The whole thing gave me a headache.

I tried to stay in one position through the trip, even though my muscles had started to get cramped and stiff. I didn't want them to know I was awake.

How long would a good faint last? Would it be too much to still be unconscious when we arrived at wherever it was we were going? Since I had no frame of reference, I was going to have to wing it.

I put my fist in my mouth to quell the scream of anguish I felt building within me. Micah said they would have to kill him to hurt me.

Where is he? I screamed in my mind.

I'm following behind you at a discreet distance. It heartens me to know you care so deeply for me, my love.

I sighed with relief.

Micah? Thank God! I was afraid they'd killed you.

He chuckled mirthlessly. The sound brushed my mind and comforted me.

They think they have *killed me, but it takes a bit more than a bullet to the heart to stop my kind.*

A bullet to the heart? I swallowed thickly and wondered if he meant his kind as in all vamps or just the ones that came here from wherever it is they were from.

All of us, Tasha.

I could feel his laughter as well as hear it. It went a long way toward alleviating my fears. It also helped make me feel a bit more positive about my situation.

I'm so glad you think this is funny. It's not like the resident vampire in my life has been very forthcoming with loads of knowledge, you know.

I wanted to seem angry, but I was too relieved to pull it off.

You have seen into my mind, Tasha. You have the ability to get any information you require from me. You only need to look within me and yourself for it.

By then I'd had enough of the conversation and his attitude and longed for a bad connection. I felt his chuckle brush my mind again and made a face.

The car I was held captive in slowed and turned right. I could tell that well enough, unless they were driving in reverse, which I highly doubt.

They are coming to a halt. You must pretend to be unconscious.

I already deduced that, Sherlock. Anything else?

Yes. No matter what may happen or what you may hear, you must believe that I am very close. That I will allow no harm to come to you. Do not open your eyes at any cost. They must believe you to be asleep. Your first priority must be to close the portal. I will take care of the rest.

Close an inter-dimensional gateway and ignore whatever horrific noises I may hear, while I kept my eyes closed. Plus, feign unconsciousness while I do something I've only done twice before in my life, with the use of a hard flat surface as a prop?

I sighed. *You don't ask for much, do you?*

I ask only for the thing you were born to do, Tasha.

I was born to shop, Vlad. Not close portals to hell using only my mind and the musty air in the trunk of a car for props. I grimaced. *It smells like feet in here.*

They come.

I caught that one last thought from him before someone opened the trunk lid and the cool night air kissed my cheeks. I tried not to take too deep of a gulp of the refreshing air while still breathing in all of the fresh oxygen I'd missed from being confined. I am a bit claustrophobic. I was barely able to keep myself still. Everything in me wanted to climb from that trunk and bound into the night. But I knew that would have ruined Micah's plan. Whatever it was.

Someone reached in and grabbed my arm. Then I heard a blood-curdling scream. My eyelids fluttered wildly and I almost opened my eyes. But Micah told me to keep them closed. So I did. Even though it was one of the hardest things I've ever had to do in my life.

I attempted to find the portal and kept my eyes shut as I concentrated on only that. Perhaps I'd hoped it would keep my mind off whatever was going on outside the trunk as well.

My stomach ached and I pressed my hands to my middle before I made the pyramid with my thumbs and forefingers to get a location on the portal. It was right here. I could feel it. If I got out of the trunk, I could see it. Walk to it, feel the energy that poured from it. I could draw energy from it to make myself stronger.

It is the glamour of the Dark One, my love. Do not allow it to entice you further. You must close the portal.

Micah's voice in my head was a soothing balm. The smooth, rich baritone helped me to ignore the screams of terror outside of the trunk. My lids fluttered again, but I was able to keep them closed. My mind centered solely on closing the open gate.

I visualized a steel door over the portal and mentally tried to slam it closed.

It didn't want to budge. I concentrated harder, unable to understand why I couldn't force this one to shut. I took a deep breath and tried to convince myself I could do it.

I'm a friggin' Guide, I can do this.

Use me.

Micah's voice startled me. I wasn't sure what he meant. He forced a bit of his energy into me and it clicked. I opened myself up to him and drew more energy from him. I could feel his massive strength ebb as he shared it with me.

Again, I visualized the door. This time it slid closed. I still had to force it, but it did finally slam with such force I heard a loud bang.

The kidnappers screamed in protest as the door hurled shut and welded itself tight as the portals seemed wont to do when they were finally sealed.

The terrifying noises became almost too much for me to bear. A part of me almost wished someone would close the trunk lid on me again. I didn't want whatever it was to get the idea that I was a bad guy, too.

A part of me suspected that the very thing I feared was Micah. That it was a side of him I still haven't seen. His silence told me I was right.

Suddenly everything became quiet. Eerily so. I wondered if I should open my eyes. I was just about to open them when strong arms lifted me from my makeshift cage.

Do not open your eyes yet. Please, little one, listen to me without argument, just this once. These men were the ones who sent the revenants after you. Their leader was a Rogue. You have no reason to fear any of them any longer. They are no longer of this world.

Micah's thoughts caressed my mind even as I felt the illusion of his voice in my ears and his warm breath upon my neck.

I decided quickly to relax and settle myself within his embrace. By then I knew if I couldn't trust him, I couldn't trust anyone.

Your confidence humbles me.

Oh, shut up.

I waited silently, patiently, as he carried me through the dense underbrush that surrounded the area where the portal had been. I rested my head on his shoulder, tired. I'd been through so much in the last few days, a part of me wanted nothing more than to sleep. I kept my eyes shut tight and finally relaxed. I was lulled into dreams by Micah's gentle embrace and the sultry breeze of the unusually warm, spring night.

I WOKE SOME TIME later in the hotel. Micah had placed me on the king-sized bed. He sat on the edge of the bed, his back to me and held his head in his hands.

I reached out and placed my hand on his back. "What's the matter?"

"I fear our relationship is doomed to end before we truly begin it."

I peered up at him through the veil of my hair before I pushed it out of my face. "I thought we had already begun it."

"That is only because you are so young." He turned toward me and I glimpsed his near perfect profile. "You have not been taught our ways. A fault that lies with your father. He should have told you of the blood ties."

I bit my lip. Blood ties?

"Perhaps he should have told me, but you're just as bad. You've had several opportunities to enlighten me on all things vampiric, yet you continue to choose to leave me ignorant." I sat up and threw my legs over the side of the bed. "You say the information is there and mine for the taking, yet a part of you holds something back."

I stood, walked around the foot of the bed and paced in front of him. "Have you given any thought at all to the fact that I can't read you all of the time? And it's not because I don't want to."

My sore body protested as I knelt in front of him, rested my hands on his knees and looked into his eyes. "I've tried to read you, several times, Micah. I think you block me somehow because you don't want me to see that part of you. Just like you didn't want me to see that part of you tonight, when you told me to keep my eyes closed." I tilted my head and looked into his eyes. "I think you're afraid to let me see what you really are. What you can do."

Micah looked up, so obviously startled, I had to smile. "The idea never occurred to you, huh?"

He shook his head. "I never thought to question whether or not I allowed you access." He sighed. "But now that you mention it..." His voice trailed off and his eyes took on a faraway look.

My lips thinned. I tried not to be angry. I really did. A part of me resented the fact Micah didn't trust me enough to show me who he really was.

Disgusted, I stood, turned and walked into the bathroom. I needed a shower and I needed to think. I closed the door behind me and locked it. I knew the thin wooden door wouldn't keep him out if he truly wanted to be with me. But I trusted him to respect my privacy. Even if he didn't trust me enough to accept him for who, and what, he was.

Micah knocked on the door and I almost ignored him, but thought better of it. I leaned against the door as I rested my hand against the smooth, lacquered surface. "Yes?"

"We need to talk, Tasha."

"Yes, we do." I rested my head against the cool wood. "But as long as you keep things from me, talking will get us nowhere."

Why couldn't we trust each other and put our differences and our secrets behind us? As long as Micah refused to air his, there was just nothing to say.

Chapter Thirteen

"**W**HAT DO YOU WANT, TASHA, BLOOD?"

I almost made the mistake of saying something crude about his eating habits, but bit my tongue instead.

"I want the truth. All of it. What you are, exactly what you can do. Everything." I felt him sigh on the other side of the door more than I heard it.

"I will try."

I shook my head. "No, you will not try. You will do," I said, grimly. "If you try, it gives you an out and I refuse to give you one in this instance. Either you will or you won't. That is all."

Too many others had gotten around me that way. It wouldn't happen again. Not this time and not with Micah.

"As you wish," he sighed.

I heard the knob rattle and looked down to see it jiggle back and forth.

"The door is locked."

"Of course it's locked. I want some privacy." I glowered at the door, then paced away from it. "And don't you dare use your...your...powers or whatever you call it, to get in here either. I'm trusting you to respect my wishes and stay the hell out of here while I'm taking a bath."

Another sigh. "As you wish, little one."

God, how I wished he'd quit saying that. He wasn't my slave and I damn sure didn't need everything I wished for. I just wanted honesty from the man I shared my bed with. I didn't think that was too much to ask.

I turned and stomped over to the whirlpool bath and smiled to myself. I had to hand it to him though. The man sure knew how to pick a good hotel. The dives I'd landed myself in on my own were little more than no-tell motels. A few of them were so bad I think I was lucky to have my own bathroom.

Warm spirals of steam filtered up as I climbed into the large tub I filled with jasmine scented hot water and turned on the jets. I lowered my abused body into the soothing hot water with a sigh. The warmth of the water soothed me as I relaxed into the pleasant spray of the Jacuzzi's jets and closed my eyes.

I know I dozed for a while. I'm not sure how long before Micah's frantic knocks on the door rudely awakened me. I sat up with a splash as a thin column of smoke made its way through the crack under the door.

No wonder Micah had been so frantic. The hotel was on fire!

Water splashed everywhere as I stood quickly. It sloshed on the cream tile floor and thick green rug beside the tub. I hopped out of the bath, reaching for the towel I laid out, and watched, entranced, as the smoke thickened into a column and stacked itself into a shape.

My mouth fell open when the column of smoke suddenly appeared as Micah. His face was a mask of utter fury as he stood before me clenching and unclenching his hands at his sides.

"Why didn't you answer me?" he growled. His eyes glittered dangerously as he advanced on me slowly.

A couple of minutes passed while I stood and gaped before I finally came to my senses and clamped my mouth shut.

"I was sleeping."

"In the tub?" he asked, incredulous.

"Yes, in the tub." I glanced toward it. The jets still bubbled merrily. "I was tired." I stated the obvious.

Heat suffused my face when I became aware of my nakedness. It was amazing that I could still be modest with him. Intellectually, I knew he knew my body better than I did myself, but I still grabbed the nearest towel and wrapped it around myself. I looked up into his heated gaze, drew the towel around myself just a bit tighter and held it to me like a talisman.

Something different smoldered in Micah's eyes now. He advanced on me slowly. He matched each of my backward steps with a forward step of his own.

"I was worried when you didn't answer. I thought perhaps you'd drowned."

I shook my head and backed up a few more steps. "I'm fine, really."

I nervously wet my lips. My tongue darted out from between them to run the length of my bottom lip.

The action drew Micah's attention and I could actually feel the temperature in the room rise several degrees. I felt the heat of his gaze almost like a touch.

Goosebumps rose on my arms and legs. I put my hand out in front of me in an attempt to stop his purposeful advance.

"I don't think this is a good idea, Micah," I nervously backed away. I tried to put a little more distance between us, my right hand held out in front of me. "We just had an argument. I don't think we should just jump in the sack like nothing happened. We need to work this out."

Micah leered, then moved closer. "What better way to make up?"

The fire in his eyes was enough to warm me to my toes. I was almost tempted to drop my towel, but I steeled my resolve. I wasn't sure that it was even my own urge. I knew Micah could have easily put the desire deep within me. When I gave myself over to him, I wanted to be sure it was my idea.

My towel disappeared. I looked down at myself in wonder. When I looked up to Micah, I watched, wide-eyed, as his clothes followed my towel into oblivion.

He arched one finely sculpted brow.

"Well, you wanted to know what I could do. Would you care to see more?" He waggled his brows playfully.

I looked down the long lean length of him and paused when I reached the part most worthy of my attention. I licked my lips and his cock jumped with anticipation.

"Oh, yes." I wanted to see much more, and I couldn't wait.

"Why do you always seem to have so much power over me?" I asked him much later.

He shrugged. "It is the same for me with you."

He trailed his hand down my back and rinsed off the soap that he'd lathered on me for the umpteenth time. I looked at my fingers and decided it was time to get out of the water. They were all wrinkly. I'd definitely been in the tub far too long.

I just needed to dry off and get some much-needed rest. I was so tired I could sleep the clock around.

"We'll never make it back to Grand Rapids at this rate. Not that I'm in any hurry to be interrogated by the police." Micah held my hand as I stepped out of the tub.

My stomach grumbled. "What's for dinner, count? I know you can get yours off the hoof, so to speak, but I prefer mine a bit more done."

Micah heaved a mock, exasperated sigh as he stood to climb out of the tub. I could tell he wasn't really upset with me, mostly because a part of his anatomy was still extremely happy to see me.

"Would you like to enjoy your food a bit more...rare?"

"Eeew, yuck! Me eat rare meat?" I shook my head, my hand over my mouth and suppressed a gag. "Don't make me sick."

I left the bathroom and shuddered at the thought. I walked toward the bed and my bag when an entirely new change of clothes appeared on the bed. I stopped and stared at the expensive-looking floor-length gown.

Hmm. Not bad. That might be a handy trick to be able to pull off. "Um, thanks, Micah, but it's not quite my style."

More clothes appeared until the bed was covered with a wide assortment of expensive-looking clothes and undergarments.

The clothes were lovely. Prettier even than the new things I'd just bought. There were no brand names on them, but the silk suit and blouse had the look of a familiar designer's style.

I smiled inwardly. It could prove to be interesting to have a...lover who had such extraordinary powers. I deliberately ignored the word husband as the word danced around inside my head.

What if you could have those powers for yourself? The thought came unbidden and unexpected. I turned, frowning, and wondered if the thought had even been mine at all.

I dressed in silence as Micah watched. My shyness, while still not gone, had abated somewhat. At least my self-consciousness had subsided enough that I felt relatively comfortable in Micah's presence.

I pulled the decadent stockings up my calves, reveling in the feel of the smooth silk as it caressed my legs. The shoes were gorgeous three-inch pumps that put my head at Micah's chin when I wore them. I never felt so small, or so feminine, in all of my life.

"Come, let us find a good place to eat," Micah said as he took my arm and led me from the room.

He gathered my things and carried them easily in one hand as we left the hotel. He deposited me in the passenger seat of a sleek, black Jaguar with dark tinted windows. I looked over to the spot where I'd left my car and gasped.

"My car is gone!"

"Yes, it is," Micah agreed, slanting a glance at me from the corner of his eye. "I had Veronica, my driver, take it back to your home. It was only a matter of time before the police stopped you, you know."

I settled back into the seat. I knew he was right. I just didn't want to be without my car. My car was my sense of independence.

"You may use this car as your own. Any of my vehicles are now yours to drive."

He turned toward me and I wished I could see his eyes. They were hidden behind a pair of extremely dark glasses. I couldn't tell a thing from the lower half of his face, which he held in an expressionless mask.

I thought about his offer for a moment as I looked around the gray leather interior. Me, drive a Jag?

I closed my eyes and shook my head. Stranger things were known to happen. Hell, stranger things drove Jaguars. I quickly censored the thought and shot a glance toward Micah.

If he'd picked up on my last thought, it hadn't insulted him. If anything, it amused him. He drove silently, a half smile on his face.

"Okay. It's time for a few lessons." I figured if we had to be stuck in the car for a while he could teach me a little about all of the other dimensions.

"Lessons?"

"Yes. It's time you brought me up to speed on inter-dimensional gateways."

"Oh, that. What do you want to know?"

"First of all, how many dimensions are there, does anyone know?"

Micah took a deep breath. "There were three-hundred and sixty, at last count."

"Three-hundred and sixty?" I gasped. My mouth hung agape for a minute before I clamped it shut with a sharp clack of my teeth. I sat and tried to digest that for a while before my next question.

"Are all of the dimensions filled with evil entities?"

He shook his head. "No. As a matter of fact, most dimensions are filled with people, humans, much like yourself."

Well, that was a relief. "So I guess I'm just lucky that the only open portals I've found are to the bad places, huh?"

Micah pressed his lips together. I decided not to push him. What I'd just learned was enough to think about for a while.

"WHERE ARE WE GOING?" I finally asked about an hour and a half later. I wanted to eat. My stomach had grumbled its protest for an hour or more and we didn't seem any closer to a pit stop now than we did before.

"I told you, to get something to eat."

Micah kept both eyes on the road and I sighed with exasperation.

"I realize that physical hunger isn't really a problem for you. Besides, you had that little snack I gave you last night. But it *is* a problem for me." I closed my eyes, took a deep breath and tried to fight down the nausea brought on by my too low blood sugar. "I have to eat something soon or I'm going to be sick."

Micah sighed and made a U-turn. "There was a convenience store back this way about five minutes. I'll stop there and get you a coffee and a doughnut. Will that be enough to hold you for another hour or so?"

I nodded gratefully. Glad he'd seen it. I was too far into a hypoglycemic episode to have noticed.

Twenty minutes later, I sighed with happiness. My stomach, while still not full, was no longer attempting to digest itself, at least, and I sipped my twenty-four ounce cup of coffee happily.

"So," I said, in between sips. "Where are you taking me?"

Just looking at Micah made me hot and I squirmed in my seat. I admired his perfect profile. How I'd gotten so lucky as to attract such a perfect male specimen as him, I'll never know. But I will be eternally grateful. I frowned at the thought.

Eternity.

Micah had that. In twenty or thirty years, if I was lucky enough to live that long, I'd be an old woman. And Micah would still appear as young and as vital as he was now. Anyone who saw us together would think I was his mother.

What would Micah do after I was gone? Would he find another mate? Could he? Or would he spend the rest of eternity alone?

That was a good question. I sipped my coffee and wondered about it, ignoring the scenery we passed as we continued to head east, toward Michigan. Back to the life I'd been so desperate to leave behind.

We stopped at a small restaurant somewhere just outside of Chicago. The name was a bit odd. The sign over the door read—The Lone Wolfe Café. The owners were friends of Micah's. Apparently, he'd arranged to eat and rest here for a while, or longer if need be.

He helped me out of the car and held my arm in the way, as I realized, he did when he wanted others to know I belonged to him.

"Tasha, this is my good friend Damien Wolfe. Damien, my mate, Tasha."

His friend grinned at me. It was an open, likable grin and I found myself returning it.

"Your mate, huh?" He slapped Micah on the shoulder. "You didn't tell us you'd met your mate," he grinned. "Shay will be thrilled." He turned the wattage up on his grin and aimed it at me. "Shay is my mate."

My mouth fell open and I quickly snapped it shut.

"Your mate? Are you saying that you're a..." I looked at Micah, not sure how much I should say.

He laughed. "Oh, this is great. You're a neophyte." He winked at me conspiratorially. "Just what Micah needs to loosen up. He's always been a bit too serious."

Damien turned, led me into the building and invited Micah in so he wouldn't be stuck outside.

"You and Shay are going to get along great."

"Who and Shay are going to get along great?" asked a beautiful, young, very pregnant woman.

Damien leaned down, kissed the woman on the top of the head and smiled. He put his hand on her rounded stomach. "How's the baby?"

She pushed his hand away with a grin. "You know very well the baby is just fine." She looked over at me with interest. "Who's your friend, Micah?"

"My mate."

"Your mate?" she squealed and danced over to give us both hugs. "I'm so happy for you, Micah. It's about time." She smiled at us and her almond shaped eyes crinkled at the corners, giving her an exotic look.

"Grandfather did say you would find your mate. I'm so glad he was right."

"He usually is," Damien said, nuzzling her neck.

She looked from Micah to myself. "Oh, my goodness, you both must be famished. Come. Let's get you something to eat. You both look rather weak."

Well, I had to admit to feeling more than a bit peckish, but I wondered how they could be the same as Micah and not realize he wouldn't need food.

They took us into the kitchen and I understood. Shay reached into the refrigerator and pulled out four sixteen-ounce bottles filled with blood. She handed one to her mate, then one to Micah and she turned to me, her hand extended. I just gaped at the blood with horror.

Micah, Bless him, stepped up and took the bottle. "She hasn't Chosen."

"Oh, my." Shay turned stricken eyes toward me. "I'm sorry. I just assumed..." Her face turned red, she took the extra bottle from Micah and returned it to the refrigerator.

109

She bent and pulled a packaged sandwich from another shelf and held it out. "I hope you like chicken salad."

My mind reeled. What had Micah meant when he said I haven't chosen yet? "Chosen what?" I asked, turning to Micah. "What haven't I chosen?"

"You haven't chosen to accept The Gift."

"The Gift? What gift?" I frowned, wondered if I'd finally lost my mind.

Damien took Shay's arm. "Let's leave them for a minute, Baby. I think I know why Micah brought her here."

I turned toward Micah and asked, "Why *did* you bring me here?"

He shrugged. "For help, support? Hell, Tasha, I don't know. I guess I thought if you saw Shay, still so young and beautiful, it would help you choose."

"Choose what?" I had a horrible suspicion of what this was about to lead to, but nothing, and I repeat, nothing could have prepared me to hear what he was about to say.

"Remember what I told you about people who had been turned?"

I nodded. Of course I remembered. How could I forget something as terrifying as that?

Micah took a deep breath and looked at me, his gaze almost pleading. "They chose to accept The Gift when it was offered to them."

I swallowed thickly. When had my life turned into a bad science fiction episode?

My first thought was that it had to be more like a curse. What would it be like to be doomed to live forever, always alone? But then again, if I accepted The Gift, I wouldn't be alone, I'd have Micah. And he would never be left alone again either.

I turned away from him and tried to think. "I don't know if I can, Micah."

He reached out and ran his hand down my back, his touch meant to soothe. "You do not have to make the decision, now. You can wait. Think about it. Think of all of the wonderful things you could do. Things you've never even dreamed of."

The thought of staying young forever and to never be sick again, were both potent lures. They were even more of a lure than being able to fashion my own designer knock-offs in the blink of an eye.

I was tempted, for about a split second, until I thought of Camen and his lack of control.

Chapter Fourteen

"No, I'd only have to worry about whether or not I would become addicted to adrenaline laced blood," I said as I neared hysterics at the thought of becoming like the vampire who tried to kill me.

"I would never allow that to happen to you. You must know by now that I would never abandon you to that fate. I would teach you as I have taught countless others."

Well, there was that. I bit my lip deep in thought. I looked down at his hand, to the small plastic bottle he still held and I wondered what it was like.

Micah smiled sadly. "For you it is abhorrent. For me, it is better than chocolate."

I shook my head. As a certified chocoholic myself, I just knew that couldn't be right.

He stepped closer, reached up with his free hand and tucked a stray lock of my hair behind my ear.

I closed my eyes. God, I was so tempted to accept his offer to live forever young. More than anything, I never wanted be alone again. Micah stepped closer. He cupped my cheek, looked into my eyes, then kissed me on the forehead.

"No pressure, Tasha. Just consider it. Please?"

What could I say? I just looked at him and nodded, thinking of Shay's ethereal beauty. And I wondered if being a vamp would enhance my looks at all. So far, all the vamps I'd met were stunning. Did that mean I would be, too?

Then it struck me and I looked at him, my eyes wide. "Shay is pregnant."

Micah nodded slowly. "Yes, this will be her third child."

So, I could still have kids. That was another plus. "How long before I can't have children?"

Micah shrugged, "Our kind can only get pregnant when we choose to. There isn't a female alive who has tried to have a child and failed."

I glared at him. "That is not an answer."

"I'm sorry, little one. It is the only one I have. Patrice is one of our oldest females. Her youngest child is twenty three."

"Oh." I sucked my bottom lip into my mouth, thinking. "How many children does this Patrice have?"

He looked a bit uncomfortable. "Remember, I have told you, you cannot get pregnant unless you wish it," he warned.

"How many, Micah?"

I crossed my arms over my chest. "I want a house full, Micah. I always have."

"Seventeen."

My eyes rounded at the number. Even I didn't want that many kids. I cleared my throat. "Did you just say seventeen?" I croaked. It was a wonder I could talk at all, considering the fact that my tongue was attached to the roof of my mouth.

Micah smiled, obviously pleased to give me news about being a vampire that I could see in a positive light.

"She is nearly one thousand years old, Tasha. She wanted to be sure our race would not die." He leaned against the wall and shoved his hands in his pockets. "There are many of us who have not found mates. Or they have lost them. Some of us decide to end our existence after they've lived so long with no one to love them."

I watched as he pulled his hands from his pockets and clenched and unclenched them at his sides. He had it bad. I could tell he wanted to take me into his arms, but didn't want to coerce me in any way. Thankfully, he wanted to let me make this decision on my own and I could only respect him for that.

"So this Patrice took it upon herself to populate an entire race?" I knew that was stretching it a bit, but seventeen kids was a lot by anyone's standards.

"She vowed to have one child every fifty years and her mate agreed."

Have a child once every fifty years? Did I want to make that kind of commitment? Could I have six children, one after the other and take three hundred years off after that?

Micah shook his head. He'd obviously read my mind again. "There is no rule which states each couple must have a child every fifty years. It is totally up to the couple." He laid his hand on my shoulders and I looked up into his eyes.

"We don't even have to have more children if you don't want to."

What?

"Did I just hear you right?" I asked him. I bent over and put my head between my knees because I felt faint. "Did you just say I wouldn't have to have any more?"

Looking nervous, he pulled away and shoved his hands back into his pockets. He moved his fingers around inside and I heard the muffled sound of jingling coins. He cast his gaze around the immaculate kitchen. I followed the path of his gaze for the most part as it darted from the butcher-block island in the middle of the room to the stainless steel appliances, everywhere but my face.

"Well?" I prompted.

He closed his eyes and took a deep breath.

"The other night, when we were...when you thought... Damn it!" He scrubbed his face with his hands and paced away from me.

I have to admit that I was at least a little intrigued. I'd never seen Micah so nervous before. And he'd never cursed in front of me either. Well, not out of the bedroom anyway. A part of me wanted to prod him a bit more, but I wanted answers, not an argument. So, I waited. Albeit a bit impatiently, but I waited just the same.

"Oh, hell," he ranted, as he turned and paced back toward me. "The other night, when we made love, you expressed a small desire to have my child."

I nodded, "Yeah. So?"

"When a Guide expresses such a desire during intercourse with their Cartuotey mate, it releases an egg in the female and primes the male's semen to be fertile."

I rolled my eyes and he scowled, leaning close to look into my eyes.

"Just because you don't know much about your power, does not mean it does not exist, Tasha."

He pinned me with a dark stare and I found myself waiting, almost breathlessly, for him to continue.

"Your powers surge at that time. It produces an extremely fertile egg, which allows you to become pregnant if my sperm reaches its destination."

"You said if," I pointed out. I wasn't sure what the feeling in my stomach was yet. Was it relief or disappointment?

"We won't know for a few more weeks." Micah's gaze never left me as he shook his head. "It is early, but there is a heartbeat. I can hear it." He smiled. "Do you want to know what it sounds like? It is very strong. This child is stubborn, just like its mother."

I slapped my hand onto the top of the counter next to me as my knees buckled with shock. He rushed to me, wrapped his arm around me and helped

113

me to one of the stools next to the island.

"Then y-you weren't joking earlier?"

"No. I wasn't. I would never joke about something as important as my child."

"I'm really pregnant?" I'm not sure what my garbled, high-pitched question sounded like, but that's what I tried to say at any rate.

Micah nodded. He slowly released me when he realized I wasn't going to faint, fall off the tall stool and hurt myself. I sat with my eyes closed and took slow, deep breaths and wondered whether it was a boy or girl. I was sure Micah couldn't know the answer to that.

I rested my hands over my stomach. I would never be alone again. Well, not as long as I carried this child.

My eyes flew open and I scowled at him and dropped my hands from my waist before I fisted them on my hips. "That's not fair." I accused, then glared at him through narrowed eyes.

Micah watched me for a minute, his brows drew together and he looked confused. "What is not fair?" he finally asked with a frown.

"That you can hear its heartbeat already." I glowered at him. "I won't be able to hear it for weeks, but you," I said with no little measure of disgust. "You can hear it and it's only a few days old." I crossed my arms and scowled at him. "You make me sick."

"You can choose to not have it, if that is your wish."

Where in the heck did that come from? How did he come to the conclusion that I didn't want this baby from that outburst?

"What? Me kill an innocent baby? My innocent baby?" I asked, outraged he could even think I was capable of such a thing. My arms slid down over my still flat stomach and covered it as if the action alone would protect my unborn child.

Personally, I'd always been against ending the life of a fetus. To me, the conception itself was a miracle. Yet, I'd never believed it was my right to force my views on others. Who am I to force someone to bring an unwanted child into the world? There were too many unwanted children already.

Apparently, Micah took my reaction as a good sign. He sat down on the stool next to me and covered my hand with his much larger one. The warmth seeped through to my stomach and caused a fluttering sensation in my middle that I knew had nothing to do with a baby.

"You must be sure, little one. I will not abandon my child, nor will I force you to give it up. If you choose to keep this child, know this, you also choose to honor our wedding vows. Till death do us part, and for my kind, that is a very long time."

I cast my gaze to my lap and stared at his large hand covering mine. I couldn't bring myself to look at his face, at least not yet.

"But I'm not your kind, Micah," I replied, softly. I blinked my eyes fast. I refused to cry over something as insignificant as my being mortal like the other ninety-nine point nine percent of the people on this rock. And I wondered whether or not I would be forced to become one of them.

Micah shook his head. "No one will force you to become one of The Chosen. That is a decision only you yourself can make."

He shifted in his seat and reached up to cup my chin in his hand. He turned my head toward him and I looked up into his eyes. They burned with an intensity I'd never seen before.

"I will, however, hold you to our marriage vows so long as you are the mother of our child."

I closed my eyes for a minute. I needed to think. It was just too much.

"I'll age, Micah," I stared into his glittering black eyes. "I'll age and then I'll die. Do you really want to watch me die?"

He shook his head. "No, I do not. I do not want to watch my child die, either, as he or she eventually must if you do not choose to become one of us, but I will not settle for less. The child deserves to know both of us." He smiled tightly. "Now you have more than one decision to make. Please, choose wisely."

Micah stood and left the room, leaving me to my quiet brooding as I tried to make up my mind about such an uncertain future.

An hour and a half later, I still paced the kitchen. "It just isn't fair!"

Whoever said life was fair?

I ignored the question in my mind and continued to pace. I turned with my eyes on my feet and almost ran into Shay.

I brought myself to an abrupt halt before I mowed the smaller woman down and brought my hand to my chest as my heart slammed against my ribs.

"I'm so sorry," I sidled around her. I thought it was about time I went and found my errant husband. I smiled slightly at the mental use of those words. My husband. It was almost laughable. If anyone would have asked me a month or so ago, I would have been certain I would never be in a situation where I would use those two words together. And me and wife were two more words that had never previously struck me as being synonymous.

Shay smiled, rubbed one small hand over her rounded belly and took my hand with the other.

"Come, sit down. I think we should have a chat and get to know each other. We have much in common."

I snorted, "Yeah, right."

She grinned. "I'm serious." She looked at me thoughtfully. "I think I know why Micah brought you here."

Curious, I let her pull me to the breakfast bar and shot her a look. "Why?" I slid onto the stool I'd vacated a while ago when I started to pace and waited for her to continue.

"Why do I think we have much in common, or why did Micah bring you here?"

"Both."

I was becoming a bit irritated with Micah and his friends. It seemed none of them could give me a straight answer about anything. I've always hated when people answer my questions with more questions. It never fails to irritate the hell out of me. If I wanted to be psychoanalyzed, I'd go find myself a shrink.

Shay looked at me and tilted her head. "I used to be just like you, you know." Then she blushed. "Well, obvious physical characteristics aside." She indicated my height and hair color.

"I used to be human, too," she blurted. It was almost as if she was afraid to admit it.

I gaped at her. I wasn't sure what it was I thought she had been about to say, but it hadn't been that.

"Excuse me?"

Shay laughed. It was a light infectious sound that I was sure entranced prey easily. I shook my head to clear it.

"I met Damien a long, long time ago. He was sent to—well, you know," she blushed again.

I watched her, a bit bemused. What a feat it was to be her age and still be able to blush over losing her virginity.

Shay took a deep breath. "Any hoo, I couldn't resist him. He was so..." She shook her head and gave a half shrug. "Compelling or something. He still is truth to tell." She sighed, a faraway look in her eyes.

"Look, Shay, I'm really not trying to be rude, but, this is relevant to me...how?"

"Don't you see?" she asked. Her voice was pitched a bit high and I fought the urge to grimace at the perky sound. "I had to make the same choice."

Okay, so I had to concede the point that we did indeed have that one small item in common. But it was still just the one thing.

"Ah, but had you seen your best friend defiled by a dirt-bag drug dealer just before she died? Then killed the aforementioned jerk for raping and killing your friend? Then did you torture yourself by giving up addictive drugs cold turkey, only to almost be deflowered by a power hungry, life sucking, demon from hell?" I said it all in one breath, putting my hand out in front me. I forgot for a minute that Micah had explained that the incubus wasn't really a demon, but an evil other-dimensional being with magical powers. It still sounded like a demon to me.

"Uh, uh, sister. Aside from the fact that you used to be human—three hundred and fifty years ago, I might add—we don't have one thing in common at all."

"But you're wrong, Tasha." Shay said, taking my hand. She frowned and rubbed it between her two warmer ones. "You're hands are frozen!"

I shrugged, "It's just my nerves. My hands and feet get really cold when I'm nervous, I don't know why." I pulled my hand from hers and smiled politely. Another woman—especially one I don't know—holding my hand, makes me feel kind of creepy.

Shay waved away my apologetic look. "Don't say a word, sweetie, I understand." She patted my arm lightly. "What I wanted to say is, that we've both had to face the same thing, make this same decision." She looked into my eyes. "Is your situation different? Of course it is. You're a different person." She waved her arm. "These are different times." She stood, walked around the island and stopped to face me.

"The question I want to ask you, what I need to know is, what do you think Micah's life will be like, once you're gone?" She looked into my eyes and I had the strange thought that she was looking into my soul. "After you die, I mean. Which could be tomorrow, by the way, human bodies are so frail. You could be hit by a car and leave him alone tomorrow. He has no guarantee how long you will live as a human. When that happens, he could be alone for the rest of his considerably long life." She gave me a sad look. "But, the chances are, he'll follow you, rather than stay and continue to live an empty existence, knowing you are forever gone from this earth."

I felt my eyes widen with the horror of that statement. "Follow me?"

Shay nodded. "He'll open a vein or something and kill himself rather than choose to live through eternity without you."

"Oh, my God."

I'd never thought of that. I mentally turned back time and remembered how I felt when I'd first lost Trina. Suicide had crossed my mind more than once because I didn't want to go back to my solitary existence.

"And you think he does?"

"Hey," I gasped. "Quit reading my mind. I swear, that's so rude."

Shay giggled. "I couldn't read your mind right now if I tried. Not without a blood bond anyway. You just said all of that out loud."

I shook my head. "Figures." I put my head in my hands and rubbed my temples. "I'm getting a headache." Didn't I have enough crap on my mind already without being saddled with a friggin' guilt trip from hell?

Shay reached over and patted me on the back. "It doesn't hurt, you know." Then she smiled and shrugged. "Well, not much, anyway. Then afterward it feels wonderful. Just think, you'll never have another headache unless, of course, someone bonks you on the head. You'll never be sick, never have another period and it will be centuries before you get your first gray hair." Then she blushed. "And the ritual can be so..."

I nodded sagely and smiled. I wanted to see if she could turn any redder.

"So, it has to do with sex, huh?"

Shay's face blazed. "How did you know?"

"You're blushing again." I pointed out.

She covered her face with her hands. "I can't help it, it's my upbringing."

"And three hundred and fifty years hasn't made a difference?"

Shay scowled. "I swear I'm gonna smack that man if he doesn't stop telling everyone how old I am. Just you watch." She looked at me and gave me a conspiratorial grin. "*He's* positively ancient." Then she looked up and smiled, "Speak of the devil."

I turned to see Micah in the doorway and he looked very nervous.

"What's the matter?" I slid out of my seat and headed toward him. I tried not to give much thought to the fact that my first reaction had been to comfort him.

He looked down at me, his expression unreadable, his usually tanned face pale.

"There was a news report on the television. The police have released an All

118

Points Bulletin on your whereabouts. We have no more time to waste. We must head back to Grand Rapids today, before they find you. It is imperative that you turn yourself in. Your cooperation helps establish the absence of guilt."

"Damn it," I snarled and stomped from the room.

The other three followed and I heard Shay ask, "Why is there an A.P.B. out for her?"

Damien took her by the arm and stopped to whisper in Shay's ear. No doubt telling her what I'd done. It was too late. I'd already told her myself.

I brushed the tears from my eyes. Why should I care what she thinks? I never asked for her friendship anyway. If a person can't accept me as I am, they aren't worth my time.

"That was self defense! Surely the police know of the concept. They have to know she would have been next." Shay was so outraged, I could hear her whispered tirade as they followed me into the room.

Damien put his arms around his mate in an attempt to calm her down. "There's nothing we can do, sweetheart." He kissed the side of her neck. "We'll just let them go tell her side of the story and hope for the best."

Shay scowled. "The hell there isn't." She pulled from Damien's arms and stomped closer to me. She shook her finger in my face, ranting, and I knew right then that she would be my friend forever. However long forever turned out to be.

"We're all going to cross that stinking lake and tell those cops what they can do with their suspicions." She breezed past the two men and hooked her arm around mine.

"It was so good of you to come and stay with me during my pregnancy, Tasha. You're such good company, it's hard to believe you've been here for—" She shot a glance at Micah. "Four or five weeks should do it."

Shay shook her head. "It's hard to believe you've already been here for almost six weeks." She winked at me.

I shook my head. "I've only been off work for a month." Then I grimaced. "I'm sure I've been fired by now."

She glanced at Damien. "It's good that you had to take the ferry over there last month. What day was it again, sweetie?"

"The thirteenth." Damien said, then smiled. He looked like he was coming around to Shay's way of thinking.

Shay looked at me and raised her brow.

"My last day at work was the eleventh and ..." I paused, almost choking on the next words. "Trina was killed on the fifteenth."

"Good, good." Shay rubbed her hands together. "Even if they check our financial records it will show that Damien bought one round trip ticket and a one way from Michigan for an adult to cross. And one was a woman, if anyone should ask the ferry crew." She smiled. "My sister in law, but how are they gonna know?"

She looked at the two men who stood and gaped at her as if she'd just grown another head.

"Well, gentlemen, shall we go?"

Chapter Fifteen

I COULDN'T BELIEVE IT. SHAY DIDN'T EVEN KNOW ME. NOT REALLY. AND she was about to stick her neck out for me like this?

I shook my head and finally came to my senses. "I can't let you do this, Shay." I almost embarrassed myself by starting to cry, but thankfully, I was able to keep control of my emotions.

Shay rolled her eyes. "Honey, at my age, nobody *lets* me do anything." She marched over to the door and stood in front of it. She looked every bit like the kid she thought I was.

Damien smiled and shook his head. "Once she's set her mind on something, there's just no stopping her."

Then Micah added, "Besides, her idea is a sound one." He rubbed his chin thoughtfully. "I should have thought of that."

I rolled my eyes, tempted to hit him, and grinned at Shay. "Why do men always seem so surprised when a woman comes up with a good idea?"

"I don't know," she winked. "You'd think they would have grown used to it by now." Shay turned, opened the door and I followed her out into the afternoon sunlight.

Damien took one look at Micah's Jag and shook his head. "If you think I'm making the trip in that little thing, you're out of your mind."

Shay leaned over and whispered, "He thinks he's psychic, like his grandfather and is certain the baby is going to be born in a car. He wants to be sure it's the Lincoln," she giggled. "He's even got emergency supplies stashed in the trunk."

Damien reached into his pocket, pulled out a flip phone, pressed a button and put the phone to his ear. "Nelson. Bring the car around, we're taking a trip." He shook his head. "No, no time to pack, Shay and I will provide." He brought the phone from his ear and closed it before he stuck it back into his pocket. "Nelson should be around with the car in a minute or so."

Five minutes later, a white, stretched limousine rounded the corner. I tried not to gape. I looked from Micah's dark good looks to Damien's lighter ones.

It just wasn't fair. They were both so handsome and so friggin' rich, it should be illegal.

Micah chose that moment to smile and wink at me. I felt myself flush and I shuffled my feet in embarrassment. He must have peeked into my mind again. I don't know why it didn't seem to bother me as much as it used to.

Nelson, whom I assumed was the driver, brought the car to a smooth stop in front of us. I could have sworn it was running silent. If it was making any noise, I sure as heck couldn't hear it.

Shay climbed into the car and motioned for me to join her. Then the two men went back inside to inform the staff the owners would be gone for a few days. Shay and I sat facing each other with me facing toward the back of the limo.

"I hope you don't mind riding backward, for some reason it makes me sick." She laughed and looked a bit embarrassed. "I get sick even when I'm not expecting."

I smiled, "Don't feel bad, I'm claustrophobic. I don't know why. The doctors said it was most likely a trauma from when I was a child, but I don't remember."

Micah climbed in and sat next to me while we talked. He reached over and laced his fingers with mine as the car began to move smoothly through the parking lot.

"You were accidentally locked in the root cellar one day when you were about five."

I turned a wide-eyed stare on him. "I was?"

Suddenly, the memories of a dark, little room flashed through my mind. The darkness closed in on me, the house creaked and groaned above me and the terrifying sound of mice scurrying through the pitch-black room took me back to that place. I was little again as the familiar panic took hold of me in an iron grip.

Micah, squeezed my hand and brought me back to the present. He nodded. "You apparently followed your grandmother into the cellar and she left you to follow her back out. She didn't know until much later that the door slid closed, locking you inside of the tiny room because you couldn't reach the latch."

"Oh," I said and realization struck. "So that was why the door was removed all those years ago?"

"I heard you screaming and ripped the door from its hinges. I carried you out. You clung to me and wouldn't let me put you down. Even when you knew you were safe and when your father wanted to comfort you, you wouldn't let me go."

He released my hand to wrap his arm around me. I leaned into him. I loved the sense of security I felt whenever we were together. I finally understood why I always felt so safe in his arms.

"HOW LONG BEFORE WE reach the ferry dock?" Shay asked Nelson about an hour later. She yawned and blinked the sleep from her eyes.

"We're almost there, madam," Nelson answered from the front. He drove the car expertly, never taking his gaze from the road.

"I'm so sorry. I must have dozed off." Shay gave us both a smile, obviously embarrassed. "I seem to nod off quite a bit lately. Can we stop and get something to eat? I'm starving." She rubbed her rounded belly with a grimace. "I've had to eat more often since I became pregnant again."

Damien leaned over and whispered something in her ear and she nodded enthusiastically.

"Oh, yes. That's a wonderful idea. It sounds perfect. You know I love their place." She must have seen my confused look because she leaned forward—as far as her distended belly would allow—and explained loud enough for Nelson to hear. "Damien has just suggested we go to the Blue Moon Café, it is owned by friends of ours. They have been in Europe for the past few months. It will give us the chance to visit for an hour or two."

Her attention turned to Micah. "And I thought you might like a visit, too. I'm sure they'll want to meet your mate."

Micah nodded. "No doubt."

"Oh." I sat back, happy with the idea that my empty stomach was about to be filled. At least I hoped it was. If it was a café, surely they would have regular food, too. After all, Shay had that chicken salad sandwich stashed in her fridge.

Don't get me wrong, Micah and his friends are absolutely wonderful, but they did tend to forget that not only did I need a different form of sustenance, they also forgot I needed it more often.

Micah consumed small amounts of blood, generally once daily. I covered the spot on my neck where he usually bit me and it tingled slightly at the sensual memory of when he fed from me. But with Micah being the way he was for all of these years, he usually forgot that I, on the other hand, needed to eat several times a day.

You wouldn't have to if you became one of them.

I jerked in my seat as that thought came totally unexpected. I shot Micah a glance from the corner of my eye and wondered if he was responsible for it.

Micah leaned over to whisper in my ear. "Is it so awful to contemplate spending an eternity with me?"

I shot him a surprised stare. Was he kidding? Spending an eternity with him would be wonderful. I was tempted to say yes right then, but I thought about the blood. There was just no way I could bring myself to drink it.

"If you were one of us, the act would not seem so repugnant to you." He smiled and kissed the back of my fingers. "As a matter of fact, I can assure you that you will find it most enjoyable."

I turned my head away from his compelling eyes to look out the window at the approaching darkness. Like he'd said before. This was a decision I needed to make on my own.

But when I turned and looked into his eyes, it was easy to make the decision. The stark need I saw in his inky stare was enough to make me agree. God help me, but I wanted to spend an eternity with him.

The Blue Moon Café was definitely not what I expected. Located in an older section of town, the café was tucked into the bottom floor of an ancient, three-story colonial. The top two stories served as living quarters for the owners.

The huge dark gray painted building boasted a light blue moon mural, which decorated the front. It was expertly painted in such a way that I could almost see the face of a man in it.

A sign on the door read—Welcome to the Blue Moon, where everyone with good in their heart is welcome. Micah explained that it was a message to all vampires. They could enter without a formal invitation as long as they did not intend to harm anyone.

Clever.

Inside, the ground floor held tables and chairs set in arcs, or half moons. Several round tables that served as full moons sat in the corners. The ceiling, painted midnight-blue, boasted fiber-optic stars, which twinkled merrily even in the light of day.

I couldn't help but gape when I walked in. The interior was just so much...more than I expected.

"I love to see a person's first reaction to this place," Shay said with a smile.

She leaned closer to whisper in my ear. "If you think this is something, wait till you see the front when we leave. They used glow in the dark paint for the moon and the fiber-optics are mounted outside, too."

I hoped I'd get a chance to look at it before we left. It sounded spectacular.

Damien left us to walk to the crescent shaped bar and rang the large bell that hung from the wall.

I peered around the empty café and wondered where all of the customers were.

Micah wrapped his arm around me and kissed my neck. "The café doesn't open for another hour yet. Richard must have seen us arrive and buzzed the door for us, either that, or Elisabeth did."

"Oh," I said and wondered if I was going to get anything to eat after all.

Micah chuckled. "Of course you are. They're probably just getting dressed. I'm sure the kitchen staff is already here preparing for the dinner crowd."

I nodded. "Of course. They wouldn't have expected four early dinner guests."

"There you all are. I started to think you'd fallen from the face of the earth."

I turned at the sound of the voice. Stunned, I stared openly at the incredibly beautiful woman who walked into the room. Were all of these people gorgeous?

I watched the woman as she entered, all six feet of her. Her long hair fell to her waist in ebony waves, framed a heart-shaped face with sky blue eyes, which I was sure, held Micah's a bit longer than necessary. I stamped down the green one-eyed monster and told myself to behave.

You are so not jealous.

My husband released me, to hurry into the woman's embrace.

You're still not jealous.

I stood back and bit my tongue. I waited, sure that was a logical explanation for his behavior. A very tall man, Richard, I assumed, soon joined them. He hugged Shay and shook the men's hands before he pulled them both to him in a hearty embrace.

"It's been awhile, hasn't it?" the man asked.

"Of course it has, Richard. What do you expect when you drag my little sister all over Europe for months on end?" Micah laughed and slapped his brother-in-law on the back.

I looked from my husband to the woman who now looked me up and down with interest. I blushed. I'd been jealous of his sister?

"Who's your friend?" She circled around me and I fought the urge to turn with her to watch her every move. She was every bit as compelling as her brother.

Micah stepped back to my side and smiled apologetically. He wrapped his arm around me in a belated show of support.

"I am sorry, Tasha." He drew me closer, then turned toward his sister. "Elisabeth, Tasha is my mate."

I watched, nearly enthralled as a smile brightened her face and she rushed over to hug me.

"Welcome to the family, little sister. I believe we will get along famously."

I swallowed thickly at her welcoming attitude. A month ago, I had been alone. Now, it seemed I had friends and a family again. I looked over at Micah with tears in my eyes. I had him to thank for it.

My stomach picked that time to grumble a loud protest of its deplorable lack of sustenance and I blushed when five sets of eyes turned my way.

"Sorry," I excused myself. "But I do have to eat every five hours or so and it's been at least six since that sandwich I had at your house." I looked at Shay, hoping for a bit of help.

Elisabeth stepped up. "Of course, you must be famished. All of you." She handed me a menu, "Order whatever you like, it's on the house." She giggled and leaned over to squeeze my hand. "Why wouldn't it be? You're my new sister."

I blinked back some pesky tears, overwhelmed at her unconditional acceptance. After I composed myself, I perused the menu for a moment before I chose the bacon cheeseburger and fries. I planned to chase it down with a cola since anything stronger was out of the question, since I'd become pregnant.

"Anyone else?" Elisabeth asked before she left for the kitchen.

"A cheeseburger does sound good," Micah said with a thoughtful look on his face. "I'd bet it's been at least a year since I had one."

Elisabeth looked toward Shay and Damien. "Shall I make it four, with the works?"

The others nodded and we moved to sit at one of the round tables for eight.

An hour later I had to admit, the food was great and the hospitality even better. The small restaurant opened before we'd finished and the full dinner crowd poured in. Elisabeth and Richard greeted their regulars like family and even toasted an older couple on the arrival of their new grandchild.

"How do you do it?" I leaned over, to ask Elisabeth.

"Do what?" she smiled, encouraging me to continue.

"How do you keep people from realizing you don't age?" I whispered, sure that, sooner or later, the multitude of people who frequented this place would realize that the two owners never got any older.

"Oh." The smile left her face and she looked a bit melancholy. "We don't. In fact, in a few years, we'll have to close down or sell." She gazed lovingly around her. "To tell you the truth, I'd almost rather just close down. If we sold it, it just wouldn't be the same."

I nodded. "You're right. I think you and Richard make it what it is."

Elisabeth leaned toward me and looked deep into my eyes. "Have you told him yet?"

I frowned, then looked from her to her brother. "Told him what?" I asked, not sure I even knew what she meant.

"Have you told him that you have chosen?"

I pulled away and looked at her. I wondered if she could read my mind because of the blood bond I shared with her brother.

Elisabeth laughed and shook her head. "No, I cannot read your mind. I know what you're thinking because it's written all over your face when you look at him."

"Oh." I bit my lip and fiddled with my napkin. What more was there to say?

"You're welcome to do it here," she smiled and blinked back tears. "I would be honored to be able to attend and preside over your handfasting."

That word got Micah's attention and he turned to look from me to his sister.

"Who's handfasting?" Micah's eyes met mine and I felt him touch the outer edges of my mind, but he waited for an invitation.

I smiled, opened my mind to him and poured all of my love into his consciousness. He needed to know I was ready to make the commitment he wanted from me.

Micah took a deep breath. His eyes shining, he took my hand in his and kissed my palm reverently. "You will never regret it. This I swear to you."

Chapter Sixteen

W E LEFT THE GROUND FLOOR, CLIMBING THE KITCHEN SERVICE STAIRS to the upper level and living quarters. Their home was just as conservative as the café was whimsical.

The parlor held a baby grand piano with a pair of wing chairs that faced each other in three of the four-corners of the room. A fireplace sat against the far wall, its huge mantle boasted a beautiful seascape above it.

The glossy, blonde, hardwood floor was covered by a massive Oriental rug in the center. Round tables were set under each tall window, a vase of flowers on each one, seemed to invite the outdoors in.

"I hope this will do." Elisabeth said apologetically. "It's too bad we aren't in England. The cottage there would have been a better choice for a handfasting." She sighed dreamily. "It's so old fashioned. I swear it was built for a ceremony like this."

I peered around the room, trying not to stare at the fireplace that dominated one wall. A long sofa in front of it, invited me to sit and soak up the warmth of the non-existent fire. The faux bearskin rug on the hearth added a bit of old fashioned charm.

"Do for what?" I was curious, now. The house was a showplace. I couldn't imagine it not doing for anything.

"For your handfasting, of course." She tilted her head at me. "You did say you wanted to do it here, did you not?"

I frowned. Actually, I didn't say that. Or at least if I did, I couldn't remember it. But, as I looked around, I realized that this was as good a place as any. Actually, it was probably better, since his family and friends would be here for him.

"Well, I suppose..."

Micah smiled softly and took my hand at my hesitant reply.

"You do not have to do this if it is not your wish, sweetheart." His black eyes bored into mine and I felt his resolve not to force me into anything that would make me uncomfortable.

I bit my lip.

How can I turn a guy down who constantly puts my comfort and needs before his own?

I couldn't.

I turned and looked up at Micah with tears in my eyes and finally said it. "I have Chosen, Micah." I knew the words weren't needed since I'd already shared that information in my mind, but it was still nice to say it out loud.

I wrapped my arms around his neck and pulled his head down to mine, not caring we had an audience. After an eternity, or at least what seemed like one, someone, I think it was Richard, cleared their throat and I pulled from Micah's arms, my face hot with embarrassment.

We followed his sister and her husband to the fireplace and watched curiously as Elisabeth pulled a small, intricately carved wooden case down from the tall mantle.

She opened the box and pulled out a wide, blood red cloth and a small, clean white-handled knife. The cloth, a shimmering scarf of crimson silk was about a yard long. Gold thread fringed each end and the three-inch long tassels gleamed in the bright light.

Elizabeth held it up and gazed at her brother with tears in her beautiful blue eyes. "I made this for your handfasting ceremony years ago." She looked down at the cloth and fingered it reverently. "I hoped you would find your mate and I would be honored to have you use it one day."

Elisabeth stepped in front of me and smiled apologetically.

"I must cut your palm and you must repeat the ritual words as I say them. Then," she turned toward her brother. "Micah will say his words and I will cut his palm. I will then bind your hands together with this cloth and the blood exchange will be made. Tomorrow you will be one of us. Your life force will be bound to Micah's if you were truly meant to be my brother's mate." She looked into my eyes. "Do you agree?"

"Yes." I nodded and swallowed around the lump in my throat that formed when she mentioned there was possibility I could not be Micah's mate. I looked up into his eyes and knew what my life would be like without him. It would be Hell. I'd already been there and was certainly in no hurry to return. I had to belong to him, that's all there was to it.

Elisabeth took my trembling hand in hers and held it palm up. She looked up at me and smiled.

"Tasha is your full, given name?"

I shook my head. "Natasha is my given name. My full name is, Natasha Katarina Hinkey."

She smiled slightly. "What a beautiful name. Were you named after someone?"

"My grandmother. My father named me after his mother."

Elisabeth straightened and became a bit more serious. "Natasha Katarina Hinkey, you have made your choice?"

She seemed to expect some sort of answer so I nodded.

She gave me an encouraging smile. "Now that you have made your choice, you must recite the vows of The Chosen."

I nodded, unsure of whether or not I should say anything.

"You must repeat these words as I say them."

She grasped my hand in a firm grip, pulled my fingers back and stretched my palm out.

"My blood to your blood. With the gift of my blood, I offer my life into your safekeeping. By taking your blood, I accept the offer of your life. Our blood blends, mixes and changes us. It creates one life in the place of two. We shall become one new, complete being with one heart and one soul. Together we are one. I have chosen Micah Maximillian Dartrazinski."

I felt a little jolt of fear as she positioned the knife over my exposed palm. I hoped it was a sharp one. Experience told me that getting cut with a dull knife was very painful. I winced as the blade approached my skin.

Micah made a small sound and I looked up into his eyes. The fear suddenly left me and I couldn't look away. I'm sure he compelled me to help me with my fear.

My smile wobbled a bit before I began to repeat the ritual words. "My blood to your blood. With the gift of my blood, I offer my life into your safekeeping."

With those words I felt the pressure of the knife blade slide across my skin. I felt no pain and I wondered, however briefly, if Micah somehow held me enthralled so I wouldn't feel the bite of the blade against my hand. "By taking your blood, I accept the offer of your life. Our blood blends, mixes and changes us. It creates one life in the place of two. We shall become one new, complete being with one heart and one soul. Together we are one. I have chosen Micah Maximillian Dartrazinski."

Elisabeth turned to her brother. She released my blood-covered hand to hold the knife poised over his large square palm. He smiled at me and winked.

"My blood to your blood. With the gift of my blood, I offer my life into your safekeeping," he recited the words as his sister took the knife and dragged the blade across his palm.

She took our hands in hers and pressed them together. Elisabeth bound them tightly with the red cloth.

"By taking your blood, I accept the offer of your life. Our blood blends, mixes and changes us. It creates one life in the place of two. We shall become one new, complete being with one heart and one soul." He paused for a moment and smiled again. "Together we are one. I have chosen Natasha Katerina Hinkey."

My eyes gazed deeply into his darker ones and I reveled in the love I saw reflected in the dark chocolate depths.

I looked down at our joined palms tied together with the blood red cloth. A tingling, itching sensation crawled up my arm, radiating up from my palm. Then I felt strangely lightheaded and my knees gave out.

"Hey," I said to no one in particular. "I thought this would make me stronger, like you guys." My words slurred together drunkenly as I felt Micah's blood go to my head like a pint of liquor.

At some point, and I'm not sure when, Shay helped Micah support me as they half carried me down a long hallway with Elisabeth in the lead.

I knew Micah was there, even though I couldn't see him. I felt his hand still bound to mine, our blood flowed between us. Micah's blood crawled through my body like a living thing, changing me as it went.

They left us alone in a huge bedroom. The California king-sized bed, dressed in blue, invited me to fall into it. I wiggled my toes in the thick pad of cream carpeting beneath my feet and frowned. When had I taken off my shoes?

I looked up at Micah, admiring his physique. I reveled in all of his six and a half feet of pure male perfection. Suddenly, I thought we were wearing entirely too many clothes. Then just as suddenly, our clothing disappeared and I stood before Micah naked and wanting. A new hunger consumed me as flames licked at my skin. How could just a touch make me quiver with such need? Were my senses already more pronounced?

His lips branded mine with hot, fevered kisses that I'd never felt the likes of before. His tongue danced around the line of my lips and I opened my mouth for him, longing to feel him inside of me. All of him. I opened my mind. I needed him, begged him to crawl within me and finally make me whole.

Micah groaned and fondled my breasts, giving each one equal attention with his free hand. The other was still bound to mine. Our blood mixed together, binding us to one another for eternity.

"I can't wait this time, Micah. Please don't make me wait. Make love to me. Now." I gasped as he licked my neck, moving higher to kiss me behind my ear.

He pushed me back onto the bed and I raised my knees, spreading my legs in invitation as he came down between them. He read my mind and thrust his cock inside me. I was already wet with desire and needed him inside me more than I had ever needed anyone or anything before in my life.

He pushed into me slowly and I savored every second of his thorough possession. He alternately suckled my breasts, his mouth and free hand everywhere on my fevered skin, brought me to the edge of ecstasy.

He rocked within me, thrusting his hips against mine, over and over, and I whimpered with the pure pleasure of having his massive shaft thrusting deep inside me.

"God, Micah. I'm going to come." I moaned against his shoulder as he picked up the tempo, his hips slapping roughly into mine. "Please." I needed the release he held tantalizingly out of my reach.

He looked down at me, his eyes aglow with passion and the blood lust I'd grown to expect from him while we made love. I saw his incisors lengthen just before he lowered his head and sank his teeth into my neck.

I cried his name. My orgasm was so intense I screamed out my satisfaction. Every muscle tensed and bunched as Micah finally took me over the edge. The combination of the orgasm and his taking of my blood became a mixture of pleasure-pain that bordered on pure ecstasy. I'm sure I died there, for a moment, and touched heaven, before he called me back to life, to him.

Micah rolled us over and I straddled his still erect staff. I'd never been on top. I grinned and rode him like I'd never done before. I leaned down, kissing his neck, his perfect chest, lapping at one flat brown nipple. I raised my head and kissed him, nuzzling his neck. My eyes widened as I felt him grow even larger within me. He turned his head and exposed his neck. His strong arms lifted and lowered me onto his engorged organ and I felt another orgasm grip me.

Micah turned and looked into my eyes. "Feed," he growled, his teeth clenched, the corded muscles of his neck bulged and his eyes were glazed over with passion. "Feed, Tasha."

I lowered my head to him, my incisors lengthened and I sank my teeth deep into the thick muscles of his chest. Memories, everything that was Micah, assaulted me. They slammed into my head with such force I nearly lost consciousness.

He must have realized what happened and shut the memories out. It left only the sensation of our two bodies joined together and the exquisite pleasure we both felt as I fed from him.

He was right, it *was* better than chocolate. I pulled my teeth from his neck and smiled as I gazed down at the two small marks my incisors made and waited for his amazing recuperative powers to repair the damaged tissue. I swiped my tongue across the tiny holes and watched amazed as they reduced to the size of pinpricks, then closed before my eyes.

Micah rolled us over and I was on my back again. He threw my legs over his shoulders, pounding into me with abandon, completely out of control. He'd never been so out of control. Not once had he ever taken me to this height of ecstasy.

"Tasha," he whispered into my ear, suckling on the lobe. "I'm getting close." He pulled back a bit, then took my left nipple into his mouth and suckled fiercely. "I've never felt this with another. Your tight little pussy grips my cock until I can think of nothing but shooting my come deep inside you."

I was caught in a seemingly endless cycle. One glorious orgasm followed another as I accepted his thrusts, mindless.

I cried out Micah's name, my love for him and my pleasure over and over. "Micah, I'm coming!"

When Micah's eyes began to glow again, I knew his climax was finally upon him. I wrapped my free arm around his neck, drawing his head to me.

He sank his teeth deep into my breast, just above my heart, and I screamed our pleasure as he shared his satisfaction with me. He came then, spilling his seed, deep inside my body.

I held him close, my left arm cradled his head against my breast until he withdrew his teeth, the tiny holes healed almost instantly.

I looked over at our still joined hands with our fingers laced together. My right hand held to his left. The red cloth gave way and slithered to the floor, almost like a living thing. It fell on to the carpet, a puddle of blood red silk next to the bed.

We pulled our hands apart and I marveled at the fine cut still in the center of my palm as it healed before my eyes.

Micah pressed a kiss to my forehead.

"Thank you for choosing me, Tasha. I will never give you reason to regret it."

He rolled onto his back, taking me with him. He wrapped his arms around me and pulled me closer to rest my head on his chest.

"No, Micah." I smiled sleepily. "Thank you for saving my life, in more ways than one." I rubbed against him like a cat. I loved his scent and the smooth warmth of his skin.

I kissed his almost hairless chest sleepily. "I do love you, you know," I murmured against his shoulder.

His hand stilled over my head where he'd been absently smoothing my hair. He squeezed me a bit tighter.

"I love you, too," he sighed. "I have loved you, in one way or another, since the day you were born."

Chapter Seventeen

"WELCOME TO OUR WORLD, LITTLE SISTER," SHAY SAID OVER A CUP OF coffee when Micah and I entered the kitchen the next morning.

I blushed at her knowing smile, then frowned. "Why are you all suddenly eating and drinking?" I blurted the question out because I have absolutely no tact whatsoever.

Shay laughed. "We will, no doubt, have to spend several hours in the company of the police. We all thought it would be beneficial to re-acquire some of our more human characteristics."

"That makes sense, I suppose."

"Why don't you fix yourself something to eat? I've heard of your addiction to coffee."

I wasn't really hungry, but I've always loved bagels and cream cheese. I walked over to the counter and helped myself to a large cup of coffee. I sipped it, then looked down into the steaming dark liquid.

"I don't know why I'm still drinking this." I made a face. "I really don't even like it. I just drank it to help me when I...when I gave up drugs." My face grew warm.

"At least you don't have to worry about undue side effects. It's decaffeinated." Shay smiled and put her hand over mine.

"Yeah, I suppose." With my new vampire healing abilities, that coffee aphrodisiac idea appealed to me again. An all day round of intense lovemaking with my husband was back at the top of my list.

"There's no need to feel ashamed." She looked around the room before she dropped her gaze to her plate. "We all have at least one skeleton in our closet."

"So, manslaughter and drug addiction are mine, huh?" I asked ruefully as I picked up a bagel and slathered it with cream cheese and strawberry jam.

Shay sat across from me, finishing her breakfast. I turned and noticed for the first time that Micah hadn't followed me into the room like I originally thought. I frowned. "Where'd Micah go?"

"He most likely went to thank Elisabeth for her hospitality." She took

135

another bite of her Danish. "We have to leave soon to catch the noon ferry. This situation with the police must be handled quickly, before it escalates into something worse than it already is."

I nodded. She was right, of course. The whole situation had already reached an intensity I never expected. I just hated that the reality of my life always interfered with the fantasy.

Why couldn't I just once, have a normal vacation, a normal honeymoon or a normal life? Was I forever doomed to be always sitting on the outside looking in?

I felt Micah's pain as he touched my thoughts. I realized at once what I dreamed of was not normalcy. Not any longer, at any rate.

I immediately felt bad and flooded his mind with my love. *You have to know I didn't mean I wanted a life without you, Micah. I merely meant that I would love to be able to stay in one place for a while. I'm sick to death of worrying that the police will try to arrest me or evil entities will attempt to sacrifice me.*

I tried to make him understand the thoughts he'd inadvertently eavesdropped on. He sent his understanding back to me. It was a soothing balm to my frazzled nerves and I lifted my head and smiled at Shay.

"I hope we can get this over with, soon. I'm looking forward to an old fashioned honeymoon. I've just decided. I'm going to embrace my new life with Micah."

And I intended to celebrate every single extraordinary moment of its lack of normalcy.

With my arms held out, I tilted my head back and gloried in my newfound happiness. If my new family could be considered strange or weird, then normal is definitely overrated.

Six and a half-hours later, we were ensconced in the limo, riding east toward Grand Rapids. I stole a look at my husband through my lashes and smiled. He sat next to me and held my hand in his as I rested my head on his shoulder. I loved the newfound feeling of closeness our handfasting brought.

His breath brushed my hair every time he exhaled and I thanked God for every moment I had with him. My entourage decided to pay the extra money for the express ferry. It was something, I never would have considered in the past. It was more than I could afford, but Micah was happy to point out that money was no longer a concern of mine.

"I can't believe we just crossed the lake in a little over two and a half hours." Shay said, looking out at the shoreline as we drove away from the pier.

136

I rolled my eyes. "Maybe so, but I could have made a house payment with what we just paid for fares."

Micah hugged me to him. "You do not have to worry about that any longer. I will take care of the mortgage on your home. You will not lose it to the bank."

"Call me a diehard," I said and hugged him back. "Even with today's gas prices, it's still cheaper to drive around. The only drawback is that it's more time consuming."

We headed east on Interstate 96 toward Grand Rapids and the police department, which now had a warrant out for my arrest.

"I can't breathe." I gasped, sitting forward in the seat. I tried to get air into my lungs. The closer we got to the city, the more my heart slammed against my ribs and the harder it was for me to breathe.

"Shh," Micah whispered in my ear. He smoothed my hair and held me close in an attempt to comfort me.

"I don't know if I can do this." I raised my head, my eyes gazing into Micah's, nervous. "I don't lie well," I shook my head. "I really don't." I looked into his dark fathomless gaze, knowing my own eyes were filled with stark fear.

"What if they don't believe us?" I laughed hysterically. "And why should they? It's all lies. I did it. Every one of you knows I killed him. He killed Trina and I killed him for it. What if they arrest me?" I babbled on, almost incoherent, as I fidgeted in my seat. "I can't go to jail, Micah." I grabbed his arm, sick with fear. "I just can't. I wouldn't survive locked up in a small cell." I wouldn't either, and I knew it. My claustrophobia threatened to choke me. It attempted to squeeze the air from my lungs as I sat in the close confines of the car.

Micah grabbed me, pulled me onto his lap and held me against his chest. He whispered soothing words in my ear, calming me down.

He put his fingers under my chin and turned my head to look deep into my eyes. I felt the strong push of compulsion as he spoke. His older, stronger, more experienced powers overshadowed my newly made gifts.

"You will not panic in the face of fear, Tasha. You have been traveling these past weeks with your new husband. Only now do you return to your home to share your good news with your best friend." His dark gaze bored into mine. I felt the power flow into me, through me, as he spoke.

"We were devastated to hear the news of her death. Your husband and your new family has been with you constantly these past weeks. All of us are prepared and willing to testify that you were not even in the state at the time of Trina's death. You have done nothing wrong."

That was the story the police received from Micah. They were told I was under sedation, having just learned of my friend's death. I'm sure I appeared to be. His compulsion kept me very subdued and I agreed with everything he said.

"I think it's strange that I can't remember the interview with the police." I told Micah much later as I sat on the bed and brushed my hair in one of his several homes. I watched him work on his laptop. The sound of the rapid clicking as his fingers flew across the keyboard sounded loud even though he was across the room.

"I am sorry I felt the need to compel you, my love." He stopped typing and looked at me through the mirror, which was in front of him on the vanity that he used as a desk. "But you were panicking and I could see no other alternative."

I nodded. "I can believe it, I'm so afraid of being locked in an enclosed space it would have surprised me if I hadn't panicked." I shuddered at the thought. "I just wish I could remember what happened."

"No, you do not," Micah said, shaking his head. "They did put you in a cell for a short time."

"And you should have seen Micah, Tasha. He was all over them." Shay said, proudly, through the open door. "He made them let you out." She smiled, then closed the door and left us to talk more privately.

Micah's eyes took on an almost murderous glint. "Yes. They were determined to keep you there, by yourself, for questioning. Until I threatened to sue them." His white teeth flashed in his tanned face. "When they found out who I am and just who my friends are, they couldn't release you fast enough."

"Your friends?"

He grinned at me. "I have some very influential acquaintances."

"Oh." I left it at that. I figured I'd find out someday. Since I was still trying to adapt to my new way of life, I figured it something better left alone.

I felt a little funny and my skin began to crawl a bit like it did when I was using. I rubbed my hands up and down my arms and grimaced in pain when my stomach clenched. I frowned, looked over Micah's shoulder and glowered in my reflection in the mirror.

"I thought I was through it all." I whimpered. A tear slid down my face as I wondered if I would ever be truly free of my drug addiction.

Micah's gaze met mine over his shoulder and he stood. He folded the screen of the laptop down and left his work to join me on the bed.

"You should have told me you were in pain."

"What could you do?" I asked, pissed. "I can't believe I'm still going through withdrawal. Will it never end?"

"It is not withdrawal, sweetheart." Micah chuckled.

I looked over at him and watched mesmerized as his pulse beat beneath his skin. It called to me. I covered my mouth with my hands as my teeth lengthened and I had the almost uncontrollable urge to rip and tear at his throat.

I threw myself from the bed and ran from the temptation and Micah followed.

"You must feed, little one. I feel your hunger. I look at you and I can see your hunger." He pushed my hair from my face. "You are very pale."

I looked over at the mirror and my eyes widened with horror at what I saw there. My skin had turned white, nearly translucent, and the hand that covered my mouth trembled and my eyes glowed with an unholy light. I fought the urge to sink my teeth into my husband's neck and drain him dry.

Micah walked up behind me and took me into his arms. He turned me and bent forward so he could rest his forehead against mine.

"Remember, little one? This is what I do. I teach those, like you, to control the horrible urge you're feeling now." His hands caressed my upper arms, his touch warm and soothing.

"I don't want to hurt you." I stepped back from him and fought to get free. If he held me to him much longer, I wouldn't be able to help myself. I couldn't bear the thought that I might kill him.

"You cannot hurt me, Tasha. I am centuries older and infinitely stronger. I will not allow you to take more than I can give."

He placed his hand on the back of my neck and pushed my face into his shoulder. I stood there in his arms for a moment, mesmerized by his heady scent. His body called to mine in more ways than one and I finally gave in and sank my teeth into his shoulder to draw hard on his skin.

Micah groaned. I wasn't sure if it was with pain or pleasure as he held me in his arms while I fed from him.

The pain and the horrible itchy sensation left me and I forced myself to pull my mouth from his skin. I licked my lips. A part of me was horrified at what I'd just done, but another part of me craved more. I pulled from his embrace and stepped away. I needed to put some distance between us because I still didn't trust myself.

"I—I don't know what just happened."

"You fed," Micah smiled. "That is what happened."

I turned away, waving my hand. "I know that. What I meant was, I just...bit you. You always make me feel so, wonderful first." My face grew warm at the memory.

He gathered me close in his arms. "You did very well, little one. I did not have to stop your feeding. You recognized the feeling of fulfillment on your own." He pulled his head back to look into my eyes. "That is something to be proud of, not ashamed. Very few of the newly turned can stop feeding on their own. That is why so many of them become Rogue."

I looked up at him and allowed him to see the fear I felt for what I'd become. "I'm afraid."

"Of what?" He reached up, brushed my hair back and tucked it behind my ear. I pulled free and paced away from him.

"Of what I—"

"Of what you might become?" He interrupted, looking at me shrewdly. He leaned back against the dresser and crossed his long legs in front of him.

I nodded. How could I get him to understand the fear? The loathing I felt whenever I thought of taking blood from anyone but him. Could I hurt him, kill him? I'd never forgive myself if I did. I wrapped my arms around my middle, hugging myself at the horrible thought.

"No. You cannot," he chuckled, shaking his head. "I have lived for centuries, training those who have been abandoned by their makers."

Micah crossed his arms in front of his chest. "I have chosen to teach them how to feed without killing and how to care for themselves." He cocked his head to the right and raised one perfectly arched brow. "Do you think I would do any less for my own mate?" He pushed himself away from the dresser and padded toward me, his bare feet silent on the thick, blue carpet. He stopped a foot in front of me and held his arms open, welcoming me into his embrace, welcoming me home.

I hesitated for a moment before I bit my lip and stepped into his arms. He wrapped them around me and I stood surrounded by his scent, enveloped in his warmth, like I'd just been covered by a warm blanket.

I've never been so comfortable with a man in my life. I'd never even been this comfortable with my father.

Micah's warmth seeped into my bones. It relaxed me and I let him hold me close as I leaned into his hard strength, absorbing his essence.

He rubbed my back, his hands sliding lower, working their magic on my abused muscles.

"I don't know if I can make love again," I mumbled into his shoulder. I looked up at him and felt the need to apologize.

Micah smiled, his eyes crinkling at the corners. "This does not have to lead to sex, Tasha. I have gone years without it before. A few days will not hurt me now."

"Years?"

Why had he gone years without having sex? Now that I knew what it was like, my new husband was going to pay hell for a few days off.

He flashed a grin my way, letting me know he'd been camped out in my mind again.

"A few days will be no hardship for me. I have centuries of practiced control." His hand reached down to curve around my bottom. "You, on the other hand," he leaned down to kiss my neck and I moaned.

I looked up him and swallowed convulsively. "That is *so* not fair," I scowled as I tried to tamp down the answering need that blossomed within me. The warmth of desire already pooled between my legs.

Micah took pity on me and pulled his hand back up to rest against my lower spine.

"I apologize for teasing you, little one." His smile flashed again. "It's just such a pleasure to have you with me. I find that it is difficult to control those urges."

"Oh," I nodded sagely. "I see. Mr. I-Have-Centuries-of-Control is having problems keeping his hands off me?" I teased.

Micah's eyes darkened. "You don't know the half of it," he growled, just before he dipped his head and kissed my socks off.

Chapter Eighteen

"So, where are we meeting Shay and Damien?" I asked Micah over dinner that evening. I hated to admit it, but I kind of missed Shay's quirky sense of humor. I hadn't seen her since yesterday when they'd dropped us off to go spend the night in another of their houses an hour or so north of the city.

Micah sipped his soup and gave the bowl a suspicious sniff. "We're meeting them at Demon World."

"Oh. I've never been there, but I have heard of the place." Demon World is a fitting name for a bar that catered to vamps, I suppose. "Is it nice?"

He hedged around the question a bit, just enough to make me feel uncomfortable about going. I looked at him and narrowed my eyes.

"What?"

Micah shrugged. He'd put a little too much effort into making it look careless. I lowered my gaze to my bowl of soup.

I smelled a rat and wasn't altogether certain that the odor wasn't coming from my bowl.

"It's mainly a place where our kind goes to let off some steam."

Did he mean Rogues or other Cartuoteys just looking for a bit of excitement?

"Are humans allowed there or is it a strictly vamp club?" I knew the answer, yet I wondered if he felt man enough to tell me the truth. I watched as he fiddled with his spoon for a minute, then I took it from him before he made a mess.

"Didn't your mother ever teach you to never play with your food?" I teased, holding the spoon just out of his reach. I waited for his answer, my brows raised in question.

"Actually," he drawled, "She made sure we played with them, daily, so they would not fear us."

I dropped his spoon on the floor and stared at him. He can't be serious! Then I slapped my hand to my face as I remembered. I have no idea how a fact like that could have slipped my mind.

I never once questioned his story when he'd told me the first vamps were aliens. I assumed he told me the truth. After all, if there were such crazy, unbelievable things as vampires, why not aliens too?

That's it. They're bloodsucking aliens from the planet Jugularia. I fought the urge to laugh hysterically.

"I—I'm sorry."

I'd completely forgotten the fantastic story he'd told me last week. Had it been a week already? It was amazing how fast the time had passed since he'd waltzed back into my life. I left my apology at its simplest, my face blazing with mortification.

"Do not worry, my dear." He flashed those incredibly white teeth of his in my face again. "I did not take offence. I was merely joking."

"You were joking?" How could a person joke about something like that?

"I never played with human children. I was allowed to play only with the children of The Chosen. When I was fed, I drank from a glass." His face got a faraway look as he remembered.

"As children, we are much like the newly gifted. We have little control and even less patience."

"Oh." I bit my lip, deep in thought. "Does that mean our children won't be able to be around other children?" How can a kid be a kid, if they can't play?

Micah reached over and covered my hand with his. "Of course they can play with other children. They will play with other children of The Chosen."

I pulled my hand out from under his, stood up and waved my arms wildly only half aware I was overreacting and, quite frankly, not giving a crap.

"The Chosen?" I scoffed. "Do you have any idea how arrogant that sounds?" I heard my voice as it raised in pitch, even as I spoke, but was powerless to stop it. "I'll tell you how it sounds." I marched over to him and pressed my finger to his shoulder, poking him, to emphasize the point I was trying to make. "You all put yourselves above humans. You think you're better than us." I hated having to concede the point that vamps *are* genetically advanced. "And you use us." I gave him a scathing look that left nothing to the imagination as to how I felt about him at the moment. "We're little more to you than a walking Deli."

Micah turned toward me, his eyes blazing with fury. "I have never, in my considerable life, ever treated a human like a walking Deli." He raised his brow. "The entire concept is absurd." He grabbed my hand, dislodging my finger from where it still poked into his shoulder. "Our children do not play with human children, because if they lost their tempers, they could kill."

I felt the blood drain from my face. Okay, so I never thought of that.

"No. You didn't," he said, reading my mind again. "You also did not think that a child may like to show off his *fangs* to other children either. It could jeopardize our entire existence."

Holy shit, Tash, you're a know-it-all, self-righteous bitch, aren't you?

I pressed my lips together, not trusting what other font of extreme ignorance would fly from my mouth. I closed my eyes. When would I learn to hold on to my temper and not fly-off-the-handle at the least provocation?

Micah's eyes softened and filled with the affection I knew he was on the outer cusp of starting to feel for me. I knew it wasn't love, no matter what he said, but hey, I'll take whatever I can get.

"You will learn, little one. You have much to learn."

I stuck my tongue out at him. "Stay out of my head. My thoughts are my own and not for public exhibition."

"But I am not the public, I am your mate." He said the word with so much male superiority and smug satisfaction it made me grit my teeth.

"Mate, schmate. Stay out of here," I tapped my temple, "or stay out of here." My hand lowered past my stomach and tapped my crotch. "Your choice."

He shook his head and gave me an exasperated look. "You have such a colorful way with words, my love."

I laughed. "Yeah, I know. You can be a royal pain in the ass, too, sometimes. "

I turned away and bent to pick up his spoon from the floor. I gathered our untouched meal from the table and dumped the contents of the two bowls into the sink.

I have never been a fan of clam chowder anyway. It always tasted funny to me and the clams always seemed to be a cross between rubbery and slimy. Since my taste buds had been enhanced... Well, it was just plain nasty. I rinsed the bowls with water and put them in the dishwasher before I returned to the table. I leaned my hip against Micah's shoulder and wrapped my arm around him.

"You know, you drive me crazy most of the time, but I think I'll keep you anyway." I smiled down, almost losing myself in his dark walnut eyes. "So, we're going to Demon World?" I changed the subject.

"Yes."

"Can you dance there?" I knew the answer. I was just gauging his reaction. I'm not afraid to admit it. I love to tease him and I don't have centuries of practiced control. So I gave in to the urge.

"Others have danced there. Yes," he nodded and a look of trepidation crossed his features.

I grinned. Somebody doesn't know how to dance. An infant inside me chanted in a singsong voice. "But can we dance there?"

He sighed, "I do not dance." He pinned me with a glare. It was an attempt to look fierce, but he only managed to look comical.

I giggled. "You can't dance, you mean."

His eyes widened and lit with an unholy light and I couldn't be entirely sure he wasn't serious.

"I choose not to dance."

"Only because you don't know how. Come on, big boy. You can admit it."

He sat back in his chair, crossed his arms over his chest and raised his right eyebrow. "I beg your pardon, madam, but I was trained by none other than Claire Le Fluer, Louis the XVI's own mistress."

I slapped my hand over my mouth to stifle a scream, of shock, excitement, hilarity? Take your pick.

"Oh. My. God. You really can't dance?" I waved my hand in front of his incensed face. "Oh, of course you can do those prissy, dark aged, French dances, but you can't dance the way we do now."

"It was not the dark ages." He glowered at me.

"Whatever," I said waving my hand. I looked up at him from the corner of my eye and wondered if I should take pity on him and show him it wasn't really that hard.

"Can you even waltz or was that after your time as well?" I shook my head as he scowled his answer. "Guess not." I suppressed a smile, looked him up and down and pursed my lips. I walked around him in a big circle, eyeing him like a prized bull. My mind wandered to the memory of his impressive erections and I shook my head to clear it. I shrugged. I suppose prized bull was an apt analogy if I'd ever heard one.

My fingers itched with the desire to touch him. I rubbed my hands together, trying to forget the way his cock felt as I caressed him to full arousal. I wiped my sweaty palms on my jeans and tried to focus.

"Dancing. Right." I smiled a secret little smile. "This is going to be fun." I walked over to the CD player that was mounted under one of the cabinets and turned it on. Classical, good. I held my arms out, waiting. "Come on, this isn't going to hurt a bit."

Micah abandoned his chair and stood watching me, leery.

I took his hand and pulled him away from the table, then stepped into his arms. "Everything else has gotten harder over the years, but slow dancing? That's gotten a lot easier."

My head was level with his shoulder. I pressed my cheek against it and rocked back and forth to the sound of the music. I rubbed my body sensuously against his and took a deep breath, inhaling his spicy scent.

"This is it?" he asked, incredulous.

It was increasingly obvious that I'd married a man who definitely needed to get out more. "This is it," I grinned up at him. "Well, there is dirty dancing, but we won't get into that right now."

"Dirty dancing?" he asked and arched one glossy, black brow.

"I'll tell you about that some other time."

Two hours later, we met Shay and Damien at Demon World. We sat at a small round table near the back, away from the dance floor and prying eyes. I watched the people dance with my elbow resting on the table and my chin in my hand. Which ones were the real vamps?

"Why did we come here again?" I asked, raising my voice so I could be heard over the extremely loud music. I needed someone to refresh my memory. It's not like I felt the need to expand my vampire acquaintances.

Shay leaned toward me. "We heard a rumor that a bunch of Rogues hangout here." She looked at Micah, almost as if she wanted to know how much to tell me. "Our group tries to stop them before they become addicted."

I whirled around to face her. "You do it, too?"

"Most of us do, Tasha," she said with a nod. "It's the only way to keep the world from finding out we exist."

I scoffed, "Let the world know. Don't you think they can handle it?"

Shay looked at me like I was a burger short of a kid's meal. "Are you nuts?" she asked, "If we allowed the general populace to know of our existence, we would be locked up, poked, prodded and used for medical research." She reached out to put her hand on mine. "Don't you realize that? What do you think the governments of the world would give to be able to study the way our bodies repair themselves? Or they would try to force us to become some sort of super soldiers."

A picture of us all captured and mutilated so scientists could study the accelerated healing rates our bodies possessed made me swallow visibly. Not to mention the horrible thought of being pressed into Military service.

"Well, I didn't think of that before, but I am now." I gave her a sheepish look. "I never put much thought into it to tell you the truth."

Micah stiffened next to me. He stood and stretched slowly, as if he had all the time in the world. Damien did the same.

Shay looked up at them with fear in her eyes.

"What the hell is going on?" I asked, looking from them to Shay since the men were no longer talking. They acted so distant it was almost as if they weren't even in the same room with us. Yet there they both stood, their attention turned inward, like very realistic statues.

"They sense a Rogue," Shay whispered. She looked around, her green eyes wide.

"I don't feel anything."

"You wouldn't. You are a Guide. Just as they cannot feel an open portal, we cannot feel the Rogue."

I frowned. I kept forgetting that little piece of my heritage. I was a Guide. Forever doomed to closing portals to dimensions that allowed lascivious sex demons to roam the earth raping and pillaging their unsuspecting victims. And they were just from one other dimension. I shuddered at the thought of what can come from all of those other planes of existence I've heard about.

"Stay here," the two men said at once.

Micah nodded in my direction for an instant. His eyes were empty, distant, almost as if he'd already gone. Was he mentally tracking the Rogues?

"We must stay here while they find them. If they cannot be helped, they will be forced to take them to the others for punishment." Shay explained.

I sat on the chair across from her, dazed. "I think I'm finally beginning to understand. Cartuoteys are good vampires who protect humans from the bad vampires. Am I right?"

Shay shook her head and covered my trembling hand with her own.

"What?" I looked over at her, scared. I was almost too afraid to ask the question.

"They don't just hunt Rogues."

I shook my head. "Oh, don't even go there. Please," I gasped. But she continued anyway.

"Cartuoteys protect The Chosen and humans alike, from all of the evil supernatural beings."

I scrunched my eyes closed and fought the ridiculous urge to stick my fingers in my ears and sing the Star Spangled Banner as loud as I could. And I know all of the words.

"I don't want to hear this, I don't want to hear this, I so don't want to hear this," I chanted when the national anthem didn't work.

Shay continued, ruthlessly spilling her guts on all things paranormal.

"Let me get this straight," I said thirty minutes and three sloe-gin fizzes later. "Cartuoteys guard us from Demons, Imps, Goblins, Gremlins and Rogues?"

Shay nodded, "That's pretty much it." She frowned, "Well, I think there's more, but I can't remember and quite frankly, Damien shelters me from almost all of it. Being a Cartuotey means he guards us not only from the entities I mentioned, but from the fear that the knowledge of their existence would instill in us."

I sat across from her and banged my forehead on the table. "I didn't ask for this," I said and brought my head up to look into her eyes. "I didn't ask for any of this."

I reached down to rub my belly. I felt a bit queasy and I wondered if it was the alcohol. I'd ordered it before I thought of my pregnancy, but Shay assured me it wouldn't harm my new physiology or that of my unborn child.

"Oh, my," Shay said from across the table as she rubbed her stomach.

Something was up. I no sooner had that thought enter my mind, before I doubled over, crying out with agony. I couldn't stand it. The pain was so intense it brought tears to my eyes. Like my stomach was trying to digest ground glass. A portal had just been opened.

A big one.

Chapter Nineteen

MICAH! I MENTALLY SCREAMED HIS NAME AND HOPED HE WOULD HEAR me. I knew we had some sort of mental link, but I wasn't quite sure how it worked. *Someone has opened a huge portal. I can't close it on my own. At least I'm pretty sure I can't do it.*

The vibrations coming from the portal were more concentrated and a lot stronger than the last ethereal gateway and I'd needed Micah's help with that one as well.

I got the impression he was fighting for his life and I berated myself for being so needy.

You are the most independent woman I have ever known. Do not worry that you have any failings. I see none.

I tried to smile at his thoughtfulness, but I'm pretty sure it looked more like a grimace as another wave of pain hit me, doubling me over.

Shay still sat, half leaning across the table, panting into her drink as she tried to ride it out. I wasn't sure if she was in labor or just affected by the opened portal.

"We have to be proactive," I told her and slid toward the outer edge of the booth. "I can't just sit here and wait for the guys to come rescue me like some sort of damsel in distress."

She looked up. The intense pain was written on her face and reflected in her eyes. "I think I'm in labor."

"Oh, God. Just what we do not need!"

She rolled her eyes. "Tell me about it. If I am, this baby's a month and a half early."

"Jesus!" I closed my eyes. That one word was the closest I've been to a prayer in five years.

"See if you can find a doctor or a midwife in this place." She panted funny and I wondered who it was that taught vamps natural childbirth classes.

I slid the rest of the way out of the booth and looked around the noisy bar.

"Hey," I said with a scowl, "if all vampires are Cartuoteys, why are all of these guys still here?" I jerked my head, indicating the men still on the dance floor. "Shouldn't they be out helping Micah and Damien?" I glared at the men who were still dancing. Half of them looked as if they were having some sort of seizure. No wonder Micah didn't want to dance.

"Only full Cartuoteys take it so seriously. Besides, most of these people are probably human and the vampires who are made, just don't care."

"Full Cartuoteys?"

Shay pointed up. "You know, the ones from out there." She rubbed her belly. "And those born to them."

"Oh. Well, hell, no wonder there are so many Rogues running around. If the general populace doesn't give a sh...crap."

I turned from the table and walked out onto the dance floor. I tapped a few shoulders, trying to ask where to find a doctor or a midwife.

"Get lost, pitiful human," one young woman said as she turned toward me, baring her filed canines.

I grinned, allowed my incisors to lengthen and decided to have some fun. "Bite me, wannabe, if you dare."

Her eyes rounded and she apologized quickly. "Forgive me, Mistress. What did you need to know?" she asked with her head bowed.

I looked around at the rest of the couples and wondered if any of them were real vamps. And would I trust one of these kooks to touch Shay even if there was a doctor here? I sighed. What real choice did I have?

"I need a doctor or a midwife, fast. My sister is in labor." Sister? Where in the hell had that come from? Well, it felt right and I didn't have time to argue with myself about it right now.

The girl turned, stepped from her lover's arms and hurried over to the DJ's booth. She turned off the music, snatched up his cordless microphone and ran back to me.

I shook my head. "Why didn't I think of that?"

She grinned and winked before she put the microphone to her mouth. "Attention, humans, vampires and scum sucking denizens of the underworld, we are in need of a midwife, doctor or nurse. A new life trembles on the cusp of entering our magical world."

There was a small commotion back by the bathrooms before I saw the DJ. He'd hurried from the restroom. No doubt, to retrieve his microphone.

"And I'll bet he didn't even take the time to wash his hands, either. Yech!" I turned to the girl and flicked my gaze to the mic. "Get rid of it. Believe me, you don't want this guy touching you," I said as he stalked toward us.

"Uh, oh." The girl ducked behind her date. "Cover me, Billy." She brought the instrument back to her lips. "Any medically trained personnel, please report to the large table in the back, under the picture of Bella Lugosi."

The girl stuck the microphone under her shirt, hiding it from the DJ as he passed by. He headed for our table, he obviously thought he would find his microphone there.

The girl threw it when his back was turned. She covered her mouth with horror at the sound of the muffled thud that came through the speakers and the angry exclamation that followed.

"Hey, Steve?" someone called out from the area where the microphone had landed. "We just found your mic, someone just conked Carlos on the head with it."

"Yeah!" another voice called out. "And that shit hurt, too!"

We watched a well-dressed man extricate himself from the crowd and approach Shay. I moved to join her. What if he was another Rogue and I'd just led him to her? I hurried over to show my support, biting my thumbnail, nervous.

"I'm a doctor, how far apart are the contractions?" he asked as he knelt down next to her. He grabbed her wrist and took her pulse.

She held up a finger as she panted her way through another contraction. "Hee, hee hoo. Hee, hee hoo."

We waited while she repeated this exercise a few more times, then sighed with relief and relaxed when the contraction was over.

Shay looked him over, suspicious. "What would a doctor be doing in Demon World?" she asked. Clearly not sure she wanted to trust him.

He bent his head and sighed. "I don't have much of a choice. Fifteen years ago, a female Rogue thought it would be...interesting to have a male harem."

"Well at least you're not some kooky wannabe." Shay moaned, with pain, as another contraction took hold and he was all business.

"How far are the contractions apart?" he asked again.

"They're about two minutes apart, already." She turned toward me and smiled ruefully. "Sorry, hon, but you're going to have to handle this one on your own." She stood up and allowed the man to help her to her feet, his hand under her arm.

"Come on, let's get out of here and head to my car. It's bad enough that my baby is going to be premature, I definitely don't want to have it in a nightclub." Then she grinned, "Besides, Damien has the limo set up with emergency supplies. He knew something like this was going to happen." She shot me a grin and shook her head. "I used to tease him about being paranoid. I'll never live this down, you know."

I watched her leave and wished I could follow. But the dull ache in my belly reminded me there were bigger things at stake and this was no time to be squeamish.

There was an open portal out there and I had to find it. I sat back down at the table and cleared my head, concentrating on finding the open gateway. It's not an easy feat in a nightclub and with an audience. With my hands in position, I was able to locate the portal. Only it wasn't really a portal at all.

A portal, as I have been seeing them, is like an open doorway. This was a tear. It looked like a long, jagged-edged hole in the pavement of a parking lot. I frowned. I'd seen that place before. I knew where it was, if I could only remember...

I opened my eyes and saw the young couple staring at me.

"What?" I asked, almost impatiently and wondered if I'd suddenly grown a penis on the top of my head. I fought the urge to reach up and feel. That was just stupid.

"You're a real vampire," they said simultaneously. "We've never met a real vampire before." They looked at each other and nodded.

"Can you turn us?"

I shook my head. "I have no idea how, I was just made myself."

"Oh." They looked disappointed.

"Look," I said as I alternated my attention between them. "I have to go. I have to find someone." I regarded them thoughtfully. "You guys wouldn't happen to know where a purple brick building is, would you? It would have to be pretty close. Within a few miles."

The girl brightened, eager to please. "Sure! I know where it is. It's south of here on Eastern, somewhere between Thirty-second street and Fifty-fourth. I'm not exactly sure where."

"Thanks," I said with a smile. "At least it gets me close."

"Hey," Billy scowled at her. "Why'd ya just tell her like that? You could have used the information to get her to change us."

The girl rolled her eyes and slapped him on the back of the head. "Didn't you hear her say that she didn't know how? Geeze, Billy, clean the shit out of your ears!"

I left them to finish their argument and ran out to the car. I looked around inside it, hoping to find a spare set of keys. But no luck.

"That figures."

I started hoofing it down Twenty-eighth street, hoping I'd get there in time to prevent a major catastrophe.

Around Division, I felt the need to hurry and I started to run. I surprised myself with my newfound ability to run very, very fast. I just hoped no one was paying attention to the not so skinny blonde, running down the side of the road at about forty miles per hour.

I turned south on Eastern and put on a burst of speed. I tried to stay in the shadows. I ran through parking lots and people's front yards, feeling an urgent need to be there. Now.

About a block from the tear, I heard a scream. It was a woman. "Dammit," I whispered and slowed down. I knew I couldn't leave her to face whatever it was alone. What if it was another damned Rogue? The last thing I wanted was to find the woman drained dry and her throat slit from ear to ear.

I slowed down a little bit more as I approached, not wanting to pass the poor woman who obviously needed my help. I opened a gate in a nearby cul-de-sac and entered someone's backyard. The yard was full of robed people. Their manner of dress looked familiar and the hair on the back of my neck prickled.

I hoped it wasn't a trap. After my narrow escape from being sacrificed last week, this group made me nervous. Micah said I wouldn't die if I got shot, but I didn't want to test it. It could still hurt like hell. Besides, there are things in this world that are a lot worse than death.

I hesitated until I heard the scream again. The shriek was cut off, followed by a muffled sob. They'd apparently gagged her.

"It's a good thing Harvey thought to tell his neighbors we'd be rehearsing a play tonight." One of the robed figures said.

Another laughed. "Yeah, I know. Otherwise there'd be cops all over us. And I don't know about you guys, but I want my turn this time."

I stepped up behind them. What was going on and who was screaming and why? The screams sounded too real to be just an act. Besides, I could feel the woman's terror. I don't know how I could feel it. Maybe it was some newly acquired ability brought on by my change to one of The Chosen.

What the hell?

The figures all shifted and moved forward. They were standing in line!

I peeked out around them in an attempt to see what in the world was happening.

"I can't wait to finally close on that house in the country. I'll have that three hundred and fifty acres out in the middle of nowhere and we won't have to worry about how much they scream while we fuck 'em."

Excuse me? I know I didn't hear that right.

I couldn't take the screams anymore. I closed my eyes and prayed that being a vampire—no matter how newly made I was—would help me. Otherwise, I'd be next. I squared my shoulders and braced myself. I took a deep breath and screwed my courage back up into my chest from where it had fallen to my feet. I tried not to think of the consequences of what I was about to do.

I walked past the two men in front of me and they stopped talking. I kept walking and the men in the line all stopped their conversations as I walked past them, yet no one made a move to stop me.

My step faltered when I got a glimpse of the horror that awaited me if I couldn't manage to overpower all of these sick bastards.

At least twenty or thirty of the robed men surrounded a covered gazebo. Inside the small structure was an altar, surrounded by various colored candles and a pentagram was drawn on the floor with chalk. It was what I saw on the altar that made me gag.

A young woman or girl, I couldn't tell which, was tied naked and spread eagle on the top. I watched horrified as one grunting man pumped in and out of her abused body, shooting his semen onto her exposed breasts. When he left her, another man took his place, pounding into her with no mercy as blood and semen ran from between her legs.

My lips thinned and I gritted my teeth. I fought the tears that threatened to run down my cheeks when I met her hopeless, tear-filled eyes. At least she was still alive.

I looked around at the robed figures, amazed that no one had tried to stop me from entering. I stared at the blood stained altar knowing they had no intention of letting either of us leave this place alive.

I couldn't stand to watch this anymore. I had to do something and do it fast. There was a giant hole in the parking lot next door that led to another dimension, and I had to fix it. Who knew how many of those strange and evil creatures were being set loose on the city?

I closed my eyes and took a deep breath. I hoped like hell I could pull this off. Otherwise, I was about to be raped and murdered by a bunch of people who looked a lot like Satan worshippers. I gathered my strength, my wits and my courage about me and stepped within the circle surrounding the large, stone altar.

God help me. I hope this works.

I turned to look at every one of the men who stood around the altar and raised my arms. I almost lost what little courage I still possessed, but the looks of depravity sent my way gave me the strength I needed to go on.

"In the name of my Dark Lord, I order thee to release this human, that he may enjoy her supple body." That got their attention.

"He has answered us! He has sent an emissary!" A man called out, excited.

"Our Lord Satan has answered our prayers," still another one said.

One man grabbed a knife and held it above his head. "She shall be his."

The girl stared in horrified silence as the knife quickly made its descent toward her heart.

I reached out with one hand and stopped the man's two, which held the knife headed for her chest. The show of my vampire strength won over the skeptics in the crowd.

"No, you fools!" I called out loud enough for everyone to hear. "He has taken human form and wishes that she be taken to him. Untie her and give her a robe," I demanded imperiously.

Then I stood up straighter and willed my eyes to glow red. The crowd in front of me took a cautious step back and I fought the urge to grin with triumph.

The girl stared at me with renewed horror. I can't say I blamed her, at all. I wouldn't want to have to go through this either.

With any luck, Micah would be able to compel her and make her think this was all a horrible nightmare.

It wasn't long before the girl stood before me dressed in a blood red robe. New tears ran down her face as she, no doubt, contemplated a horrific end.

She shuffled past me and whispered the Lord's Prayer. She was obviously prepared for a horrible death at the hands of a madman who believed himself to be Satan.

I admired the way she carried herself as she refused to cower before these men and walked with her head high, only limping slightly.

She finished reciting the prayer, stopped and looked me in the eyes. Even the men had refrained from looking me directly in the eyes after their little glowing stunt.

The woman had courage and spirit. I'll give her that.

"I will not submit," she said, proudly. "He will have to force me, just as these animals have." She waved her hand toward the robed men.

I watched her, proud she still had so much spunk after everything she'd been through. I studied her for a moment, sure she was a Guide. My guess was the tear opened when her virginity was taken in the name of Satan.

If so, these sick bastards had the idea right, they just didn't have enough knowledge to steal her powers. They'd only borrowed them for a bit. Either that or she knew she was a Guide and opened the portal in an attempt to gain assistance from the creatures on the other side. Like when I called Brock a few weeks ago when Camen had attacked me.

"I wasn't really sent by Satan," I whispered in her ear.

She turned her sad, cinnamon eyes on me. "But you said you were sent by the Dark Lord."

"I said in the name of my Dark Lord." I didn't tell her, my Dark Lord was Micah and he wouldn't want anything from her.

"She lies," someone cried. "The woman lies, she was not sent by our Lord Satan!"

"Run," I screamed to her. "Run and don't look back."

It was already too late. Two men tackled her, bringing her to the ground. They ripped the robe from her already abused body. One man wasted no time as he grabbed her breast and settled himself between her bruised thighs.

Suddenly, a loud roar rent the air and the man went flying. I looked up to see another man standing over the girl as she stared at him with renewed horror.

The new man towered over the woman, his nearly seven-foot frame covered by a black leather duster. He removed his coat, dropping it over her. "Cover yourself."

The smooth rich baritone of his voice flowed over me like warm butter. I frowned at the effect it had on me. I shouldn't have reacted to it the way I did. As Micah's mate and a newly made vampire, I should have been resistant to his compulsion.

He turned my way, his silver eyes boring straight through me, the irises swirling like mercury.

I shivered uncomfortably. I looked death in the eye as I attempted to shake off the degenerate who'd just started to paw at my clothing.

I slapped at the man as he reached up and grabbed my ass. Then I kicked him away from me when he wouldn't let go. The man flew about ten feet backward.

"Hey," I grinned. "I guess I don't know my own strength."

The Cartuotey removed the remaining threat from the girl and walked toward me. I knew he was a Cartuotey. No one else could be so handsome and compelling. And no one else would have cared enough to try to rescue us from these monsters alone.

The sound of his voice was almost enough to make me want to fall at his feet and beg to hear more of its musical baritone. I shook my head to clear it of his compulsion.

The man scowled in my direction, his dark, brown brows cruel slashes over those beautiful silver eyes. He grabbed every man who tried to harm either one of us two women and sent them flying.

The sickening sound of bones as they snapped and broke was loud as he wrenched their necks before tossing them away like so much garbage. A few of them ran out through the gate, smart enough to realize they were out-matched.

The Cartuotey turned his nearly dead eyes on me once more, looking me up and down, he arched one perfect brow in question.

"Were you planning to help her service all of these men?" He brought his arm around in an arc, encompassing the area that was now littered with broken bodies.

I heard the poor girl gasp in outrage at his comment and, before I could think, before I could stop myself, my hand shot out and I slapped his too perfect face.

He just stood there and stared me, my handprint a red mark on his cheek. He lifted the corner of his mouth, in what I suppose, for him anyway, was a smile.

"That is a strange way to thank me for saving your lives." His eyes narrowed. "Go fix the tear, Guide. Why have you insisted on wasting your time to save this woman when you know you have a job to do?"

"Because, Cartuotey," I spat. "This woman is the poor, previously untapped and untouched Guide whose powers were used to open that fissure." I bared my teeth in what I hoped would pass for a smile. "I need her help to close it. How did you expect me to close it while they kept feeding it her stolen power in an attempt to keep it open?" I paced away from him and snarled, "You're such a jerk. Someone needs to teach you some manners."

His eyes widened and his attention turned back to the girl, now huddled within the folds of his long, black, leather coat, sobbing.

He sighed and stepped over the prone bodies to approach her. The Cartuotey reached down with his right hand and offered to help her up. She shied away from his touch, quickly shuffling away from him with a frightened whimper.

He looked down at his hand and wiped it on his pants, then looked over his shoulder at me. I could have sworn, for a moment, that those frightening eyes revealed a vulnerability that was previously not present.

I shook my head, determined not to feel sorry for the arrogant ass.

"Go repair the tear, Guide. Too many of the *Narctou* have escaped already."

I skirted around him, unsure if he would retaliate for my slap earlier, then bent to help the girl up.

A closer inspection of her battered face revealed her as a young woman, not too much younger than myself. It was her size that made me think she was just a girl.

"How old are you?" I gazed down as she looked up at me and pushed her hair back. I noticed the dark circles under her eyes and a swelling along her jaw. Dirt smudged her cheeks and blood trickled from the corner of her mouth.

"Twenty-four."

So she wasn't a girl then. And she was plenty old to have not been divested of her virginity before. It seemed we had a little in common.

"I know how you feel," I said as I pulled her to her feet. I didn't, not really, but I didn't know what else to say. "Just so you know, a Cartuotey," I gestured toward the man when she gave me a confused look. I was unwilling to call him a vampire. I needed her cooperation, not her hysterics. "Someone like him will never harm you intentionally." I shot a disdainful glance over my shoulder. "Even if they are thoughtless, arrogant asses."

I don't know how I knew that, but I felt that it was the truth, deep within my bones. I wrapped an arm around her and led her out of the yard toward the portal.

"What is a Cartuotey? I've never heard of them."

I sighed and tried to think of what to say to keep her curiosity at bay until one of them could explain it to her. I didn't want to terrify her and I was sure I would if I told her they would be knocking on her door to screw her brains out from time to time if she didn't use her powers regularly. She definitely didn't need to hear that. Besides, that was for one of them to tell her.

I opted for a partial truth.

"They protect us from evil entities and make us whole." I didn't want to tell her how they made us whole exactly. Those robed bastards ruined that for her.

I shot a glance her way and wondered if she would ever be able to trust a man again. Especially one with the kind of power a vampire wielded.

We walked through an opening in the fence and I pulled her down the street to show her the tear.

"They did this when they stole your power. They took the untapped power within you, which you were meant to use for good. They tried to open a portal to the netherworld." I waved my hand toward it as a goat-like creature ran out of the opening. "You can see the other-dimensional creatures slipping through, even now. That was an incubus," I pointed to the creature. "We must close it before too many more escape."

Chapter Twenty

SHE STARED AT THE OPEN PORTAL AND BROUGHT HER HAND TO HER CHEST.
"I did this. I wanted it to open closer to where I was being kept. I wanted to use one, or more, of the creatures to aid me against those...monsters." Her voice broke. "They refused to come," she sobbed. "If I had been more experienced maybe I would have been able to open the portal properly and in the right place."

She looked at me with huge, light brown eyes and I smiled softly. "You know you're a Guide?"

She nodded, new tears flooding her eyes. "My aunt and grandmother tried to keep me sheltered from all of this, but they found us." She gestured back to the house where she had been held prisoner. "I don't know how to close it." She wiped her eyes with the back of her hand. "I've never had to close one before."

"Well, you're one up on me. I just learned what I am a couple of weeks ago. At least you know what to expect." I patted her arm and tried to comfort her. "Just picture an impenetrable door in your mind and close it over the portal. That's all I've ever done and it seems to work fine. I just learned how to do this myself."

She turned a shy gaze on me. "What is a Cartuotey? You never did answer."

"They are the equivalent to supernatural policemen." I shrugged and left my explanation at that. "We have our work cut out for us here." I walked around to the other side of the tear and examined its jagged edges and wondered if we could close it. Energy popped and cracked around the edges.

"Your untapped powers could have surged as you opened the portal. When they stole your innocence. Then the men continued to feed it energy, through you, to keep it open. Now it must be drawing its power from somewhere on the other side. I need your help to close it. I can't do this by myself, it's too powerful."

I knelt down next to the tear and placed my hands on the ground near the opening.

The Narctou filtered through at an incredible rate. The vamp stood near, taking care of them as they attacked us and tried to pull us into the hole. The tear became smaller as I concentrated on it, but it refused to go past a certain point. The energy that poured from the open fissure was too great for me to close by myself.

The girl knelt in front of me and placed her hands on the ground. We looked at each other from opposite sides of the tear. She nodded and closed her eyes. We both stayed on our knees, our hands near the edge, as the tear slowly grew smaller.

The hair on the back of my neck stood on end and I felt a presence behind me. It distracted me enough to look.

Micah smiled down at me, then rested his hand on my head, stroking my hair.

"You had me worried, little love. I couldn't help you." He reached out and calmly grabbed a Narctou by the neck and hurled it back into the hole. It screamed its fury at being sent back to its own dimension where it had no supernatural powers.

I shrugged. "I knew you'd be here as soon as you could."

"Damien and I would have been too late. That was why we sent Gabriel." He turned slightly and indicated the new Cartuotey who stood several feet away. His gaze was glued to the girl who still knelt before me, her palms flat on the rough pavement.

I gaped up at him. "You sent that relic?"

"Relic?" he frowned, then looked from me to his friend.

We both watched as the man in question decapitated another *visitor* and sent its body back through the portal. I fought the urge to gag.

I rolled my eyes. "Yeah. Mr. Six-and-a-half-feet-of-total-stupidity."

"Gabriel is six-foot eight," Micah informed me.

"Whatever."

The girl cleared her throat. "It's getting bigger again. I don't know what to do to stop it."

"Dang it!" I cursed and settled back down onto the ground to finish my work. I looked up at Micah. "We'll finish this later." I gave him a meaningful look before I got back down to business.

Geeze. The man is almost a thousand years old. You'd think he'd have better taste in friends.

It took a lot of power to repair the chasm. I almost wasn't able to manage it. Not long after we began to attempt the repair the second time, I felt Micah's immense power flow through me as it rushed to help mend the dimensional tear.

His power wrapped around me and kept me safe as I pulled massive amounts of energy from the woman. So much energy that I had to wonder if she wasn't The Chosen One, my mate had mentioned, instead of me.

I came to realize then, that even though I didn't have a lot of power myself. I was able to draw it from others and channel massive amounts of it toward closing the portal.

I used both the girl and Micah as anchors to bind me to this world, even as the energy of the portal tried to pull me down.

Someone on the other side attempted to pull me through. So they would have their own Guide to open portals, no doubt. The power of the fissure seeped into me. There was a presence there. Someone wanted to turn me to the darkness that waited within the dark pit. The entity on the other side whispered unbelievable promises to me in an effort to tempt me to abandon my world and join him in the next dimension.

My hands and body tingled with the effort to hold the power at bay as it seeped through the barriers in my mind and tempted me with everything I had ever dreamed of. I gritted my teeth against it and fought the terrible urge to give up and let them come.

I ignored the horrific sounds of death around me as Micah and his friend protected us from the grotesque Narctou. Blood spattered my cheek when a leg flew past me and into the hole, followed by the rest of the limp body.

The tear slowly narrowed as the portal finally closed. When the last fraction of an inch was finally sealed, I sagged to the ground, completely spent.

The girl—whose name I learned, through the tapping of her powers was Alicia Chalmers—lay beside me, her eyes closed, her chestnut lashes dark crescents on her pale cheeks.

I lifted my hand and covered hers in a show of sisterly solidarity. We may not be related by blood, but some ties were stronger.

Then I looked up at Micah and my newly acquired canines lengthened. They shot from my gums in a painful manner. Even though he looked exhausted, he bent down and picked me up with a smile.

"You must feed, my love," he whispered in my ear. His breath brushed the side of my neck and sent a shaft of desire through me. My body clenched in anticipation as he tilted his head and exposed his neck to me.

I buried my head in his shoulder. My mouth watered with anticipation. My gums throbbed around my canines as my body begged for sustenance. I shook my head and denied my need.

"I can't," I whispered into his neck, my voice and body trembling with urgency.

I couldn't bring myself to feed in front of the others. I refused to just stick my teeth into his neck with no foreplay again. Feeding was an orgasmic experience for both parties if it was done correctly.

I glanced up at him and remembered he was my mate, not just my dinner. I shook my head, squeezed my eyes closed and realized the same determination I possessed, which allowed me to stop my use of drugs would also help with the development of my feeding habits.

Everything in my new life was ultimately determined by how well a person could control themselves and their urges.

Micah gave me a light squeeze, then released me, a proud smile on his face.

"That's my girl." He patted me on the back then quickly backed away as a scream rent the air.

I whirled around, expecting some other horror to appear, only to see Micah's friend approach and stand over Alicia. His face was an implacable mask as he bent toward her.

Alicia screamed again. She attempted to crawl away, but was too weak. She collapsed in front of him with a frightened whimper.

I ran to her, placed myself between them and looked up into those glowing silver eyes. I stared death in the face for the second time in just a handful of minutes. I swallowed thickly as he took a step closer. Terrified, I stood my ground and stared down an ancient vampire.

"Leave her be, Gabriel." The menace in Micah's voice was clear as he watched every movement his friend made and stood ready to defend me.

"The woman is mine," Gabriel bit out between clenched teeth as if he dared Micah to tell him differently. "Only my mate would have been able to draw power from me as she has."

"Perhaps," Micah agreed, then nodded his head. "But she must choose. You cannot force her." He cocked his brow at the offensive stance Gabriel assumed as he prepared to attack me. "You would not be like the miscreants we have all faced tonight and take the choice from her, will you?"

Gabriel looked from Micah to the girl on the ground in front of him. She looked tiny compared to the two men who stood over her. She even looked tiny compared to me, like a little broken doll that had been thrown to the pavement.

"Do you think she will choose you now? Let my mate and I take her. We will care for her, heal her and protect her. Tasha, my mate, will help her come to terms with what has happened tonight. Then perhaps, in time, she will come to you of her own free will."

Gabriel's gaze was still on Alicia, his eyes were unreadable and I feared the worst. He staggered back a bit. When the glow ebbed from his eyes, I realized, for the first time, how weak he really was.

"Please attend to my mate. She is injured."

I bit back a smile at that. I knew from Micah's personality how much effort it took for him to ask and not demand.

I knelt down beside her and bent to whisper in her ear. "Can you hear me?"

She nodded and licked her split, swollen lips. "Keep him away from me, please," she sobbed.

Tears slipped from my eyes and ran down my cheeks unchecked. Tears for this poor woman and for the horror and degradation she'd gone through tonight. I was amazed that she still had enough strength to help me when I needed it, strength enough to tap into a vampire's immense energies.

I put my hand on her head and wished with all of my might that I had the power to help heal her mind. To make the horror of this night lessen, if not completely go away. I pulled my hand away quickly when I noticed her wounds were closing at an accelerated rate. The split on her lip healed with no trace, in a matter of seconds.

"Micah?" My voice trembled as I stood and backed away from her. "Why is she healing so quickly?" She was a human. She shouldn't heal at such an accelerated rate. I peered down at her still form. Her wounds no longer continued to heal since I'd stepped away from her.

I lifted my hands and stared down at them with disbelief. It couldn't be me. I'd never had that effect on anyone before.

Gabriel looked from me to the girl. She still lay like the dead on the pavement. She appeared unconscious.

"Heal her, Guide."

"I have a name," I snapped. My nerves were shot and I was damn tired of his imperialistic demands. I turned to Micah. "How can this be happening? People don't just develop magical abilities like this in an instant."

Yet I had.

Micah stepped forward. "Tasha," he whispered, "you must heal her if you can." He gazed at me with hunger that made me burn and, then raised his hand to push a stray lock of hair behind my ear. "I'm not certain what has happened to you, little one. But you must help her if you have the ability."

I nodded. Of course I had to help her, but who was going to help me?

Micah rested his hands on my shoulders and I immediately felt ashamed. He would help me, of course. I just didn't know how to be dependent on him yet. He gave me a light squeeze. I settled back down onto my knees and looked at my hands with trepidation.

I placed my hands on Alicia's head again and her face healed completely. Every cut, scratch and abrasion she sported, disappeared before my eyes in seconds. I don't know what or how many internal injuries I healed.

I jumped back when her eyes flew open.

She sat up and rubbed the back of her neck. "Thank you for helping me," she said, looking me directly in the eyes again. "They would have killed me if you hadn't come along." She raised a hand and felt her lips. She looked at me with wide eyes when she realized they were no longer split and swollen.

"They would have killed you both if I hadn't come along," Gabriel added.

I closed my eyes and willed the idiot to shut up before he ruined every chance he would ever have to make Alicia his.

"Gabriel," Micah said as he gave the man an unreadable look. "I would have a word with you." He indicated that they should step away from us. They moved to a corner of the lot to talk. I could still hear them with my newly acquired abilities but, apparently, it wasn't me that Micah was worried about.

"You cannot force her to accept you, Gabriel. You would be no better than those who have stolen her innocence this night." He cocked his head the side and paused. "Someone has called the police."

Gabriel was quiet for a moment while he obviously listened to the approaching vehicles. "I hear the sirens. We must quit this place immediately."

It always amazed me that they functioned so well in today's society when they still spoke the way they did. Old habits do die hard, I guess.

Gabriel wasted no time. He strode back to us, his tone as forceful and autocratic as ever.

"We must go." His gaze flicked over Alicia as he checked her condition.

She was still conscious and was better, but to run or even walk was totally out of the question. She could barely stand.

I looked between the two men. There was no doubt in my mind which one of them would want to carry the girl.

I leaned down to speak to her. "We have to leave quickly, before the authorities arrive."

Alicia peered up at me with frightened eyes. "We have to report what happened." She drew Gabriel's coat tighter around her trembling form. "I don't know if I can stand to have them touch me. Do you think they will touch me?" She shuddered visibly and drew her knees to her chest. She rocked back and forth on the ground.

I blinked and forced back more tears of frustration. I should have been faster.

Do not blame yourself, little one. How could you have been here before they harmed her? It was her impending violation that forced her to open the portal, alerting you to their presence.

I heaved a sigh and threw Micah a thankful look. He was right. It was too late the second the gateway had been opened.

I cleared my mind and looked Alicia in the eyes. I knew what I had to do. She would never allow this from either of the men.

I took a deep breath and gave my first attempt at compulsion. "We cannot stay here. The police wouldn't listen to the truth. They would believe us to be delusional."

Alicia's eyes glazed over and she nodded. "They would think we were delusional."

"You must allow Gabriel to carry you."

She gave a little whimper of distress. I smiled softly and tried to assure her. How could I make her comfortable with the idea of being held in Gabriel's arms?

"He would never harm you." I laid my hand on her shoulder. "I will be there with you. You will not be alone with him."

Her eyes glazed over a bit and she turned to look at him. "Gabriel will not harm me, you will be there."

I stood and nodded to Gabriel. "I think she'll let you carry her now. At the very least," I dropped my voice to a whisper, "she'll be more susceptible to *your* compulsion." I gripped his forearm. "And don't you dare abuse it."

Micah took my hand in his and pulled me away from his friend. "We must

166

leave this place. Now."

The sirens were louder, almost upon us. Gabriel scooped Alicia up into his arms and we all ran to the back of the lot.

My mouth dropped open as I watched Gabriel raise himself and Alicia up over the eight-foot tall chain-link fence.

Micah's fingers squeezed mine.

"Imagine that you are as light as a feather. The wind is so strong, it carries you up and over the fence."

I felt my feet leave the ground as I did what he asked. "I'm flying! I don't believe it, I'm friggin' flying!"

He grinned at me. "I'd forgotten how to be excited about our abilities until we were brought together. You make everything new to me again, Tasha. That alone makes you precious to me."

He wrapped his arms around me and I reveled in his embrace. I didn't even realize we'd started to make our descent until my feet touched the ground.

I looked over to see Alicia and Gabriel watching us. Gabriel looked on with...longing? Alicia watched us with barely disguised disgust.

I couldn't help feeling a little bit sorry for Gabriel. He certainly had his work cut out for him. That's for sure.

Yes, he does, little one. But he will give her the time she needs. After all, if there is one thing he has, it is time.

"Come. This way," Micah pulled me behind him.

"Where are we going?" I struggled to keep up with the two men. I don't know if it was their age or the fact that they were male, but they could sure move fast.

Micah cast a glance over his shoulder. "We're going back to Demon World. Shay and Damien can give us an alibi, if we should need one."

I shook my head. "Shay's in labor. I doubt either of them will be able to help us out with that."

Micah's eyes widened a fraction. It was the only indication he gave that he was either shocked or worried.

I was tempted to touch his mind to find out which, but I couldn't very well keep demanding that he mind his own business if I wasn't minding mine.

"You must be mistaken. The baby isn't due for weeks yet." He held my hand in his and dragged me along with him at an incredible pace.

"I know. That's what Shay told me, right before she told the doctor—who just happens to be a vampire, by the way—that her contractions were two minutes apart."

"We must go to them," Micah said as he took both of my hands in his, turned them over and studied my palms.

I shook my head. "We don't know what effect, if any, I would have on her or the baby."

"We must return to them in case there are any complications."

I didn't want to go. It's not that I didn't want to help Shay if she needed it. A part of me was gung-ho about it. The other, more-sane part, was scared shitless. I was afraid I would do something horrible. Cause some sort of irreparable damage to either Shay or her child.

After we ran a few minutes, Micah lifted me into his arms and carried me the rest of the way. He still moved faster than I could, even under the burden of my considerable weight. We arrived at the club in record time.

I HAD HALF HOPED we would be too late, that Shay would have had her baby by now and they would both be fine. What I didn't want to see was a very concerned doctor and a frantic husband.

"She can't die in childbirth like a mortal, can she?" I asked, confused over the hubbub.

"No, but the baby can," Micah whispered. "They think the baby is already gone. Shay is just doing her best to push the fetus out of her womb so it can be taken care of." He rubbed my back and the gentle motion calmed my frazzled nerves.

Damn! I knew something like this was going to happen. I just knew it.

The doctor knelt just outside the door to the limo and coaxed Shay to push harder.

I tapped him on the shoulder. "May I?"

He scowled at me. "This is not the time for you to play at being a nurse."

I looked at Micah and crossed my arms over my chest. "Well, I tried." I wasn't about to start a fight about my desire to use an ability that may or may not desert me at any time. The last thing I wanted to do was raise false hopes.

Micah reached down and grabbed the man by the neck. "You will allow her to aid Shay." Apparently there was no arguing with him when he had his mind made up.

The doctor nodded rapidly. "Okay, okay. She can help her." He stepped out of the way and walked around to climb into the front seat of the limo, aided by Micah's hand on the back of his neck. On his knees, the doctor leaned over the back of the front seat to supervise.

I knelt down just outside the back door. I can honestly say I wasn't prepared for the sight that met me. The last thing I ever expected to see, in my lifetime, was another woman's bare body. Let alone find myself on my knees between her legs.

This is gross!

The doctor stuck his head over the back of the front seat.

"Put some gloves on, for God's sake. It's going to be messy, at the very least." He gave me a sober look. "Are you sure you'll be able to handle this?" He really wanted to know if I was prepared to deliver a dead baby.

I swallowed thickly. "This baby is going to be fine, if I have anything to say about it."

The doctor just closed his eyes and shook his head. To him, it was hopeless.

I took a deep breath and turned back to Shay. Maybe I was the best person for this after all. At least I had some hope.

I put the gloves on. Not so much as to protect the baby, but my mind told me how nasty this was about to get. I looked up and noticed Damien for the first time as our eyes met. I gave him a wobbly smile and looked away. I reached up between Shay's legs when he urged her to push.

After two more contractions, the baby slid out into my hands. His tiny blood-soaked body was blue from lack of oxygen. Vampires don't have to breathe often unless they want to appear human, but they do have to breathe.

The doctor held out his hands and would have taken him from me, but Micah stopped him. I used the scissors they had stored in the limo to cut the cord and I tied it off with the twine the doctor handed me.

"I don't know why you're even bothering to do that," he said, his look grim as he examined the lifeless face of the infant in my hands.

I frowned, then stepped out of the way so the doctor could attend to Shay and deliver the afterbirth. I cleaned the blood from the tiny body with the soft cloths brought to me from a suitcase in the trunk and swabbed the mucus from the boy's bow-shaped mouth.

"I don't understand." I knew it was too much to ask. My ability to heal had apparently vanished. The powers were probably no more than borrowed energy from the open portal. And now they were gone.

I handed the baby to Micah and removed the gloves. Tears ran down my cheeks as I looked at his perfect little face. I reached out and touched the soft skin of his hand and used my thumb to gently wrap his tiny fingers around my larger one.

As soon as the palm of his hand made contact with my finger, the baby inhaled deeply and let out a bellow that would make any new mother proud. His legs jerked, making a bicycling motion and he stuck his hand in his mouth and sucked on his fingers.

"My baby!" Shay cried from inside the limo. "Damien, it's our baby."

Damien left her for a moment to run around the limo and take the baby from Micah's arms. He cradled the wrapped bundle to his chest, looked at me and smiled.

"I don't know what you did or how you did it, and frankly, I don't really care. But thank you."

I gave him a wobbly smile in return. "I'm not sure what I did either."

"You healed him," Micah said.

I grimaced. I may be modest, but my mate sure isn't. "I touched him, Micah. I don't know what healed him."

I looked down at my hands and wondered if I could have gained my new powers from the conversion or if the ability to heal is just a residual by-product left by the portal when it tempted me with its power.

Micah wrapped his arms around me and grinned. "It does not matter. You will deal with this just as well as you have dealt with the other impossible things you've dealt with lately."

"I suppose." I looked over at Gabriel and Alicia. He still held her in his arms. He looked at her like he was a starving man and she was, well, lunch.

Alicia wriggled in his arms.

"Put me down!"

Gabriel held her closer to him. He didn't even appear to notice her struggles. "I would know your name before I leave you, mate."

Even I felt the compulsion in his voice. The command he gave for her to surrender her name was very strong.

Alicia must have felt better, either that, or she'd realized somehow that Gabriel wasn't going to hurt her.

She crossed her arms over her chest and scowled. "Tough crap, Goliath! Put me down."

I hid a small smile behind my hand at the look of total disbelief on his face. Someone needed to tell this guy no, on a regular basis and Alicia just might be the person to do it.

Gabriel bent his head closer to her and smiled. "Only a true mate can deny compulsion," he said, his voice smug as he set her on her feet.

"I don't know what you're talking about," Alicia sniffed as she wrapped his coat tightly around her.

She limped over and stood just behind me to use me as a shield to protect her from Gabriel's intense stare.

"I'm nobody's mate," she returned, her eyes haunted. "I will never submit to that kind of degradation ever again." She reached up and swiped a tear from her cheek. "I'll never let another man touch me like that," she said with a shudder. "Ever."

I knew she meant that now, but hurts do heal. Even grievous wounds like those she'd received today. There is no doubt in my mind that, given the determination in Gabriel's eyes, she would one day be his. It just wouldn't be tonight.

"I would know your name before you leave me, mate."

My mouth dropped open when Alicia told him to do something that I'm pretty sure is anatomically impossible. Even for a vampire. I took her manner as being too prim and proper for that kind of language. But, I guess not.

She looked around. "I don't know how I'm going to get home." Tears streamed down her face. "I'm not even sure I have a home to go back to."

"Why?"

She turned those haunted cinnamon eyes on me.

"They took me from my home. They..." she choked on a sob. "They killed my aunt and grandmother when they tried to protect me. I don't have anyone anymore. I'm alone now."

I shook my head. "No, you're not. You have us." I smiled a bit sadly. "You can stay with us as long as you need to." I shot Micah a nervous glance and hoped he wouldn't mind that I'd just opened our home to her.

He winked, letting me know it was okay.

I looked up at Gabriel's somber face and smiled. If the loneliness that Micah had gone through was any indication. The poor man needed some hope.

So I threw him a bone. I wrapped my arm around her and winked at him. "Come on, Alicia, let's get you home."

171

Epilogue

SIX WEEKS LATER:

MICAH HAD BEEN IN TOWN, OVERSEEING SOME BUSINESS VENTURE AND was on his way home. Alicia was with Shay and Damien. They said something about going to the movies.

I sat on the sofa in the living room and waited for my husband like an unwrapped Christmas present. Well, an almost unwrapped present.

My skin still glowed a soft pink from my warm soak in the small swimming pool that Micah called our tub. My cheeks were hot, flushed with a mixture of desire and embarrassment as I waited for Micah to return. I only hoped he would get here fast before I lost my nerve and ran upstairs to put some clothes on.

After my long, hot soak in the massive tub, I dressed in a new emerald-green crotchless teddy. The matching garter belt held up my black fishnet stockings. My feet were encased in a pair of three-inch black stilettos that I'd purchased before we were married.

The staff was gone since I gave them the night off and I waited, rather impatiently, for my best friend and lover to return.

Micah found me waiting on the sofa. My legs were spread wide and my hand lazily caressed my pussy. His mouth dropped open when he entered the room. His Adam's apple bobbed as he swallowed visibly and watched my index finger circle my clit in a leisurely exploration.

I stood up slowly. I wanted to be sure he got a good look at all of my exposed attributes. My hands traveled up over my stomach and cupped my breasts. The movement accentuated my exposed cleavage and drew his attention to my hardened nipples. I smiled an invitation as I sauntered toward him.

"Hello, lover."

I wet my lips. My tongue trailed along my lips in a blatant show of my

172

desire. A movement low on his body drew my gaze and my eyes lowered to his crotch. I wished his clothes away as I trembled with suppressed need.

His cock bucked and swayed with anticipation as I approached. My husband was definitely happy to see me.

"Natasha, you look—"

I put my fingers over his lips as he drew me into his arms. I didn't want talk. I wanted action.

He inhaled deeply, took my fingers into his mouth and suckled my essence from them.

"That's so sexy, Micah," I gasped. I pulled my fingers from his mouth and trailed my hand down the smooth skin of Micah's chest. His breath rushed out in a hiss as my fingers lazily circled his flat, brown nipples.

Micah's hands brushed lightly over my back. They skimmed down over my hips to caress the partially exposed cheeks of my ass.

"How did you know this would turn me on?" he asked, his eyes glazed with desire.

"I'm your woman," I said and pulled from his arms for a moment to turn in a slow circle in front of him. "And I'm dressed in this." I modeled the teddy, making sure to trail my hands over my body as he watched before I stepped back into his arms. "Why wouldn't you be turned on?"

I reached down and grasped his shaft. My thumb caressed the tip and rubbed the little pearl of moisture away. He was already straining to hold back his orgasm. Good. It was about time I got to drive him wild.

"Ah, that feels good." He sucked his breath in through his teeth. The muscles in Micah's neck bulged as he fought for control of his body.

The pictures that danced through his mind were erotic. My skin heated to a burn when I realized this was one of his fantasies come to life.

With his hands still caressing the cheeks of my rear, Micah slowly released each strap of the garter. Then he knelt in front of me and peeled the stockings from my legs. He took his time as he pushed the netting down to let his fingers glide over my heated flesh.

"I've imagined this," he whispered. His breath brushed against my upper thigh as he kissed around the strap of the garter.

I lifted my left foot while he removed my shoe and stocking before placing it back on the floor. Micah's eyes were glazed with need as he forced himself to take his time with the other leg. He rolled the netting down over my calf and caressed the arch of my foot as he pushed the stocking from my toes.

I shook with need and pent up desire. My legs almost gave out. I put my hand on the wall and buried the other in Micah's hair to steady myself.

"Yesss," I hissed out my pleasure as his tongue flicked through the folds of my nether lips and caressed my swollen clit before he cupped my ass in his hands and buried his face between my legs. He sucked my clit into his mouth and nibbled lightly on the swollen nub. I was so turned on it didn't take long to reach the edge.

I'd never climaxed standing up before, but I guess there's a first time for everything. "Micah!" I screamed out his name, a warning as I stumbled when my legs gave out and I almost fell.

He scooped me up in his arms and carried me back to the couch where he sat me down and spread my thighs. I felt the heat of his gaze like a touch.

"Let me watch you," he urged, taking my hand. He placed it over my glistening, dew-covered curls and watched as I plunged my fingers into my honeyed slit.

I slowly parted my nether lips and my fingers reached unerringly for the little nubbin that I knew would send me over the edge once more.

Micah knelt between my spread thighs, his face tight with passion as he watched me pleasure myself.

"That's it, baby. Bring yourself to it."

I groaned as my fingers slid over my hardened clit. It throbbed and twitched with each little flick of my finger.

Fire climbed up my legs, crawled up to lodge in my belly as I brought myself closer to the edge.

"You're getting closer now, aren't you?" Micah panted. "I can see it." He reached up with both hands and squeezed my nipples through the lacy fabric of my teddy.

I closed my eyes, reveling in the sound of Micah's raspy, breathless voice.

"Aiieee!" I squealed, as he drove himself deep inside me.

The shock of his sudden possession sent me over the edge. I quickened my fingers on my clit as he rammed himself into my clasping vagina.

"Fuck me!" I demanded as another orgasm overtook me.

"Yes, Tasha," Micah groaned. "Come for me. Tighten that little cunt around my cock."

He drove his thick length into me and I screamed out another climax as his hips ground into mine. His balls slapped my ass as he pushed himself into me, up to the hilt. His blood-engorged shaft bucked inside me and filled me with his seed. He rested his damp head between my breasts, his breath coming in short gasps.

It was a heady feeling to know I'd driven him so far over the edge that he was gasping for breath.

The sound of the front door closing filtered down the hall and through the still open formal double doors.

"Shit, Alicia's home. I didn't expect her, this early. She's supposed to be at a movie with Shay and Damien." I rushed around and frantically picked up our clothes.

Micah chuckled softly and dressed us with a thought. The only evidence of our recent activities was the faint smell of sex that I hoped Alicia's senses were too dull to pick up.

I needn't have worried.

"I hate that man!" Alicia exclaimed as she climbed the stairs, heading straight for her room. "I absolutely detest him, the chauvinistic pig!"

I sighed and leaned over to give Micah a soft kiss on his lips. "Call Gabriel and tell him her favorite flowers are daisies.

He looked at me and raised his brow. I just shrugged.

"Look, I don't like eavesdropping on her thoughts. You, of all people, should know how I feel about that."

I'd thought about it earlier when Gabriel talked with me on the phone. He'd asked me to find out what her favorite things were. It was a necessary evil as far as I was concerned.

She didn't know it, but Alicia needed Gabriel as much as he needed her. There wasn't another man on this Earth who would be as patient or kind with her while he waited for her to overcome her fears. My experience with Micah told me that much.

"Tell him he's going to have to be very patient with her, but she does care for him a little. She has a tiny bit of affection peppered with a hint of attraction and healthy lust. She doesn't like it that she wants him, but she can't stop herself."

I wanted to refuse to make excuses for my behavior, but I felt I should explain.

"After being in your mind, I couldn't bear the thought of him continuing to face the future alone." I shrugged at the question in my husband's eyes. "No, I still don't like him. I still think he's an ass, but he saved my life. I felt I owed it to him to at least give him a little hope."

Micah nodded. "He has that now, and given time, Alicia will agree to be his mate."

To be continued...

THE CHOSEN

ALICIA: THE AWAKENING

PROLOGUE

WHEN I WOKE TIED NAKED TO AN ALTAR, I STRUGGLED AGAINST MY bonds then stilled when six robed men walked into the room. Heat rushed through my body and I blushed, angry and self-conscious about my nakedness.

"What do you want from me?"

The leader, dressed in a black, gold trimmed robe, looked like the nightmarish vision of a Hollywood special effects artist. Long, lank, greasy brown hair hung from his head in disheveled clumps. I could easily see his yellow fingernails, more like talons really, were at least three inches long as he fondled the amulet suspended from a chain around his neck. The very air around him crackled with menace. He turned his dark gaze on me, an evil chuckle issuing from his bloodless lips as he elbowed the man at his side.

"It is time to call our dark lord forth." He looked around and pointed through the slats of the covered gazebo they'd put me in. "We will take your virginity in the name of Satan. When your latent powers are released, a gate will be opened and he will be called forth into this realm."

I lifted my head, the only body part not strapped down to the altar. "Like hell you are! You guys are insane!"

I looked past the slats to the group of men waiting in the yard outside the gazebo and shuddered. There were no illusions. These men were about to rape me.

"Help me!" I screamed. Unable to tell if there were homes nearby or not, I screamed as loud as I could anyway.

The leader laughed. "No one will help you. Anyone within hearing distance thinks we are rehearsing a play."

My heart slammed in my chest as I realized the next few minutes would be the last I would ever know. Tears ran down my face as I prayed they would a least make it quick. Another glance at the line of men outside the gazebo told me it was most likely wishful thinking.

Suddenly, another man arrived. I felt his presence like a warm blanket surrounding me. He wasn't wearing a robe and a sliver of hope grew inside my breast. Tall, blonde and silver eyed, he was the most handsome man I had ever seen. Dressed in khaki slacks and a baby blue shirt, he could have just stepped from the cover of a fashion magazine. Broad shoulders nearly brushed each side of the doorframe as he strode through. He exuded masculinity and power clung to him like a cloak.

I felt his gaze rake across my naked body like a touch. I squeezed my eyes shut, refusing to look at him. I fought my insane attraction to the newcomer. He was here to take my virginity. Tears of frustration slid down my cheeks. How could I think any of these monsters were handsome?

My eyelids flew open when he rested his warm hand on my shoulder and I watched as he cast his cold, silver gaze around the inside of the gazebo and smiled. The white flash of his teeth looked detached, didn't reach his eyes. Instead, they warmed, glowing with a strange, orange iridescence.

I watched with growing horror as the newcomer turned into a real monster—a werewolf. His teeth lengthened, his body contorted, became more compact. Thick fur grew over his once smooth flesh. He was no longer a man, but a large, golden wolf. The wolf attacked and killed my captors before he turned back into the man.

As the man, he had taken on a slightly different appearance. He was no longer detached and cold. Ruthless. Instead, his heated gaze warmed my blood. It slowed, flowing thick through my veins, burning through me like molten lava. My heart hammered against my ribs when he looked at me.

His heated gaze blazed a scorching trail over my bare body, devouring every inch of my exposed flesh. Blood pounded in my ears as he approached. When he stood beside the altar, he leaned down to release my bonds.

"I've been searching for you forever." He lightly pressed his mouth against my lips. The warm moist pressure was soft, gentle, the touch feather light.

Heat pooled in my middle, flared out to consume every inch of my body. The warmth of his touch suffused me, filled me, as the kiss overwhelmed my senses and took my breath away. I closed my eyes, enjoying the sensation of his kiss.

"Who are you and why have you been looking for me?" I asked as soon as his lips left mine. I didn't know this man from Adam, but I allowed his kiss because something about him screamed that he belonged to me.

The man released the bonds around my wrists, tangled his fingers with mine and pressed my hands against the cold, stone altar. He held me pressed against the frigid cement but I'm not sure it was against my will. Something told me I would follow this man anywhere, do almost anything to be with him.

He raised his head to look into my eyes before his silver gaze moved over my face. He stared at my parted lips then lowered his head once more.

"You are my mate," he breathed against my mouth, his tongue caressing the seam. "You are the woman I have waited lifetimes for." He moved his mouth to my jaw, then down to my neck, caressing the curve of my throat.

"Lifetimes?" I panted then turned my head, exposing my neck to give him better access.

That molten silver gaze burned a fiery trail over my flesh. My nipples hardened, gooseflesh rose on my body. I squirmed as unfamiliar warmth pooled between my legs.

"You are mine. You belong to me." He threaded his fingers through my hair, tipped my head back. Pinpricks of sensual pain darted over my scalp and I moaned.

His hips surged forward, the evidence of his desire pressed against my nether lips and I gasped. My head thrashed, cushioned by the palm of his hand.

"I am not yours. I belong to no one but myself. I don't even know you."

"You know me. You have loved me before." His eyes darkened and filled with pain. "But you did not love me enough. You have never loved me enough. But it is my fault, I have failed you."

He stared down at my breasts. My nipples hardened, heat pooled low in my middle and my breath hitched. My body tingled and burned for this man. How could just one heated look from this strange, powerful man have such an effect on me?

"What do you want?"

I squirmed beneath him, scared. Excited. Horny. God, I couldn't believe how much I wanted this man and I didn't even know him! How could I fight him when I had to fight myself as well? I wanted this man—no—I needed this man with an intensity I never dreamed possible.

My traitorous body thrust my hips up to meet his as he pressed the bulge beneath the zipper of his pants against my weeping sex. The cold metal caused a sweet abrasion that wasn't quite painful and my body shuddered, craving so much more of his touch.

"This," he said before he bent his head to my breast. His mouth laved my nipple and I groaned. "And this." He moved from between my legs to lie beside me, his hand moved up my thigh and he slid his fingers through my nether lips.

"You're so wet." He brought his fingers to his face, sucked them into his mouth. "Mmm... You taste exquisite. Tell me you want me." He nuzzled my ear. The motion caused me to shiver. Gooseflesh covered my arms and legs.

He moved back to my cheek then kissed me again and thrust his tongue into my mouth. He drove me so close to the edge of ecstasy that I nearly tumbled over the precipice. Practiced fingers slid over my sensitive skin and nearly drove me wild.

"Yesss," I hissed against his lips.

His mouth left mine to suckle my breast again. First one, then the other he used his teeth gently, expertly, until I threw my head back ready to scream my climax to the world.

Beep. Beep. Beep.

THE ALARM WOKE ME. It was another damned wet dream. In real life, I knew the man who played the hero in my dreams. In real life, Gabriel had not gotten there on time to stop those lunatics from raping me. Nor was I so free with my kisses or my body. Even in my dreams.

If the alarm hadn't awoken me, I would have refused him as I always did. As usual, I would have sent him from me with a painful erection because I'm a coward.

My flesh tingled all over. The lingering sensation of my dream Gabriel's touch made me shiver with a confusing mixture of fear and desire. My body wanted him with a force that was difficult to deny. But in my head, I was just plain scared.

My body hummed with desire. The dreams always left me frustrated and wanting. I'd hate to know what it would do to Gabriel. I felt bad for my dream man. Since I was a coward, I always left him wanting. It was just a good damn thing they were only dreams.

I rolled over, glanced at the clock on my bedside table and groaned. It was time I got up and into the shower. It was my wedding day and I was already late.

Chapter One

I WALTZED INTO THE DIMLY LIT CHAPEL AN HOUR AND A HALF LATE AND stared into icy, silver eyes. I glanced at Tasha and Micah, our only witnesses, and tried to smile through the almost paralyzing fear.

Tasha grinned and gave me a thumb's up sign. The action seemed strange coming from such an elegantly dressed woman in the rose-filled chapel. I didn't put too much more thought into it as I gazed around the interior of the church.

Whoever took the time to decorate the place, did a wonderful job. A veritable rainbow of expensive, aromatic flowers rested on almost every flat surface.

Many long stemmed roses braided together created a rope of fragrant blossoms that draped over the ends of the pews. An excess of colorful rosebuds and blooms hung from the backs of the wooden seats. They should have signified a glorious occasion, but only served to remind me of my impending loss of freedom.

The plethora of foliage lent the chapel a certain old-fashioned charm. Who was the lucky girl that got his kind of loving attention? I barely stopped myself from snorting. It certainly wasn't me. I was sure of that.

My marriage to the giant, albeit gorgeous, blonde man standing beside Tasha's tall, tuxedo-clad husband was nothing but a lie. A sham. A pretend marriage, a pale imitation of what it should be.

This was a marriage of convenience and I entered into it for my own selfish reasons. Gabriel's motives were his own. He never told me why he was willing to marry a woman who would most likely never agree to a physical relationship. On that, like most other things about him, he had kept his own counsel.

Slowly, I strode down the aisle, crushing fragrant rose petals beneath my feet. The action seemed symbolic, serving only to remind me that last spring saw the crushing of every hope and dream I had ever held dear.

I thought about being polite and almost apologized for my tardiness until I met Gabriel's icy gaze.

"You're late," he bit out between clenched teeth as he held his smile in place. "You were supposed to be here almost two hours ago. Where have you been?"

As usual, that deep baritone slid over me like warm honey. Warmth heated my middle and I grew damp. His voice, no matter the tone, never failed to touch me in places better left alone.

I deliberately ignored the flash of those white teeth. His smile always made him seem younger and more approachable. Too bad, his smile looked fake.

As I shuffled toward the dais, I tried to convince myself that, no matter how handsome the man was, he meant absolutely nothing to me. Nothing at all.

"You should be glad I'm here," I said with false sweetness.

Sure that it wasn't the brightest move I'd ever made, I continued down the aisle. I agreed to it and I have never gone back on my word. So, I stood next to the man I promised to marry and tried to stop shaking.

If I had learned one thing about him in the last six months, it was that this man would not hurt me. Well, at least, he wouldn't hurt me on purpose. I'm sure he could hurt me if I suddenly became stupid and allowed it by falling in love with him. I would just have to remember to keep my emotions in check.

I glanced at the balding preacher and scowled uncharitably. "Can we get on with this, or not?" I snarled.

He coughed, his stomach shaking beneath his robes, then cleared his throat, "If this is not what you wanted, miss, now is the time to..." His gaze nervously darted around the room. He studiously avoided looking at my affianced, as if not seeing Gabriel standing there would give him the courage to refuse to marry us. But somehow, I doubted it.

I shot my husband-to-be a dirty look through narrowed eyes. I wasn't happy about the situation. I made sure he knew how I felt and I refused to let him forget it.

"What I want has little to do with it, now."

The preacher's gaze bounced back and forth between the two of us. His gaze rested briefly on my stomach before his face reddened, his eyes bulged and he coughed.

"Oh, my... I think we'd better get on with it, then."

The wide-eyed look on his face told me he thought I was in a family way and I started to set him straight. Thinking better of it, I kept my mouth shut instead. He would most likely balk at marrying us for convenience. People just didn't do that sort of thing these days. It's not as if I had another choice.

Fanatical associates of the people who murdered my aunt and grandmother kept returning to my house, trying to find me. I knew I couldn't continue to live with Tasha and Micah for the rest of my life so I had a choice to make. Go home and wait for those crazy monsters to kidnap me again or marry the insanely handsome man who stood at my side staring at me with those glacial eyes.

My stomach churned. Because of circumstances beyond my control, I had to live with people I barely knew. In a place where I was also required to accept charity, where I couldn't work and pull my own weight. I had no way to support myself. I had to quit my job when some of the fanatics tried to abduct me from where I worked. The last thing I wanted to do was further endanger my friends.

So I faced the continuous worry of being nabbed by Satanists who wanted to kill me or living with Tasha and Micah like some spinster aunt for the rest of my life. This marriage was my only other option.

Tasha cleared her throat beside me and gave me a warning glance when I turned. I knew that look. It screamed, *Get on with it!*

"You look nice," I whispered, shocked to realize that I wanted to squeeze her hand. I hadn't voluntarily made physical contact with anyone in months. "Thanks for being here for me."

Tasha smiled. "Of course I would be here, silly. That's what friends are for."

Her gaze flicked to her handsome, dark-haired husband and she smiled. I had the ridiculous notion that they had somehow learned to communicate without speaking.

"Don't be stupid," I mumbled.

"Did you say something?" Tasha asked, turning back toward me.

"No."

Admit to having such fanciful thoughts? Not in this lifetime. My hands trembled, my fingers fiddling with the dangling baby's breath in my bouquet.

I gritted my teeth in a parody of a smile and tried to look happy as the preacher droned on and on about marriage being a sacred institution.

Still smiling, I ignored the preacher's monotonous speech about love and marriage. I leaned toward Gabriel and whispered, "I certainly hope you weren't planning on a wedding night, mister." I shook my head with a scowl. "Because it's never happening."

Gabriel just looked at me with something...feral in his gaze. I don't know why, but I was relatively certain I knew what that look meant as well.

Want to bet? comes to mind.

I know my eyes bulged as he pulled a two-carat heart-shaped diamond ring from his pocket, followed by two plain gold wedding bands. I knew Gabriel had money. I just didn't realize he had *money*. That ring must have cost a fortune.

The minister—who stopped droning for the moment—looked at me expectantly. He tugged on his collar, pulled a kerchief from his pocket with his other hand and dabbed at the perspiration that ran down the side of his face. That collar must have been hot and horribly uncomfortable. I wondered absently how long he wore it on an average day.

Tasha nudged me in the side and gestured with a nod of her head. "This is where you repeat after him," she whispered, taking the bouquet from me before I shredded the beautiful flowers in my nervousness.

I realized then that *she* must have been behind the appearance of the bouquet in my bedroom and the flowers here in the chapel. I would have to thank her for that later.

"Oh!" I turned my attention back to the preacher, ignored the arched, flowered trellis that surrounded him and blushed. "I'm so sorry, sir, I was um...daydreaming."

He smiled kindly. "That is to be expected, my dear."

I put the thought of flowers and Gabriel's finances out of my head. Besides, I was not marrying the man for his money, just his protection. I would never feel safe anywhere else, even in my own house. Even *I* knew that he'd risk his life to protect me. He'd done it once already. It was probably a good thing I couldn't remember everything that happened that night. I had enough nightmares as it was.

There was little choice in the matter. My choices were marry him, go home or stay with Tasha and always be the fifth wheel. I looked up at my soon-to-be husband and quashed the little hum of desire that shot through me. I fervently prayed that one day I could overcome my hesitance. With the way he affected me, at least this way I had a shot at a family if I could manage to conquer my fears.

The preacher reached out and patted my arm. My skin crawled and my stomach churned at the contact. It was all I could do not to shrink away from his touch.

I knew the old man meant well, on some level. But, part of me still hadn't gotten over the unspeakable violation I experienced six months before. Perhaps I never would get over it.

Swallowing my protest, I gave the man a shaky smile and repeated after him. "I Alicia Marie Chalmers take Gabriel Lucian LeBlanc for my lawful wedded husband..."

The words droned out of my mouth with the same lack of enthusiasm as the middle-aged minister's previous speech. Then, after what seemed like an eternity, I was finally finished.

I don't remember Gabriel saying his vows. Although I'm sure he did. Because soon, too soon, the preacher smiled down at us and informed him that he could kiss the bride.

Oh, God. It was all I had time to think before my husband's head lowered to mine and he placed a feather soft kiss on my lips. I knew he had to do it. It would have looked odd for me not to want him to kiss me. Especially after I allowed the minister to believe I was pregnant with his child.

I licked my lips. He tasted a little of cinnamon, with the hint of something else I couldn't identify and I wondered what kind of toothpaste he used. Whatever it was, I liked it.

He stared at me for a moment, his eyes shuttered. I tried to read him again but, as usual, failed miserably. Reading him was the one thing I had continually failed at since I learned how to use most of my powers. The very same powers my Aunt and Grandmother never wanted me to learn to use.

I'm sure they never wanted me to be gang raped either, but *that* is another story.

Still, the kiss wasn't as bad as I thought it would be. I pulled away from my new husband and shuddered at my mental use of the word. I was comforted that, at least, in this day and age, he couldn't demand any conjugal rights. It still didn't make me any less nervous.

If there was one thing I'd learned over the last few months, it was that men like Micah and Gabriel were somewhat above the law. Either that or they just kept finding ways around it.

I looked up into his eyes again and saw...pain? Whatever it was, he masked it before I could really get a good look. Why did I get the feeling he'd read my mind? I shook it off. It was an absurd notion anyway.

"That's just ridiculous," I told myself in a near whisper.

Gabriel leaned closer to me. His warm breath fanned my cheek and I fought the urge to pull back.

"Not if you believe."

His gaze raked my face and, for a moment, settled on my lips. They tingled a bit in remembrance of the soft kiss he had just placed upon them. I lowered my gaze to stare at my feet as a small, traitorous part of me wondered what it was like for a man to physically love me. Not just to be screwed, fucked or whatever other crude word can be used. But to be actually made love to.

I shook off the curiosity and forced myself to remember the pain of the horrifying night I had lost my innocence to a group of Satan worshippers. I certainly didn't want to experience that ever again.

First, the group of men murdered my aunt and grandmother. Then they tried to use me as a sacrifice to release their Dark Lord—whom they believed to be Satan—from his imprisonment in another dimension. It was all so fantastic, for a while I thought I'd gone mad. I refused to go through that again. I would rather die first.

No. I *would* die first.

Tears filled my eyes and I wished them away. I'm not sure why, but they came so easily these days. Lost in thought, I jumped when Gabriel lightly touched my hand.

I ignored the man I now called husband as the preacher shook his hand and congratulated us. My obstinate mind refused to release the memory of that gentle kiss he had pressed against my lips.

"Would you care to pay your respects to your aunt and grandmother? I have roses in the car."

Gabriel's fingers tangled with mine for an instant. He lifted my hand to his lips, pressed a kiss to the back of my hand, and then dropped it before I could pull away. I didn't know what it was about the man, but he had the uncanny ability to know exactly when I've reached my limit.

I nodded my assent and marveled that he remembered I visited their graves once a week on this day. With everything that happened, even I had forgotten. Yet he hadn't.

"I remember everything about you," he breathed into my ear. "As I promised, I will care for you till death do us part."

Warm breath fanned my cheek. Little shivers of delight dancing up my spine, caused goose bumps to follow in their wake. I frowned at the strange sensations he made me feel in the pit of my stomach without even trying. I didn't want to feel anything where any man was concerned. Especially desire.

A soothing balm moved within my mind, helping me to relax. I wondered, however briefly, if he had anything to do with it. I shook my head again and brought myself back to my senses. I'm not usually one for fanciful thoughts like those.

Gabriel still stood silently, his arm out, waiting patiently for me to take it or not. He had to know the likelihood that I wouldn't, but he still waited. I admired him for that.

I took it. Sort of. I placed my still trembling hand on his solid forearm over his suit jacket. I felt his smile all the way to my toes as he led me back up the aisle. Warmth spread up my arm from where my hand rested on his sleeve. Gooseflesh rose on my arms as we exited the chapel. My face heated and my body burned. Heat pooled in my middle as I tried to ignore how close he was to me. How could such an innocent touch and a smile affect me that way?

Chapter Two

W E EMERGED FROM THE CHURCH AND STROLLED SLOWLY INTO THE
bright afternoon sunlight. All the while, I told myself that we were doing
nothing more than keeping up the pretence of being a loving couple for the
aged minister.

"Wait a minute," I said, pausing just outside the chapel. "Aren't we
supposed to sign papers or something?"

I have never been to a wedding before, but I do watch TV. I stopped and
looked up into his liquid silver gaze.

Gabriel smiled and I closed my eyes out of self-defense. I had to admit that
I loved that smile. The man was so handsome he was nearly a God. I may not
have wanted anything to do with men, but I still knew a prime example of
manhood when I saw it.

Let's face it—I was scared, not dead.

"We have already signed them. I'm sure you don't remember because you
have been so distraught over our marriage." He gave me a sympathetic look
and covered my hand with his own. "I would have taken away your fears if it
had been within my power to do so."

He removed his hand when I started to pull free of the contact. The
warmth of his touch lingered on my fingers even after he let me go.

Baby steps. I reminded myself and left my hand resting lightly on his arm.

"I'm sure you would have, these are my demons. I'm the one who is going
to have to exorcise them from my life. No one can do it for me."

He lowered his head in a slow nod. "As you wish."

I blinked slowly. I finally understood what it was that Tasha found so
irritating about that particular phrase. I could wish for so many things.
Wonderful things. Impossible things. However, it didn't make them any more
likely to be mine.

I could wish that Aunt Mag and Grandma were still alive or that I never
allowed them to sacrifice themselves for me in the first place.

Hindsight *is* twenty-twenty and I knew that the price they paid for my life had been too high. I would never be as strong as they were and I feared I wasn't worth it.

Unshed tears burned my eyes as Gabriel ensconced me into his sleek, black limousine, and I waited for Tasha and her husband, Micah, to join me.

I gasped at the huge bouquet of my favorite roses that sat on the seat. I ignored the other two bouquets—one white, the other red. Instead, I picked up the large bundle of peace roses and buried my face in the fragrant blooms.

The other couple sat across from me and then Gabriel slid in next to me, facing the front. I chose to ignore him by keeping my face buried in the fragrant blossoms.

Tasha leaned forward, rested her hand on mine and said, "I know you didn't want to do this. But we have to go to Europe and settle a few things with Micah's estates." She cast a glance at her husband, before she turned back to me. "We couldn't leave you alone."

I laughed. It sounded hollow even to my ears. "Of course you couldn't. I'm still not stable and could end it all at any time." It was an attempt to sound flippant, but the ever-present resentment that she thwarted my suicide attempt six months ago, was still a bit raw.

"It's not that," Tasha denied, then blushed. "Well, it's *mostly* not that. We were afraid that someone would try and kidnap you again while we were gone."

She looked at me with tears in her eyes then lowered her gaze to stare at her hands in her lap. "I couldn't bear for you to go through that again."

She felt responsible for what happened to me and, selfish bitch that I am, even after six months, I still hadn't disabused her of the notion. A part of me blamed the world for what happened that night.

"I should have gotten there sooner," Tasha mumbled. "If I had only been ten minutes faster, you wouldn't have gone through any of that."

Her tears were familiar and real. Suddenly I was tired of making the poor woman feel bad. It wasn't her fault. Torturing her about it wasn't going to change the fact that it happened and I would remain forever changed. Forever soiled. Even after six months, I still showered at least twice a day. I never felt clean anymore.

Gabriel shifted next to me as if he wanted to say something, but refrained.

Sighing, I finally forgave her for not getting to me before those monsters stole my innocence. I also forgave myself for not being strong enough to prevent the events that transpired that night. Not that the fault really lie with either of us.

For a while, we'd both blamed her inexperience and lack of speed in identifying the open portal in time. I figured it was finally time to let her off the hook.

"You couldn't have found me any sooner, Tasha." I gave her a wry smile and shrugged my shoulders. "There was no way for you to know what was happening to me."

"I should have found the tear faster," she said as she wiped the tears from her eyes. She relaxed against her husband, rested her head on his shoulder and entwined their fingers together.

"You must listen to her. I have told you the same as well, my love," Micah chimed in.

He gazed at her with so much love in his dark eyes, I felt...jealous or something. I'd never been attracted to Micah, even with his tall, dark good looks, but a part of me wanted the kind of relationship they had.

Micah rested his hand over Tasha's swollen belly and whispered something in her ear. They shared everything. Their happiness, their tears. They even managed to share the child that still grew within her womb.

Suddenly, I realized that I wanted that rare intimacy that two people who really care for one another share. The only problem was that no matter how much I wanted that kind of life, I feared it more.

Gabriel, on the other hand, was another matter entirely. The man was always as cool as January in a crisis and as hot as any raging inferno when he looked at me.

Quite often, the man had me both shivering and simmering at the same time. How he managed it, I would never know.

Tasha lifted their clasped hands, pressed a kiss to her husband's knuckles, then smiled up into his eyes. I looked on with some measure of envy and wondered if I would ever be comfortable enough with my husband to be able to do that. I fought the urge to steal a peek at him as he sat beside me.

Gabriel shifted and rested his hand next to mine. Our fingers almost touched and the warmth of his hand seeped into my fingers. I resisted the wild urge to cover his hand with my own. I wanted to be closer to him. I even wanted to feel the safety of his embrace, but I feared the implications of that action more. The last thing I wanted was for him to expect more than I was willing to give.

Returning my gaze to my friend, my thoughts returned to our previous conversation, and shook my head. There was no way she could have found the dimensional tear any faster than she did. I knew it, even if she didn't.

I waved my hand in front of her face. "Hello! I was the one who caused the tear in the first place. Remember? I attempted to open a portal to draw the other-dimensional creatures forth. I knew enough, even then, that if I opened a gateway to another dimension, the entities who exited through it would be bound to me and would have to do my bidding." I inhaled deeply and sighed.

"I did it hoping to order them to my aid. How could I have known that in my inexperience I could open it just anywhere?" I shrugged. "Although, I should have known anything could happen. Every time my aunt and grandmother opened a portal, it usually came with the disclaimer, *Do not do this at home,* or something as equally annoying."

I had to try it. My life depended on getting help from somewhere, anywhere, fast. In fact, I would most likely be dead right now, if not for that novice attempt to open the portal. Otherwise, Tasha, as a neophyte Guide, would never have found us in time and those monsters would have killed me soon after they had opened their own portal.

Sometimes I wondered if I would have been better off. However, those times were constantly becoming fewer and farther between and I didn't miss them a bit.

For the most part, I like my life. I even liked the part about having to marry an overbearing jerk with delusions of numerous sexual encounters with me. Which, unbeknownst to him, were in his dreams.

Gabriel leaned over and I suppressed the ridiculous urge to scurry across the vehicle and join Tasha and Micah on the other seat.

"Perhaps, if it is necessary," he breathed into my ear. His voice, as always, was deep, husky. It touched a chord deep inside me that only he had been able to stir to life.

Little flames of desire crawled through my belly, licking at my flesh. Warmth pooled in my middle and my nipples hardened to tight buds.

Clenching my teeth, I looked out through the window and fought the surprising impulse to climb into his lap and kiss his socks off.

Instead, I made a face, glared at him and swatted him on the leg. "Cut it out."

I rubbed my ear to remove the tingling sensation of his warm breath against my skin. If I didn't know better, I would think he knew exactly what that did to me. I scowled. It irritated me, that's what it did. And, if I keep telling myself that, I just might start to believe it.

Making a face, I ignored the knowing smirks from the two on the other side of the limousine. I refused to give them the satisfaction of knowing he'd aroused me in the slightest. I rubbed at the goose bumps on my arms and glowered at them both instead.

"No comments from the peanut gallery either."

Tasha sniggered and leaned farther into Micah's side. He leaned down with a smile and placed a chaste kiss on the top of her head.

"I hope you two will be able to work out your differences by the time we get back."

Her gaze darted between us and she released Micah's hand. Unlatching her seatbelt, she moved across the floor to sit beside me and looked deep into my eyes. She took my hand in hers and squeezed.

"Gabriel is quite possibly the only man who will ever truly understand who you are and where you're coming from." She glanced over at her husband before she continued. "He was there that night, too, remember. He has his own monsters to deal with."

Her gaze flicked to Gabriel for a moment.

"Like me, he has to deal with the guilt of not getting there sooner himself. Give him a chance." She smiled sadly. "You don't have to sleep with him to get to know him better." She shot a glance across my lap to Gabriel. "And God knows he's certainly old enough to have patience with you."

She squinted and made a little moue in his direction. Then she leaned closer to me and said, sotto voce, "He's older than he looks, you know, but *that's* his story to tell."

"Now why doesn't it surprise me to find out he has secrets?" I made a face then looked at him. "And you didn't deem it necessary for me to know these things before we were married?"

"I don't think he wanted you to know until you were married," Tasha said with a grin. "There are a few other things he's going to tell you about Micah and me as well."

She sat up with a grin and neatly changed the subject. "Oh, look! We're back at our house." She checked her watch. "I'd love to invite you in, but we have just enough time to pick up our bags and head to the airport."

She squeezed my hand again and smiled. "This is your wedding day. Go, have some fun. I'll instruct our driver to take the rest of your things to Gabriel's..." She cut herself off. "Your house, first thing in the morning."

Quickly kissing my cheek, she waved gaily as she stepped from the vehicle. "Have fun getting to know each other."

"Yeah, right," I grumbled, as she pushed the door shut in my face. I looked over at my new husband and tried not to scream out my frustration.

Gabriel just smiled at me, "Where would you like to go for dinner?" he asked, reaching across the seat in front of us to knock on the glass that separated us from the driver.

The partition slid down. "Yes, sir?"

"Take us over to the cemetery, Carlisle, you know which one," he said, then settled back into the seat next to me.

Of course, he knew which one. It was the same cemetery he followed me to every week for the last six months. His excuse was that he feared for my safety.

I feared for my sanity, the man was driving me nuts.

The glass silently slid back into place. Gabriel had released my hand while he talked with the driver and I took the opportunity to scramble across to the other seat.

I needed to keep a safe distance from him. His presence did strange things to my insides when he was that close to me.

I raided the small refrigerator and poured myself a glass of champagne.

Gabriel frowned, "You are too young for spirits."

I snorted. "If I'm old enough to be married, I'm old enough to get plastered on my wedding night. Besides, I'm of legal age and I have been for a long time." He's lucky I didn't go for the several bottles of liquor I saw stored in there.

I watched as his expression changed. I still couldn't read him, but I was at the point where I didn't give a damn what he thought. It was a lot more fun to contemplate not remembering what happened tonight.

So what if I get falling down drunk? Maybe he won't want a drunken wife and will leave me alone. At least for tonight. I knew forever was out of the question. He didn't strike me as the kind of man who would break his wedding vows. He also didn't strike me as a man who would take those vows lightly.

"Why do you still fear me?"

He tilted his head to the side. He looked confused and maybe a little hurt. Like he couldn't understand how I could possibly resist his charm, or something equally narcissistic.

I stared at him with disbelief. "I can't believe you felt the need to ask me that question." I knocked back another glass of champagne. False courage was better than no courage at all. In my opinion anyway.

Shaking head, I looked out the window and watched the passing scenery with disinterest. I waited a few minutes before I turned back to him. Tears filled my eyes as memories of that fateful night flooded my mind.

"You were there. How do you think *you* would feel if someone did that to you?" I wiped the tears from my cheeks. "They took something precious from me. Something that was mine alone to give." I glared at him. "Tell me! How would you feel?" I poured myself another glass.

He pinned me with his silver-eyed gaze. "I would not know. A man tends to deal with these things differently. Although I do think I know how you feel."

"You can't know how I feel," I snarled before taking another big gulp of my drink.

Looking down, I was surprised to see the bottle was already empty. I reached back into the refrigerator for the other bottle of champagne I saw, pried the cork free and poured more into the plastic soft-drink tumbler I used as a flute.

"Like you said, you're a man. Men did this to me. So don't presume to know how I feel." I refilled my glass again and set it, quite forcefully, in the cup holder built into the armrest.

His effort to understand was pissing me off more than anything else. I crossed my arms and stared out the window to avoid his probing look.

He straightened himself in the seat. The black leather creaked and squeaked beneath him. I tried not to think about how he moved to make those noises. What he would look like. How his well-defined muscles would ripple beneath his clothing. I also tried not to think about what he expected of me tonight.

My skin crawled at the memory of the robed men who killed my family. They were fanatical Satan worshippers, dressed all in black. I tried not to remember their rough, pawing hands, their stinking breath, how they climbed on top of me and took turns to ram themselves into my virgin body.

I squeezed my eyes shut, wished for the hideous vision to go away. Would there ever be a time when I would be free of the waking nightmare?

Wrapping my arms around my middle, I swallowed repeatedly to keep myself from being sick. The unspeakable memory of that dreadful night always made me sick to my stomach.

I glared at him. I hated him for a moment. He was a man and I grouped him in with all other males.

"You don't know!" Tears streamed down my face and I swiped at them with the back of my hands. "How could you ever understand the—the humiliation, the outrage I feel at being such a victim?" I forced myself to look into his eyes. "They *raped* me, Gabriel! Don't you see? They made me choose.

They put me in the position of having to choose between my safety and the life of another."

Then those monsters had killed my family anyway. That's what hurt the most. No matter what I did to save their lives, it hadn't been enough. It would never have been enough.

The vehicle came to a halt and I looked out over the headstones, my gaze unerringly drawn to those of my grandmother and aunt. I picked up my drink, downed the contents then set my empty glass aside. I stumbled from the car and ran to the gravesites of my dearest friends.

I stood and stared at their graves for a long time. I barely blinked as I read and reread the inscription on the headstones. I vaguely remember telling Tasha what they would have wanted them to say. If it wasn't for her, I'm sure they would be in unmarked graves.

I don't know how long it was before I finally sank to my knees then broke down and cried. They were my family and I loved them. Why did they have to die and leave me alone to mourn?

Gabriel joined me after a while. With him, he carried the white and red roses I always took to the graves, but had forgotten this time. He sank to his knees next to me, no thought for his tuxedo, and handed me the flowers. I put them in the brass vases on the graves and swallowed around the lump in my throat.

"Thank you," I mumbled, disgraced that I treated him so badly and he was still there for me, doing things for me.

Why was he always near, caring for me when I made no effort to care for him in return? I didn't deserve him.

At least I felt bad for using him. He was convenient. It was the only reason I had married him. What really hurt, though, was he knew it.

Chapter Three

THE SUN SAT HIGH IN THE SKY WHEN I WOKE UP THE NEXT MORNING. IT BEAT through the curtains, making the room warm. I frowned and wondered why no one thought to close the blinds last night.

I raised a trembling hand to my pounding head and moaned. I recalled bits and pieces of my arrival at Gabriel's home the night before and groaned with mortification.

The staff stood quietly in the foyer, lined up to meet their employer's new wife. If I remembered correctly, they'd looked on with barely controlled curiosity, mixed with a healthy dose of contempt.

I couldn't say I blame them. I was so drunk by the time we arrived Gabriel probably could have poured me into a glass if he would have tried.

"I shouldn't have drunk all that champagne on an empty stomach," I said to myself as I threw the covers back and sat up gingerly.

You should not have consumed two whole bottles of champagne, then chased them down with a half-pint of bourbon on an empty stomach.

The thought, which had come both unbidden and unwanted, sounded suspiciously like my husband.

"Oh shut up, smarty-pants," I told my imagination.

Standing up slowly, I curled my toes in the thick rug next to the bed, carefully attempting to acclimatize my still pounding head to the change in altitude. Normally it wouldn't be a problem, but today was definitely a day to err on the side of caution.

I looked down at myself for the first time and paused. My wedding dress was gone. Instead of the dress I had been married in, I wore my favorite nightshirt, yet I had no memory of putting it on.

"What the hell?"

I stared at my attire with the certain knowledge that Gabriel had undressed me. The same man, who had promised not to touch me in a sexual manner, unless I specifically asked him to do so. My skin crawled as the memory of that horrible night six months ago came back to me.

Remembering the hard grip of the cruel men as they pawed at my sensitive flesh made my skin crawl. My breasts ached in remembrance of the painful pinches and bites.

I heard the lewd remarks as if it were happening all over again. Sobbing, I begged the sweating, fat, middle-aged men to leave me alone as they waited their turn to violate me.

Stumbling blindly to the bathroom, I stripped my clothes off with each step as I headed for the shower. I turned on the water and climbed into the stall even though the water was still ice cold.

The cold spray beat down on me and cleared my head. Bathing always seemed to help remove the memory of their rough, grasping hands. I sat on the floor of the shower as the water beat down on me. I brought my knees to my chest and tried to exorcise my demons.

THE WATER HAD LONG since gone cold again when Gabriel found me still huddled on the floor of the shower. I sobbed out my fears and frustration as I tried to hold on to what little was left of my sanity.

I was too exhausted to fight when he picked me up with no thought for his designer suit. He cradled me in his arms and carried me into the bedroom.

He sat down on the chair next to the window with me in his lap and whispered to me, comforted me. His big hands gently stroked my wet hair and back, neither of them traveling any lower than my waist or further forward than my shoulders.

I crossed my arms modestly over my bare breasts and wished for my clothing. After my sobs subsided, he stood, carried me into the bathroom and lowered my feet to the floor. My toes curled in the plush mint-green rug next to the tub. I stood cowed, waiting for my husband to demand his conjugal rights.

"You have no faith in me at all, do you?" he asked, pulling a thick towel from a cabinet.

I stood silently while he wiped me down, his touch no more personal than my doctor's touch had ever been. After he toweled my hair and torso, I watched as he bent, picked up my foot and ran the towel down my leg and around my foot to my toes. I almost flinched when I noticed a muscle tick in his jaw. He was angry.

After I was sufficiently dry, he led me back into the bedroom, walked to the dresser and retrieved some of my under things. He stopped a few feet away and held out his arm.

"Put these on," he said gruffly and then shoved his hands in his pockets. "I am many things, Alicia. Some of them you may even deem monster, but none of them include the title of rapist."

I turned away from him and donned the underwear he brought me. "I—I'm sorry, Gabriel, I just can't..." I cast a glance over my shoulder and pointedly glanced toward his groin.

His silver-eyed gaze bored into mine, but he never once tried to look at my body, even though I knew he wanted sex from me. He looked so angry, his eyes nearly glowed with intensity.

"And I have not asked you to, not yet. Be assured, that when I do, you will be ready."

He arched a perfectly shaped brow and the corner of his mouth turned up in a wry grin.

"I want more than sex from you, Alicia. I want your acceptance, your trust and your love. And the one thing I can afford to do is wait."

I nervously licked my lips and watched his eyes darken as they followed the trail of my tongue.

"I—I need to get dressed," I stated the obvious.

He bowed his head in the affirmative. "Yes, you do." He gave me a lopsided grin and handed me some clothes. "I hope you don't mind, but I took the liberty of getting you a wedding gift. I'd like to show it to you later."

He held up his hand when I would have said something. "I know you do not think of this as a true marriage, but when you have lived as long as I have, you will understand how I know we were meant to be together."

I rolled my eyes. "Yeah, right, like another ten, or fifteen years is really going to make that much of a difference."

I was fishing and he knew it. He'd never told me his age and the one chance I had to find out for sure, I had been so out of it I forgot to check.

I wish I could remember signing that damned marriage certificate. It would have had is birth date on it, I'm sure of it.

He bared his teeth in a shark-like grin. "Get dressed first, then we shall talk." He left the room, leaving me to dress in private.

I MET GABRIEL IN the hall just outside the door to my room. It was a good thing he was there, too. I wouldn't have been able to find my way around the house without a guide. It was huge, and to think, I had thought Micah's house was big.

The antiques on the hall tables made me nervous. Having been clumsy all my life, I knew it was only a matter of time before I tripped and broke something expensive.

He led me down the stairs and into the library. I stopped when we entered and stared in awe at the hundreds of books that lined the fifteen-foot tall shelves.

"Holy sh—cow," I barely stopped myself from swearing. I picked up that bad habit from Tasha. She has a potty mouth from hell.

I glanced at Gabriel from the corner of my eye. He was grinning again and I decided I liked it when he smiled and vowed to try to get him to do it more often. I waited for him to seat himself on the long sofa in front of the fireplace, then took the empty chair opposite him. I frowned.

He looked nervous. I couldn't help the thought that a man as powerful and as good-looking as he, had no reason to be nervous about anything. His grin got broader and I had the distinct impression he had been reading my mind.

"I have been," he said and leaned forward to rest his elbows on his knees.

The wrinkled, water-stained condition of his beautiful suit did not escape my attention and I felt guilty. It had probably cost several hundred dollars.

"Do you feel better?"

"What?" Since I had been thinking about his suit, I was sure I had missed something.

"Do you feel better?" he leaned further forward in his seat. "When I came to you earlier, did it comfort you, in some small way?"

"I...well, yes," I stammered, not sure where he was going with this.

"Then that is all that matters." He looked down at himself. "Do not worry about my suit."

"But—but it must have cost you hundreds of dollars. How can I just forget about it?"

He smiled softly. "I have already forgotten about it. Don't you know that you mean more to me than a sixteen-hundred dollar suit?" He looked up and winked at me. "You will always mean more to me."

My mouth dropped open and I snapped it shut with an audible clack. "But—but sixteen-hundred dollars?" I almost choked on the words.

He ruined an expensive designer suit and he thought it was worth it because he made me feel better?

He nodded his gaze meeting mine. "Yes, and I would do it again and again if necessary." He tilted his head. "Have you not realized how I feel about you?"

I shook my head, my eyes widened, still dumbfounded by his revelation. I don't know if it was the knowledge that he had ruined such an expensive suit just to comfort me or if it was the cost that stunned me to silence.

He leaned further forward and rested his elbows on his knees. "You are more important to me than a thousand of these suits."

I didn't know what to say to that, so I just sat there staring at him in stunned silence. Besides, after that revelation, there was just nothing left to say.

Gabriel leaned back in his seat looking nervous. "There is something between us that must be said. You must understand what I am and what I do."

I shrugged. "I already know what you do, Gabriel, you're a *Cartuotey*, like Micah."

I have found, through my limited experience that a *Cartuotey* is a paranormal cop, for lack of a better word. They keep everyone from realizing that the evil entities from other dimensions exist.

He nodded then cleared his throat. "Yes, I am."

I watched fascinated as he removed his tie and unbuttoned the collar of his shirt. Somehow, the fact that he was exposing all of that tanned flesh didn't alarm me.

"A *Cartuotey* is destined to have one mate. Without that mate, he or she is fated to live life never knowing the joy of unconditional love. I can love, but will never be truly loved in return by anyone other than my true mate." He fidgeted for a minute before he continued.

"There are very few ways to tell one's mate. The most common is physical contact." He stopped for a moment, most likely searching for the right word.

"You mean sex," I finished for him.

He gave me a curt nod, clearly uncomfortable bringing that subject up with me.

"Another less common way is for the *Cartuotey* and the Guide to spend enough time together that the Guide falls in love with their mate, thus negating the need for physical contact to make the identification.

"When a Guide falls in love with a *Cartuotey*, a connection is made. It is a mental connection that identifies them as the one." He gave me a crooked grin. "At that time, the Guide does not fear a physical union. Besides I would not have such a strong mental bond with you if you were not my mate."

"In other words, they fall tail over teakettle in love with their mate whether they really *like* him or not?" I asked incredulous. "Pardon my language, but who thinks up this shit, anyway?" Then I thought of something that I needed clarified. "What do you mean by mental bond? Is a *Cartuotey* mate always a Guide? "

I almost swooned at his nod. Did that mean if I'm not his mate, there could be another *Cartuotey* waiting out there who might not be as patient with me?

"Yes, a Guide is always a mate. As to the bond, our mental bond allows us to communicate through our minds."

Immediately beginning to shake, I waved my hand in his face. "I can't handle anymore, right now. Can we take a break from reality for a bit? Let's concentrate on fantasy, just for a little while." I wanted nothing more at the moment than to go home, throw myself on my bed and cry.

Gabriel stirred in his seat, but remained seated. "You are home."

I jerked my head up. "How do you do that?" I demanded.

He grinned. "How do I do what, read your mind?" He winked at me. "I know everything you're thinking. I know the inside of your grandmother's house almost as well as you do. How you love the rolling hills behind the farm, the rough country between the trails. How you always adored the smell of her kitchen."

"How...how can you know all that?"

I searched my mind, tried to remember if I had told any of that to anyone. I hadn't, I *knew* I hadn't.

Gabriel sighed. "I do not wish to frighten you, but you must know this. Regardless of my feelings, you have a right to know."

I felt a degree of trepidation at that remark and was almost afraid to ask, "I have a right to know what?"

He rubbed his hands over his face. I wasn't sure if he was tired or scared. "I am a vampire." He took a deep breath, looking resigned. "All *Cartuotey* are vampires."

My mouth dropped open and I had the ridiculous thought that it was becoming a regular occurrence lately. I shook my head with disbelief.

"I've married a madman." He was beautiful and patient, but he was definitely a couple of sandwiches short of a picnic.

He sat there, looking at me with his eyebrow still raised as if *I* was the person who needed their head examined.

201

"I can prove it," he said, looking at me rather desperately. "Would you like me to?"

What was I supposed to say to that? I didn't know, so I didn't answer him. Mostly because I didn't know which was worse, being married to a man who is delusional, or actually being married to a vampire?

I stood up and ran from the room. I found my way back to the bedroom he'd given me, threw myself on the bed and hugged the pillow, thinking.

Sometime during my pondering, I fell asleep and began to dream. I like dreaming. Well, to be more specific, I like lucid dreaming. In a lucid dream, I can be things and do things I cannot or will not do in real life, like fly. It's really kind of freeing. I would suggest everyone try it at least once.

Anyway, I digress. The dream had my husband in it. Surprise, surprise. Only he wasn't the tough, overbearing, macho, rarely smiling Gabriel who was a major pain in my ass. But one who was free with both his conversation and his smiles.

He gave me a look that could melt stone and my dream body responded enthusiastically. Very enthusiastically. Heat pooled low in my stomach and I actually enjoyed his nearness, instead of fearing it. Why, I couldn't, begin to fathom.

I watched entranced as he moved slowly, approaching me as if he were afraid I would bolt like a scared doe. In real life, I'm sure I would have but this was a dream after all. I could do anything in a dream.

He moved closer, his every move fluid and full of male grace. His muscles rippled temptingly under the transparent white silk shirt he wore and I swallowed thickly. He stopped in front of me, gazing down.

"Are you just going to stand there?" I asked, placing my right hand on his chest and gazing up into his eyes.

He looked surprised. I would have understood that, had this not been a dream. I decided not to worry about it. It wasn't real, so why bother?

He lowered his head toward mine. "I'm going to kiss you," he said, then paused. "Do you wish to stop me?"

He looked down at me, one eyebrow raised. I had the ridiculous urge to tell him that if he continued to do that, his face would freeze that way.

He grinned then and I had the distinct impression my dream Gabriel could read my mind as well. His head began its slow descent again and my lips tingled in anticipation of his kiss.

I didn't say why I felt so free in the dream. There were no fears, no shudders of distaste when he touched me, only pleasure as his lips caressed mine. He lifted his hands, feathered his fingers through my hair and tilted my head to the side, for better access. His tongue touched my lips, begging for entrance to my mouth.

This tender seduction was nothing like the violation I had experienced six months before. Gabriel was so caring, so gentle. He pulled his lips from mine, allowed them to hover just above my mouth.

"There is only you and I here, Alicia. Bury those horrible memories. That time is long gone. Come away with me on a sensual journey where I will show you how real love should be," he breathed against my lips. "Allow me to touch you, to love you."

I moaned in response as one of his hands lowered to my back. He stroked my sensitive flesh, his hand circled down to the rise of my rear. He was so gentle it brought tears to my eyes. This is the way my first time should have been.

"As far as I am concerned, when we do finally make love, it *will* be your first time. You are as pure as a newborn babe, my heart. Never doubt that." His hand gave my butt a squeeze before he lifted me and pressed me against the hard evidence of his desire.

"Do you feel how much I want you?" he asked, his lips trailed against my neck. The semi-rough abrasion of his cheek against mine made me shiver. Little flames flew through my bloodstream winging their way lower, to my womb and it clenched with suppressed need.

I nodded, "Yes, I feel it." Panting with desire, I reached down, pausing for a moment before I tentatively grasped his growing penis through his slacks and he groaned.

Gabriel pulled back and rested his forehead against mine. "You don't know what you do to me." He took a deep breath, moved his hands up to rest them on my shoulders. "I have to stop."

"Stop? Why?"

The first time I had ever really wanted him to touch me and he backed off. Did I do something wrong? Tears of frustration burned my eyes. He didn't really want me. He was just teasing me.

"Of course I want you. I just do not want to rush you. You need to understand there is such a thing as control. A man who has honor can assert that control." He stood, reached over to lift my chin with his fingers and looked into my eyes. "He does this even when he wants nothing more than to do what he knows is wrong at the time."

"It's not wrong." I shook my head. "How can it be when I want you to?"

Was I whining? God, I hoped not!

He shook his head. "You are not truly ready. When you are truly ready, we will consummate our marriage and you will no longer fear me." He stepped back, studied my face, still staring into my eyes. "I will come to your dreams again, sweetheart, never doubt it. And one day, you will welcome me."

The fantasy faded and I blinked my eyes and realized I was awake. My body still hummed with desire and my panties were wet with the evidence of my need.

I never, ever expected to feel this way about any man. This all-consuming hunger, this yearning, was all so very new to me. I wondered, however briefly, if the real Gabriel was as good as the one in my dream.

Chapter Four

A SOFT KNOCK ON THE DOOR BROUGHT ME FROM MY SLEEP. I SAT UP IN the bed, stretched then pushed the hair out of my eyes.

"Yes?"

The door opened a crack and a young woman peered into the room. "Hello, I'm Cassie. I'm your personal companion."

"Excuse me? I have a personal companion?" I asked, frowning. "Do you mean like a maid or something?"

The woman's face reddened a bit. "Yes, I suppose, if that's what you want to call me."

It didn't take a rocket scientist to figure out that she found that particular title demeaning.

"I don't need a maid." I looked around the room, trying to screw up the courage to extend an olive branch, so to speak. "I do need a friend, though."

She smiled, looking relieved. "I can certainly be that."

I stood up, walked over to one of the chairs in the sitting area and sat down. I waved my hand to the chair opposite me.

"Have a seat."

"Thank you." She sat on the edge of the chair across from me, her spine stiff.

"Relax, why don't you? I don't bite."

She grinned. "I'm sure you don't. If you don't mind my asking... How did you meet Mr. LeBlanc?" She stared at the wall, a dreamy expression on her face. "Was it romantic?"

"Hardly," I replied, immediately uncomfortable. Did this young woman have the hots for my husband?

I hope not.

I shook my head and pushed the jealous thought aside. I didn't give a crap about him so what did I care if she was attracted to him? I realized when I asked myself that question that I did care. Very much. I would have hated to kick her ass, seeing as we were just becoming friends and all.

"Let's just say he saved my life the night we met and leave it at that. I—I..." I looked down at my feet. "I really don't like talking about it."

I was not about to tell a complete stranger about my sordid past. I didn't want, nor need, her sympathy.

Cassie reached across the empty space that separated us to pat my knee. "If you ever feel like you want to talk, I'm here for you. I'd like to be your friend." She stood and smoothed down her slacks. "I've forgotten my organizer in my room. If you don't mind, I'd like to go get it then schedule some activities to keep us busy."

I pressed my lips together and narrowed my eyes. "You mean that Gabriel would like you to keep me busy."

The thought had me gritting my teeth. If that—that *man* even dreamed of being with me, the way Micah was with Tasha he certainly had another think coming. I was not about to let the man tell me what to do on a daily basis. Just because Tasha decided she liked it, it certainly didn't mean I would.

A blush dusted Cassie's cheeks. It might have made her look a bit attractive, or pixie-like, if she wasn't so busy attempting to look innocent.

"I didn't say that."

"You didn't have to."

"He thought you might get bored during the day and suggested we work out a schedule of routine activities." She tried to make excuses for his highhanded tactics.

I scowled, stood up and stalked from the room. "Where the hell is he?"

Cassie hurried to catch up with me. I had a distinct advantage since I was about four inches taller than she is even though I'm not tall by any means. My longer legs ate up the distance quickly.

The muffled sound of her hurried footsteps following behind irritated me. It was if they didn't trust me enough to leave me to my own devices.

Was he afraid I would make off with the good silverware or something? The thought gave me pause. Maybe he didn't trust me to be alone. Not because he thought I would steal anything, but because I did try to kill myself, after all.

"He's not here. He had a business meeting. He wanted to be sure..." Cassie let her voice trail off as if she realized she was about to say too much.

"He wanted to be sure of what? That I would still be here or that I wouldn't suddenly decide to try to kill myself again?" I asked with a snarl then turned to confront her. "Where is the bastard?" I stopped my tirade at the expression on her face. "What?"

"He didn't tell me that you'd tried to…" she put her hand over her mouth as if to say something so horrible would somehow make it true.

"He didn't tell you I tried to kill myself with an overdose of sleeping pills six months ago?"

She shook her head. "Why would you want to do such a thing?"

"I did it because I've been having a hard time coming to terms with the fact that I'm still alive and my grandmother and aunt are dead, because of me."

"Did you kill them?"

I looked at her, startled. "Of course not!"

"Then they aren't dead because of you."

"They sacrificed themselves for me."

Cassie nodded as if she suddenly understood. "They gave their lives to protect yours and you repay that debt by making an attempt on your own life? That definitely makes sense." She shook her head. "It sure sounds like a poor way to thank them if you ask me."

"I—I never thought about it that way."

I *hadn't* thought about it that way. My attempt to kill myself *was* a poor way to thank them for giving their lives for mine. They had wanted me to live. Maybe it was time I attempted to make something of my life.

Cassie smiled sadly. "When we're hurt, we seldom think of the things that others, who care about us, do." She reached out and grasped my elbow as we approached a door.

"This is my room. I would like to go in and get my organizer, if you don't mind. I'm rather lost without it."

I nodded. "Sure, go ahead."

As soon as she was out of sight, I walked down the hall at an accelerated rate.

"I don't need a babysitter, dammit! I refuse to let either of them force me to have a constant companion." I couldn't stand the thought of never having time to myself.

"Who gives a shit if Mr. High and Mighty isn't home?" I mumbled to myself. The two of us would have a nice little chat later. I picked up my pace even more when I heard a door shut on the second floor and *my companion* call my name.

I told her I didn't need a keeper and I damn well meant it. There was a lot of thinking I wanted to do and I certainly couldn't do it here. I ran out through the back door and into the garden behind the house.

A stream bubbled merrily in the woods behind the back garden. A small, wooden footbridge spanned the narrow ribbon of water. I hurried across the bridge, ignoring the handrail and the siren's call of the cool musty scented water.

The water called to me, begged me to take off my shoes and sink my feet into its cool depths. I ignored it and kept walking deeper into the forest.

The air was so clean here and the woods seemed friendly, not frightening in the least. Still, I kept to the path. The last thing I needed was to get lost. I didn't want anyone to think I'd made another attempt on my life. They just might decide to have me institutionalized.

I needed to think and I wanted to be alone to do it. I couldn't do that back at the house with Cassie's constant presence. The more I thought about it, the angrier I got.

"How dare that jerk hire someone to keep tabs on me?" I mumbled to myself and stomped over to a large flat rock that hung over a small glassy pond.

The large flat stone looked inviting, so I sat down. The water was cool and the day unseasonably warm for mid-September. Giving in to temptation, I took off my shoes, dangled my feet in the cool water and settled down to do some serious soul searching.

I laid back, put my hands behind my head and relaxed. A cool breeze blew over me and I inhaled deeply. The scent of pine and moss tickled my nose. The calming sound of the forest relaxed me and at some point, I started to doze.

"CASSIE IS WORRIED SICK about you." Gabriel's voice woke me from my light slumber.

My heart nearly jumped into my throat at the thought that anyone could have snuck up on me. Trying to act nonchalant, I sat up, looked up at him and gave him a one-shoulder shrug.

"She'll get over it."

He sat down next to me, obviously careful not to get too close lest he scare me away.

"*I* was worried about you."

"You'll get over it, too." I glanced down at my feet as they dangled in the water. I'd come to a decision after Cassie's comment. I thought it only fair to tell him. "I won't make another attempt on my life, Gabriel."

He held my gaze for a moment. "I apologize for my efforts to keep you busy. I don't want to lose you."

"Your trying to keep tabs on me, you mean," I argued, angry that he thought I was dumb enough to believe that. "I don't know why you even bothered. You don't even know me."

He turned to look out over the smooth water of the pond. He brought his foot up onto the rock, wrapped his arms around his knee and watched as a fish—a trout I think—jumped out of the water after a bug. It did a graceful somersault in midair, then fell back into the glistening water.

"I know I love you. That is all that matters." He stood, gathered my shoes to slip them on my feet when I pulled them out of the water. "I cannot bear the thought of losing you." He put my left shoe on, then stopped what he was doing to look into my eyes. "I ask that you accept that weakness in me."

I reached down to grab my right shoe. "I'm not a child and you needn't dress me like one."

Meeting my gaze, his eyes stared into mine. They burned with a light I wasn't sure I wanted to understand. I think it was desire. If it was, it was nothing like anything I had ever experienced before.

"No, you are most definitely not a child. You are a woman," he said, leveling his gaze. "You are my woman and I cherish you."

When he offered me his hand, I sat and stared at it for the longest time. Did I want to take it? Accepting his hand was a lot more than it seemed. Letting him take my hand in his was akin to saying I trusted him. Did I really want to give that impression?

"I offer you my hand in friendship. It is all I ask, for now. It will be enough to know that you will at least try to trust me."

I looked back up, met his silver-eyed gaze for a moment and knew he meant what he said. He wanted to hold my hand, nothing more. I slowly raised my hand, placing it in his much larger and warmer one.

"Come. Let's go back to the house. It will be dark soon.

Nodding my assent, I fell in step beside him.

"May I request one thing of you?" he asked, as he continued to lead me back to the house.

I watched him from the corner of my eye and wondered if I should pull my hand free.

"It depends on what it is."

He grinned. "Smart girl. Never agree to anything until you know the terms."

Stopping, he pressed a quick kiss to the back of my hand and released it before I could pull free of his grip.

"Please do not travel so far out of sight of the house while you are alone again."

"I thought you weren't going to infringe on my freedom?"

He shook his head. "I'm not, my heart. There are bears and other wild animals in these woods. It is too dangerous for you to wander about unprotected."

Unprotected.

The word shimmered between us, making me shiver as I thought about all of the things that could have happened to me while I was being childish. The people who killed my family could have found me while I slept. What if I had awoken tied to another altar, stripped of my clothing while they did unspeakable things to my body?

"Oh." I bit my lip. "I wouldn't have wandered so far from the house had I thought about it."

Something dark flickered in his eyes and I got the impression that he didn't believe me.

"Don't you dare give me that look, dammit! I know I've been thoughtless and just plain stupid in the past. But that doesn't mean I *still* have a death wish." I had the ridiculous urge to give him a good smack somewhere tender.

"Cassandra made a very valid point with me this afternoon and I'm inclined to agree with her."

Gabriel cocked his head to the side and studied me for a minute. "What point was that?"

"That Grandmother and Aunt Margaret wanted me to live. I would not be thanking them for their sacrifice if I committed suicide." I shrugged. "They obviously wanted me to live and I've decided that I don't want to squander the gift they paid for with their lives."

He seemed to breathe a sigh of relief.

"You're glad?"

"I'm ecstatic," he said with a smile.

The action transformed his face, made him look younger, almost boyish. I started to walk again and he fell in step beside me before he took my arm and stopped abruptly.

I turned, pulled my arm from his grip. "What's wrong?"

I ignored the beautiful ferns and flowers that grew wild in the forest to look up into his eyes.

He took my hands in his. "You are the greatest gift I have ever been given. I treasure every moment I am fortunate enough to spend in your company. I do not expect you to believe how precious you are to me." He looked away, but not before I saw what I'm sure was pain flash in his beautiful eyes.

"Do you think..."

When he paused, I wondered what he wanted to say that would make him that nervous. I had never seen him like this before. Usually, the man exuded self-confidence.

I tore myself free from his searching gaze and stared at his tanned throat just above his collar. I had a good idea of what he was about to say and I wasn't sure I could tell him the truth, no matter how much I wanted to.

He swallowed and I watched his throat work. "Do you think you could ever trust me?" He hurried to add, "I can wait, forever if necessary. I only ask for hope."

What could I say? I could only tell him the truth. He deserved at least that much.

"I—I don't know."

His eyes darkened to a steel gray as he watched my tongue moisten my lower lip. It was the same reaction my dream Gabriel had when I had done the same in my sleep. Suddenly, the brave part of me, the part that wanted to go on living, decided to trust him, just a little.

"Will you..." I swallowed around the lump that had formed in my throat. "Will you kiss me?"

What are you saying? My mind raged. *You are out here in the middle of nowhere with him. He could do anything and you wouldn't be able to stop him.*

Nothing but trees and forest surrounded us. Small animals rustled in the underbrush. Rodents, squirrels or chipmunks raced through the tall, dry grass and a soft breeze rustled the leaves on the trees. It blew through the forest, carrying the scent of pine and wet moss. I ignored the remote area we were in, tilted my had back and stared up into eyes which had widened at my unexpected request.

"Are you sure?"

With that selfless thought, with those three simple words, he gave me something I never thought I would have since the night those men brutally raped me.

It was a gift we could both cherish. Trust in him and a hope for the future.

Chapter Five

"**Y**ES," I SAID, SMILING SOFTLY. "I DO BELIEVE I AM."

My stomach clenched, felt as though a hundred butterflies took flight inside me when he slowly lowered his head. The press of his lips against mine was soft, feather-light. Like warm wet silk sliding over my mouth.

His lips caressed mine softly and I wondered at the gentleness. My first and only experience with men had been violent, brutal. Horrible memories of that fateful night invaded my mind intruding on my dream and I placed my hands on his chest to push him away.

He lifted his head and looked around us. He waved his arm, indicating the tall swaying trees covered in a canopy of green and full of life. He shuffled his feet, stirring the brown leaves and pine needles on the ground.

"There is only the two of us in this place, Alicia. There is no one else. No monsters hiding in the bushes, no fanatics to try to take you from me. Do not let the dreadful memories of that terrifying night ruin our time together."

He raised his hand and tenderly brushed a stray lock of hair from my face. I trembled beneath his compassionate touch. God, how I wanted to be able to consummate our marriage, but I was just too damn scared.

What he said was so similar to what my gentle dream Gabriel had said, that my mouth dropped open with shock. I did little more than stand there, gaping at him.

He quickly took advantage of my surprise and kissed me again. His tongue swept inside my mouth, examining my teeth quite thoroughly. I fought the slight panicked sensation and tilted my head back. I wanted this. It was an experiment.

Even though it was a rather pleasant event, I would have pulled away if he had wrapped his arms around me. The action would have been too much like a forced plunder. Gabriel knew exactly what he was doing. He kept his hands at his sides and left the choice to continue or end the kiss with me.

I think I could have loved him for that alone but, coupled with his seemingly endless understanding, I'd begun to think perhaps everything would eventually be all right. My mind wandered and I wondered if I would be able to love anyone ever again. Would I be afraid to? Everyone I have ever loved has ended up dead in one way or another. I felt cursed.

I backed away, ending our mutual exploration and cleared my throat. "I'm sorry. I don't..."

He put a gentle finger against my still moist lips and I paused.

"Don't say it. Never say you're sorry. You have nothing to apologize for, my heart."

I flicked my gaze down to his crotch and quickly avoided his gaze by looking over his shoulder. I asked, "What about that?" My hand waved in the general direction of his hardened penis.

He gave me a lopsided grin and chuckled. "*That*," he said, "is my problem. Do not let it worry you."

Gabriel offered me his hand. I hesitated for a minute, then took it. We walked slowly back to the house in companionable silence.

THERE WAS A KNOCK on my bedroom door and it woke me. Yet I knew I was still asleep. The sensation was strange. Somehow I knew was dreaming again.

My stomach clenched as I thought about my dream Gabriel's heated kisses. I sat up, brushed the hair out of my face and the sleep from my eyes.

"Who is it?"

"It's Gabriel. May I come in?"

My stomach knotted with a mixture of anticipation and anxiety as I remembered the kiss in the woods with the real Gabriel. That was only an example of what awaited me if I could manage to overcome my fears.

That kiss had been real, not contrived to be everything I wanted like the one in my dreams. I ignored the answering heat that pooled in my middle and made my nether parts twitch.

"Yes. Come in."

He opened the door and strode into the room. The man was pure unadulterated sex. His form-fitting black jeans left almost nothing to the imagination and his t-shirt looked like it was two sizes too small. It showed every ripple of muscle, every indentation. His darker nipples showed through the stretched thin material, making my stomach clench.

The man looked good enough to eat. I watched him nervously. Would he kiss me again? I swallowed thickly. Would my dream Gabriel show me what it was like? Could he show me the way love should be between a man and a woman? Most importantly, would I be too afraid to couple with him, even in my dreams?

"Such thoughts you have, Alicia," he admonished. "Do you think the only thing on my mind is burying my cock in your tight little pussy?"

I flinched at his use of profanity. "Isn't that what all men constantly think about?" I walked to the other side of the bed. I needed some space and having the bed between us gave me some semblance of security.

"No, Alicia," he shook his head and stepped around to the foot of the big four-poster bed. "Most men, honorable men, think of how to pleasure their lady. They strive to bring her to her pleasure, have her scream out her ecstasy to the heavens. They do not merely think of gratifying themselves."

He moved closer and I fought the urge to take a step back, but that would have put me against the wall and I didn't want to feel trapped.

"I would show you how an honorable man behaves, if you would only allow it."

I shook my head. "This is a dream. It's not real. And you're not really my husband."

He held his arms out to his sides. "But I am. I am the Gabriel of your dreams, come to fulfill your every desire. Your every fantasy."

I didn't have any fantasies. I wasn't sure I dared to. What if things got out of control and I couldn't stop him?

Tears burned my eyes when I thought of all I had lost. I would never have a real family again. How would I ever be able to have children if I couldn't bear a man's touch, let alone be intimate with one?

He reached out and took me in his arms. "Of course we can have a family." He pressed a chaste kiss to my forehead, splaying his large hand across my back. His hand moved in soothing circles as he held me close. I relaxed a bit, resting my head against his chest. His heart beat steadily beneath my ear. Strangely, the sound of his even pulse soothed me, comforted me.

"I will not say your fears are groundless. We both know that is not the case. I know why you fear a physical relationship with me." His hand skimmed over my hair. "I can wait until you are ready to share your body."

I fought the nearly overwhelming urge to sob onto his shoulder. Instead, I pressed my ear tighter against his chest and stared down at the thick comforter that covered my bed and allowed him to hold me. Just for a moment.

"I wish you could have gotten there sooner, Gabriel." Tears ran down my cheeks, soaking his t-shirt.

He took a deep breath and sighed, his hands still moving over me in slow soothing caresses.

"I wish I could have spared you the horror and degradation of that night, as well. It is over, regardless. And no matter how much we may wish it to be different, no one can change that night."

He stood straighter, put me at arm's length and looked into my eyes. "You must be strong and continue your life. You must know that your grandmother and your aunt would want you to learn to live and love again."

I reached up and brushed a stray wheat-colored lock of hair from his forehead, wrapped my hand around the back of his neck and brought his head down to mine.

Gabriel's kiss was everything I hoped it would be. His firm lips pressed against mine and I shivered with unexpected delight.

Gooseflesh rose on my arms and heat pooled in my middle, a reaction I had come to expect while kissing him. His arms slowly wrapped around me, caressing my back and hips. When his tongue caressed the seam of my lips, I took the hint and opened for him. His slow exploration of my mouth was heady and made me feel giddy. My knees buckled and I felt half-drunk with the sensations he introduced in me.

The fire within me burned brighter, flames licked at my flesh until he pulled me up against him and pressed his growing erection against my stomach.

I panicked.

Tearing my mouth from his, I pushed against his chest. "Let me go!"

He released me immediately. "I'm sorry, Alicia. I certainly didn't mean to frighten you." He watched me warily, his breathing uneven.

"I—I..." My hand covered my mouth as tears filled my eyes.

My horrified gaze slid down to the evidence of his desire. His cock jumped behind his zipper in response to my gaze and I felt my face heat with embarrassment.

"I didn't want...I didn't mean to..."

How could I tell him I never meant to be a tease? How could I ever explain that a part of me wanted him with everything in me? Yet, I was still scared. Sex hurts too much. I have never been able to understand why any woman would enjoy it.

"It is not always painful, Alicia."

I jerked my head up and wished he would stop reading my mind. It was still hard to believe he could do that. I didn't put any credence to what he'd said about being a vampire. They certainly did not exist. Even if it was true, and he was a vampire, he would still be the man he had always been. The man I was foolishly beginning to care for.

"Forgive my crude language, my dear, but you were raped, fucked, screwed or whatever crude word you would use to describe it. But you were not made love to."

He brought his hand up and gently stroked my cheek.

"Whatever we should choose to call it, when we finally do merge our bodies, we will be making love. It will never be anything but that."

The butterflies in my stomach took flight again as he leaned over to gently kiss my lips. I was still terrified of him, but his gentle and understanding attitude made me want to try. I didn't know a man could be this tender. Even Micah wasn't this gentle with Natasha.

"Since this is *my* dream, you'll do what I want?" I asked, circling around him.

He nodded.

"Whatever you wish."

The soft glow of the lamp on the other side of the bed softened his features, but still left enough light to look deeply into his eyes.

I believed him.

"Take off your shirt."

He reached up, slowly tore his shirt down the front, then pushed it off his shoulders and dropped the garment onto the floor. It fell in a pile of white cotton at his feet.

I stared in rapt fascination as he tore the shirt and exposed every inch of his tanned chest. Golden hair lightly dusted the exposed flesh, tapering down to disappear beneath the waistband of his slacks.

"May I?" I asked as I lifted my hand toward his chest.

Gabriel nodded, swallowing convulsively when I stroked his torso. The fine hairs sifted through my fingers as I explored his hard, well-defined pectoral muscles. He drew a sharp breath when my fingers circled his flat brown nipples. He groaned and his breath quickened when I drew my fingernails across the small male nubs.

Muscles bunched and quivered as I let my hands make their slow exploration across the expanse of his washboard abs. His stomach clenched and his member moved beneath his slacks. The movement intrigued me. Was it involuntary?

He nodded. "I have little control over my cock when you touch me like that."

Stepping back alarmed, I put my hands behind my back and stared at him, my eyes wide. "You promised!"

He sighed. "I said I have little control over my cock. Not my actions, Alicia. There *is* a difference."

His breathing was uneven and I marveled that I could do that to him. He was older than me and I could only assume, more experienced. The man had a ton of control and it only made me want to trust him more.

He looked me in the eyes. "Yes, I do have a lot of control. You needn't fear me."

His mouth turned up at the corners and he raised his brow as if daring me to make a move.

"This is *your* dream."

I watched him standing in front of me for a minute as he patiently awaited my next move.

His eyes darkened to a stormy gray when I slowly ran my tongue over my lower lip, nervous. The lids lowered and he stared at me with those half-closed eyes. I wished he would stop that. He made me feel...I don't know...sexy or something.

"I can't stop looking at you. You *are* sexy." His voice flowed through me. Touched me in places I never knew existed before that moment.

I jumped when my clit throbbed at the way he looked at me. It surprised me. How could I ignore that look when his heated gaze warmed me to my toes?

"Kiss me," I demanded. "But don't touch me anywhere else."

Gabriel devoured me with his gaze. I felt each of his heated looks like a physical caress. He bent slightly at the waist, lowered his head and gently pressed his mouth to mine. The warm touch of his lips sent the butterflies in my stomach reeling. Warmth seeped between my legs and I wondered if this was what it was like to truly desire someone.

He sucked my tongue into his mouth and caressed mine. I trembled with the need to have him wrap his arms around me. He didn't. He merely stood close to me and held his arms to his sides, keeping his hands to himself as I instructed. Soon, too soon, he lifted his lips from mine and feathered tiny kisses across my cheek and jaw. The raspy brush of his five-o'clock shadow against my flesh only heightened the sensation.

"If you want me to touch you, you only need to ask."

He moved to kiss my eyes, then moved back to my mouth, jaw and finally to my neck. My legs almost gave out and I threw my arms around his shoulders before I fell.

"Hold me, don't let me fall," I panted in his ear, my breath coming in short gasps.

Gabriel brought his hands up and grasped my waist. He held me up, kept me from melting into a puddle on the floor at his feet. His touch felt impersonal compared to the sensational press of his lips against my fevered skin.

"Please, Gabriel, hold me."

His fingers tightened on my waist. "I am," he murmured against my neck as he feathered more soft kisses around my ear. "If you wish for something else, you need only ask. Your wish is my command." The last he whispered in my ear and my legs gave out. His hands tightened on my waist, but he still held me so impersonally.

"I—I want you to..." Unsure how to word my request, I paused and swallowed my fear. This was just a dream. I only hoped it didn't become a nightmare. "Hold me. Caress me like a lover would." I pulled back to look in his eyes. "Caress me the way you would if you didn't have to worry about my fears."

He closed his eyes for a moment. "A lover would hold you like this." He wrapped his arms around me and drew me up against his hard frame. His fingers splayed across my back, his hands gliding down over my rear.

"This is how I would touch you." He breathed against my neck and moved his hand up to cup my breast as his lips moved lower to my collarbone.

His hard shaft pressed into my bellybutton and, for the first time since I lost my family, I wasn't scared of that part of the male anatomy.

"Touch me," he whispered.

I let my hands slide over his shoulders to his chest and down the flat plane of his well-defined stomach. The muscles jumped beneath my fingers as they skimmed above the waistband of his slacks. I smiled to myself when I realized he was ticklish.

My hands shook as I contemplated reaching down to unzip his fly and release his large erection from its fabric prison. Did I really want to go that far?

It's just a dream.

"It is just a dream," Gabriel echoed my thoughts.

I moved my hands back up to his chest to play with his hard nipples.

"Touch me...there."

"Touch you where?" he asked.

I frowned. "I don't believe this. You're going to make me spell it out for you, aren't you?"

Gabriel rested his forehead against mine and looked into my eyes.

"I am yours to command, my love. But command me you must."

He kissed me again, plunging his tongue in and out of my mouth until I pulled away.

"I want you to..." My face burned, showed my mortification. "I want you to play with my nipples. Suck on them." My own words drove me wild with a desire I never thought myself capable of experiencing.

Chapter Six

GABRIEL PUSHED HIS HANDS UP. HIS FINGERS BRUSHED MY STOMACH UNDER my shirt and my muscles clenched. The heat of his hand warmed the underside of my breast, through my bra, and I almost begged him to touch me there.

My nether parts twitched with anticipation and I brought my hands to the front of my blouse. I stared into his eyes as I slowly unbuttoned my top. His breathing became erratic when I uncovered my lacy bra and he buried his face in my cleavage with a low groan.

"Yes," I sobbed, when his mouth closed over my left nipple.

His tongue laved the little bud through the white lace of my bra while his teeth gently abraded the hardened bud. His fingers squeezed my other nipple, pulling it gently to copy the suckling sensation of his mouth. My hips undulated against his.

"Gabriel, please!"

I wasn't sure what it was I asked for. I didn't know. I only wanted him to show me how love should feel.

"What do you want, my love?"

"Love me."

"I do love you, Alicia, more than life itself."

I nearly groaned with frustration. He had to know what he was doing to me. He had to know I was burning up inside and I didn't know what to do to stop it.

"Touch me. Show me what it's supposed to be like." I sobbed into his shoulder. "Show me how to..." *be a real woman.* I couldn't force myself to say it. "Please."

My dream man took pity on me. He slid his warm hand under my nightshirt, over the quivering flesh of my thigh. His long fingers found their way beneath the elastic of my panties and he expertly stroked my throbbing sex. He thrust his fingers deeper within my slit, circled the aching nub with his fingers and I screamed.

"Gabriel!"

Tears ran down my face as a pleasure unlike anything I had ever felt in my life washed over me, through me, like a tidal wave. It was a pleasure so intense I thought I would die.

Is this really what it feels like to make love? My mind whirled as the sensations he introduced me to, almost took priority over my common sense.

"What's happening to me?" I cried, as the intense pleasure swept me away I couldn't think anymore. My emotions ran so high, it was a wonder I could breathe.

Gabriel lifted his lips from my breast and blew on the hardened nub. "You are coming, Alicia. You are having your first orgasm. Relax. Allow yourself to accept it." He kissed me again. His tongue slid into my mouth, his teeth softly nibbling on my lips.

I came down from that euphoric place crying his name in ecstasy.

Does the rest of the act feel as wonderful as this? I asked myself as I stared deep into his eyes.

He smiled softly, pressed my still trembling hand against his straining erection. "It's better."

I woke up with my body screaming for release. My nipples were hard, straining against my nightshirt and my clit twitched out a rhythm that matched that of my dream Gabriel's fingers on my flesh.

"Dammit!"

I lay in my lonely bed, my heart slamming against my ribs. My breasts were full and aching. Both nipples pebbled against the thin cotton of my nightshirt, the brush of the soft material against my sensitive flesh drove me wild.

Curious, I reached up and felt them. A shaft of desire tore through me as I rubbed the hardened peaks. It didn't feel the same as when he did it. The feeling wasn't nearly as intense as before and my clit still throbbed at the memory of my dream Gabriel's touch.

Alicia.

The sound of his voice was almost ethereal. I heard it within my mind, not with my ears. Maybe I was still asleep after all.

On the other hand, I could be a fantasy. Do you want me to be your fantasy, my love?

I latched onto that thought and imagined the sound of his voice as I reached up to caress my nipples through my shirt. Experimenting, I rolled them between my thumbs and index fingers.

The warmth of my desire rushed between my legs and my fantasy man whispered into my mind once more.

Reach down between your legs and feel how wet you are. How your body dreams of mine. How it creams for my touch. Know that the wonderful sensations you felt in your dream are real.

It seemed so real. The whiskey smooth timbre of his voice was compelling. It set my blood on fire. It moved through my veins slowly, like lava, before it finally settled between my thighs.

I reached down, slid my fingers through the wet folds of my nether lips and caressed my clit, mimicking the movements my husband's fingers made in my dream.

My eyes flew open when I felt his lips close over my breast. It felt so real, yet I was still alone. The pleasure pain of his imagined teeth on my nipple sent me careening over the edge.

"Gabriel!" I sobbed out his name. A delicious feeling of warmth swept through me and the little nubbin began to spasm beneath my fingers.

"I—I..."

You are coming, my heart, and you are awake. This is no dream.

My breathing came in heavy, erratic pants as I pulled my wet fingers from my slick pussy and lay gasping on the bed. My legs were spread wide like the sacrifice I had been about to become six months ago, but I was too tired to care. I drifted to sleep while I enjoyed the illusory sensation of my husband's strong, safe arms wrapped around me.

The rude, incessant buzzing of my alarm permeated my sleep. I rolled over and groaned. My body still felt heavy with desire and I wondered if making love with Gabriel would be at least as good as my dream.

Better.

The echo of my dream Gabriel whispered in my mind. My face heated when I thought of what I had done to myself the night before. I was going to be horribly embarrassed if he could really read my mind. The thoughts in my head were anything but tame.

The dream I had the night before awakened something within me I never knew existed. Something I never thought myself capable of doing. It awakened a woman who wanted to be sexually aware, even at the expense of her own sanity.

When I dressed and went downstairs for breakfast, my thoughts drifted back to the wonderfully talented fingers of my dream Gabriel and I wondered how I would keep my husband from reading my mind.

My body creamed at the thought of what transpired in my fantasy and I realized, at that moment, there was hope for me after all.

I walked through the large house. There never seemed to be anyone about. He had a staff. I remember meeting them. Yet they never seemed to be around.

I shrugged, walked through the large parlor, past a huge grand piano that my fingers itched to play and headed to the sunroom. Someone, perhaps Cassie, had told me that was where I would find my husband in the mornings.

Bright sunlight greeted me when I entered the solarium. My husband sat at the table, a newspaper in front of his face, a glass of juice at his elbow.

"All right, Dracula, I'll bite. Why are you drinking orange juice instead of blood if you're a vampire?"

He lifted his glass, took a sip and grinned. "I like it."

Well, that was as good an answer as any, I suppose. It was going to take a whole lot more convincing on his part before I bought in on this vampire crap though.

Soft strains of Bach reverberated throughout the room. I looked but I couldn't see the speakers anywhere.

I grimaced. It figured. I should have known. I knew he always seemed like the staid, boring, classical music sort. That was just great. My life was going to be very lively with him.

Gabriel looked over his paper, picked up the remote for the CD player and pushed a button. A hard rock song from the late seventies started to play. I listened to the well-known band singing about a fire station while the sound of sirens echoed throughout the room.

That was more like it. I frowned. Had he just read my mind again? I turned my thoughts away from the previous evening's night's enlightening activities and concentrated on the weather instead.

He glanced up at me again. "You look...rested. Did you sleep well?"

Boy did I! Blushing, I nodded, noticing the fine lines of strain around his mouth for the first time. Was he not feeling well?

"You don't look rested. You look tired," I said gazing out the window into the back garden. "Should you even be up? I mean, if you're a vamp and all, shouldn't you avoid the sunlight?"

I knew he was about as much a vampire as I was. I probably shouldn't have encouraged him.

He just shrugged and kept his eyes still on his paper.

"Are you feeling okay?"

He nodded. "I feel wonderful. Thank you for asking." He gestured to the antique walnut sideboard against the wall. "There are donuts on the server. Have some."

I glanced over to the plate of donuts and my eyes widened.

"I love éclairs." I wandered over to the sideboard, put one on a plate and made my way back to the table.

I know.

Though the words remained unspoken, they still hung thick in the air between us. He knew everything about me and I still knew next to nothing about him.

When had I become such a selfish bitch? I frowned, stared down at the delicate china plate and played with my pastry, my appetite suddenly gone. I wondered and worried about the lines around his eyes and mouth. They hadn't been there a few days ago had they, or was it me?

I thought about how high strung I felt after my dream. How I needed the physical release after I woke and I wondered if the tension I saw on his face was from having to wait so long for me to grow up.

"CARE TO GO SHOPPING?" Cassie asked from the doorway to the parlor about two weeks after my wedding. "I have some things I need to get at the mall."

I nodded, shifted on the sofa and indicated she should join me.

"Me, too."

I needed some personal items and I didn't have a way to get them. Though, I did finally find out what Gabriel's wedding gift to me had been.

He'd gotten me a sleek, black Corvette, the car of my dreams. He had obviously read my mind again. Why I still found that so hard to believe after all of the proof he'd given me, I don't know.

Even though it almost killed me, I didn't accept the car of course. I refused to keep taking from him while I still refused to give anything of myself. He deserved a partner, not a freeloader. I pressed my lips together, determined to change that.

I had a couple of weeks to think about it and came to the decision that I wanted to give him a chance. If I tried it and found that sex still hurts, at least I would know there was no hope for me. At least this infernal wondering would be over.

Cassie reached over to the end table, picked up the phone and pressed a few buttons.

"Carlisle, can you take me to the mall?" she paused for a minute, obviously listening.

"Yes, Mrs. LeBlanc will be joining me so you'll want to bring the limo." She nodded. "Of course, five minutes will be fine."

I almost asked her who was going with us, until I remembered that *I* was Mrs. LeBlanc.

"Are you ready or do you need to change?" she asked, turning her open gaze on me.

"I think I can go like this," I said, looking down at myself. "Could you... Would you mind helping me pick out a few...personal items?"

I wanted to get some lingerie and I had no idea where to go or what to buy to drive my husband wild. Something told me my request was right up Cassie's alley.

The mall was crowded. So many people were shopping for school clothes and Christmas gifts we had a difficult time making our way through the crowds. I looked around at the bizarre mixture of Halloween items and Christmas trees and shook my head. It was hard to believe the stores had their holiday decorations up already. You would think they would wait until after Halloween at least.

"There's the lingerie shop. I think we'll find everything we need there." Cassie pointed to a store a few doors down and we headed in that direction.

Suddenly, someone grabbed me from behind.

"Ow!"

Tasha and Micah insisted I take self-defense courses in case something like this ever happened. I put those lessons to good use. Turning quickly, I gave the person a good taste of my right fist. Only it didn't seem to faze him. My actions were so ineffectual he didn't even flinch.

I looked closer. It wasn't a man that held me at all. It was some humanoid type creature. It resembled a man, but there was something hideously wrong with it, him...whatever.

The creature wore dark glasses over its eyes and its gray skin screamed undead. It grabbed my arm, spun me around and dragged me backward one arm around my neck, the other around my middle. I stomped on its foot, but still got no reaction.

Cassie vigorously fought the one that captured her. However, the struggle was futile. They were both too strong for us.

I reached out with my mind and hoped my husband would hear me. Otherwise, I was sure we were both dead.

Gabriel! Help me. Help us!

Warmth flooded me as his mind touched mine. *What is it, my love? You are frightened.*

I sent him a mental image of the men attacking us and he swore. His mental use of profanity shocked me. He didn't normally use that type of language.

Fight them. I will be there as fast as I can.

Don't leave me.

I will not, my love. If I become too quiet, just reach out with your mind and follow the path back to mine. I will be here. I am coming to you now.

I turned my attention back to what was happening and watched horrified as the one who held Cassie lowered his head to her neck. His teeth elongated and I nearly fainted from fright.

Vampire!

No, he is a revenant. A vampire turned him by giving him blood. He now lives on the blood of rodents and small animals. He follows the orders of the Rogue who turned him. The Rogue has ordered him to bite Cassie in an attempt to frighten you into submission. You must not give in.

I won't let them hurt her.

No, you cannot, but you also cannot let them hurt you.

He paused and I got the impression that he was thinking. He apparently knew how to compartmentalize his thoughts. I couldn't gather a thing from his silence other than the calming sensation of his presence.

The revenant's teeth slowly lowered to Cassie's neck and she screamed.

"Help us! Somebody, please help us."

Something flew past my head. The object moved so fast I felt the air it displaced as it whistled past me. It was a knife. The force of the throw imbedded it to the hilt into the side of the neck of the revenant holding Cassie.

He growled, dropped her like a hot branding iron and reached for the plain wooden handle that protruded from his neck.

By this time, the mall patrons all ran for their lives. None of them wanted anything to do with the bloody battle in front of the cell phone kiosk.

I heard a loud, meaty thunk and a grunt. Another knife buried itself into the revenant that held me. He let me go and reached for the knife buried deep in his neck.

Cassie and I didn't wait around for them to grab us again. We ran.

"Who do you think that was?" she asked, breathless, as we ran for the nearest exit.

"I think *what* that was would be a better question." I shook my head. "I don't know and I don't care. I just want to get the hell out of here."

I grabbed my side. I've never been a runner. I'm one of the lucky ones who stay thin no matter how little exercise I get. And, since I am inherently lazy, I had always strived to get as little of that as possible.

I wasn't sure how much Cassie knew and I wasn't about to tell her what I now knew to be true. What if she went to the authorities? They would take Gabriel away and experiment on him. I certainly didn't want that.

The sense of warm arms surrounding me filled my mind. The feeling was strange since we still ran at top speed through the mall.

We continued to run toward the exit where we knew Carlisle waited with the limo. We were about forty feet from the doors when they all opened simultaneously and six tall, gorgeous men walked in.

Cassie stopped, dragging me to a stop beside her. Her eyes rounded when she saw the men closing the distance between us.

My mind froze.

All of the men had hard, implacable faces. Their long legged strides carried them to us faster than I ever thought possible for someone who appeared to be moving in slow motion.

"No," I whispered, shaking my head. "Not again."

Chapter Seven

Strong arms grabbed me from behind and I fought.

"Do not fear, little one."

Relieved, I relaxed with a sigh. It was Gabriel. He pushed me behind him and faced the other men.

"There are revenants here?" one of the new men asked. He was dressed all in black. He kept his shoulder-length dark hair swept back from his face. His chest was wide and I wondered how much he worked out. No one got muscles like these guys had by being lazy.

Cassie—who had obviously recovered faster than I did—lifted a shaking hand and nodded.

"Yes, they're back that way. Someone, I'm not sure who, saved us from them and may need help."

The man in black inclined his head to one of his companions. The other man nodded and left, walking in the direction we'd just come from.

I watched, somewhat bemused, as Cassie stared up at one of the other men. He seemed a bit shorter than the rest. He was perhaps six-foot-two instead of the more typical six-foot-seven amongst the *Cartuotey*.

He watched her intently, raised his brow and said, "Want a picture?"

She gasped and looked away. A blush dusted her cheeks and she stared at the floor, embarrassed.

I scowled at his rudeness. "Are all of you men lacking in common courtesy and tact?"

I don't know what gave me the courage to stand up to these men. They were all about the same size as my husband and we were outnumbered. I guess a part of me knew they were *Cartuotey* and would never hurt us without cause.

A few of them threw a disgusted look my way and broke off from the rest.

"We'll go see what we can do to help Sterling."

Another turned to stare at me. "Was it a Guide who took the revenants on?"

"How the hell should I know?" I said with a shrug. "I couldn't tell a Guide from a taxi driver. The only reason I can identify a *Cartuotey* is because you guys stand out like sore thumbs." I gave them all a thorough once over. "Face it, guys, there's no way you can hide what you are."

The word vampire shimmered in my mind as I looked at them all. I'd never been around so many of them before. The fact that they were all tall, compelling and so good looking they could make a Nun drool, did not escape my notice.

Vampire. The ridiculous word would not leave me alone. I scowled.

"Don't be stupid."

I heard someone murmur, "Too late."

"Hey! That's not nice." I fisted my hands on my hips and resisted the urge to kick one of them.

The man who said that stared at me with an intensity that made me squirm. "You see us for what we are because you know of our existence."

Cassie leaned over to whisper, "People who don't know of their existence mistake them for Chippendale Dancers. I know I would." She gave the shorter one another once over.

His eyelids drooped and his gaze slowly raked her body from head to toe. "You're not so bad yourself, sweetheart," he said, then turned toward his friends. "We'd better get over there and help the others and that Guide, or whoever it was. We need to get this situation under control."

The tallest of the group stepped forward and my mouth gaped open. He looked like a carbon copy of Micah, only taller.

He bowed in my direction, then lifted Cassie's hand to his lips. "It is my distinct pleasure to meet you. Please allow me to introduce myself. I am called Maximillian." He lifted my limp arm and lightly pressed his lips to the back of my hand.

Wasn't that Micah's middle name?

It was a measure of my shock that I didn't pull my hand free and he slowly released it instead. His gaze darted to Gabriel.

"Your wife is lovely. I wish you happiness and many children to fill your empty home."

Something told me there was some sort of formality passing between the two men, but I wasn't privy to their customs. So I decided to ignore them both.

I have learned that *Cartuotey* appear human, for the most part, but they were something different altogether.

Vampire, immortal.

The two words danced through my head and I dismissed them as fancy. There were definitely monsters in this world, but there were certainly no vampires.

Maximillian grinned and slapped my husband on the back.

"You are going to have a time with this one. She thinks you to be delusional. She cannot come to terms with the fact that a species like ours exists."

I waved my hand in his face. "Excuse me, but I'm right here." I scowled. "Can you at least put off certain remarks that make it seem like I'm not here until I'm *really* not here?"

The tall man lowered his gaze to meet mine. "Call me Max, please. I apologize if I made you uncomfortable."

Uncomfortable? He didn't make me feel uncomfortable. He pissed me off, that's what he did.

He grinned and shook Gabriel's hand. "We should go find the humans who have seen this and reprogram them so they will not remember the things they have seen today."

Gabriel nodded and held out his hand. "I don't like having to do that. Too many mistakes can be made while tampering with people's minds."

"You are correct, but sometimes, such as now, we have little choice in the matter." He shook my husband's hand. "I will visit you soon, my friend." His gaze flicked to me for a split second. "I will give your mate time to adjust before I make my appearance."

White, white teeth flashed in his dark face. His smile was a complete contrast to his dark skin, hair and eyes. It was amazing how almost every one of these men resembled someone of Latin descent, yet they denied any relation and claimed to be vampires.

He turned and addressed the other *Cartuotey* who awaited his order.

"Come. We must find the humans who have seen the revenants and instruct them in what to remember of this day. They must not recall what they have witnessed here."

My gaze followed the small group as they went in search of the people hidden throughout the mall. I thought it strange how they seemed to know where each one of them hid.

They stood outside the entrance to the stores and beckoned the people out. They all shuffled out of their hiding places resembling zombies.

The ridiculous word, *vampire*, shimmered in my mind again and I shook it off.

Man, if I started believing that, someone just might lock me in a loony bin, please!

"You are not crazy, my love," Gabriel said, drawing me under his arm.

I didn't protest. I wanted nothing more in my life than to feel safe and being under Gabriel's physical protection did just that.

He looked surprised when I wrapped my arm around his waist and rested my head against his shoulder. I can't say I blame him. This was only the third time since we met that I had touched him voluntarily.

"Would you care to finish your shopping? I shall stay so you can continue without another incident."

His gaze roamed over my face, rested on my lips for a second then moved back up to my eyes. I tried to read him again but as usual, there was just nothing there.

I looked over at Cassie and she grinned. "I think this is the perfect opportunity for you to get those items you were talking about. How convenient that he should be here to give his opinion on your choice."

He looked between the two of us, his expression suddenly wary. "This isn't going to require me to hold purses or feminine hygiene products, is it?"

I glanced over at my friend and we both giggled. "No. I think you're safe there."

WE RETURNED HOME ABOUT two hours later with several bulging bags and one very edgy man. More pronounced lines of stress marked his face than before. His face seemed almost haggard and gray. I worried about that and wondered if he was ill.

"I think you need some rest."

I pressed my hand on his forehead, expecting him to be hot. He was cool to the touch and apparently not coming down with anything.

Gabriel backed away and gave me a half smile. "I'm fine."

He raised hands that were loaded down with bags filled with clothing he had insisted on paying for. "Shall I put these in your room?"

I nodded my head. "Yes, please."

What was I saying? I wanted them in his room. Didn't I? All day I had been trying to convince myself to go through with my plans. Now, faced with the real possibility that he would touch me in places I would rather keep hidden from the world...I chickened out.

"As you wish." He let his breath out on a sigh. "I shall see to it immediately."

He was disappointed. I know he had hoped that I would move my things into his room. Perhaps I just wasn't ready.

Cassie stepped up behind me. "I thought…"

I turned to her. "I know what you thought." I paced away. "What can I say? I thought I was ready, too. Then suddenly, I just…wasn't."

She wrapped her arm around me. "I'm sorry, hon. I'm sure you'll be able to overcome that fear sooner or later." She gave me a thin smile and a light squeeze before she stepped away. "I can't tell you sex doesn't always hurt. I don't know that for sure. I only know that as soon as my Mr. Right comes along, I'm going to be ready to try." She looked into my eyes. "That's the question you're going to have to ask yourself. Are *you* ready to try?"

That was a very good question.

"I…I need to think. Will you tell Gabriel I went for a walk out back when he comes down?" I did need to be by myself for a while. I also wanted to be with him. What was I going to do? "Tell him…" I paused. "Tell him I'm not running from him. I want him to come to me."

She followed me into the kitchen. Before she closed the door behind me, she said, "Good luck. I hope you find what you're looking for."

I turned to look at her.

"Yeah, me, too."

The garden was beautiful, as usual. I slowly made my way through the fragrant rows of roses and night blooming jasmine. I strolled slowly through the garden, my mind in a whirl. I needed this short time alone to think.

My footsteps were nearly silent as I wandered over the grassy trail through the backyard across the footbridge and toward the woods beyond.

It was so beautiful I didn't realize I had wandered so far from the house. I felt relaxed, serene. The farther I wandered away from the main house, the more peaceful I felt.

It was almost as if something pulled me farther and farther away. I paused, listening intently, when I thought I heard someone call my name.

"Yes? Is someone there?" Was it my imagination or did I really hear someone calling me? "Gabriel?"

The pull became stronger and I started out again. It was as though invisible strings had attached themselves to my middle and they steadily pulled me into the woods beyond the back garden. Soon, I didn't care that I had heard someone call my name.

There were too many other things on my mind. The way the wind lifted my hair from the nape of my neck. The scent of wet earth and loam beneath my feet and the pine trees swaying gently over my head tickled my nose.

I stopped, held my arms straight out to my sides and closed my eyes. The life of the forest seeped into my pores. I breathed it in. Something about the woods drew me deeper and deeper within them.

Come to me.

"Gabriel?"

It didn't sound like my husband's deep baritone. But, who else could it be? He was the only person who had ever talked to me mind to mind.

Come to me.

I bit my lip. "How strange..."

The voice was in my head, yet I got the impression that it came from somewhere in front of me. It couldn't possibly be Gabriel, could it?

The hair on the back of my neck prickled and my skin began to crawl. Suddenly, whatever it was that called me seemed malevolent.

Evil.

The voice became more urgent. *You must come to me or all is lost!*

I snorted. "Like I really give a good damn about all being lost." I started to turn around but something seized my will.

Abruptly, I began to shuffle toward the voice. The horrible, compelling strains coerced me into padding closer and closer.

I ignored the direction in which I headed as my feet padded unerringly toward the disembodied voice. All I could think was that something forced me to approach a creature I knew was evil.

"Oh, God," I whimpered.

My gaze darted around the woods. I saw nothing but the forest and lush ferns carpeting the ground.

You will find me. You are close.

The voice was male. I was certain of that. My limbs shook as I realized that I knew nothing about the man who drew me. Yet, my feet still shuffled toward the horrible place.

Come to me.

I opened my mouth to scream for my husband but nothing came out. My mouth flapped open and shut like a fish out of water.

You will not call to him, my dear. Come to me!

The voice demanded obedience, the owner imperious. It was as though he expected me to obey him as if it was his due. I screamed out my fear in my mind.

Gabriel, help me!

Do you really think I would allow him to hear you? You will come to me now!

I dragged my feet, grabbed tree branches. Still, my feet plodded toward that horrible voice. It was if my will was still my own, but my legs and feet wouldn't obey. I did anything and everything I could think of to keep from going to the creature who called to me but my struggles were useless.

Soon, I stood on the bank of the little pond where I had rested not so many days ago and stared into the red-rimmed eyes of a real vampire.

Blood ran from his mouth. It dripped from his stained, elongated incisors. He smiled at me. The slight curve of his lips was little more than a mockery of what it was supposed to be.

"Come to me and give me your power, Guide."

I shook my head, even as my feet took me ever closer.

Two revenants appeared from behind the bushes to my left and shuffled toward me to grab me by my arms.

The vampire stood. His tall, once elegant frame covered by a perfectly designed tuxedo.

I almost rolled my eyes. How cliché.

He snarled at me. "I may be cliché, darling, but I'm still your worst nightmare."

Actually, he wasn't, but I was afraid if I told him what it was he would make that happen as well.

An evil grin spread across his face. "Ah, your worst nightmare is one of my fondest dreams. In fact it's one of my fondest memories." He licked his lips. "I can't wait to taste you." He breathed in my ear and made my skin crawl. "I intend to sample all of your body's fluids."

Oh, God.

"Your God can't help you now. He does not wish to help you. If he did, *I* and those like me, would not exist." He turned toward his revenants. "Take her to the warehouse and ready her for the ceremony."

"Not again. Not again." I chanted, struggling, just before I lost consciousness.

I woke strapped to an altar. I knew the people who murdered my Aunt and Grandmother found me again and it was only a matter of time before my life would come to a horrific end.

At least I had the odd comfort that I was still clothed. Still, it was merely an inconvenience for my captors that I knew, from experience, could be omitted by the careless slide of a sharp blade.

My body shook with the fear of knowing I would soon face the same kind of fanatics who took my innocence last spring and I cried for every missed opportunity that I'd had to find out what real love is.

Chapter Eight

I'M SO SORRY, GABRIEL. IF I COULD DO THINGS DIFFERENTLY, I WOULD. I put everything I had into reaching him. He had to get my last message. I wanted him to know that I did not leave him voluntarily.

Let me in, my heart.

Gabriel? I hardly dared to hope that I had gotten through to him. *Is it really you?*

Yes, my heart. It is really me. I cannot find you. I need to see through your eyes.

I can only see the inside of this room. I heard the vampire tell his revenants to take me to a warehouse, but other than that, I have no idea where I am.

I almost giggled at the thought that I had finally gone irrevocably insane. I closed my eyes, filled with the shame of my weakness.

I lost consciousness when I knew what they planned. I paused, showing him my failing. *I won't survive another assault, Gabriel. I know I won't. It will drive me mad.*

You will be fine, my heart.

His mind touched mine again and filled me with warmth. I felt his arms wrap around my trembling body even though he was not in the room with me. It was a strange comfort.

"No." I struggled against the bonds that held me. "*I feel it. I'll go mad and I will open a gate to some horrible, horrible place. If they have already violated me when you arrive, kill me.*

I felt him pause. *I cannot do that for you, my love. I am not strong enough.*

I snorted. *You're a vampire. Of course you're strong enough.*

I will never be strong enough to kill the woman I love, Alicia. Do not ask me for something I cannot give.

Then tell someone else to do it! I snarled at him mentally. *I can't live through another violation. If you will not kill me, then I will leave my body to float*

236

around aimlessly for eternity while they use it for whatever nefarious purpose they have. If I do, my body will die leaving my soul trapped in limbo, I will never incarnate again. Is that what you want?

I stopped, shocked that I had even thought of that. Something within me told me it was possible though.

Gabriel couldn't hide his indecision. I felt it. He didn't want to lose me. I knew that. I certainly couldn't just lie here and let them do unspeakable things to my body.

I refused to let those monsters steal what little confidence I had regained over these last few months. That hard-earned confidence was so long in coming.

Gabriel?

Yes, my love?

Can you do things with your mind?

I had been wondering about that. He read my mind so easily, what would stop him from doing other amazing things?

Things? What things?

Yes, things. Can you open doors, stuff like that? You know, telekinesis.

Yes, I can. Why?

I raised my head and looked at my bound wrist. *Then help me out of this. I would rather go down fighting than just lie here and wait for them to come back.*

I felt his pride in my willingness to fight as the leather strap that bound my wrist loosened, then opened for me. I turned my head and looked at my other arm and that strap fell to the floor almost immediately.

Nice trick. Care to teach me how to do that?

He chuckled. *I could, but you would have to agree to become like me first.*

I paused at that. Become like him? I didn't know if that was possible. Did I really want to become like him? I thought about his strength and the things he could do with his mind.

"Oh, yeah. I want that." *When can we do it?*

His shock reverberated through our bond. *You want to become one of The Chosen?*

Should I not want to? He seemed almost scared. What wasn't he telling me?

Others may change you if you pay them to, but I will not agree to change you until you are ready.

What makes you think I'm not ready? I asked as I sat up to release my feet from the straps that held them bound to the altar.

It's just a good thing they didn't think Gabriel would be able to reach me. Otherwise, they may have used something more difficult to release.

You must handfast with me. I will not change anyone but my true mate. If you choose to remain separate from me, you will do it as a human.

Now that pissed me off. He wouldn't change me until I had sex with him. That thought really jerked my chain.

That is not it. I will only change my true mate. You must bond with me in a handfasting. When we handfast, our bodies will call to each other and bring us together.

We will have sex whether you want it or not. Therefore, you must be sure you want it or I will not change you. I will not have you looking at me the following day with those haunted eyes and call me the monster I am afraid I would become if you refuse me.

What if I choose to have sex with you? I had to know what he was trying to say.

The handfasting ritual is a true mating. It ties our life forces together and we will live and die together.

I bit my lip as I thought about that. A true relationship with him would be wonderful. I knew now that my life, any life, was too short to succumb to such unreasoning fear. Because of that fear, if I died today, I would never know the intimate touch of my gentle husband.

The bond he wanted to share with me wasn't half as frightening as the idea of sharing our bodies. The fear of a physical union was one phobia I was determined to overcome.

Get me out of this mess and we'll talk about it.

As you wish.

That had better not have been a smartassed remark, mister. I'm not up for it.

I looked around the room where they had held me prisoner.

My captors left me strapped to a large cement slab with brownish stains on it. I shuddered and tried not to think about what those stains were.

A large pentagram covered the floor in the center of the room. Someone drew it in—what looked like—dried blood. Candleholders, large and small, set around the outer edges of the circle. Melted wax of various colors stained the cement floor.

A large challis and mean looking double-edged knife sat between two of the points. I turned and noticed the door ajar and peeked through the crack.

Apparently, my captors didn't think I was capable of escaping my bonds because there were no guards standing about. It was as if they had left to gather the rest of their group, leaving me here to wait in fear.

Ha! I would laugh in the face of death. It's being raped again that scared me shitless.

They were right. *I* wasn't capable of escaping my bonds—at least not by myself. I'm sure they weren't counting on Gabriel helping me either. Like me, they probably didn't know what he was capable of doing. I was determined to find out though.

I slipped through the door into the main area of the building. The outer area was quite large. It was probably the warehouse the vampire talked about. The rafters stood a good twenty feet over my head. The sides of the structure—that I could see anyway—were made of metal.

Hundreds of large crates filled the area. If they hadn't held me prisoner in that other room, I would have believed this was a legitimate warehouse.

Climbing on top of a few crates, I looked out through the nearest window and tried to figure out where I was. I sent what I saw to Gabriel through our mental bond.

I hoped he knew where I was because I certainly had no idea. I saw nothing but rolling hills. A tall radio or cellular tower rose over the forest in the distance, but besides that, there was nothing to see but grass and trees.

Do you know where I am?

I felt him connect his mind with me as he attempted to *see* through my eyes.

Yes, I think so. Hang tight. I should be there soon. I am already close. That is why we are able to communicate. I would not have picked up your call if I had not already been near. He paused for a second. *I would know exactly where you are at all times if we were truly bonded.*

Another reason doing that handfasting ritual thing was a good idea. If anyone tried to take me from him again, he would be able to find me no matter where I was.

That is definitely something we need to talk about when you get me back home.

We are not going back to the house.

His tone brooked no argument. Not that I would have argued. The fanatics knew I was staying there, obviously.

Figures.

They have found a way to get to you there. I must take you to where they will not think to look for you, at least for a while.

And where's that, Goliath? I raised my brow and sent the image of my action to him.

He paused at my use of that name and I had to grin. I knew he didn't like it. But that's what made it so darned fun.

Besides, the man *was* huge. All over.

We are going to go visit some friends of ours in Europe.

Tasha and Micah? I asked, excited at the prospect of seeing my best friend. They were the only people I knew overseas. *Woo hoo!*

I could ask her for so much advice. I knew she wouldn't tell me to just go ahead and sleep with Gabriel and I was sure she'd tell me the truth about sex. I couldn't believe she'd lie to me about something like that.

At least I hoped she wouldn't.

A noise came from just outside the window to my left and I ducked, pressing myself up against the wall. Apparently, they had left a few guards after all. Several gunshots startled me and someone squealed before I heard something hit the side of the metal building.

I tried to link with Gabriel and found nothing but a huge void. Either he blocked me, was unconscious or he was dead.

"He's unconscious," I told myself as I looked around the large enclosure for a weapon.

I couldn't overcome the ghastly feeling that he was injured. What if one of those monsters had shot him and he was out there, lying in the dirt, helpless or dying? The thought of my husband lying on the ground unconscious, bleeding out, spurred me to action. I had to help him.

I ran back into the room where they'd kept me tied up and skirted the blood stained altar. I picked up one of the large, brass candlesticks with one hand and the double-edged dagger with the other.

I ran back out into the main room, headed for the door. It crashed open and a body flew into the building, landing at my feet. The man's head lolled to the side at a peculiar angle. I tilted my head and stared at him in horror for a minute when I realized he was dead, his neck broken.

Swallowing the bile that rose to the back of my throat, I backed up a few steps when the silhouette of a large man blocked the doorway. He held a body over his shoulder. With the sun behind him, I wasn't sure who it was, but I had an idea. "Gabriel?" I whispered his name, then choked out a horrified gasp when the second man's body hit the cement floor with a sickening thud.

I retched when his head turned and empty eyes stared my way. Blood covered the man's neck and chest. It looked like someone ripped his throat out. Yet, even dead, the man looked evil.

Closing my eyes, I took a deep breath and tightened my grip on my weapons.

Gabriel sighed, wiped his bloody hands on his slacks and pushed his fingers through his hair. "You would fear me now?"

I swallowed and looked away from his pain-filled eyes. "You—you killed them."

"Of course I killed them," he said, his voice a bit harsh. "Do you think they would have hesitated to kill either of us?"

He reached up to press his hand over his chest near his left shoulder, close to his heart.

"Oh, my God! You've been shot!" I fought the overwhelming urge to go to him. I bit my lip. "You need to put direct pressure on that so it will stop bleeding."

"They almost managed to hit me once when they shot wildly as I took them." He pointed to the first man he had thrown into the building. "That idiot shot me through himself before I broke his neck."

"I guess he figured he was dead anyway..."

He nodded. "That was my thought exactly."

My grip on the weapons in my hands tightened and loosened as I stood there wanting to go to him. I was torn. My experience with him told me he was a gentle man but I had never thought him capable of such violence. What else was he capable of doing?

"I am capable of many things, Alicia. You must know there is nothing I wouldn't do to ensure your safety."

He looked down at the man covered in blood and nudged him with the toe of his boot.

"Had I not been shot, I would have broken this one's neck as well." He looked back up to meet my gaze. "But I had to have the blood. I need my strength if I'm to get you to safety." His lips quirked at the corners and he raised a perfect brow. "Would you have wanted to be the donor?"

I bit my lip. Wasn't that how it was supposed to be? He saved my life. It was my turn to save his then. I swallowed around the lump in my throat.

"Yes. Yes, I would have," I said, lifting my chin to meet his gaze. I don't know who was more surprised with my statement, him or me.

Gabriel held out his hand, looked down at it and shook his head. He closed his eyes and took a deep breath. Suddenly, he was clean. His clothes had changed and the hand he still held out to me was clean and free of blood.

I gaped at him as a new red stain bloomed on his left shoulder through the white shirt he just changed into and I gasped.

He grunted when I ripped the shirt off one of the dead men and pressed it to his shoulder. He looked down at me, raising his hand to cover mine.

He gave me a half smile. "I'm sorry, sweetheart, but no matter what we may wish, the wounds are not so easily taken care of."

He half turned and tilted his head toward the door. "We must leave. Now. The others are returning."

I looked around the warehouse and bit my lip, frowning. "I know I saw something flammable in here. We should burn the place to the ground."

He strode up to me, lifted me into his arms and grinned.

"We don't need flammable liquids."

I opened my eyes wide and raised my brow.

"Why not?"

He looked out through the door at the approaching darkness. "Promise me you won't be frightened."

"Too late, Einstein, I'm already there." I wrapped my arms around his neck and rested my head on his shoulder.

He shook his head, kissed me on the forehead and sighed. "Please remember it is me you are with."

"What do you mean? Don't forget what is you? Of course I'm not going to forget I'm with you. You're standing right next to me," I said as he set me back onto the floor.

He stepped away from me for a minute and winked.

My eyes widened as I watched my husband do something that I had previously thought impossible.

"Oh, my God!"

Chapter Nine

I SQUEEZED MY EYES SHUT FOR A MINUTE AND SCRUBBED MY FACE WITH my hands.

"I know I didn't see what I think I just saw." I pushed the hair back from my face and vehemently shook my head. "I've gone mad. I've gone completely and utterly mad."

You have not gone mad, Alicia, Gabriel chuckled into my mind. *Climb up onto my back.*

"What?" I held my hands out in front of me and backed away from him. "No. I don't think so. Horses I can do. But...but..." I waved my hand toward him. "You're a dragon, for goodness sake!"

I paced back and forth in front of him. I don't know how he expected to get out of here. He was bigger than the doorways. Even the large roll-up door on the end of the building for loading trucks was too small for the new body he had acquired.

He ducked. Even at the peak, the twenty-foot-high ceiling was too low for him to stand completely up. His triangular shaped head turned and he looked at me with glowing yellow eyes. He bowed low and bumped my shoulder with his nose.

Climb onto my back, you little chicken. He looked down at the weapons I still held in my hands. *Keep the knife and ditch the club.*

"It's not a club, it's a candlestick."

You could have fooled me. The thing looks like a baseball bat.

I dropped the candlestick on the floor at his direction and held up the knife.

"So do I cut off a piece of your heart for myself and that's how we live and die together?"

He shook his large head, bumped me and nearly knocked me down.

You have watched entirely too much television. Now, climb up onto my back.

I do not want to have to carry you. I cannot guarantee that I will not cause you injury.

He lifted his large, clawed foot.

I took a deep breath. *When did my life start looking like an episode of* Special Unit?

I put the thought of one of my favorite TV shows—that the network cancelled without warning—out of my mind and shook my head.

Gabriel lifted one of his larger back legs a little and made a step for me to climb onto his back.

"Lord, have mercy! You're going to tell me everything you can do when we get ourselves out of this mess," I grumbled as I settled myself between his two large wings.

My mind is an open book to my bonded mate.

"Oh, I get it. I don't get to know unless I let you change me." I grinned and gave his back a smack.

"Hey, your scales feel weird. And while we're on the subject, can you be any color you want or are you always this peculiar shade of green?"

He snorted.

I can be any shade of any color I choose. I just figured this was a good shade. Since this is the color you will be soon after we take flight.

"Flight?" I squeaked. "Okay. You got me there. I probably will turn that exact shade of green right before I throw up on your back."

I'm not sure, but I think he cringed at that.

Hold on, he said just before he took a deep breath and blasted one side of the building out. He half walked, half crawled through the large hole.

I got the feeling he moved slower than normal because I was on his back. I had pulled something out of his mind from when he had done an amazing thing like this before.

He had just jumped up and crashed out through the roof of the building. He couldn't do that this time. This time he had to worry about me sitting on his back.

I felt his love for me through our bond and wondered if it was something he had projected to me or if it just slipped out through his protective barrier.

Gabriel stretched to his full height as soon as we cleared the building. He turned, lowered his head and took another deep breath. Flames shot from his mouth and nostrils, into the warehouse. The crates caught fire and the metal squealed as it heated.

A stiff breeze carried the stench of burning flesh to me and I wrinkled my nose. The muscles in his back tensed and he pushed off from the ground. As quick as a snap, we were in the air, flying over the burning building.

I spied the headlights of a slow moving vehicle about a quarter of a mile away and wondered at the fact that he'd heard them coming several minutes ago.

Gabriel made a sharp turn and my body shifted on his back. Afraid I would fall, I leaned down and wrapped my arms around his neck.

Since my arms wouldn't go all the way around the thick column, I held on the best that I could as we flew over the darkened city.

"Aren't you afraid someone will look up and see you?"

I didn't worry about anyone seeing me on his back. There was no way anyone would see me from the ground.

Most people never look up. They go through life with blinders on. They are in too much of a hurry to stop and look up at the beauty of the night stars. He gave a mental shrug. *If they do see me, they will most likely think they are seeing things anyway. Besides, who would believe they actually saw a dragon?*

"Me?"

You would not have believed it before either. You are just now coming to terms with what I am.

Well I had to agree with that. A few months ago, I never would have believed vampires existed either. Hell, I still didn't really believe they existed until one kidnapped me and Gabriel further proved it by having some lunatic shoot him before turning into a dragon. I suppressed a hysterical giggle at the thought.

I tried not to think of the man he'd killed and the blood Gabriel had on his mouth when he carried the body into the warehouse.

Tilting my head back, I inhaled deeply. The smell of freedom was a wonderful scent. The night breeze ruffled my hair and cooled my cheeks.

He continued to fly south, away from the building toward the city and I marveled at what it looked like at night from the air. I had never had the opportunity to get a glimpse of Grand Rapids from this height. I steadfastly refused to climb onto an airplane.

I know the statistics are that automobiles are technically more dangerous than planes. Plus, more people die each year in cars and all that yadda. However, I wouldn't be in control of an airplane. In a car I was usually in control and in a car, if the engine failed, it was a rather short fall to the ground.

He landed on the roof of a tall building and I climbed down off him before he changed back to his human form. I reached up, opened his shirt and took a good look at his chest.

"Wow. That's something," I said, my hand rubbing over his shoulder and chest as I stared at the bullet that had partially worked its way out of his skin. "How long before that's completely healed?"

He shrugged. "About six or seven more hours would be my guess. I would be healed now, if I had more blood."

I studied him for a moment. "If I gave you blood, would it hurt?" I bit my lip, nervous. I wanted to help him, but I'm a big baby when it comes to pain.

He stared into my eyes. His silver eyes glittered with something I wasn't sure I wanted to understand. My comment must have been some sort of weird ritual consent or something. I shivered with a mixture of anticipation and dread.

Cool air lifted my hair, felt like a soft breath against my skin. I felt my nipples pebble as the thought of his mouth on my neck made my womb clench.

"Are you sure you want to do that? If you give me blood, it will tie us irrevocably for the rest of your life. Even if you decided to leave me, we would always be connected through our blood bond."

I shrugged, trying to make the action look nonchalant. "Won't the same thing happen if we handfast?"

Turning, I slowly walked to the edge of the building, put my arms on the protective rail and looked out into the night. He followed me to the edge and I turned to look at him.

"Yes."

He reached up to brush a lock of hair from my face. He slowly fingered the slight curl before tucking it behind my ear.

"The handfasting ritual is a loving, passionate connection between mates. It will make you a vampire, much like me. You will need to consume blood to survive."

I swallowed and tried not to cringe. "Well, I assume that if I was like you the action wouldn't seem so repugnant."

He stepped up beside me. "It would not be abhorrent. Feeding with a…loving partner is a very pleasurable act."

My heart slammed in my chest. My hands clenched at my sides and I paced away, then turned to look at him.

"It's sexual?"

246

He nodded. "It is more than that. The bond is a connection between mates we cannot deny. You would want to join with me, often." He leveled his gaze. "And I would want to join with you, always."

That was something to think about now wasn't it? Not once did I think that being like him would make me want sex. Even crave it. How could a person like me survive if the act itself turned out to be repulsive?

He turned his back to the rail, leaned up against it. His shirt fell open and I saw the bullet still lodged in his chest. That hole wouldn't be there if not for me. Gabriel had gotten that little piece of lead when he came to my rescue. He just stood there, leaning against the wall. He waited for my decision, giving me any pressure.

I took a deep breath and let it out on a rush. He suffered because of me. Could I do no less than make sure he was at least as comfortable as I could make him? "It won't hurt and you won't take too much?"

He pushed away from the rail. "I will never hurt you. I give you my word."

I stepped closer to him, released a few of the buttons on my shirt and tilted my head. "Well, there you go, Vlad, have at it." I made a face. "Or should I call you Drac? You did turn into a dragon."

He chuckled. "Close your eyes."

When I did as he asked, his hands cupped my face. His soft lips feathered over my eyelids, down over my cheeks then pressed against my lips. He bit my lip gently and I gasped. When my mouth opened, he took advantage, sliding his tongue between my lips.

I groaned as the wet velvet sweep took me by surprise. Heat pooled in my middle and moisture seeped between my legs. Too soon, his lips left mine and he nibbled and kissed his way to my neck then up to my ear.

"You are so beautiful, Alicia. You taste exquisite," he breathed against the outer shell.

My legs almost gave out at the sensation of his tongue caressing my ear, the gentle suction on the lobe. My head dropped back, leaving the curve of my neck exposed.

His mouth trailed back down to my throat and he suckled there for a moment. His hands moved over my back, making soothing circles, relaxing me.

Before I knew what was happening, one split second of pain gave away to a pleasure so intense, I think I had an orgasm standing in his arms. I'm not sure though, I felt half-drunk, as though I was in some sort of weird trance.

He lifted me and in my trancelike state, I forgot this was real and not another of my erotic dreams. I wrapped my arms around his neck, my legs around his waist and rode him.

Gabriel held me tight, one hand held me by the back of the head. The other rested under my rear and his hard shaft pressed against my nether parts. Joy swept through me as I realized that I wasn't scared of him, of what he wanted to do.

We ignored the sounds of the city below us. Traffic moved through the city and horns honked. Tires screeched below just before a dull thud sounded in an accident.

Soon, he pulled his head back and licked at the skin of my neck. He raised his head and kissed me again. It was a long, drugging kiss. I'm sure it touched both of our souls. I knew it touched mine. I would never be the same again.

I feathered my fingers through his hair and opened my mouth to deepen the kiss. Did it matter that he was a vampire? Did I care that he had turned himself into a dragon?

No.

He was still the same man I had fallen head over heels in love with. I pulled my head back and stared into his passion glazed eyes, speechless.

"What's wrong? You look surprised."

He didn't reach into my mind and take the information he wanted and I kissed him for that. It was another long, drugging kiss that left us both breathless.

"I just realized something," I said, after I reluctantly pulled my lips from his.

"And?"

The tension built within him as he fought against his desire to peer into my mind even as he kept his thoughts open to me. He respected my privacy and waited for me to tell him.

"I—I think I love you."

My heart filled with wonder as I gazed deep into his beautiful eyes. They turned molten silver at my declaration.

He lowered his gaze and stared at my lips in rapt fascination. "Say that again, please."

"I love you."

It was easier to say the second time around.

He threw his head back and laughed happily. "That's what I thought you said." He twirled us around, making me dizzy.

I have never seen a man so happy in my life. Delight shone on his face. The positive energy pulsating around him could have lit up a Christmas tree. I was shocked that I even saw it.

Chapter Ten

I MOVED MY HAND THROUGH THE GLOWING COLORFUL WAVES AROUND his body. The bright colors rippled and swayed with the fluttering of my hand. The night breeze filtered through it, and it danced merrily with the small gusts.

"No one ever told me I would begin to see auras. Is that natural for a Guide?" I asked, still watching him, awed that I could see the amazing light show his aura provided.

Small starbursts exploded around him and I wondered what my own aura looked like.

He shrugged. "Every Guide has their gifts. Yours may be seeing the aura. You will know when people are sick, lying, nervous, or any other emotion once you learn to identify what it does to the energy field around the body."

"That's cool, I suppose. As gifts go, it isn't a particularly great one though. I would have preferred telekinesis." I sighed. "Oh well, you can't have everything."

Since I didn't know how to read auras, but I knew my husband's personality, I figured the bright colors and starbursts were a good thing. I am thinking darker colors are going to mean illness or evil.

Suddenly, I realized the position I was in and felt my face heat. "Um..."

"Yes?" he said with a smile. "Is there something wrong?"

I unwrapped my legs from around his waist and let him lower me to the floor, roof, whatever.

"We seem to have gotten a little carried away. I'm sorry." My cheeks burned with my embarrassment.

"I'm not."

Gabriel wouldn't let me apologize. He placed his fingers over my lips and smiled.

"After the declaration you just made, you could do just about anything right now and I wouldn't be upset." He gave me a squeeze.

The light reflected from his eyes filled me with happiness. Maybe we did have a shot at a life together. It was like Tasha said to me on my wedding day. He was probably the only man in the world who would be this understanding and this gentle.

I blinked back the tears that threatened to embarrass me.

"Shh, Alicia, do not do this," he said, wiping the tears away with his thumbs when they made their way down my cheeks. "I cannot bear to see you cry."

"I'm happy, Gabriel. I'm crying because I'm happy."

I leaned into him, wrapped my arms around his waist and inhaled his unique scent.

"You are the best thing that has ever happened to me. I don't deserve you."

And, I didn't. I couldn't think of one thing I have ever done in my life that would have made God give me such a wonderful man to love.

He gently probed my mind, then smiled. "I am the one who does not deserve you, Alicia." He pushed the hair from my face and cupped my cheek. "I will cherish you like the treasure you are until my dying breath."

He kissed me gently then. So gently, tears pooled in my eyes again and made my vision go blurry. I pulled back, gave him my best wobbly smile and he kissed me again, so tenderly I thought my heart would break.

I don't know what alerted him to the fact that we were no longer alone on the rooftop. He suddenly raised his head, turned and pushed me behind him so fast I almost tripped over my big feet.

You have lovely feet.

How do you know? You have never seen my feet.

I beg to differ, wife.

I stuck my tongue out at his back.

I saw that.

You did not! You have your back turned to me.

Okay then, I felt it. Now behave. We are no longer alone. He moved restlessly in front of me and I wondered what put him on edge.

I changed the subject. *Do* not *remind me about my first night in your home, husband. You just might make me mad.*

I felt his eyebrow rise in my mind more than I saw it.

I shudder at the thought.

Oh, shut up! The man drove me nuts half the time. Nevertheless, I loved him and I took this opportunity to tell him so again.

"I do love you, Gabriel. I don't care that you're a..."

"Blood sucking fiend?" He turned slightly to look into my eyes.

"I didn't say that."

Did I even imply that I thought him to be a monster? I frowned. Perhaps I did the first night we met. That night was little more than a blur.

I do remember being frightened of him. But, I was frightened of everything for a while. I looked up into his eyes, rested my hand against his clean-shaven cheek and smiled.

"You forget. I have met real monsters. No matter what nature has made you and no matter what the thoughtless may have called you in the past, you are the gentlest man I have ever met." I leveled my gaze so he would know that I meant what I said. "I have never thought of you as a monster."

The unmistakable sound of clapping came from the corner of the roof over his left shoulder. Gabriel turned and shoved me more squarely behind him, placing himself between the unknown person mocking us and me.

His soothing presence in my mind kept me calm. Now that I knew what he was, I also knew there was no way anyone would ever be able to take me away from him. Not for long, anyway.

"How touching." The strange female voice was filled with sarcasm.

Gabriel relaxed a bit, but still stood in front of me, pressing me into the wall behind my back. I rested my hand against the firm muscles of his back needing the comfort of his solid form beneath my hand.

"What do you want, Micella?"

I peered around him, wanting to see the woman who had enough courage to mock a being as powerful as my husband.

Long dark hair hung over her shoulders in glossy waves that framed her stunning face. She was easily one of the most beautiful women I have ever seen.

She was also one of the most malicious looking women I have ever seen as well. Her eyes were dark and hard, as though she had seen and done things that would change a person's view on life forever. Perhaps she had.

Her aura was cloudy. Murky. A bit like muddy water. It reminded me of a trip to Lake Erie when I was younger. The landscape and shore was beautiful but the water looked polluted. Perhaps her mind was just as polluted as that lake had appeared to be.

She licked her lips rather noisily. "A bit of your...dinner would be nice."

Gabriel's anger and distrust were tangible. His aura had grown in size, instead of rising three feet above his body. It appeared to surround us both in a protective shell, a circle about twelve feet in circumference.

I looked up at it in awe. The hair on the back of my neck rose and I felt the power stirring in his aura. My skin began to tingle as if I had just stepped into a pool of carbonated water.

Do not move. The mood she is in is volatile and I do not want to hurt her if I can avoid it.

"How sweet, Gabriel."

Her gaze flicked over me briefly then she dismissed my presence as though I was beneath her. Almost as if I were nothing more than an insect that she would like to squash.

"Are you really afraid I'll attack your little snack?" She made a face. "Getting a little selfish in your old age, aren't you?"

She sauntered toward us and chuckled. She stopped just before Gabriel and rested a hand on his chest. I got a glimpse of her sultry look from my husband's mind before he blocked me.

"Why don't you get rid of your little *friend* so we can reminisce?"

I narrowed my eyes and thinned my lips. *Reminisce?*

She meant nothing to me, Alicia. Surely, you didn't think I have remained innocent throughout my many years on Earth. You know I am Cartuotey. You know what it is we are required to do.

Well, you've got me there, I grumbled into his mind. *It doesn't mean I have to like it, you know.*

Is that jealousy?

I could almost feel his smile. *Oh, shut up!*

She leaned forward and whispered something in Gabriel's ear. He stood straighter, then moved back a bit before drawing me up beside him and under his arm. The gesture struck me as possessive and protective.

"I'm sorry, Micella. I should have introduced you to my *wife* sooner."

Her eyes widened and her gaze left his face and she trained it on me.

I fought the urge to squirm under her scrutiny. Instead, I stood taller, squared my shoulders and wrapped my arm around my husband's waist. I gave her the most sickening sweet smile I could muster and introduced myself.

"I'm Alicia. It's so nice to meet you, Micella. Gabriel has told me so much about you."

Little liar.

I ruthlessly pinched his side until I felt his mental wince, then I turned up the wattage of my smile.

I may be a liar, but you are a dog, Gabriel. A real dog. How many women

253

have you been with anyway?

He chuckled. *Do you really want to know?*

I bit my lip. *Wait a minute. Let me think…uh, no.*

"You dare to laugh at me? You think this is funny?" Micella snarled at Gabriel.

She turned her terrifying gaze on me and I fought the urge to run screaming for my life. Something told me if I ran, she would be on me in a heartbeat, her teeth buried in the soft tissue of my neck as she ripped my throat out.

Her eyes began to glow an iridescent red in the darkness. Her beautiful face turned ugly. Already long canines grew longer, giving her a freakish look, like something out of a science fiction movie.

Gabriel shoved me behind him again.

"I laughed at something private my mate said. It had nothing to do with you, Micella. Do not force me to hurt you."

I rested my forehead against his back and breathed in the spicy scent that was uniquely his. He backed up again, his body crowded mine against the cold, hard brick wall at my back.

I bit my lip in an effort to keep my mouth shut. The last thing I wanted to do was to incite her further.

She will not harm you, my heart. Never fear.

I don't fear for myself. My hand lifted, almost of its own volition and rested on his hip. *I'm afraid that you will never forgive yourself if you have to hurt her because of me.*

No, Alicia. I would never forgive myself if I allowed her to harm you. Your safety is all that matters to me.

I made a face. *Is she like you? I have assumed so, given her earlier comment about you sharing your snack. Namely me. Well, that and her glowing eyes kind of gave her away.*

He chuckled into my mind and it relaxed me. The sound of his laughter soothed my frazzled nerves.

He must have done something to me. He had to have. Suddenly, I was as calm as I would be if we were at home, sitting in the living room, sipping iced tea or playing a trivia game. No. Scratch that. I don't ever want to play a trivia game with a vampire. I still had no idea how old he was and his age could give him an unfair advantage.

How old are you anyway? I asked with a frown.

I felt his amusement at my sudden curiosity. *Why do you want to know?"*

Because I want to know how many college courses to make you pay for before I can play a trivia game with you, you goon.

He made a strange noise and I frowned. *Did you just snort?*

I do not snort.

I felt more than heard his laughter and I grinned, glad that I could make him feel such happiness. When the feeling was gone, my consciousness dragged me back to our present situation, kicking and screaming.

"Don't you *dare* ignore me, Gabriel!"

Our attention was back on Micella. The woman was a real threat. I don't know why I had been able to forget that. Was it because I was with Gabriel? Did he really have some sort of mental power that allowed him to take away my fears?

I had reached a point where I didn't really care. Whatever the reason, I was not safe and I wouldn't be until this was all over.

Gabriel reached down and laced his fingers with mine. *Never fear, my love. No harm will come to you as long as I live.*

I whimpered at the thought of losing him. Something horrible could happen to him and I would be alone again. I didn't want that.

The sensation of his arms wrapping around my shoulders startled me, because his back was to me and one of his hands still held mine with our fingers interlaced. I pressed my cheek between his shoulder blades and tried to have faith in my husband.

I am a very hard man to kill, Alicia.

That does not make me feel any better you know.

"Damn it, you two, I will not be ignored! Do you hear me?"

Micella was in a rage. She knew we communicated with each other using our minds and she definitely didn't like it.

"Listen to me, you little slut. He can speak like that with any woman he takes blood from." She sneered. "Wife or not. If you were his true mate he would have changed you."

I think you'd better do something about her, honey. We don't have all night.

Her tirade, meant to make me uncomfortable, only served to make me feel better. He wanted to change me, he had already said as much.

Hmmm...Honey, I like the sound of that.

I wanted to revel in my newfound love for him. For once, I wanted to *show* him how much I cared. I couldn't with an audience. My feelings and old hurts were still too new and too raw to put them on display.

Gabriel sighed then spoke as if he were speaking to an incorrigible child.

"I am centuries older than you, Micella. Please do not force me to show you the things I have learned about killing in my considerable existence."

Micella sneered then stepped back. "She will be unprotected one day, Gabriel." Her voice distorted as she changed shape into that of a large raptor. "And that day will be her last."

Chapter Eleven

I HEAVED A SIGH WHEN SHE FINALLY LEFT AND DISTURBING THOUGHTS RACED through my mind.

"You're *centuries* older than her?"

No wonder Tasha said he was old enough to have learned patience. My thoughts centered on my best friend's words. She knew about him. That meant...

"Tasha is..." My gaze darted around the rooftop before I managed to gather my courage to look into his eyes. "Are Tasha and Micah..." I couldn't force myself to voice the question even though, deep inside, I knew the answer.

He nodded. "Yes, Alicia. They are both like me. Though Tasha was a Guide, like you, before they handfasted and linked their lives together last winter."

"Tasha really is around my age then?"

I didn't know why the thought of her being so much older than I am bothered me, but it did.

"She is your age," he said with a nod.

"That's good," I mumbled.

Now that the danger was gone, shock set in. The world began to spin and my head felt muzzy. I watched, stunned, as the ground moved slowly up to greet me.

WHEN I WOKE, IT was to the sound of a news anchor's voice droning softly in the background. I heard something vague about vampire murders. However, I was too out of it to pay attention.

My head ached and I wondered if I hit my head when I fell. I reached up to feel for a lump. There was none. I smiled. Of course there wasn't.

Gabriel must have caught me. He would never let me hit the floor as I first imagined. My stomach growled loudly, reminding me that it had been way too long since my last meal.

The sterility of my surroundings lent to the idea that I must be in a hotel room. There was a small desk with a ladder-backed chair in the corner and a large, curtained window let in way too much light for my pained head.

Rolling over, I noticed an occupied easy chair on the other side. My husband sat in it, his eyes closed, his long legs outstretched. I frowned. He couldn't possibly be comfortable.

Standing, I stretched and headed toward the bathroom. A shower was in order and I needed to use the facilities. Not necessarily in that order.

The shower did a lot to clear my head. I stayed beneath the hot spray long enough to wash my demons down the drain for a few more hours.

After my shower, I dressed in the clean nightshirt I found waiting for me on the bathroom counter then decided to take a nap. I figured being unconscious doesn't have quite the same recuperative powers as actual sleep, since I was still exhausted.

By the time I exited the bathroom, the sun was high in the sky. It warmed the room to an almost uncomfortable level and made it too bright to sleep. I closed the blinds and drapes, turned the thermostat down a few more degrees then approached Gabriel slowly.

He looked so peaceful and strangely, innocent, sitting in that chair with his eyes closed. I stepped between his legs and tapped him on the shoulder. His eyes opened slowly and he looked up at me curious, at first.

"Is there something wrong?"

It was almost as if his words galvanized him to action. He stood abruptly and pushed me behind him and I almost fell onto the chair.

"No. There's nothing wrong. I just thought..."

Unable to finish my sentence, I swallowed around the lump in my throat. I was about to pass a point of no return. What I had been about to say would lead me to an invisible line I still wasn't sure I was ready to cross.

Even though I wasn't sure I was ready, he was exhausted. It showed in the fine lines around his mouth and eyes. He had aged in the last few days and it showed. Besides, it wasn't fair for me to get the comfortable bed, while he slept on the chair.

"I thought maybe you might like to—to join me on the bed."

He stood up straighter and looked at me. I spied a sliver of hope in his eyes and I hated to dash it.

"Are you sure?"

"Yes...no..." I paced in front of him. "Hell, Gabriel, I don't know."

Swallowing my fear, I led him to the bed, pushed him down into a sitting position and sat on his knee. "I—I want to make this a real marriage someday and we have to start somewhere." I motioned to the bed.

"This seems as good a place to start as any. I'm not sure I'm ready for the physical part yet so I'm asking you to wait on that." My gaze darted from him to the bed and back again. "Do you think you can sleep next to me and not do anything I don't want you to do?"

His Adam's apple bobbed in his throat and he nodded. "Yes. I can sleep here with you without ravishing you, if that is what you're asking."

My face heated at his words. Ravish seemed like a more antiquated and civilized word than rape but it still meant the same thing.

"Good."

I cleared my throat and started to stand but he pulled me back down to his lap. I stiffened when he wrapped his arms around me but relaxed after he gave me a quick peck on the cheek and released me.

He settled back with his head on the pillow and was asleep before I rounded the foot of the bed to climb into the other side. I stayed awake for a while and marveled that this perfect, handsome man was mine before I slipped back into my dreams.

THE BLANKETS WERE IN a pile on the floor when I woke on my side of the king-sized bed. Gabriel still lay next to me, sleeping. I looked toward the window. It was dark out and the hotel was quiet.

It must be late.

I climbed out of the bed, made my way to the chair I had found my husband sleeping in earlier and sat down. Everything had this surreal quality to it and I wondered if I was dreaming again.

My answer came when I suddenly felt invisible lips on my skin. My nipples hardened and my breath hitched.

"Oh, God," I moaned. "Not now."

Not while I was sleeping in the same room with Gabriel. If I wasn't able to wake up and I did finally awaken still beside him in the throes of an orgasm. I would be mortified.

Long fingers gently slid up my thigh, pushed around the elastic of my panties, through the folds of my nether lips and circled my clit.

My hips undulated above the chair, my heels digging into the thick carpet. In my other dreams, I had some semblance of control. Not this time. I couldn't turn it off.

Before, I had been able to end the dream and wake myself up. Then I would either work myself to an orgasm or suffer through the frustration of not getting a release.

It was different this time. I couldn't force myself to wake up. Soon I would need more. More stimulation, more heated kisses. My invisible dream man wouldn't be enough for me anymore.

Only the real, tactile sensation of touch would make this burning need go away. My hand trailed down over my stomach, my fingers delving beneath my panties, into my sex.

I stole a quick glance at Gabriel. He lay there, his eyes opened, watching me. His shuttered expression told me nothing. How long had he been awake? Did he see what I had been doing? Had my moans awakened him?

My face burned. He had to know. How could I convince him I wasn't the shameless hussy I apparently appeared to be? More importantly, did I really want to convince him of that?

The mental picture of our naked bodies entwined on the bed was nearly my undoing. I whimpered softly as the need to orgasm took control of my reason.

I searched his gaze. Those usually expressive eyes told me nothing as I stared deeply into their depths.

Was I awake? God, I certainly hoped not. I looked down at myself, at my hand buried between my legs. The fingers of my other hand rested on one of my nipples giving proof that I had stroked the hardened peaks of my breasts.

Somehow, I had fallen asleep in this chair and fondled myself until I woke us both up. I thought about how I must look with my fingers buried between my legs and tears burned my eyes.

"Oh, God."

My cheeks warmed as his gaze held mine. I sat immobilized. There was no mistaking what I had been doing to myself and no way to deny it.

A sexual awareness had awakened within me and the tension of my unfulfilled dreams kept building. Would I wake up one morning and find that I had lost control of myself? Would I give my body to the first man available because my husband wasn't present? Or, would I have the courage to cross this room and finally put both of us out of our misery? Was I brave enough to crawl back into that bed and let my husband teach me about the ways of love?

He read my mind again. He must have. Without saying a word, he sat up and held out his hand. I stared at it. Knew the decision he asked me to make would not be an easy one.

My body kept me rooted to the spot. He dropped his hand, grabbed the hem of his shirt and ripped it over his head.

"Come to me, Alicia. Please do not continue to torture us both this way."

I shook my head. "I—I can't."

Other than allowing me to get to my feet, my body still refused to cooperate. I stood in front of the chair and stared at his perfect, tanned torso held prisoner by my own traitorous body.

He raised a brow. "You can't or you won't?" He leaned back on the bed, his elbows supporting him. The muscles in his arms bulged, his pecs rippled and I felt my gaze drawn to his enticing, bare, washboard stomach.

Short golden hairs covered his abdomen. A light dusting of hair covered his chest, circled around his flat brown nipples. The fine blonde down tapered to a vee that narrowed then disappeared beneath the waistband of his slacks.

I closed my eyes. Just for a moment. The aesthetically beautiful expanse of his chest was almost too much for me to take. He had given his word not to touch me unless I wanted it and that was probably why he didn't undress when he climbed into bed earlier.

"Why can't you come to me, Alicia?"

Concern showed in his eyes. He was so thoughtful, worried so much about my feelings. It surprised me that he could seem so unconcerned about the large bulge beneath his waistband.

"That is my problem not yours, sweetheart. Do not let it concern you," he said with a soft smile.

The words, so similar to those uttered by my dream Gabriel, reminded me that this man had promised he would not take more than I was willing to give. Only one question remained. Could I trust him to keep that promise?

"Give me a chance, Alicia," he said as he held out his hand again. "Allow me to show you what love is."

Tears of fear and frustration ran down my face and I wiped them away with the backs of my hands.

Gabriel took a deep breath and let it out slowly. "I cannot make that decision for you. This is one you must make on your own."

He sat up then stood. I looked away, trying not to stare at his exposed chest. I refused to think about the sensations fluttering around the inside of my stomach. Biting my bottom lip, I squeezed my eyes shut.

"At least let me comfort you." He walked over to where I stood, lowered himself back to the chair, where he knew I would feel safe.

I moved to stand between his legs, my head bowed with shame.

"I'm sorry. I didn't mean to do that." I gestured toward the lower half of my body with my hand. "I was sleeping." The last came out on a sob. "God, Gabriel, why do I do that in my sleep?"

He drew me down onto his lap and wrapped his arms around me. "You need release. You need a real orgasm."

He pushed my head back down to his shoulder when I raised my head to tell him that I'd made myself come.

"Masturbation is only a pale imitation of what we could achieve together."

"This is only going to get worse, isn't it?"

I rested my head on his shoulder. Why didn't he get angry with me? Any other man would have lost his temper by now. Another man would have ranted about how I'm a prick tease.

"Sh..." He breathed into my ear. "Do you trust me?"

Chapter Twelve

DID I?

That was a good question. I thought for a minute, then nodded.

"Yes." I think my answer surprised us both. His hands stilled on my back for a moment.

He swallowed and nodded.

"Good." He leaned me back over his arm. "Now relax." His hands started to move in slow circles over my back and hips and I allowed myself to relax into him.

He shifted and moved me on his lap so my head rested more comfortably against his shoulder then buried his face in my neck.

"You always smell so good."

The term good-enough-to-eat popped into my head and I remembered our activities from the night before. A rush of heat pooled in my stomach and blossomed out to my pelvic region.

Moisture rushed between my legs and my nether parts twitched out the same rhythm his tongue made as it danced across my sensitive flesh.

He kissed my collarbone and jaw, working his way up to my lips. I moaned as he pressed his mouth against mine. Taking advantage of my opened mouth, he plunged his tongue inside.

My flesh heated. Goosebumps rose on my skin and my womb clenched with need. I wanted to lose myself in the kiss. Desperately, my arms snaked around his neck, my fingers tangled in his hair and I moved to straddle his hips.

"This feels so wonderful. You make me feel so cherished. I wish the whole act felt this good."

I forced the words out when his lips left mine to travel to my ear. Following his lead, I sucked the lobe of his ear into my mouth and bit down gently.

My neck tingled and burned every time his lips trailed over the spot where he had fed last night. I felt strange inside, kind of nervous and sick, yet not. The muscles in my stomach clenched and I realized this was true desire on a level I had never reached before.

It surprised me to discover that I really wanted Gabriel. I wanted to find out what was about having sex that everyone loved so much.

I would give him this one chance. To satisfy my curiosity and to help him with the release I knew he hungered for, I decided to go through with it, to trust him, just this once.

With that monumental decision made, I settled deeper within his embrace and gave my all to the kiss he slanted across my lips.

He pulled me closer. His fingers slid past the elastic of my plain white panties and caressed my rear. I whimpered and ground my sex against the bulge beneath me.

Do you want me?

The question shimmered in my mind. I wasn't sure if he had really asked the question or if it was my subconscious mind asking if I was able to continue.

"Yesss," I moaned as his mouth closed over my nipple, through the soft material of my new silk nightshirt.

The sensation was similar to what I had felt in my dreams but this... this was so much more.

This is real.

My body grew wet with need as his mouth drew on the sensitive peaks. His fingers slid past the slick folds of my nether lips and I cried out.

I thrust my fingers through his hair and held his head to me. I never wanted him to stop. My dream Gabriel hadn't been lying when he said a real coupling was better than my dreams.

I nearly jumped from my skin when his expert fingers circled my clit. The sensation, akin to a small electric shock, surprised me.

"Yesss," I hissed, driving my hips down onto his hand. "I didn't think—"

He pressed his lips firmly against mine. Thrust his tongue into my mouth before he moved back to my neck and ear.

"I never knew—" I gasped when his mouth closed over my nipple again. He lavished attention on first one, then the other.

A familiar pressure began in my pelvic region while a strange heat filled my lower extremities. Flames continued to lick at my flesh as I rode his experienced fingers.

"Come for me, Alicia." He moved his mouth back up my neck and breathed the words in my ear. "Show me the fiery passion I feel buried deep within you."

My head thrashed back and forth. What was it that he wanted from me? I couldn't think. I couldn't breathe. I could only...feel.

"I want you to come for me, my love. Then I want to bury myself deep inside you and make you scream with ecstasy."

He pulled his mouth away from my ear to look deep into my eyes. He stared into my eyes, searching my gaze, looking for something. Perhaps it was fear.

"Does that frighten you?"

His hips thrust against me as I ground myself into his hard cock and shook my head, my actions belied my words.

"Yes. It scares me to death but I've never wanted anything more in my life."

I whimpered softly when his fingers found an especially sensitive spot. I ground my hips against him again. I bent my head, suckled his neck.

"God, that feels good, Gabriel."

"Will you come for me, love?"

"Yes!" I screamed against his shoulder and rode his hand.

He thrust a finger deep into me, rubbing a sensitive bundle of nerves inside me to heighten the sensation and I groaned against his throat. My hips jerked involuntarily and I shuddered as his fingers brushed over my clit once more.

Gabriel stood easily with me in his arms. I wrapped my legs around his waist, giving little thought to the fact that I had just opened myself to him.

If he decided to drop his pants and thrust his hard shaft inside me. I wouldn't be able to stop him. Truthfully, I didn't know if I would want to.

The thought struck quickly and without warning that, with his massive strength, he could have done that at any time since I moved in with him. Yet, he hadn't.

Tears burned my eyes as I realized my trust in him was not misplaced. I wrapped my arms more securely around his neck, buried my fingers in his thick hair and whispered into his mind.

I want you to show me what it's like.

He laid me down onto the big bed, his hands reached for the waistband of his slacks and he paused.

"Are you sure?"

I looked up into his swirling silver eyes and nodded.

"You could have taken what you wanted from me at any time, regardless of my feelings. Yet, you didn't." I sat up then reached up to smooth a stray lock of hair from his face. "I've come to the realization that if I can't trust you, I can't trust anyone."

His hands shook as he unfastened his pants.

"You will not regret it. I swear."

My eyes widened when his pants slid over his narrow hips and revealed the size of his hardened member. I swallowed and blinked slowly.

Six months ago, I would have found that part of the male anatomy disgusting. Yet, Gabriel's massive shaft didn't generate that type of response.

He rested his forehead against mine and smiled. *For that, I will be forever grateful.*

My gaze darted back up to his face as my cheeks warmed. I nervously licked my lips and gave him a wobbly smile.

He lowered himself over me, settling his hips between my spread thighs. I fought the urge to close my legs and tell him I had changed my mind. I couldn't do that to him. I gave him my word and intended to keep it.

He stared into my eyes. His glowed red and I knew he struggled with his inner beast. Still, I wasn't frightened. No matter what he looked like, nothing could make me believe he would ever hurt me.

"It will most likely kill me, but I will find a way to stop if you tell me to."

He bent down, lowering his head to lap at my nipples, first one then the other. My arms wrapped around his neck and I thrust my fingers though his hair. My head thrashed on the pillow and my hips bucked of their own volition.

Wasn't that silly? Even *I* knew there was no turning back, now.

"Show me what love is, husband," I said as I cupped his cheek and gently kissed his lips. "Love me."

"I do," he breathed against my neck.

"Make love to me, Gabriel." I amended my instructions.

He tilted his head into my hand then kissed my wrist.

"Your wish is my command, wife."

The next kiss was long. He thrust his tongue deep into my mouth. I suddenly felt strange, drugged, as if all of my inhibitions had been swept away by that one meeting of our lips.

His mouth left mine to trail kisses over my cheek and neck. He worked his way slowly down my body to my hips and I wondered why he still hadn't thrust inside me yet.

Because you aren't ready, he whispered into my mind. Aloud, he said, "Do you trust me?"

"Yes, amazingly enough, I do," I answered with a nod.

My womb clenched when I realized what he had in mind. I opened my mouth to tell him not to bother, that I was ready for his possession but he spoke first.

"Good. Hold that thought."

He lowered his head to my already creaming sex. His warm breath stirred the short curls just before his tongue stroked the tiny pulsing nub.

I mewled incoherently as he sucked the swollen bud into his mouth. My hips bucked up, my fingers thrust though his thick hair and I held his head to me as I screamed through another orgasm.

Gabriel crawled back up my body and kissed me again. The head of his cock pressed against my vaginal channel.

"Let me know if I hurt you." He pushed forward slowly, easing his shaft into my painfully empty body.

Sweat beaded on his brow. A testament to the tight rein he had on himself. The muscles in his neck bulged and his face was tight with a near grimace. If I didn't know that men found this so enjoyable, I would have thought he was in pain.

He pulled out then surged forward again, moving his thick shaft deeper. Each time he reentered my clasping channel, he sank his huge erection deeper inside me.

It felt good. Too good. And I was no longer frightened. Not of him. I would never be frightened of him again. Finally, I raised my hips on his downward thrust and seated his shaft all of the way inside me.

His hands grabbed my hips and held me still for his slow invasion. He set an unhurried pace that quickly drove me over the edge. Still, I knew there was something more. Something he held back because he was afraid he would hurt me.

"Please, Gabriel," I gasped. My head thrashed on the pillow. "Show me everything."

"Wrap your legs around my waist," he growled against my breast.

I did as he asked and gasped when he thrust deeper and sucked my nipple into his mouth. The sharp abrasion of his teeth, felt so good. I never thought something that could hurt, no matter how little, could still feel so good.

"I need..." I let my words trail off. I wasn't sure what it was I needed.
More.

My heels dug into his back and I brought my hips up to meet his. He thrust deeper, harder. His sac slapped against my rear every time he rammed himself inside me.

The delicious pressure built again and I was on the urge of another orgasm. My heart slammed in my chest and I screamed my pleasure when he lost all control and pistoned his cock into my slick channel over and over before he finally sank his teeth into my neck.

The mixture of pleasure pain sent me over the edge. My vaginal walls clasped around him. Strangely, I felt my inner walls grasping his hard member. He somehow shared the sensation with me as his cock erupted. Warmth filled me as he spilled his seed deep within my body.

Gabriel's mouth still worked gently at my neck. The euphoric sensation rushed through my blood and increased both our pleasure. I could feel him within me, yet I was him and could feel my vaginal walls tightening around his shaft, milking the seed from his body.

Somehow, our minds had linked together. His thoughts and memories raced through my mind. I could feel everything he felt, remember every memory as if it was my own. I saw every virgin he had ever deflowered. Every kill he had ever made was open to me. I could see his life before.

Most of all, I felt his loneliness and the despair he felt every time he lost one of my previous incarnations. My heart broke for the incredibly lonely man he had become. It surprised me to realize how much I wanted to erase his memories of such a lonely existence.

I called a mental retreat. He'd been around a long time. There was a chance that he hadn't always been good. My trust was still too new and too fragile to risk by exposing myself to his violent past. I didn't want to see him do anything that might require an explanation.

Soon, his teeth withdrew from my neck and his tongue swirled around the puncture wounds, soothing the slight sting. I lay limp beneath him like a worn rag doll. I fought to catch my breath and our labored breathing filled the room.

"Wow. That was..." My voice cracked. "That was incredible." I swallowed. My throat was sore and I wondered why.

Gabriel raised himself up on his elbows, looked down at me and smiled.

"Yes it was." He leaned down to kiss the tip of my nose.

"I need a drink. My throat is sore."

"I don't doubt it," he chuckled. He shifted to move off me then stood and walked over to the small table by the door. "With the way you were screaming, your throat may be sore for a while."

My stomach picked that time to grumble out its protest that I hadn't had anything to eat since the day before. Choosing to ignore his last remark, I glanced toward the dark window and frowned.

"How long have we been here?"

The wide expanse of his well-muscled shoulders held me nearly spellbound. I stared at his back and licked my lips. My eyes traveled over his tanned body, following the long line of his spine to his perfectly rounded ass. I smiled, thankful that the man obviously didn't have a shred of modesty.

Shifting myself into a sitting position, I watched as he grabbed a bottle of carbonated water from the table and brought it to me.

"Thanks." I tipped the small bottle back and nearly drained it of its contents. "I'm glad there's more. I think I could drink a gallon of this stuff."

Gabriel smiled, reached out and pushed a stray lock of hair from my face.

"The loss of blood will make you thirsty. I'm sorry I have fed from you twice in such a short time. I shall attempt to refrain to do so in the future."

I shook my head, my cheeks burning. "Does it always feel so—" *wonderfully erotic* "—so...nice with everyone?"

He nodded. "It does. Some of us think it is to ensure compliance from our prey. If it is pleasurable, a person is less likely to protest. Also, we mostly take from opposite sex prey. For example, I only take blood from a man in an emergency."

"Why?"

"Feeding makes both sexes feel... desire. It makes a human male question his manhood when he feels desire for a male *Cartuotey*." His face went blank for a moment. "It is difficult and dangerous to totally remove someone's memory. When we try, we take the risk of causing permanent brain damage. That is why most of us avoid feeding from the same sex." He shrugged then added, "Except Rogues and those of us who enjoy same sex partners. Even then they choose their prey carefully."

"Oh."

My stomach grumbled again and he grinned.

"I apologize. I should have ordered you something to eat this morning."

"This morning? How long have we been here?

"About thirty-six hours. I apologize. I'm still not used to—"

"Hanging out with someone who needs to eat?" I asked with a grin.

"Something like that." He grinned and reached over to the nightstand and grabbed the phone. Picking up the receiver, he placed it against his ear and punched the zero.

"Yes, this is Gabriel Leblanc in room twenty-three ten." He looked over at me as though asking what he thought I would like to eat then winked. "Would you have room service send up an assortment of breakfast items please?"

He paused, listening.

"Have them leave it inside the sitting room if I don't answer." He glanced over at me. "Just charge it to the room. Thank you."

"Sitting room?"

I looked around and spotted a set of double doors that had escaped my notice before. A lot had escaped my notice, before. The large, bureau against the wall between the bathroom and sitting room doors and the large armoire that held the TV and DVD player had both been missed.

"How big is this room, anyway?"

He grinned at me and shrugged. "I wanted to pamper you." He walked to the bathroom and donned a white, terrycloth bathrobe.

He carried another, smaller one back to wrap me in its warm soft folds.

The robes must have been on a warmer, something else I had apparently missed. Heat seeped into me and I realized I had been a bit chilly.

When I would have walked to the door to see the rest of the room, Gabriel scooped me up in his arms and carried me through the set of double doors and I gasped.

"Put me down before you hurt yourself."

My face burned with mortification when he laughed.

"Hurt myself? Sweetheart, I can bench press a truck."

"Oh."

I turned my head, determined to see the room as he carried me down a short hallway to an upper, inside balcony.

A long row of large picture windows stretched out before us. Our room was obviously on the East side of the hotel. The sun peeked over the horizon, kissed the edge of the city below with its golden light. Night purple with morning orange and yellow streaks lit the sky and my mouth dropped open in awe.

"It's beautiful," I whispered like a child in church. "I've never seen anything so lovely in my life."

"I haven't either," Gabriel agreed.

I turned to watch him, but he was looking at me and my face warmed as I realized he'd stared at my rapt expression when he'd made his comment.

He kissed me gently. "You are so beautiful, Alicia. I'm already looking at the most beautiful thing in this world. I'm the luckiest man alive."

The heat of my blush grew stronger and I buried my face in the crook of his neck.

Chuckling, he carried me along the inside upper balcony to a set of winding stairs.

Disappointed in leaving the splendor of the sunrise, I sighed. I didn't complain, though, because I wanted to see the rest of this veritable palace, he called a hotel room.

Once we were downstairs, he sat on the plush, leather sofa still holding me in his arms. I marveled at the strength it took for him to be able to do that.

"What next?" I asked with my head still on his shoulder.

"We make our way to England."

I sat up to look him in the eyes. "Are we going to stay with Tasha and Micah?"

He shook his head. "No. I have a home there. We will be joined by a few of my...associates who will stay with us to assist in keeping you safe."

He stroked my hair. The sensation was soothing and I relaxed against him.

"We can visit Tasha and Micah, of course." I felt him smile. "If you wish to visit them. But first, I shall call my associates and ask them to secure the castle first."

"Associates and not friends?" I wondered at that. Didn't he trust them? "They won't be living with us, will they?" My body stiffened of its own accord and my breathing suddenly became labored and erratic. Then my mind latched on to an irrelevant fact. "You own a castle?"

He chuckled, pulled me to him and rubbed my back. "Yes, I own a castle. As for my friends, I hesitate to call them that because we have not seen each other for such a long time. They will stay in the gatehouse and the rooms over the stables, my love." He held me to him until my trembling subsided.

Tears ran down my cheeks and I bowed my head. I didn't deserve him and I knew it. At present, my biggest fear didn't come from the men who would be staying with us when we arrived in England. My greatest fear was that Gabriel would realize the same thing. I didn't deserve his love and probably never would.

"Sh...stop such upsetting thoughts, Alicia." He cupped the back of my head and brought it to his shoulder. "I love you more than life itself. Nothing, not one thing will ever change that."

Someone knocked on the door and he glanced at me. "That would be our breakfast."

Thumbing the tears from my cheeks, he smiled and gently kissed my forehead before he set me on the couch.

"Don't move. I'll be right back."

He strode around the corner and I settled into the comfortable warm, buttery leather sofa to wait for my breakfast.

The murmur of voices reached me before Gabriel's thoughts burst into my mind.

Run! Go up the stairs and out through the other door. I will catch up with you in a few minutes. I can take care of myself, he said when I hesitated. *Just run!*

A spitting noise came from the hall. I leapt from the couch and ran up the stairs, ignoring the long line of windows that had so captivated me just moments before. I knew that sound. It was a horrible sound. I heard it several times the night my aunt and grandmother were murdered. It was gunshots through a silencer.

My mind reached for Gabriel. Instead of his calm, soothing presence, I felt an emptiness I couldn't bear to contemplate.

Tears blinded me as I quietly crept into the bedroom to gather my clothes and shoes. They were dirty, but they were all I had now. I didn't even have my husband any longer.

His constant soothing presence that had been in my mind over the last few weeks was gone. I'd never even realized he had been there, dulling my fears and pain until his calming presence was no longer there.

Nothing was left but a sea of fear and uncertainty without his calming presence. His absence was like a big gaping hole in my psyche. I berated myself for allowing him to put himself in danger by marrying me. I should have known those fanatics would never give up.

Slipping out of the suite through the bedroom upstairs, I ran to the nearest public restroom to get dressed. After changing and wasting a few precious moments on useless tears, I washed my face with shaking hands.

I searched the bathroom for something, anything, I could use as a weapon. There was nothing. When I realized my search was fruitless, I did the only thing I could think of to disguise myself. I wet my hair to give it the appearance of a darker color.

Looking in the mirror, I squared my shoulders then strengthened my resolve and slipped out through employee's entrance of the hotel.

Those fanatical bastards just killed my husband. I should have been more careful. I should have known my happiness was too good to last. My jaw clenched and I ground my teeth together.

Gone was the frightened rape victim who was afraid of her own shadow. In her place was born one pissed bitch with her mind bent on revenge.

Chapter Thirteen

"You can't do this," Cassie argued as I snatched up my purse from the table, ready to go out and use the credit cards Gabriel had given me.

I needed some weapons. Since I couldn't go back to my childhood home, where Aunt Mags had a veritable arsenal, I would have to purchase them. The credit cards would come in handy. I turned and glared at her.

"Don't tell me what I can or can't do. Those assholes shot my husband. I can feel his absence. If he isn't dead, he soon will be. They have him. They'll kill him," I snarled. "I refuse to stand by twiddling my thumbs while those fanatics kill the man I love then try to kidnap me again."

As if in slow motion, she picked up the remote and turned off the T.V., the silence was deafening. I never realized how much I'd come to rely on Gabriel's presence to sooth my mind until now. My thoughts raced. Was he alive or dead, was he being tortured, mutilated?

A hysterical scream bubbled up from my chest and I clamped my lips together to hold it at bay. Losing control was not an option. I needed to stay focused.

What if he was still alive and held in the same compound those creeps held me in the other day? That warehouse he burned down wasn't the only building there. He would need blood...lots of blood. He would need transportation quickly before they killed him.

Cassie stood and paced away from the sofa. I gritted my teeth and ignored her calm in the eye of the storm attitude. I just wanted to find a gun, any gun and run out of here, chasing after the men who shot and held my husband.

There had been nothing on the news. No reports of a body found at the hotel. That told me those damned devil-worshipping fanatics had him.

There was a very good chance he was still alive. Maybe he was too weak to link with me through our bond. Maybe he was unconscious or, maybe, too large of a distance separated us. I refused to believe he could be dead.

"You should at least ask for help." Cassie picked up the cordless phone on the table next to her. She held her hand out, as if to hand it to me.

I ignored it. "Who would I call? I don't know anyone *to* call."

I thought briefly of my friends in Europe. I had no way to contact them though.

Tasha gave me a number where I could reach them but I threw it away in a fit of anger not too long after my wedding. What can I say? I was stupid.

"I do," she said softly. "I'm a Guide, too. I was raised a Guide." She pressed her lips together in a thin smile. "I'll call my brothers. They'll know what to do."

"You do that," I said with a nod. "Have them come and protect you. I'm going after those bastards before it's too late."

I took a deep breath. I hated so many things about this house when I first came here, but it had never included the way it smelled. Somehow, it always smelled faintly of Gabriel's after-shave. The scent comforted me in a strange way. Almost as if it told me, he was still alive, just waiting for someone to help him.

Tears threatened to fall when that familiar scent hit me. Why had it taken so long to realize we had a chance of a life together? Why did I always have to lose everyone I love?

I went upstairs to shower and change. I needed to see if I could find him. I would have to search for open portals and I couldn't do it when I was so distraught and dirty that I could smell myself. I wrinkled my nose and clomped dejectedly up the stairs.

LATER, AFTER MY SHOWER, I sat at one of the small tables in Gabriel's bedroom. Somehow, I felt closer to him there. His scent permeated everything in the room. If I closed my eyes, I could almost pretend he was on the bed with me, sleeping, just out of reach.

Through wallowing in my own pity, I settled down to find an open portal. Usually, where there were evil fanatics, an open portal was not far away.

I couldn't find an open gate close enough to the city to believe he was kept at any of them and I frowned. Forgetting the others, I decided to let the other Guides handle those. I wanted to find my husband first.

I felt a bit guilty for ignoring those other gates. I knew my job. I knew what I was born to do. This time, this one time, I came first and my love for my husband came first. I refused to let him down.

If, after I found Gabriel in one piece, and still breathing, I just might trot on down to close the portals if they were still open. God help those communities if they were.

My hands shook as I packed a small bag of things I thought we might need. I grabbed a cooler and a few twenty-ounce bottles of what I suspected to be blood from a refrigerator in his room.

I still wasn't sure I could find him. I determined to give it my best shot. Having been able to watch where we were going when Gabriel flew us out of there, I had a direction for a place to start, at least.

I ran down the stairs, my wet hair flying out behind me and started for the foyer.

Cassie grabbed me by the arm as I opened the front door.

"Just hear them out. If you don't like what they have to say, then go ahead and go off by yourself." Her hands squeezed my upper arms as she held me in place.

"I can't say I wouldn't do the same if the man I loved was in the hands of lunatics. But you have to know that going off by yourself is a suicide mission."

I winced at the tightness of her grip and she let me go.

"Sorry." She dropped her hands and wrung them together in front of her. "At least try to get some help. What if Gabriel *is* still alive? Getting yourself killed won't help either of you, will it?"

She was right and I hated to admit it. There *was* a possibility, no matter how small, that my husband still lived. It was that possibility that kept me going. It kept me from lying down on the ground and screaming until my throat was raw.

It also kept me from running into the kitchen to grab a large knife to slit my wrists. Somehow, loving Gabriel had made me stronger.

Something kept telling me he was alive and in pain. I needed to try to go to him, to find him, as soon as possible. Something also told me I would know if he were truly dead. It was what kept me going. It's what kept me functioning instead of cowering in a corner like some abused puppy. This hesitance I felt made me believe he was alive but unconscious.

"Okay," I said on a sigh. "Call your damned friends. Get the friggin' National Guard if you want." I looked her in the eyes. "But if they can't be here by nightfall, I'm going it alone."

Smiling, Cassie gave me a quick hug, grabbed the cordless phone and ran into the living room. When she returned fifteen minutes later, she set the phone down on the polished table and smiled.

"They're coming." She walked into the kitchen, poured herself a glass of cola then returned to the dining room to sit in the chair across from me.

"My two brothers, Mark and Matt are on their way. They're bringing a few friends along."

I nodded, suppressing a shudder. "How many men?" I asked pressing my lips together. I steeled my resolve. These men were coming to help me, not hurt me. I had to keep reminding myself of that.

It was time I became stronger. There's only so much fear and self-loathing I can take and I finally reached my limit. It was about time I shook off that paralyzing fear.

Circumstances last spring made me a victim. My fear *kept* me a victim. I refused to be one any longer. The thought of no longer living in dread of another attack was a freeing thought and a weight lifted from my shoulders.

Within two hours after making her call, Cassie's brothers arrived on the doorstep. They were eight men, all together. Eight strange, armed men standing in my foyer. Men I had to learn to trust.

Every one of the Guides were loaded down with their favorite types of ordinance. Looking them all over, I found the tallest one had the biggest selection. He looked familiar and I recognized him from the mall. Along with the other, shorter *Cartuotey* that seemed to take such an interest in Cassie that day.

Finally pushing the frightened little girl into a small closet in my mind, I looked up at him and grinned. "You can't play if you don't share."

He just looked at me and raised a glossy black brow but stood silent.

Another male stepped forward. He was blonde, not as tall as the brunette was, but had a commanding presence just the same. The man exuded confidence.

He wore his rather long, sandy-blonde hair pulled back behind his shoulders and secured with a tie. Before, I had always thought long hair looked feminine on a man, but not with this one.

"Nathaniel Longstreet, Ma'am. Your husband is a friend of mine. I'd be honored to fight in your stead." He held out a big, beefy hand. I flinched back before I bit my lip and slowly took it.

My face pulled into some hideous form of smile as I tried to overcome my fear of these men. *They won't hurt you. They won't hurt you,* the chant played like some sick litany in my mind.

"I don't think so, *Mr. Longstreet*," I said, shaking my head. "You're not leaving me here to twiddle my thumbs and wait to see if you can find him. I have a good idea where they have taken him and I can't tell you where it is. I can only show you."

I took the time to glare every one of them in the eyes. "I'm going with you or I'm going by myself. Either way, those bastards have to see that I'm through cowering. I am through being a victim. If they can't see that I'm going to put up a fight the next time they try to take me, they'll never leave me alone." I stared every one of them down. "I'm through with being their victim. I'd rather be their nightmare instead."

Rubbing my hands together, I grinned at the tall guy with the black hair again. He had wonderful taste in weapons.

"Hey, stretch. I think I'd like the Uzi. It's short, compact, full of punch and doesn't tend to jam as much as the M-16." Then my eyes lit on something even more to my liking. "Scratch that," I said, pointing behind him. "I'll take the AK-47 you have strapped to your back instead."

One of the other men stepped up. His hair was a plain, dishwater blonde, nothing exceptional. It was his eyes that caught my attention. If eyes really were the window to the soul, then this guy was a glacier. I have never seen such cold, ruthless eyes on anyone.

"Look, lady, you can't go with us."

"Mattie." Cassie stepped up beside me, a warning in her voice as she glared at the strange man. "You promised."

He turned to look at her. "Stay out of this."

She gave him a determined look. "Kiss my ass, Matt. She has a right to go. We're talking about her mate, here." She glared up at the man who I assumed was her brother.

"We'll work this out. There are still a couple of hours till dusk." She turned to me. "How far do you think this place is?"

I shrugged. "Not far from the downtown Marriott as the crow flies." I closed my eyes, thinking. How fast had he been flying? Pretty fast. "Maybe it was forty or fifty miles, now that I think about it." He had flown pretty darn fast because he wasn't afraid of people getting a good look at him.

"Crow flies?" One of the other five men stepped forward and asked.

I waved my hand. "Don't ask." Good grief! I certainly didn't want to go into that.

A thought occurred to me and I wondered if maybe the woman from the other night had anything to do with all of this.

"Do any of you know a woman by the name of Micella?"

The men shook their heads and I sighed. Well it was worth a shot.

278

"This woman... bumped into us the other night. She wasn't very pleasant. She is a vampire and not a very nice woman at all. She—she acted as if she wanted to kill me. She even suggested that Gabriel share me with her." I felt my face heat. "And I don't think she meant for sex."

Another man stepped forward. Of an average height for a man and a Guide, about six feet tall, his broad shoulders tapered down to a narrow waist and flat stomach.

His shock of red hair fell over his face in an adorable but annoying way. Some woman was going to love to hate that hair. Sky blue eyes gazed into mine as he held out his hand.

"Dalton Hunter, Ma'am." He turned and indicated the taller redhead next to him. "This is my brother, Jake. I..." He paused and gestured to his brother *"We* may have an idea who you're talking about. We don't know what she calls herself, but we do know where vamps like her tend to hang out."

Jake gave me a thin smile. "They like to hang downtown at a club called *Demon World.*"

"I've heard of that club," Cassie cut in. "Isn't it supposed to be for weirdoes and freaks?"

"I better never catch you there," Matt said, stepping forward with a fierce look on his face.

"Like I'm that stupid." She rolled her eyes, obviously annoyed that her brother would think she'd go to a place like that.

Jake stepped forward and pinned me with a stare. "What better place is there for a vampire to hang out?"

"Yeah, with all the Goth people there and the weirdoes who believe themselves to be real vampires, the place is a smorgasbord for the true vamps," Matt piped in.

Backing up, I slumped down onto the couch. I looked around, surprised. I didn't realize that I had slowly backed myself into the living room.

It made sense though. These men kept getting closer to me. It isn't any wonder I inexorably found myself backing into the next room.

"Let me guess." I rested my head in my hands. "Rogues like to hang out there too?"

"Of course," They all said in unison.

Now how did I know that?

Another hour later, we had introduced ourselves and started to formulate a plan. Of all the men gathered here, four struck me as capable enough to go in and take those bastards down.

They were *Cartuotey*. How I knew that was beyond me. They all looked like any other of the men, except... only their auras were different. The other men's auras were a glowing rainbow of purples, blues, greens reds and yellow.

Diego Cartucco's, Myles Haversham's, Nathaniel Longstreet's and Joshua Holcomb's auras shouted *Cartuotey*. Laced with a bright white, orange gold and silver they shone brightly around them. It was a veritable lightshow. They resembled Gabriel's. They weren't the same, but similar.

I really needed to get a book on auras so I would know what I'm seeing. I'd already figured out that a dark aura was an indication that you were not speaking to a nice person. My meeting with Micella taught me that.

It wasn't hard to pick Cassie's other brother out of the group. He was Matt's twin. The short *Cartuotey*, the one who seemed to have the hots for Cassie was Joshua Holcomb.

He was a shy looking boy next-door type who struck me as the kind of guy who would stand here wondering how the hell he ended up mixed up in this crap in the first place. However, he was a vampire, so I knew better.

"I can't thank you enough," I said, looking at them all in turn. "For coming to my and my husband's aid." I looked at my watch. "Well, gentlemen, we need to have a plan. Our time is running out.

ANOTHER TWO HOURS LATER, we had our plan worked out and our weapons loaded. The large man with the AK-47, who I learned was Myles Haversham, was kind enough to loan one of his weapons and a few extra clips to me.

"I figured you'd give me a hard time about borrowing this," I said as I took the heavy semi-automatic rifle from him. "Most men don't want to be around a woman with a gun."

He lifted his right shoulder in a casual shrug, looked down at me and grinned. "I figured you knew your way around weapons when you said that bit about the M-16 jamming. Besides, anyone could make one lucky guess on the types of guns I carried, but getting them all right was an indication that you knew your way around them."

"Why do you even carry guns? You're a *Cartuotey*. You don't really need them. I've seen what your kind can do."

"You've seen what your husband can do. The full *Cartuotey* and their mates are a bit more... talented than the rest of us. They can shift into anything they want."

"Full *Cartuotey*?" I'd never heard the term before. "I thought either you were a vampire or you weren't."

"A full *Cartuotey* is bred, not turned. I was turned but I didn't become rogue. I'm basically immortal, strong as ten men and I heal quickly but that's the extent of my powers. Diego and Nathaniel are full *Cartuotey*. I'm sure you noticed that they aren't carrying weapons."

I had, but I attributed it to their being of the undead.

Myles laughed. "Undead, I like that."

"Stop reading my mind, you creep! That's rude!"

"I don't read minds. You project."

"Well, ignore it, then."

"You know a lot about guns," he said, changing the subject.

I nodded. "You could say that."

Aunt Mags had an arsenal in a secret room beneath the basement. Oh, how I wanted to go home, get some of the C-4 she'd acquired, and blow that place to kingdom come. Plus, I'd really love to get my hands on one of her P-ninety clones and her extra clips.

Gabriel burned what had appeared to be the main building they had held me in, but the compound had three more large buildings. God only knew how many fanatics frequented that place or what they kept hidden in the other buildings he didn't have the time to destroy.

Myles rode with me when we left. It was the first time I had driven my new car. He squeezed his tall frame into the passenger seat and gave me a smile. "Nice car."

I smiled, a bit wistful. "Yeah, isn't it? It was my wedding gift."

He nodded. "I know. He told me. He worried you'd never drive it."

Maybe he had worried more that I would never accept him. I wondered if it was his way of saying that without airing our dirty laundry.

Chapter Fourteen

"I HAD...ISSUES." I SHRUGGED AS I BACKED OUT OF THE GARAGE. "I HOPE everyone is ready."

Shifting the car into drive, I mashed my foot on the gas pedal and the car screamed down the long driveway, we were out to the road in no time.

The others were keeping up nicely as I looked into the rearview mirror and smiled. *Good.* I certainly didn't want to waste any more time by losing someone.

We sped North on Highway 131. The stereo blasted out one of my favorite Halloween songs. This time, I just couldn't get the same feel good feeling from it.

I frowned.

Halloween? Was it so close already? What would Gabriel say about my habit of dressing up and joining the children on the streets as they went from house to house begging for bits of candy?

I certainly didn't ask for candy anymore but I still liked to dress up and join the children. At least I used to. I'd thought about starting to do it again this year. I don't know if I'll ever be able to recapture that sense of innocence again. After knowing Gabriel, I wasn't sure I wanted to.

He'd get a kick out of my costume, though, I'm sure of it. My slinky, blood red dress and matching cape would probably make him drool. It was the long, pointed teeth that would make him laugh. Not that I needed them anymore.

I shot Myles a glance and my face burned. I had forgotten what he was. I'm sure he read my mind.

He grinned unrepentantly. "I can't help it. Like I said, you project." He pressed his lips together, obviously trying not to laugh.

"Oh, shut up, Myles." I scowled at him. "And don't you dare say a thing. If I want Gabriel to know I'll tell him."

You'll tell me what? Who is there with you?

Slamming my foot on the brake pedal, I pulled off the pavement onto the shoulder of the highway.

Tears filled my eyes and I started to scream and jump up and down in my seat. "He's alive, he's alive! Thank God." I looked over at Myles. "Gabriel is alive."

He tensed and looked out the window into the darkness.

"He must be close. Where is he? We must be headed in the right direction if we're close enough for you to communicate with him."

Closing my eyes, I reached out to him. *Myles is with me. He wants to know if you know where you are. He says we must be close.*

I got the impression of weakness and pain. Locked in a dark room, with no windows, he had no idea where they held him. He was injured and needed to feed so he could heal more quickly.

His vampire hunger wrapped itself around me. The incredible burning pain nearly made me cry out before he suddenly took control and blocked me from feeling most of it.

Still, his hunger was there, lurking in the background. He needed to feed, badly. My neck throbbed where he had taken blood from me and my stomach clenched. Liquid heat pooled low in my middle and I berated myself for the sexual nature of my reaction at a time like this.

He chuckled softly into my mind. *It is good to know I can stir such a response from you, even in my condition.*

Shut up and tell me if we're on the right track.

He smiled into my mind. *Myles was right. You are close or we could not communicate. I am too...weak for my senses to reach very far.*

It took a lot for him to admit that to me. He knew how much I'd counted on his protection before.

Good. I'm glad I'm close. That just means I'm driving in the right direction.

What? I felt his agitation. He stirred, attempting to use his powers to free himself.

Save your strength. You'll need it when we get there.

We? Who besides Myles is with you? There had better be more than just the two of you.

A few Guide friends of Cassie's brothers' and few more friends of yours are coming with me.

Friends of mine? His agitation subsided a bit now that he knew I wasn't coming to him alone. *Who?*

Diego Cartucco, Nathaniel Longstreet and Joshua Holcomb.

Waves of relief came from him and he relaxed. *I don't know this Joshua, but I think the other two can be trusted, as well as Myles.*

That's it, darling, save your strength. I have a feeling you're going to need it.

I pulled back out onto the highway and the others followed.

Myles had been kind enough to use his cell phone to call the others and tell them why we had stopped so abruptly.

"How is he?" he asked after I pulled onto the road and got back up to speed.

"He's in pain." I bit my lip, worried. "He tried to keep me from knowing, of course, but I felt it, though. Not to mention, he's weak—very weak. He needs to feed so I don't know how much help he'll be when we get there."

Myles cast a glance my way. "He'll be of help. You'll be there. He won't allow any harm to come to you as long as he lives."

He turned to gaze out his window at the passing scenery. I assume vampires can see better in the dark than humans but I don't really know for sure.

"I kind of get the impression that he was upset that I'm coming with you."

"Of course he would be upset. He sees it as you're handing yourself over to them on a platter. As vampires, we are nearly invincible. There are only a few things that will totally incapacitate us."

"Just a few?" I asked, sarcastic. "Apparently bullets are one. What are the rest?" *Stakes, beheading?* I suppressed the urge to laugh hysterically.

My fingers tightened on the wheel. Why does everyone think they get to tell me what to do? First, it was my relatives, even after I reached the age of majority, then Tasha and Micah, closely followed by Gabriel.

I thinned my lips. Who did he think he was, anyway? I don't know him from Adam and he presumes to reprimand me for attempting to save my husband?

"Gabriel is the oldest friend I have. He helped me when I was first turned. He taught me how to feed, how to not become one of the monsters of legend. Of course I would take it upon myself to protect his mate in his stead."

His tone did little to lower my hackles. I was pissed. What was it about me that made everyone want to put me in a padded box for fear I would break?

I paused. *Because you would have.* The thought surprised me. I had been strong, if rather naïve, before the attack. Still, after... after I had been a big baby. I can see that now.

Taking a deep breath, I blew the bangs out of my face and glanced over at him.

"I'm a grown woman, Myles, Mr. Haversham."

I blushed at the use of his given name it was one thing to think of him as Myles, but something totally different when speaking to him. He was my elder—by how many years? I was afraid to ask.

"I do have *some* experience with defending myself, as long as I'm *allowed* to do so."

Gram and Aunt Mags knew that I was a crack shot. I could have picked off every one of the men who had kidnapped me and killed them. However, they still wouldn't let me have a gun. They were too worried about my feeling guilt over killing one of those assholes.

I don't think they put in a bit of thought about the guilt I would feel over their deaths. Or, the utter despair, humiliation and sense of violation I felt at being gang raped.

My grip tightened on the steering wheel again until I was sure it would bend from the sheer force of my anger and hatred of the fanatics who repeatedly insisted on trying to sacrifice me to the devil.

I slanted a glance his way. He still sat stiffly in his seat, his manner brooked no argument but... I *have* said I was never one to take a hint.

I'm a great shot, Mr. Haversham."

"Call me Myles."

I nodded. "Okay, Myles. I'm not kidding. I really am a great shot. Given the right weapon and sight, I can hit a ping-pong ball at two hundred yards. So, you see, you don't even have to let me get close."

"You still don't understand, do you?"

He turned to look at me, acting as though I was some slow child. The weight of his gaze bore down on me and I almost gave in, almost relented.

"They never wanted death to touch you. Your family sacrificed themselves to keep it from touching you. Gabriel would sacrifice himself to keep it from touching you. Because they love you. I know how they think. Your husband, as a full *Cartuotey*, doesn't want death touching his mate."

"It's already too late for that," I said turning off onto exit 120. I turned right, heading East on highway 46 toward Lakeview, made a left onto Federal Road, then a few minutes later, I made another right.

I don't know how I knew where I was going. I just did. It was almost as if Gabriel were leading me. I felt a... pull toward something. I hoped that something was my husband.

The rough dirt road nearly bounced us off our seats. I slowed down. I didn't want to damage my car. We needed it for a getaway.

"Didn't you know?" I finally asked him. My face burned with mortification as I contemplated airing my dirty laundry. "We met six months ago. Gabriel swooped in out of nowhere to save me from—"

Do not!

The sheer magnitude of Gabriel's anger stopped me from finishing what I was about to say.

Why not? It's not like it's some sort of secret. I scowled and turned down another, rougher dirt road. After driving several hundred feet, I pulled off into some bushes and motioned the others around me.

I wasn't aware that you were so ashamed of me.

Gabriel tried to calm my mind. But being without his soothing presence over the last few days, had taught me how to eject him. I did.

It hurt that he was so ashamed of me, of what happened to me that he would stop me from telling his friend. I fought the tears that threatened at his betrayal.

It didn't stop me from wanting to save him. I still loved him and I didn't want him to die. But, I couldn't live with him again. I wanted his love, not his pity. It's just too damned bad I didn't notice the difference between the two before.

Chapter Fifteen

"WHAT NOW?" I ASKED MYLES WHEN WE GOT OUT OF THE CAR AND collected our weapons from the small trunk.

"We walk the rest of the way to the compound," Jake said, shuffling up behind us with a big pack slung over his shoulder. Somewhere along the line, he'd donned a bulletproof vest.

I frowned when I realized I forgot to tell Gabriel the others were with us.

Dalton walked up behind him, slapped him on the back. "Just about ready to roll, brother?"

Jake nodded and turned to walk back to the car.

Diego strode up behind me and started to take my weapons.

"Oh, no you don't!" I jerked them back and glared at him. "No one is going to stop me from going in there. Besides," I said, smiling sweetly. "You guys still don't know where he is."

If I had to, I would keep that information close to my chest until it was too late for them to stop me from accompanying them.

Diego held up another bulletproof jacket. "I was trying to help you with this."

My smart-alecky smile abandoned me as I realized he was giving up his own safety to protect me and I was being bitchy with him.

"Oh! Uh, thanks, Mr. Cartucco."

He offered to take my weapons again and I handed them over to put the jacket on.

"Call me Diego. You will see much more of me over the years, no doubt. After you've chosen."

"Chosen? Chosen what?"

He didn't answer. I'm not even sure he heard my question. He immediately turned and called to the others.

"I can find him now. We're close enough." He flicked his gaze over me then handed the gun and the clips back after I fastened the jacket.

"Make sure she stays in the rear. The last thing I want to do is explain to her mate why we allowed her to get in harm's way."

"Allowed?" I snarled. "*Allowed?* You don't have the right to allow or disallow me anything, mister."

I drew the forty-five Myles had given me to strap to my hip and everyone backed away. It would have been comical if I hadn't been so damned pissed.

"No one tells me what to do."

Alicia.

Leave me alone, damn it!

Do not do this, Gabriel whispered into my mind.

His pain was intense. So intense, I felt it. My left hand strayed to the center of my chest, above my heart.

They had shot him very close to the heart. He couldn't heal properly without blood and his captors weren't forthcoming with sustenance for him. I can't say I blamed them. I certainly wouldn't have trusted a vampire.

I do not blame you for feeling betrayed, my heart.

Don't call me that! Have you forgotten? You don't get to call me nice names like that anymore.

I looked up to see everyone leaving. Gabriel had done what he had intended. He'd distracted me enough so the others could go.

Joshua was the only one left with me, watching me warily as if he thought I might shoot him to go gallivanting off on my own.

Shooting one of them had never been my intention. I had fully intended to shoot myself. I'm so tired of being afraid, of hiding my past and always, always left out of the loop because someone else wanted to protect me.

Trust me.

I did and look where it got me. You're—you're ashamed of me. I swiped at the tears that ran down my face with my free hand. Bitter tears caused by his betrayal.

Never that, dear heart. I didn't want you to tell him because I know you are so ashamed of it yourself. You feel that what happened to you colors you in some way. That it makes you unworthy of friendship or love. Just like you want me to love you for who you are, I want my friends to come to like and respect you for who you are in your heart. Not because they pity you.

I lowered the gun and tucked it back into the holster. Shooting a disgusted look over at Joshua, I said, "Come on, or we're going to miss all of the action."

Turning my attention back to Gabriel I frowned and blew the bangs from my face.

Just because I'm taking your word for it, it doesn't mean you're out of the doghouse, buddy.

I wanted answers for a good many things.

I want you to tell me all about your world as soon as you heal.

His relief was so great when he realized I finally had my emotions back under control that *I* nearly slumped to the ground.

The first thing I want you to tell me, is how you link to me the way you do. I complained. *You're damned lucky I like it. Otherwise, I would have done this a long time ago. Now stop spying on me and get some sleep.*

You would have done what a long time ago?

I cut him off again. He had been about to demand an explanation. Well, he got his answer. But, I'm sure he didn't like it.

The two of us ran through the woods, dodging the thorny vines of the wild blackberries and raspberries. We had fallen way behind the others since Gabriel took it upon himself to distract me. I wasted many precious moments arguing with him.

We had just caught up with the others when they dropped down, crouching behind some bushes at the edge of a large clearing.

"How many do you see?" Matt asked Mark who had a pair of night vision binoculars against his eyes.

I frowned, alternatively glancing between the two brothers. Was it Mark who held the binoculars? I shook my head. It didn't really matter.

Nathaniel, who also had a pair, lowered his to let them drop and hang by the cord around his neck.

"I see seventeen. There's no way to go in there without someone raising the alarm."

Jake sighed. "We certainly can't take them all out at once."

The others nodded their agreement. I sidled between Myles and Diego to see what they were talking about that had them whispering.

I'm nosy like that.

I jerked Nathaniel's NV binoculars to my eyes and watched the guards make their rounds, below us. The compound, about a half mile North of us and down the hill, was lit up like daylight.

Spotlights, hanging from tall lampposts, attached to the roof of every structure, shone brightly down into the center of the buildings to give the appearance of daytime.

We would never be able to sneak in there with all of those guards walking about to raise the alarm over any movement out of the ordinary.

Several armed guards patrolled the perimeter. The interval at which each man made his pass was so tight they barely missed each other.

A sniper would only be able to hit one or two of them before another guard stumbled upon the bodies and raised an alarm.

"Damn it! Why couldn't we catch a break here?" Nathaniel grumbled.

I looked between the men, eyed Matt's sniper rifle, an M40A1 a rifle usually used by the Marine Corps and grinned. He had it set up on a bipod and ready to go.

It looked strange with the weird muzzle attached to its barrel. I tilted my head, trying to figure out what it was. A silencer, maybe?

"Diego, Myles, Nathaniel?"

They turned. "Yes?" Myles asked raising his brow.

"What?" Diego and Nathaniel asked, warily.

"If someone were able to pick off those men one by one, would you three be able to step in and remove the body before the next guard happened upon it?

They nodded. "Of course we would." Myles said then looked at Diego. "What do you think, old man, are you up to it?"

Diego said something to Myles in Spanish that I'm sure wasn't very nice.

"Right back at you," Myles said then looked at me and winked. "How *was* the inquisition, anyway, Diego? Did you burn many heretics?"

Diego snarled at him and went off on another barrage of Spanish.

"Come on you two. Try to show some restraint," Mark said to the two men. He turned to Diego. "I know you're most likely used to people not understanding what you say when you swear in Spanish, but..." He glanced at me and quirked his lips in a half grin then mouthed the words *play along*.

I hate to be the one to break it to you but—"

"I understood every word you said." I clucked my tongue. "Really, Diego, such language."

He reddened and I couldn't resist rubbing a little salt in the wound. I had recognized a few words, but not many.

"What was it you said about Myles, his mother and a barnyard animal?"

Diego choked and Mark shook his head.

"There you see? You have totally shocked Gabriel's mate. What do you think *he's* going to say about that?"

Diego shot me an apologetic glance. "I'm—I'm sorry, Mrs. LeBlanc."

I crossed my arms over my chest. "Don't apologize to me, Diego. Apologize to Myles. It's his mother you've maligned."

When Diego turned to give Myles his apology, the man punched him in the stomach hard enough to make him grunt.

Then he smiled. "Apology accepted. Now let's get down there so our marksman can start picking them off."

The three of them made their way silently through the bushes, down the slope and to the edge of the compound in no time. The shadows in the woods covered their movements quite nicely.

"Okay, Mark. Can I have a go at your rifle? Please tell me that weird looking thing attached to the end is a silencer for it. Otherwise we're only going to get one shot off before they raise the alarm."

Mark shook his head. "Uh, uh. No way. I'm the sharpshooter here."

"We can't afford for you to miss, damn it! Can you hit those men from this distance? Do you *know* beyond a doubt that you can hit them? I *know* I can," I argued. "If you miss and hit something else, we could be discovered. We can't afford that."

"I can do it," he snarled, already checking his load, setting up for the shot.

"You'd better be able to, mister. That's my husband they're holding down there. I won't have you risking his life."

He rested on the ground, waiting for the all clear to go after his first target.

Diego radioed up, "We're in position, Mark. You have a go for your first target."

Mark took aim and pulled the trigger.

Chapter Sixteen

THE RADIO CRACKLED.

"What the hell are you trying to do, kill us? That shot almost hit Diego. Give the damned gun back to Mark, Alicia. I thought you said you were a crack shot?" Myles snarled over the radio.

I grabbed Jake's radio and pushed the talk button.

"That *was* Mark's handy work, you chauvinistic pig. If I had the gun the man would be down. *I* allow for distance and drift."

I let my thumb up off the button, then immediately pushed it again.

"Are those guys wearing armor?"

"Yes, ma'am, they are. So you're going to have to aim high."

I threw Jake's radio back at him and kicked Mark's foot.

"Move it. You're not going to endanger my husband or the others again."

Mark made a face and got up. "All right, I'll give you a shot. But if you miss—"

"I won't," I interrupted. "Like I said, I allow for distance and drift. Anyone can shoot a stationary target at one-hundred yards. It takes skill and practice to do this, and—not to sound self-important—those are two things I have plenty of."

I settled down on the ground behind the rifle and waited to acquire my target.

"Tell Diego to get ready." I paused, thinking. "Tell him that in deference to my husband's wishes, I'm not going to kill them. Since Gabriel doesn't want me to kill, I'm just going to take them down. Those three can do the rest." I shrugged at the telling silence. "Ask Gabriel, not me. I'll only kill these guys if I have to."

"They'll cry out if you don't kill them."

I shook my head. "No they won't. The chamber pressure on this rifle is fifty-thousand PSI. Those men will either be unconscious or too busy trying to catch their breath. They may be wearing vests, but the impact from this high powered rifle, even at this distance," I patted the stock of the weapon and smiled. "Will certainly take their breath away."

After changing to a new clip so I could keep track of the rounds I used, I settled back into position and took my shots. Two to the chest in quick succession and the man dropped like a rock.

Diego moved in, grabbed the man, threw him over his shoulder in a fireman's carry and ran for the cover of the woods.

His quick response made the way clear for my next target. Myles lay in wait as I set up for my next shot. The man rounded the corner of the building, walking the same fateful path as his fanatical buddy before him. The next guy was a bit bigger, burly. After three successive shots, I had him writhing on the ground, no doubt, trying to breathe.

"You should have killed that one," Jake hissed, watching through his binoculars. "He's warning the others. I can see his hand on the radio."

"He's talking into a useless radio, then," I said with a snort. "I knew he wouldn't go down easy. So, I took the radio out first. I told you, I've made a promise to my husband. I won't kill unless I have to. So far, I haven't had to."

"Damn! She *is* good," Matt muttered to Mark who just nodded and gave his brother a noncommittal grunt.

I sat up, looked at Mark and raised my brow. "Do you have any more clips? If not, I've just wasted my time." I pulled the empty clip and tossed it at a very surprised looking Matt.

"Did you think I didn't know the clips only hold five shots? I'm a woman, not a moron, you know." That was something I couldn't say about my companions on either count.

Nathaniel was trying to communicate with my husband and find out which building he was in. We sat and waited for Diego's signal that he was in position and ready to extract the next body.

The woods were too quiet. I knew it was because we were there, humans in an animal world. Still, the night noises seemed muffled and I wondered whether the *Cartuotey* had anything to do with it. I shrugged. Probably not, but it was something to think about.

Gabriel's presence shimmered in my mind with a sense of humility and pride. He had been watching us, monitoring me through our mind link, no doubt.

I apologize, Alicia. I shall never underestimate your abilities again.

My face heated at his compliment as three clicks came over the radio, indicating that one of our men was ready for another extraction.

It was a good thing I delayed the shot. Two men had been able to pass while we waited for their signal and I wondered how long it would take someone to try to communicate with the missing men.

I took the rest of them down, much the same way as the first few. They all rounded the corner of that building to meet their fate and I didn't have to kill any of them.

Thank you, Gabriel whispered into my mind.

For what?

For not killing them.

I frowned. *I swear I will never understand men. I had the impression you wanted them all dead. If you didn't, I think it's too late now. I'm almost certain Myles, Diego and Nathaniel have dispatched them to meet the object of their devotion.*

He was silent for a moment, as if he was trying to find the right words to say what was on his mind. Hell, he probably was. What do I know?

I did want them dead, if, for no other reason than endangering your life by bringing you out here again. I did not want you to be the one to do it. I never want you to have to face the guilt of ending another person's life. Believe me, there is much guilt associated with making a kill.

His arms wrapped around me and I marveled that he could embrace me from a distance like that, especially since he was injured.

Try as I might, I couldn't manage to return the favor.

You could if you would consent to become one of The Chosen.

Gooseflesh rose on my skin as I contemplated his offer. Become like him? Did I really want to? I don't know why I kept flip-flopping in my decision. First, I did then I didn't. I was beginning to irritate myself.

You do not need to make the decision now, my love. I can wait.

I felt his smile and the sensation of his hand caressing my cheek. *You have several years to age before you will become too old for me.*

Too old for you? I asked indignant. *Look who's talking, Mr. I've been around since...since the civil war.*

It pissed me off that I couldn't think of anything better to say. Not to mention that I still didn't know how old he really was.

Mark looked at me funny. "Are you talking to him? Is he all right? We can go in if he thinks it's needed."

Gabriel chuckled into my mind. *I have been around since before the crusades, sweetheart.*

294

Just shut up and stop bragging. Believe me, your age is certainly nothing to be bragging about, mister.

I changed the subject.

Cassie's brothers want to know if they should go in or if the three of you can handle what is left of these guys.

Tell them to stay with you, for now.

How are they going to know which building you're in? Has Nathaniel found you yet? I asked, biting my lip.

Not yet, but they will know.

He cut himself off from me then and I resisted the urge to scream.

Every time he left my mind, I felt alone, abandoned. I steeled my resolve not to cry like the baby everyone apparently thought me to be.

He's probably doing something incredibly stupid that's causing him pain. That is why he cut himself off from you. He is not dead.

I turned to look at Matt. "He said he's sure the four of them can handle whoever is left. Just stay here in case he's wrong."

Matt nodded. "That sounds like a plan."

The bushes rustled behind us and Joshua went to investigate.

Stupid? Me? I am never stupid, Gabriel chuckled.

No. You're just overbearing, macho chauvinistic... Need I go on?

He didn't answer.

"I didn't think so," I muttered.

My head jerked back a bit when someone gently tugged my hair.

"Hey!" I turned around and scowled at Matt and Mark. "What did you do that for?"

They both raised their hands palms out. "We didn't do anything."

Dalton chuckled. Then they all looked at each other with big stupid looking grins on their faces.

Joshua joined us from the bushes. He jerked his thumb back in the direction from which he came. "It was just a raccoon." Then he looked at me, his expression somber. "He must be healing if he can tease you like that from a distance."

My eyes narrowed and I squinted at them.

"You'd better not be talking about who I think you're talking about."

They all burst out laughing, shook their heads and walked away to give me some privacy with my husband. Not that they could hear our conversation anyway.

Stop pulling my hair.

Who, me?

Don't play that innocent act with me, you goon. I know you're the one who pulled my hair. The others ratted you out.

He pressed an imaginary kiss to my lips and I went all tingly inside. Warmth spread through my middle and my womb clenched. *I don't know how you do that but I hope you never forget how.* I sighed into his mind.

Am I forgiven?

Forgiven for what? I asked dreamily then blinked my eyes open.

For pulling your hair.

Ha! I knew I would get you to admit it. I smiled, smug.

When are your companions going to break me out of here, you lazy woman? I'm languishing away in this place while you sit up on that hill teasing me.

I clamored to my feet, grabbing the rifle and bipod. *Who are you calling me lazy? I'm the one gallivanting around the Michigan woods shooting people so your friends can make dinner out of them. You're the one lying about on your backside, too weak to break free of whatever restraints that are holding you. Don't you dare call me lazy, you—you vampire.*

He chuckled into my mind and I grinned. I loved the way he did that. I would never be alone again.

That's my girl. I always knew you were stronger than you gave yourself credit for being. You only needed to remember you had such strength within you.

What are you doing? I got the impression he was distracting me so I wouldn't know what he was up to. Suddenly several gunshots sounded and I felt every round from those shots hit Gabriel's already weakened body. The bullets, too numerous to count, sank deep into his flesh.

Run, little one. They've allowed us to speak to draw you in. Warn the others. You must not come for me. It is what they want. This is a trap!

I shook my head. *Don't you dare give up on me now, you son-of-a-bitch.*

"Come on," I shouted over my shoulder. Gabriel said this was some sort of trap. "We can't let him be right."

I motioned to the others to follow me. They caught up then passed me.

"We can't allow you to take point, Alicia. Your husband would have our heads." Matt said, pushing me behind his brother and him to walk between the remaining Guides and looked between Jake and Joshua, the remaining *Cartuoteys.*

I looked over at Jake. "Why don't you go down there and help? You're a lot faster than the rest of us, certainly you could help do some damage."

He grinned. "I thought you'd never ask." Then he grabbed me, threw me over his shoulder like a twenty-pound sack of dog food and ran down the hill.

Gabriel's mind touched mine. *They are the strength of this unit. I should have been able to detect the presence of a rogue sooner. I am sorry I have failed you. Myles and Diego are still trying to get to me. I think Nathaniel is down. I am afraid they too, will die. Please forgive me for allowing this.*

I felt his resignation, his sense of failure. He thought they were taking me to the compound to sacrifice me. There was one thing they didn't know. I was not centuries old and bred on honor and keeping my word. Being the self-centered bitch that I am, I was willing to break a promise if it meant keeping us all alive.

Joshua, if that was even his real name, followed behind us. He kept looking over his shoulder to see if Matt and Mark had been able to recover from the hard shove he'd given them down the hill. I was just glad that's all he did. I would have hated to have to tell Cassie her brothers were dead.

Carefully, I reached up to feel my right hip. Thank God, I could still reach it. I pulled the .45 free from its holster and shot Joshua between the eyes.

I don't know if a bullet to the brain will kill a vampire, but it's certainly going to slow him down a bit. Not to mention hurt like hell. I watched as Joshua jerked, fell to his knees then slumped to the ground onto his face.

One down two to go.

I couldn't see Dalton anywhere. I don't know where he disappeared to.

"Don't even try that with me," Jake snarled. "Give me the gun."

In your dreams, buddy.

I tried to censor my thoughts then realized I didn't have to. Gabriel was there, preventing the Rogue from knowing what was in my mind. In fact, he projected thoughts that weren't even mine to the creep.

Oh, no! I dropped the gun. What will I do? I'll never get away from this monster now.

I almost laughed aloud at the helpless-sounding thoughts Gabriel sent into the sucker's head. I was glad to know that when it came right down to it, my husband was willing to help me kill someone, regardless of the promise I had made.

Jake laughed aloud, the sound full of malice. "Hell, why wait? Everyone knows you won't allow him to touch you. Your powers now will be almost as strong as they were when you were still a virgin. Didn't anyone tell you? You have to remain sexually active or use your powers daily to release them. Otherwise, you're still a target."

He shook his head as he dropped me on the ground and grinned evilly at me as he contemplated what he was about to do.

I purposefully fell on the right side of my body so he couldn't see the gun.

He reached for the button on his jeans. "You know, it's amazing how easy it is to make people believe you're something you're not. All we had to do was play nice and not carry any weapons. Suddenly, we were above reproach."

He tugged his zipper down and dropped his pants around his ankles. I tried not to look at his crotch. At the way his prick danced in the moonlight as he readied himself to rape me.

"This is going to be fun for both of us, baby." He grabbed his erection and shook it at me. "You're going to open a gate for me because I'm going to fuck your brains out, then shoot my load."

"Me first!" I snarled, sat up and quickly drew the gun while he still stood several feet from me, his pants bunched around his ankles.

I pulled the trigger repeatedly. Shooting the man in the head until the clip was empty. I stood, grimaced then kicked his lifeless form.

"So, tell me. Was it good for you?"

Chapter Seventeen

I LOOKED UP TO SEE MY HUSBAND STANDING BEFORE ME. HIS CLOTHES WERE torn and filled with bullet holes. His face was drawn and white, gaunt. He needed to feed. Badly.

I already have. He turned to look at Myles and Diego. *They provided for Nate and me. It seems a very beautiful woman gave them quite a feast tonight.*

I ran into his arms and buried my face in his neck. "You still need more." I pulled back to look into his eyes so he would know my offer was sincere and without fear. "I'm offering if you need it."

Heat pooled in my middle at the thought and my face burned.

"I'm sorry. I shouldn't be tempting you at a time like this."

"Not to mention when you have an audience," Myles grumbled good-naturedly.

Diego sighed. "I guess I'm the only one in any shape to take care of this mess." He cast a glance to a blood covered Nathaniel looked over at Myles. "Come on, you can help me carry the bodies to the building at least, then I'll torch the place."

Myles nodded, picked up Joshua and followed Diego with Jake down the slope to the compound.

"You broke a promise."

I nodded. "Yes I did. It's not something I make a habit of doing though."

"Good." He swallowed thickly. "The ritual binding is nothing more than a promise between two people to always care for one another. I would hope you wouldn't enter into it lightly."

I sighed. "I killed those two because they had every intention of killing us both. Not for any other reason. Usually, when I make a promise, I keep it."

He rubbed my back, soothing me. It was so much better to have him in my arms for real, instead of just the illusory sensation of his arms holding me.

"We need to find Matt and Mark and make sure they are both okay. I'd hate to have to tell Cassie that something happened to them." I frowned.

"Me too." He kissed me then set me from him to search for the other men.

The hair on the back of my neck prickled. "Where's Dalton? If Jake was a rogue..."

Gabriel closed his eyes, his aura getting larger as he reached out with his powers. "He's gone. He probably ran when he realized that the others were overpowered."

"I thought they were Guides. Their auras weren't like yours. They weren't dark like Micella's were. I don't understand."

"The aura can be manipulated. Never rely solely on that for a character reference. You must always get to know someone before you pass any kind of judgment on them, good or bad."

I nodded. "I supposed you're right. A dark aura could mean illness not evil."

"Exactly."

We walked back up the hill keeping our eyes open for Matt and Mark. Thank God, they were what they appeared to be. Cassandra would have been devastated otherwise.

We found them lying in a heap in the brush along the hillside. They were shaken but relatively unhurt, thank goodness.

I bent down to pick up his equipment. "I'm just glad you two are all right." I handed Mark his rifle. "Thanks for letting me use this."

He took it and hung it over his shoulder by its strap. "You're welcome. I'm glad you're a better shot than I am."

"No you're not," I said with a grin, giving him a shrewd look. "My aunt gave me a cheat sheet on math and physics when I was younger. I still have it somewhere. If you like, I'll run you off a copy. Allowing for windage is nothing more than a math problem." I winked. "It works great for pool, too."

Mark elbowed his brother in the side.

"Did you hear that, dude? She's going to give me a cheat sheet on physics. I'll be able to beat you at pool, now."

"In your dreams, rat boy." Matt pushed him up the slope.

I stopped mid stride. "Who's going to take Jake and Dalton's SUV out of here?"

"I'll be surprised if it's still there with the others. Dalton *has* been gone a while. Definitely long enough to have retrieved their car," Mark said with a grunt as he stepped into a hole.

We topped the hill and saw that our vehicles were there waiting for us. As Mark predicted, Dalton's truck was already gone.

Strong energy fields surrounded all three of the remaining vehicles and I paused. My body shook as the energy fields grew larger.

"Don't go near the cars!" I screamed my warning to the twins as they raced toward their vehicle.

Their constant competitiveness would get them into trouble one of these days. But not today.

"What's wrong?" Gabriel wrapped his arm around my shoulders and hugged me to his side.

"I—I don't know. The cars look funny." I tilted my head to look up into his eyes. "They didn't have auras before. Now they..." I shrugged, looked back at the cars and sent him a mental image of what I saw.

He stepped forward, leaving me to stand just behind him. My legs gave out and, with Gabriel's help, I settled myself on the thick branch of a fallen tree.

"She's right. Something is wrong with the vehicles." He pressed his lips into a thin smile. "Dalton, no doubt."

Matt set his gear down with the exception of one small bag and continued toward the parked cars.

"Don't," I called after him.

He turned to address us all. "This is my day job. It's what I do. All of you stay at a safe distance until I'm done. I don't need any distractions."

"Day job?" I threw a questioning glance at Mark. "What does he do for a living?"

The corner of Mark's mouth lifted in a grin. "He's a cop. Bomb squad and S.W.A.T."

"C-cop?"

Suddenly, I found myself sitting with my head shoved between my legs.

"Breathe," Gabriel whispered in my ear.

"No wonder..." I gasped, trying to catch my breath. "No wonder he had a gun not available to the general public." I glanced over at the rifle I had used. "Some people get nice replicas that look like the real thing but I *knew* that," I pointed to the weapon, "wasn't a replica."

I pressed my lips together in a tight smile, trying to keep from having a breakdown.

"Aunt Mags used to be a Marine. She had a lot of friends who stayed in the Corps. They taught me everything I know about weapons."

Closing my eyes, I took a deep breath. *Okay, Alicia, get it together. This isn't just about you.*

When I opened my eyes, I finally had my emotions in check. I stood up, leaving the bug infested log, strode over to my husband and watched.

Matt was on the ground next to my car, his arm up underneath it.

"I hope he knows what he's doing," I whispered to the others.

"He does." Mark walked over to join us then watched his brother with obvious pride. "He's the best."

After a minute or two, Matt scooted away from my car and sat up. He held something in his hand. From a distance, it looked like a small package.

He set it on the back of my car then strode over to the SUV parked in front of it. It didn't take him long to remove the devices from the other vehicles since they were larger than my car and sat higher off the ground.

He put the square objects into his truck and strode back to us.

"All set?" he asked, giving me a strange look. "How did you know someone had set explosive devices on the cars?"

I bristled at his accusatory tone. "Hey, don't try to blame that on me!" I waved my hand toward the road. "I was with you, remember? Have you forgotten that the first bomb you pulled was from *my* car?"

I paced back and forth, taking great delight in crushing the dried pine needles beneath my feet. Why do men always target the obvious?

Gabriel straightened to his full height. The air of menace surrounding him was not something to ignore.

"You would do well to not accuse my mate again."

Matt looked between us, raised his hands palms out and immediately apologized. "I'm sorry. I guess it's the suspicious cop in me."

Mark stepped up, slapped his brother on the back and gave him a hug. "You had me worried there for a bit, bro. Try not to take years off of my life, next time, huh?"

I took a deep breath, shrugged out from under my husband's arm and went to Matt, my hands held out in front of me.

"I—I killed two unarmed men out there tonight. You're going to want to take me in."

His gaze flicked over me, then to Gabriel and the others. He turned away and started to gather the gear he dropped earlier.

"In my opinion, a Rogue or a revenant is already dead." He jammed the extra clips that had dumped out onto the ground, back into his bag. "You just laid them to rest as far as I'm concerned."

He stood and strode toward his truck. "Let's get the hell out of here before I have to explain this to some of my friends. They're going to pick up our trail from the compound in no time."

Chapter Eighteen

"LET ME SEE YOUR CHEST." I RIPPED OPEN GABRIEL'S BLOOD SOAKED shirt and pushed it off his shoulders.

Angry red welts marred his perfect chest. A few more peppered his hard, washboard abdomen. His breath hitched as my fingers trailed over his golden skin, inspecting his injuries.

My lips curled in a small smile as his flat, brown nipples pebbled beneath my fingertips. A part of me wanted to lean forward and lick those small, pert nubs, but we had an audience.

His face was still gaunt. "You need to feed," I invited, my voice husky with desire. That thing I felt awakening in me must have been my sexual awareness of my husband. I craved his touch, hungered for it.

He leaned forward, kissed my forehead and pulled me to his side.

"You should be careful, Cassandra, they may set their sights on you after we've gone."

I wrapped my arm around his waist, resting my other hand on his flat stomach. I don't know what came over me. Before, I couldn't bring myself to touch him. Now I couldn't seem to keep my hands to myself.

Cassie nodded. "They may decide to come after me," she agreed. Her face split into a grin as she pulled out one of her brother's semi-automatic pistols. "But if they do, they're going to be in for one hell of a surprise."

I frowned. "I'd feel better if you would go stay with your family."

She gave a wry smile. "You, of all people, should understand why I don't want to do that."

"I do," I said, nodding. "But it doesn't mean I have to like it." I looked up at my husband. "After all, look what I've done to assure my own safety."

Tilting my head, I studied the woman who had fast become one of my closest friends. "Diego said he will stop by and check on you from time to time."

She wrinkled her nose. "I'd rather it was Nathaniel." She winked at me.

"He's kinda cute."

I had to hand it to her. She was handling Joshua's betrayal quite well. She had a full-blown crush on him.

Gabriel raised his brow. "Why Nate?"

She blushed. "Oh, I don't know. I have never really been attracted to the tall, dark and handsome type. I really prefer blonds." She flicked her gaze to Gabriel and rolled her eyes. "I know you're taken, so get that nervous look off your face."

I'm not sure whose relief was more palpable, his or mine.

She shook her head. "You two should go get some rest. You have a long trip in front of you." She turned to grab a soda from the mini bar. "Are you taking a commercial flight or a charter?

Gabriel grinned and my heart stuttered in my chest. How the man could turn me on with a look was beyond me.

"We do need to get some rest," I cast my gaze over to my husband and winked. "We're burning darkness."

I certainly hope he got the hint. You would think, for a man who could read my mind, he certainly wasn't picking up on my needs, tonight.

Gabriel winked at me and grinned. He bent, picked me up and headed for the stairs. "You're right. We should go get some rest." *Tonight, the night is ours.*

He caressed the tip of each of my breasts with a look I felt all the way down to my toes. Still carrying me, he climbed the stairs to his room. We would spend our last few hours in this house making memories. Good memories if I had anything to say about it.

The door opened as we approached it and I shook my head. "You're going to teach me how to do that, aren't you?"

He chuckled. "Of course. After you have chosen to become one of us."

"I already have." Pouting, I crossed my arms over my chest.

The action pushed my breasts together and up, drawing his attention. My nipples pebbled against the abrasive white lace of my bra as his gaze fired my blood.

A slow grin spread across my face as I remembered all of the sexy nightwear in my closet that awaited a night like this.

He set me on my feet, cupped my head in his hands and kissed me softly. A slow burn began in my toes, working its way up through my extremities to settle in my middle.

"I, um...need to go to my room for a minute." My face heated as I thought about what I would wear to surprise my husband.

"You're not..." he cleared his throat, looking uncomfortable. "You're not going to—"

"Run?" I finished for him with a smile. I shook my head. "Definitely not. I just want to shower first. I looked down at my grungy clothing. "You have to admit I could use one."

"You don't need to. I mean I could..." He paused and waved his hand in front of me, obviously uncomfortable with making the offer. He was probably afraid of scaring me off.

I shook my head. "No, thank you. I think I'd rather cleanse myself the old fashioned way."

He bowed his head slowly. "As you wish."

Turning, I gave him a soft smile and a wink. "Don't worry, I'll be back." I sauntered to the door connecting our two rooms, allowing my hips to sway gently with each step.

When I reached the door, I turned and gave him the sexiest look I could muster then left the room.

After my shower, I applied scented lotion to my body and donned the white corset we purchased at the mall. Over that, I wore a white lace negligee and matching robe. The garter-belt and silk stockings finished my ensemble. I never felt so sexy, so decadent, as I did when I slipped on the three inch stiletto pumps.

Before returning to Gabriel's room, I splashed cold water on my burning face and told myself that I *did* have the courage to go through with my plans.

I nervously approached the door that separated our rooms. Resting my forehead against the cool wood and my hand on the knob, I took a couple of deep breaths. My fingers tightened on the knob, I turned my hand and slowly opened the door.

He was facing away from me as I entered the room. I took the opportunity to admire the broad expanse of his muscular back. My gaze lowered to rest on his well-formed ass. I swallowed thickly and cleared my throat.

He turned as if in slow motion. The wine bottle he held in his right hand slid from his grip and shattered on the hardwood floor. A red puddle formed around his feet. His Adam's apple bobbed in his throat as he swallowed repeatedly, obviously speechless.

"You—you look..." *Ravishing.* The word hung between us for a moment. It was almost as if he had said it. I heard his voice say the word in my mind. "Beautiful."

"Beautiful?"

That certainly wasn't the word I would have used. Slutty. Whorish. Like a five-dollar hooker. Now, those words fit. I don't know about beautiful.

He glanced down at the mess on the floor and waved his hand. The broken glass and puddle disappeared and my jaw dropped.

"Handy trick you have there. You're definitely going to teach me how to do that," I said, pointing.

He chuckled. "Everything, my love. I'll gladly teach you everything I know."

His intense gaze devoured me as he approached. His movements were slow, as if he was afraid he would frighten me and I would run screaming from the room. Perhaps he was.

Embarrassed, I lowered my gaze to his chest. His shirt was unbuttoned halfway down and revealed his extremely buff torso.

Blonde hairs lightly dusted his chest, his tanned skin, a dark contrast against the gleaming white of his shirt.

He'd changed. The blood and holes were gone but there was still evidence of his earlier battle. The angry red welts from before, were now pink and mostly healed.

My thoughts flashed back to the *wine* he'd been drinking when I entered the room and I wondered if it had really been wine at all.

Was there blood in that bottle?

"It was blood," he answered my unspoken question.

"I told you that you could..." I let the words trail off as I raised my hand to my neck and covered the tingling spot where he had fed before.

My face heated and I turned away, humiliated. He didn't have to feed from me if he didn't want to. Maybe I taste funny or something.

He walked up behind me, grasped my upper arm and turned me around. I refused to look up into his eyes. I fixed my gaze on the center of his chest and tried not to cry.

"Goodness, Alicia. The thoughts you have." He pulled me into his arms and held me close. "You definitely do not taste funny. I drank the bottled blood because I hungered greatly. I feared for you."

He drew in a deep breath then sighed. "I could kill you if I took too much. I do not want that. With my hunger and the fact that I already crave the sweetness of your blood, I feared I would harm you. Taste funny?" He rested his cheek against my head and laughed softly. "You taste exquisite."

I rubbed my face against his chest, delighting in his warm, sandalwood and citrus scent.

"I love you." My declaration was louder, stronger than it ever had been. "I want to be like you. Make me like you."

He sighed with relief. I felt the tension drain from him as if I had removed a great weight from his shoulders.

"I am delighted you want to become one of The Chosen. I have waited so long to hear those very words come from your lips."

He set me from him and ran his fingers through my hair.

"I cannot change you tonight."

"Why?" I bit my lip, worried. Was he having second thoughts?

He chuckled. "Second thoughts? After waiting several lifetimes for you? After watching you die, time and time again because previous incarnations of you refused to accept the gift?" He shook his head. "Not hardly. There is a ritual involved. We need a third party, someone to help us say the vows, like a Christian minister. Only this is not a Christian ceremony at all. It has been this way since before your Christ was born."

"Oh." I looked down at myself and laughed. "I guess right now is out of the question, then."

His lips quirked and he raised his brow. "Indeed."

His scorching gaze burned a trail over my body, lingering over my breasts. My nipples hardened against the stiff material of the corset.

I shifted uncomfortably. I had tied the sides of the corset tight, to push my breasts over the top, giving myself the cleavage I otherwise lacked.

His glittering gaze rested on the rise of my breasts, where they spilled out over the top of the corset. My flesh tingled and burned as his intense stare seared my flesh, traveling lower before moving back up to look into my eyes.

He held his hand out.

"Come to me."

I licked my suddenly dry lips and rose to my feet. I slowly walked over to stand in front of him.

Reaching up, his hands skimmed over my arms, his fingers closed around my biceps, he pulled me down onto his lap and wrapped his arms around me.

I leaned into him, buried my face into the crook of his neck.

"You smell so good," he said, inhaling deeply "I could sit here forever and be happy, just smelling your skin."

I squirmed on his lap as his cock grew hard and pressed against my hip.

My hand slid up his arm and over his shoulder to cup his cheek. Leaning into him, I brought my face closer to his and pressed our lips together.

"I didn't realize you were all talk and no action, husband," I teased.

Before I knew it, he stood with me in his arms and rushed over to the bed. Laying me down on the thick goose-down comforter, he covered my body with his.

His talented mouth slid sensuously over my skin. "You wanted action." He practically breathed the words into my ear. "I shall show you action."

Butterflies took flight in my belly as he trailed kisses over my face, neck and shoulders. He lapped at my hardened nipples before drawing each turgid peak into his mouth, suckling lightly.

Tiny invisible threads of desire flared out from the firm tips, reaching deep into my belly. Every draw on my breast tugged those threads causing my desire to flare higher, hotter.

I felt strange. Almost sick, my stomach churned as my need climbed and he took me to a new level of desire I had never reached before.

My heart slammed in my chest as his hands skimmed over my burning flesh. He touched me everywhere—in secret places I never even knew existed.

Long fingers separated the folds of my nether lips as his mouth drew on my right nipple. His teeth nibbled and teased, kneading the tender peak.

"Do you like this?" He blew across the moistened nub.

"Yes." My head thrashed on the comforter. My cheeks burned with desire and embarrassment as I answered his question.

He drew my nipple back into his mouth and sank his fingers deep into my between my legs. "Tell me what you want me to do."

My face burned. I couldn't voice my needs. This wasn't my dream Gabriel, this was really happening. I found I couldn't be so vocal, so demanding in real life.

"Tell me."

Chapter Nineteen

"I-I can't."

"Why can you not tell me what it is you like, what it is you want? How will I know, if you do not tell me?" He moved his finger a little, barely brushing the quivering nub. "Don't you like this?"

Like it? I loved it. I just couldn't bring myself to tell him with words. I tried to tell him with my body instead. Rolling my hips up, I tried to force the contact my flesh craved. It didn't work.

"Yes, I like it. Please, Gabriel," I sobbed.

"Then tell me." He nibbled the underside of my breast. "Tell me to rub your clit. It is that simple. Tell me you want me to bury my cock deep into your tight, little pussy. Tell me and your wish is my command."

Tears of frustration leaked from the corners of my eyes. Would he leave me in need if I couldn't say it? Could he really be that cruel?

I fisted my fingers in his hair, pulled ruthlessly on his head until his lips hovered over mine again.

"Please," I whimpered.

I felt almost devoured by his gaze. My body reacted instantly to his heated stare and my womb clenched. The tips of my breasts hardened to painful peaks and my clit twitched beneath his unmoving fingers.

"Tell me," he murmured against my lips.

"Stop teasing me, dammit!" I pushed him away, screaming out my frustration.

My chest heaved from my exertions, my breath coming in short gasps. He'd taken my desires to a new height. One that frightened me because I realized I would do almost anything to find relief.

"Tell me," he lapped at my nipple, drew the hard peak into his mouth and suckled it.

Suddenly, some previously barred door in my mind slammed open. A new awareness swept over me. A previously unexplored and untapped area of my mind awakened with an intensity that made me quiver and shake.

Gone was that frightened little girl. That shy timid victim existed no longer. In her place was a woman with wants and desires, a woman who was totally aware and finally unafraid of her own sexuality.

"Yesss," I hissed out between my clenched teeth.

His mouth felt wonderful on my flesh. I took a moment to enjoy it. No longer frustrated, I was about to give him what he wanted and was sure he would finally give me relief.

Covering his hand with mine, I pushed his fingers against me.

"Move your fingers, dammit. Stroke my clit and make me come before I scream."

I giggled softly at that. He would make me scream when I came, so either way my poor husband was in for an earful. I think I shocked him. He lifted his head, his mouth leaving my breast and I whimpered.

He didn't make me ask for it, his mouth quickly returned to my breast and I arched up into his embrace. Long fingers slid through my slick folds as he thrummed the little nub.

My hand slid from his when I realized he'd gotten what he wanted. My hands fisted in his hair, alternately caressing and pulling as I held his head to my breast.

A tingling heat began in my toes, worked its way up my legs and throughout my body until I burned all over. Insensate with desire, I craved the mind-blowing orgasm that I knew was just out of my reach.

"Gabriel!"

I screamed his name as he took me over the edge. He held my clit between his fingers. It pulled slightly as it pulsed with the force of my orgasm.

His mouth left my nipple and he moved his head lower. Kissing my stomach, he sank his tongue into my navel. It seemed to dance over my flesh as he worked his way down my body.

I reached up and pushed the damp hair from my face. I knew what he had in mind. I didn't think I would survive it. Pausing, he gave me a reprieve.

"What next, my love?"

"Fuck me." I blurted it out. I was through being shy. Through with being embarrassed or scared of my sexuality.

"With what?"

You have got to be fucking kidding me.

I lifted my head off the mattress to look at him. He returned my gaze with one brow lifted. He brought his hand from between my legs, still wet from my juices.

"Should I fuck you with my fingers?" He licked the crease of my hip. "Should I use my tongue?"

"You're going to kill me," I panted. "I want you to fuck me. Slide your cock into me, please!"

He smiled softly and I scowled. He was enjoying this way too much and I vowed to myself to make him pay for this someday.

"Fuck you where?"

"Arrgh!" I screamed out my frustration, spread my legs and spelled it out for him, since it seemed that was what he wanted. "Fuck me, dammit! Slide your cock inside my pussy and fuck me!"

"That wasn't so bad, now, was it?" He grinned then and I wanted to hit him.

He leaned back, tore the white lace thong from me as if I had taped it on then slid into me slowly.

"I love the way your folds spread for me, hugging my cock as I push inside you."

He reached between us, fingering my slick pussy. His finger circled the small pulsing nub of my clit. It twitched, begging for his touch.

"Wrap your legs around me, love."

His voice had a slight accent. I rarely heard it when we talked under normal circumstances, but it seemed, he couldn't mask it when he was fully aroused.

I tossed my head on the bed and cried out when he finally buried himself all the way inside me. His sac slapped my rear as he drove into me.

He looked into my eyes and slid in and out, grinding his pelvis against me on each forward thrust.

"Is this what you wanted?"

"Yes." I tightened my legs around him lifting my hips to meet his every downward plunge.

He slid into me again, groaning. "You're so wet, so tight, Alicia." He leaned forward, lapped at my nipple.

I reached up, brushed the hair from his face and wiped the thin layer of perspiration from his brow.

"Love me," I whispered against his ear when he leaned forward to kiss my neck.

He pulled back, brushed my wet bangs from my face and looked into my eyes. "I do love you, Alicia. More than you know." He kissed me tenderly.

I looked up at him and smiled. "I love you, too." I gasped when he grasped me behind the knees and pushed my legs to my chest.

The change in position allowed him to sink his massive erection even deeper inside me. Leaning forward, his lips covered the tip of my breast, the abrasive scrape of his teeth and the rough brush of the stubble on his cheeks added to the sensation.

I jerked against him, raised my hips higher during his downward thrust, needing a more forceful possession.

My head thrashed back and forth. "You're going to kill me, dammit," I panted. "What are you waiting for?"

How much more would he tease me before he allowed me a release? I didn't know how much more of this slow, gentle possession I could take.

"Tell me," he insisted again.

This time I didn't hesitate. I gave him what he wanted. If he wanted me to talk dirty to him to get what I wanted, what I needed, I damn well was going to do it.

"Ram it into me, you prick! Have mercy, Gabriel. Give it to me!"

"I'm afraid of losing—"

"Control?" I asked. "I *want* you out of control. Please, Gabriel. You're killing me."

My whole body shook with the need to come. My climax was so close, just out of reach. It was there waiting for...something.

His hard cock slid in and out of me, the slick cream from my grasping sex covered his thickness, dripping down onto his balls. I felt the wetness as they slapped against my rear where he pounded into me.

His breathing was harsh as his body labored over mine. He drove into me with a force that rocked the heavy four-poster bed. The headboard banged out an uneven rhythm against the wall.

Reaching up, I wrapped my arms around his shoulders, digging my nails into his back.

Finally, his thoughts, his feelings flooded into my mind. Countless memories flew through my head. I saw his youth, his horrible, lonely and endless existence.

Two women whom I didn't recognize loved him, and then left him. Two women he loved. I didn't recognize either of them, but their souls and memories were one.

Mine.

Tears ran down my face as I finally learned who my husband really was.

"Enough," he said, then kissed me gently. His memories receded, replaced with pure sensation. I felt his pleasure. I felt the way my channel clasped his cock like a slick velvet fist. How my climax made my vaginal walls milk his shaft.

His sac ached with the tremendous need to climax, yet he held back, waiting to bring me pleasure first. He withdrew, then slowly sank himself into me again and started the wonderful cycle of sensation over again.

"God, you're good," I panted as he drove deeper within me. His balls slapped my rear. Impossibly, his cock grew larger, pulled at the extra bit of flesh around my clit. The base of his cock rubbed the little swollen nub every time he drove inside me.

"Gabriel," I screamed his name as another massive orgasm gripped me.

"Alicia, love," he groaned against my lips. His mouth moved over my jaw to my neck. He lapped at the sensitive skin just below my ear.

He lost control then, I think. He pounded into me as I'd begged him to do. I screamed out my pleasure as he sank his teeth deep into my flesh.

His body jerked over mine and he repeatedly pounded his erection into my body as he fed from me. I wrapped my arms around his head as a strange languor stole over me.

"I'm so tired," I whispered, then frowned when my hands fell from his head and my legs dropped from around his waist. I wanted desperately to hold him, but was just too tired.

My head fell back on my shoulders when he lifted me to sink his teeth deeper into my throat.

I had the fleeting thought that he had lost control and was draining me dry but was just too tired to care. I barely felt him swipe his tongue over the wound his teeth left in my neck and his frantic call came from so far away.

If I was about to die...well, what a way to go.

"Alicia!"

Chapter Twenty

I FLOATED NEAR A THIN, THIN LINE SOMEWHERE BETWEEN LIFE AND death, wakefulness and sleep. It was a strange place where Gabriel both begged and threatened me. I shook off the ridiculous notion that he would do either.

My husband just wasn't the type of man who would beg for anything and he would never threaten any woman, let alone me.

"Thank God," Gabriel sighed when I opened my eyes. He sank to his knees on the floor beside the bed, reached up and caressed my face with his thumb. His fingers feathered through my hair and he looked...old somehow.

"I'm thirsty." I licked my lips.

He brought a cup to my mouth. I tried to gulp down the cool water, but he would only let me have a few sips.

"Easy now," he said softly. "Try not to take too much at once. We don't want you to be sick."

I looked up at him.

"What happened?" My voice cracked, my throat was so dry.

He looked away, a muscle ticked in his jaw. I cast my gaze around the darkened room and smiled softly.

"Wow! Now I know you're good. You fucked me so senseless, I passed out." I shifted, trying to sit up. "How long was I out?"

Judging by the level of darkness outside the window, I would guess at least a couple of hours.

He gazed into my eyes, his expression somber.

I frowned. For someone who just screwed his wife senseless—not to mention to a state of unconsciousness—he certainly didn't look too proud of himself.

"Never again," he growled, shaking his head.

"What? Never what again," I asked warily. I shook my head, trying to clear it. "Boy, am I dizzy."

He shook his head and cursed under his breath.

"What is it?" I asked with a frown.

"I will never take your blood while I hunger, ever again."

A sense of resignation settled over me as I finally remembered the events from earlier. My hand flew up to cover the spot from where he had fed.

"You almost took too much, didn't you?"

"I almost killed you, that is what I did," he bit out between clenched teeth.

I couldn't bear his tortured expression any longer. I reached up to smooth the lines of strain and worry from his face.

He pulled away and stood up. "Some protector I turned out to be." He turned his back to me, stuck his hands in his pockets. "I almost killed you."

I shivered and gooseflesh rose on my skin as I remembered our earlier activities. "Yeah, but whooo boy! What a way to go."

"I'm not kidding, Alicia. I could have killed you."

Taking a deep breath, I found the strength to sit up. "I know you're not joking. Neither was I." Shifting, I tried to move the pillow behind me to make myself more comfortable.

He was there in an instant, helping me. He fluffed the pillow and placed it behind my back, seeing to my comfort as he always did.

"You're—you made a mistake." I almost made the mistake of saying he was human.

"It was a deadly mistake, an unforgivable mistake. One that cannot be repeated."

I grabbed his hand, pulled and held it against my cheek. "You already know I'm not afraid of death. The only things I am afraid of is being violated again and living a life without you in it. Don't you see? If my death would have helped you, healed you, it would have been worth it and I would have called it good."

He sank to his knees beside me again. "How can you forgive such an unspeakable act?"

"Because I love you."

"I can't—I won't endanger you that way again," he said, pulling away. "I don't even trust myself to be this close to you while I hunger."

I gritted my teeth as I watched him withdraw. Reaching out, I grabbed his shoulders and tried to shake him but he didn't budge.

"Listen to me, dammit!" I snarled. "I'm so tired of this shit. If you're not going to stay close to me, who is? Who's going to protect me, no one?"

I swung my legs over the side of the bed. The sheet fell away from me, revealing the corset that we never removed in our rush to taste one another. My breasts spilled out over the top, jiggling as I tried to shake him again but I just didn't give a good damn.

"If I'm to have no protection from now on, you might as well finish me off."

Denial flashed in his eyes and he shook his head. He would have said something, but I held my hand up in his face.

"I'm not finished yet, so keep your mouth shut."

Stopping for a moment, I took a deep breath and rested my hand on his chest.

"I love you, Gabriel. I don't want to live without you." I looked up, gazed into his beautiful swirling silver eyes. "If you would have killed me tonight, you would have continued until all those monsters were dead. You would have lived on and I would have considered my sacrifice well worth it."

Reaching up, I wrapped my arms around his neck and drew his head down to rest on my breast. "I would have given my life for yours back at the compound. What makes you think I would do any less here at the house?"

Smiling, I added, "So, the next time you almost drain me dry, swipe a couple of pints of that blood you keep stored and give it to me. Just make sure it's O positive."

I let my smile grow to a grin and winked. "Who knows? You might get lucky and give me the blood of a nymphomaniac or something."

He wrapped his arms around me, trembling. "I don't believe you forgive me."

"What's to forgive?" I asked with a snort. "You give me the best sex known to womankind and you think I should be upset?" I shook my head. "You should be so lucky. You may have just created a monster." I winked again. "A sex monster."

He grinned. "Sex monster? I think I like the sound of that."

I rolled my eyes and snorted. "You would."

He stood, looking serious. "We should get dressed. We must leave soon."

"Leave?" I frowned. "It's in the middle of the night. Won't they expect us to try and sneak out of here in the dark of night?"

"Yes, he said with a nod. "That is exactly why we must go now." He donned a pair of black jeans he pulled out of thin air and shrugged into a long sleeved black shirt. Stopping, he waved his hand and clothes appeared on the bed. All black and all my size.

Whistling, I sauntered over to the bed, picked up a pair of black crotch-less panties and matching bra.

"Have high hopes for later, do you?" I turned to him, my eyebrow raised.

He actually blushed. "You could say that."

"Can't blame a guy for hoping, I guess."

I slipped into my clothes as quickly as I could. I'm not as comfortable with my nudity as he obviously was.

"What?" I asked when I noticed his intense stare.

"You are so beautiful. I love the way your chestnut hair glistens in the light. The fire of your cinnamon eyes when you are angry. How they light with desire when I stroke your sex."

He kissed me slowly. It was a totally tongue-free kiss and so tender it brought tears to my eyes.

"Did I hurt you?"

He looked stricken, upset with the thought that he could have brought me pain.

"Of course not. I just..." What could I say? I already told him I didn't deserve him. "Forget it. We need to get moving."

Thankfully, he didn't push me for an answer. He merely agreed, took my hand and led me to the door. "Have I told you I love you today?"

"You just did," I said with a grin.

Leaning up on my toes, I gave him—what I hoped was—a toe-curling kiss.

"If you keep squeezing my rear like that, I don't think we'll be going anywhere soon."

Embarrassment scorched my cheeks and I pulled my hands back so fast you would think it had bitten me.

Gabriel threw his head back and laughed. It shocked me. I didn't think the man could get more handsome. I was wrong.

That didn't excuse his invading my thoughts again.

"Hey!" I gave him a shove. "How many times do I have to tell you to stay out of my head?"

He chuckled. "You didn't mind it earlier."

I made a face and narrowed my eyes. "Watch it, mister."

Warmth stole through me when he wrapped his arms around me, resting his hands on my rear. "Our mind link is to help you understand our relationship better, among other things."

"Other things?"

"When you become one of us, you will need the link between us to learn faster." He kissed the tip of my nose. "I do love you, Alicia. My hope is that

317

you never doubt that."

"I haven't doubted that for some time." Turning, I faced the window and looked at him from the corner of my eye. "I have, however, doubted your sanity a few times."

He pulled me closer, wrapped his arms around me and pinched my rear.

"Ow!" I swatted him then rubbed my right butt cheek. "That hurts, dammit!"

I stuck my tongue out at him and watched the color of his eyes change from pale silver to a stormy gray. I loved the way I could make him want me like that. A few weeks ago, that would have scared the hell out of me. Recently, though, it just made me hot.

He leaned down, pressed his lips to my ear. "We must get moving, my love."

The stubble on his cheek, coupled with the warmth of his breath on the sensitive skin of my neck, made me shiver with anticipation.

"We'll finish this," he kissed my neck, his lips and tongue doing wonderful things to my neck. "Later."

The door opened behind me and he backed me out into the hallway.

"Yeah, okay." I agreed with a nod. "But I want to stop somewhere where we can be handfasted."

"That anxious to get it over with, are you?" He gave me a half grin that didn't quite reach his eyes. "If you are unsure..."

The impression of pain flickered in my mind before he severed the connection between us. I reached up to smooth the frown from his brow.

"No. I'm in a hurry because I will be stronger after you make me a vampire."

Did I just say that? One of these days, I'm going to have to come to terms with the fact that I wanted to live with Gabriel for the rest of my life. Hell, let's face it. I wanted to live with him the rest of *his* life.

I reached up to smooth the frown from his brow and wondered if he kept peeking in on my thoughts because he was insecure about our relationship.

Pulling from his embrace, I paced away from him. "The way I am now, I always need to rely on you for just about everything. Not that I don't want to rely on you," I hurried to add. I walked back to him, rested my hands on his chest and looked up into his eyes.

"It's strange to think that a few weeks ago it would have bugged the heck out of me to tell you that. Now, I don't find it distressing or horrible in the least. But, you have to admit, it would be easier if I could defend myself. It would be so much easier for the both of us. To tell the truth, I'm kind of looking forward to truly mating with you."

"That is a sound argument."

"Don't go all logical on me now. I didn't realize I was arguing a case."

He took a deep breath and blew it out on a rush. "You were not. I just thought you would like Tasha to be there for the ritual."

I pursed my lips and tilted my head to the side. "Well, there is that." He was so thoughtful it almost made me want to cry.

Did he really want to wait until we reached England, or did he want to defer the handfasting because it was what he thought I wanted?

There *was* one other possibility. Maybe he didn't plan to change me at all.

After all, he still held himself from me except when we were making love. It was almost as if he couldn't keep me from his thoughts when he was extremely aroused.

Chapter Twenty-one

STAY CALM, ALICIA, THERE'S A LOGICAL EXPLANATION FOR WHY HE WANTS TO wait. Don't jump to any conclusions. I frowned at my inner monologue.

"Okay, we can wait. I'm guessing there's some reason you would rather handfast in Europe, so I'll defer to your better judgment on this."

"Thank you." He pressed a quick kiss to my lips and led me down the hall to the back stairs.

"We must make it appear as though we are attempting to slip from the house unnoticed." *We will communicate through our mental link and, like it or not, you must allow me into your mind to protect you from others reading your thoughts.*

I rolled my eyes and sighed. *Well, I don't have much of a choice, now, do I?*

It was amazing how easily I accepted speaking mentally with Gabriel.

We opened the door at the bottom of the stairs and crept into the kitchen. The cook was already at work setting bread dough to rise.

What is she doing here so early? I glared at him, crossed my arms over my chest and tapped my foot. *Let the poor woman sleep.*

She likes what she does. I have spoken to her several times on this matter. I cannot convince her otherwise.

I looked up at him, confused. *Can't she see us?*

No. I am shielding us from notice. The less we say to those we leave behind, the better. The less they know, the safer they are.

Oh, I never thought of that.

We continued to move through the kitchen to the back door.

I don't believe we're doing this just to put on a show for those damned freaks.

The show, my love, is to draw them from those under our protection.

I loved the way he said *our protection* like I was already one of his kind. He always seemed to know what would make me feel better.

He stopped, cupped my cheek and looked into my eyes. *If the others see us leave, they will follow and, with luck, leave Cassandra and the others we leave here alone.*

I didn't think of that either.

He thought of everything and I thought of nothing. I felt so stupid.

You are many, many years younger than I am, my heart. Why do you insist on believing you should think like an ancient?"

I know you didn't just call yourself ancient. I rolled my eyes, pushed past him and sidestepped when Rosa almost stomped on my foot.

I forgot she can't see us. I turned to him and raised my brow in that annoying way he was so fond of doing. *Where to now, oh ancient leader?*

I think the word is fearless. Fearless leader.

Hrmph. That's what you say.

He gave me a shark-like grin and I winked at him.

My heart skipped several beats when he grabbed me and planted another toe-curling kiss on my lips.

Silver eyes clouded with desire stared deeply into mine when he lifted his head. His lips still glistened with moisture from our kiss and his heart slammed erratically beneath the palm of my hand.

We must leave.

It sounded an awfully lot like he wanted to do anything but leave.

That is so. He inclined his head. *We must be far from here when the sun rises.* He frowned. *I never should have brought you back here.*

I'm glad you did. I wanted to tell Cassie goodbye. I didn't want it to look like we had just disappeared off the face of the Earth. She wouldn't have known where we went.

It would have been safer for her if she did not.

I gave into the urge to reach up and smooth a stray lock of hair from his forehead. The silky strands sifted through my fingers before stubbornly falling back over his left eye. *You need to get that cut.*

He took my hand in his and kissed the back of my knuckles. *Time to go.*

Taking a deep breath, I squeezed his fingers and let him lead me to the door.

The slight breeze the weatherman predicted from the North carried the musty scent of the forest. The cool air lifted the hair from my neck and I shivered in the darkness.

Gabriel conjured up an old-fashioned looking cape for me and draped it across my shoulders.

Thank you. I pulled the heavy silk lined wool around me, snuggling deeper into its warmth. *Does that come naturally or is that something I'm going to have to learn how to do?* I reached out, resting my hand on his arm. *You are definitely teaching me how to do that at the first opportunity. I'll save a fortune in clothes.*

As you wish.

I made a face at the annoying phrase and hurried to keep up with his long legged stride.

We slipped silently through the yard and around the back of the garage. The side door opened as we approached.

That's so cool!

The more Gabriel used his unique powers in front of me, the more I wanted to be like him.

When we stopped, just outside the side door, he wrapped his arms around me from behind, his hands lightly cupping my breasts. My nipples tightened, hardening into diamond-hard peaks aching with the need to feel the warmth of his mouth.

You shall be like me as soon as we can manage to perform the ritual safely, my love.

The door opened silently and we entered the dark garage.

I can't see in here.

If it had been dark outside, it was black as pitch inside.

Gabriel immediately merged his mind with mine and suddenly I could *see* through his eyes.

This is so strange.

Everything was as clear to me as if the lights were on. The only difference, I could see things from several inches higher than usual.

So this is what everything looks like from up there, huh? I asked with a grin.

He chuckled into my mind, his fingers tangling with mine as he led me around several cars to a beautiful, red Porsche 911.

I whistled, and then slapped my hand over my mouth. *Sorry.*

He grinned and opened the passenger door for me. I slid into the car and shivered against the cold leather seat.

Aren't you afraid we'll destroy this beauty? I know I would be terrified.

322

No. He shook his head. *They will disable it while we are in the hotel, thinking to strand us. We will depart from our room, leaving no trace. Carlisle will pick up the car sometime tomorrow.*

He slid easily behind the wheel and the car started smoothly while he fastened his seat belt. The things he could do with his mind still amazed me.

When he finished with his own restraint, he glanced over at me and frowned. My seatbelt wrapped itself around me, fastening itself snuggly over my hips.

"Thank you," I whispered. "Show off."

"It is more than likely that our enemies will be out there, waiting for us to leave so they might follow us. They will hope to catch us unaware." He said as the garage door opened and he drove out into the darkness. "If they do not stop us tonight they will, no doubt, send their revenants to do their bidding during the daylight hours, when they are weakest."

He didn't remind me that he would also be at his weakest during the day. I've seen his weakest. He is approximately twice as strong as a human male, even at his weakest. I could have kissed him for trying to protect me like that. I refrained since he was still driving.

He reached over and rested his right hand over my left. I turned my hand over, threading my fingers through his. It felt good to be so close, so connected to another human being.

You forget, my love. I am not human.

The words spoken so softly in my mind, reminded me what my husband was and I didn't care. He was the kindest, gentlest man I have ever known. My husband was more of a gentleman than *any* human male I have ever met.

Traveling north, we sped along the highway for nearly three hours. We stopped somewhere around Traverse City, I think. He parked in the underground parking lot of a large, upscale hotel.

"We will only remain here long enough to make our enemies think we are trapped here for the daylight hours. Rogues tend to forget that it is only they who are so susceptible to the sun's damaging rays."

I opened the door to get out of the car. Before I could move, he was there, beside me, helping me from the car.

"How did you—" I shook my head. "Never mind."

Of course, he was fast. I had seen it before, on the night we met. I forgot that, just like I chose to forget almost everything from that horrible night.

He pulled me into his arms. "Do not dwell on those memories, my love. It breaks my heart to feel your distress."

How could I continue to reprimand him for peering into my mind when his every thought seemed to revolve around my comfort, safety and well-being?

I snuggled further into his embrace, taking advantage of the heat radiating from his body. "How do you stay so warm even when it's so chilly outside?"

His hands skimmed over my back, gooseflesh followed in their wake. A heavy streak of desire shot through my system, my nether parts twitched and my sex grew slick with need.

Burying my face in his chest, I grinned, embarrassed. It seems the poor man *had* created a monster.

"We can regulate our body temperature, to an extent."

"To an extent?" I pulled back, tilting my head to the side.

He shrugged. "If it were extremely cold, we would still need a coat or cloak, for no other reason than to keep up the appearance of being human."

"Hello, Mr. LeBlanc. How are you doing this fine evening?"

The door attendant, a fifty-something man, with friendly green eyes, graying hair and moustache ushered us into the building.

"Let's get you two out of the chill night air." His gaze flicked over me briefly before he turned to lead us into the lobby. "You should have warned us that you were coming, sir. We have your room available, but due to a convention in the area, we have no room for the young lady."

"She'll be staying in my rooms with me, Burton. You needn't disstress yourself."

"Oh!" The man cast another glance my way, his eyebrows raised. "Very well, sir. I didn't mean to pry, sir. I just... It's just that you never..." The man's gaze traveled back and forth between us, his face growing red.

Gabriel clapped the man on the shoulder. "It's perfectly fine, Burton. Allow me to introduce you to my wife, Alicia."

Burton's eyes lit up. "Why that's wonderful. I've always said you needed to settle down. Too many years alone clouds a man's judgment. You should know that."

He quieted as we entered the main lobby. I dodged a bellhop hurriedly pushing a cart behind a woman in high heels who nearly ran across the marble floor to the opened elevator.

"I'll just get your key, sir." Burton walked off. I took the moment to study his ramrod straight spine as he approached the front desk.

Turning, I raised my brow. "Why do you get the royal treatment?"

He grinned then winked at me. "They like me."

"Yeah, right."

I turned to the large fountain in the middle of the marble tiled lobby. A mermaid sat on an outcropping of rock, a waterfall cascading behind her. Her outstretched hand dipped into the falling water, parting it for a small bird perched on the tip of her tail. It was beautiful.

"This must have cost a fortune." I looked around the opulent lobby. It must cost a pretty penny to stay one night in a place like this. Not to mention that, he had a room kept for him.

I felt him behind me. His warm breath stirred the hair on the nape of my neck. Heat pooled in my middle and I couldn't help but think we'd be lucky if we made it to our room if he kept that up.

"The fountain?"

I nodded. "Yes. It's the most breathtaking fountain I've ever seen." I circled around it. "Don't you ever wonder how much something like this costs?"

"One million, four-hundred- one thousand two-hundred sixty-three dollars and fifteen cents after tax." He reached out to wet his hand beneath the spray of water.

"How do you know? Did you design it?"

He shook his head, tucked me beneath his shoulder and kissed the tip of my nose.

"No, I bought it."

"You bought..." I felt my eyes grow round at his statement. "That means..." I cleared my throat. "You own this hotel?"

He grinned and hugged me closer. "I own the chain."

My knees buckled. I would have fallen if he hadn't scooped me up into his arms. My eyes glazed over when I looked down at my ring and thought about what went through my mind on our wedding day.

"I—I've read about you. You're the man everyone says has the Midas touch." I squirmed in his arms, unable to look into his eyes. My gaze focused on his neck, watched his throat work as he talked.

"Is that a bad thing?"

"I—no. Hell, Gabriel, I don't know. How will you ever know if I truly love you? I could have married you for your money."

He chuckled. *Perhaps. If I were human. My gifts make it easy to know your innermost thoughts, remember?*

Crossing my arms over my chest, I was glad for a reason to be upset with him again. I looked at him and smiled with false sweetness. "Stay out of my head, if you know what's good for you. You goon," I hissed, then balled my hand into a fist and thumped his chest good and hard.

I shut up when I noticed Burton heading our way. The man didn't need to know that the newlyweds were already fighting. Hell, the honeymoon was barely over.

Speaking of honeymoons...

We will have plenty of time for that on our trip to Europe.

Ha! That's what you say. I think we're going to be too busy running from Rogues and revenants to have a good time.

The sensation of his fingers plucking at my nipples suddenly took me by surprise.

I slapped him. "Stop that."

Burton cleared his throat beside me. "I have your key. Do you have any luggage, sir?" He asked, his eyebrow raised as if he knew there would be no need for luggage.

"No." He gave Burton a meaningful look. "This was an unexpected trip and we shall not stay long."

"Ah, I see, sir." He turned and led us to a special elevator, inserted the key and waited for the door to open.

"Rogue following you, sir?"

My mouth fell open and my eyes widened. My gaze darted from my husband to the doorman then back again.

"He is a Guide, my love. He knows about my kind and helps protect us from the Rogues and their minions."

"How many of you are there, anyway?"

It was hard to believe that I had lived my entire life without knowing about vampires. I knew other Guides existed, but I certainly didn't know on how grand a scale.

Gabriel tilted his head, deep in thought. "There are about three thousand *Cartuotey* and at least thirty thousand Guides."

"That many?" I felt my eyes go round at the thought.

He looked around us. "This conversation should not be taking place here."

Chapter Twenty-two

MY GAZE DARTED FROM THE FRONT DOORS TO THE CHECK-IN DESK. Many people milled about, bustling from one side of the lobby to the other, all in a hurry to live their lives, all of them ignorant of the danger that surrounded them on a daily basis.

I used to be one of them. One of the lucky ones. One of the ignorant hordes of people who didn't know about all of the monsters that roamed the earth.

Pain filled my mind for a split second. Then Gabriel cut his mind off from mine. Gabriel severed our mental link, hurt.

The absence of his thoughts touching mine left a huge gap in my mind.

Grabbing his hand, I laced my fingers through his. *I didn't' mean to hurt you.* I put all of my love into my thoughts. I wanted him to know he was the only light in my otherwise dark existence.

He squeezed my hand and looked down at me, his expression somber, silver eyes gray with sorrow. *You need not worry, my heart. The loneliness and insecurity are my failings, not yours.*

No, they are mine, Gabriel. You wouldn't have been so lonely for so long, if not for my weaknesses in the past.

How could I let him continue to blame himself for everything? It was so unfair to my gentle husband. Besides, I was no longer the frightened child he married.

Later, when we were alone, I would let him know I didn't expect him to take the blame for everything. It wasn't that he was weak. On the contrary, he is the strongest man I've ever known. It was because *I* had been so weak for so long.

He leaned down to whisper in my ear. "This is neither the time, nor the place for this, my love."

I looked around us, wondering if anyone besides Burton overheard us.

"You're right." I took his arm. "We can finish this in the room."

Many things needed to be finished between us. My perpetual state of selfishness was at the top of the list of things to be expunged from my life.

Burton escorted us to the room, and then left us to inform the other Guides in Gabriel's employ, to expect a siege.

I eyed the blue, satin-covered bed, wishing we had the time to use it.

Gabriel wrapped his arms around me from behind. "Do not be cross with me," he said nuzzling my ear. Shivers of delight coursed through my body, causing heat to settle in the pit of my stomach.

Covering his hands with my own, I leaned back into him and rested my head against his shoulder. We stood silent, basking in each other's presence for a long time.

Gabriel was the first to speak. I had been content in my husband's strong, arms, reveling in the feeling of safety they provided.

"We must go now, my love." He kissed my temple and pulled his hands from beneath mine. "I will shield us from the watchful eyes of the Rogues. They must not know we have gone. We need to identify as many as we can. The surveillance cameras will tell us what we need to know."

"Where will we go? Do you really think we'll be safe in England?"

Taking a deep breath, he sighed. "No. They will look for us anywhere I have a home. We will visit Micah's sister in Chicago or a friend of mine in another city." The corner of his mouth lifted in a half grin. "It is fortunate that I have lived as long as I have. I have many people I call friend who would help us."

My mouth fell open and I blinked. "Micah has a sister?" It would be an understatement to say I was shocked to find that Tasha had a sister-in-law. She never mentioned her.

I frowned and rested my hand on his chest. "Wait a minute. I thought Micah was born a vampire... Wasn't he?"

"Yes," Gabriel said with a nod. "He was born a vampire, as was I."

"Do you mean that we..." I moved my hand back and forth between us. "You and I can have children?" I don't know why that surprised me. Tasha was pregnant. I just wasn't used to knowing Tasha was a vampire. I guess I'd never put the two together before.

He searched my gaze for a moment before answering with another nod. "Yes, Alicia, you can have children. That, by the way, is entirely up to you. You have the power to either keep yourself from conceiving or you may decide what day you would like to become pregnant with my child."

I sucked my bottom lip between my teeth. "This is an interesting development. That kind of takes all of the fun out of it, doesn't it?"

"Oh, no." He grinned at me then winked. "I do believe the fun is still involved to fertilize the egg you produce."

My cheeks burned and I reached out to pinch him. "Didn't you say it was time to go?" I glanced through the window at the approaching dawn and hoped that no matter how he planned to get us out of here that I would be able to handle it without going into hysterics.

He wrapped his arms around me and kissed me gently. Thoughts of our escape and visits to people I don't know flew from my mind when his lips pressed against mine.

Warmth surrounded me, wrapped around me like a cocoon. I lost the ability to acknowledge the passing of time. I was so lost in the warmth and my husband's kiss.

After what only seemed like a moment, my feet touched the ground. I frowned. When had they left the ground? I opened my eyes and looked around me.

We were no longer in the hotel room. We stood on the roof of another building. I looked out over the strange city, sure that the lights on the horizon were not the lights of Traverse City.

"Where are we?"

"Muskegon."

"What are we doing here?"

"We are going to enlist the help of a friend of mine. We can no longer wait to handfast. You are in too much danger as a human. I can show you how to protect yourself if you are one of The Chosen."

"The Chosen?"

"It is what we call ourselves because true *Cartuotey* will only choose to turn their fated mate. You are my fated mate and I have chosen to turn you." He lifted my hand and kissed it. "If you still wish to become like me."

My stomach knotted at the thought and butterflies took flight, leaving me to wonder if it was what I truly wanted. I steeled my resolve. Of course, it's what I wanted. Who wouldn't want to spend eternity with a man like him?

I raised my hand and cupped his cheek. "That is a wonderful idea, husband." I smile softly, swallowing my trepidation. "How long before we get there?"

His smile was dazzling. One day it would be my undoing, I knew it. He looked at me as though I had just given him the world. "We *are* there."

"Ooh!" I swallowed thickly. "Great. Do you think he'll mind us just showing up on his doorstep without warning?"

Gabriel shook his head. "No. He will not mind. What we are about to request of him is considered a great honor among our people."

I took a deep breath and blew the hair from my face, then licked my lips, nervous. "A great honor, huh?" I pushed the errant hair back from my forehead. "Do I know him?" That wasn't a fair question and I knew it. I had met so few of them over my lifetime.

"This is Maximillian's residence."

Well, at least it was someone I knew, sort of. I had started to like the Micah look-a-like before he had left to rid the world of a couple of revenants at the mall. I stopped him with my hand on his arm when we reached Max's door.

"How do I look?" I asked, nervously smoothing my hair and clothing. This was essentially another wedding day. I wanted to look the best I could.

"You look lovely, as always." He reached up to push a stray lock of hair behind my ear. "Your chestnut hair glows with fiery highlights. Your changing eyes dance with a dark golden light and your cheeks are rosy with the blush of your youth and modesty. You are, in a word, beautiful." He leaned down to kiss the tip of my nose. "You needn't be embarrassed. You must know I think you are the loveliest woman in the world."

I looked away, tears in my eyes. Knowing he thought that and having him say it were two entirely different matters. I *so* didn't deserve him. "I wasn't fishing for compliments, you know. I merely wanted to know I didn't look a mess."

He threw his head back and laughed.

God, I love it when he does that.

"Alicia, my love, you are beautiful at all times. I have never seen you *look a mess*. Stop worrying."

My thoughts flew back to the night we met. I knew I was a mess then.

Gabriel cupped my chin and gazed into my eyes. "You were beautiful, even then. Never doubt that." He turned to the door and held out his arm for me to take it. "Shall we?"

The door opened just as he raised his hand to knock.

"I knew someone was out here, but I can say I never expected it to be you two. Why aren't you off having a honeymoon?"

Gabriel bowed formally then shook Max's hand. We have come to ask a favor."

Max crossed his arms over his chest and leaned against the doorframe. "What kind of favor, old friend?" He blinked slowly, the expression on his face and the wild pulsing of his aura made me believe he knew what my husband was about to ask, or he at least had a good idea.

Gabriel tucked me beneath his shoulder and smiled down into my eyes before he returned his gaze to his friend.

"We ask you to handfast us."

Max stood up straight, backed away from his door and extended his arm toward his living room. I felt my eyes widen with surprise when he moved away and I saw inside. I never expected a bachelor to have such a well decorated home.

His living room, decorated with a modern flair, was a dream. The floors, made of tumbled, cream marble gleamed in the soft light from the lamps on the glass-topped tables.

A circular, blue-white rug sat beneath a rectangular chrome and glass coffee table. Behind that stood the sofa, a decorator's dream in modern design, seven feet of decadence covered in buttery, light cream-colored leather.

Glass topped tables flanked the ends of the sofa that faced the large fireplace. Two side chairs of a matching design flanked the fireplace facing the long sofa.

"Come in, please." He waited for us to enter before he asked, "What brings you to me for your handfasting? I thought you would want to wait until you reached England and your family for that."

His curiosity wasn't lost on me. I watched his aura pulsing with the excitement of Gabriel's request. He attempted to appear calm, but his aura told me our request had him totally jazzed.

My gaze darted to Gabriel. I didn't know he had family overseas. I bit my lip as my cheeks warmed again, we really needed some alone time.

Visions of the both of us naked, in bed, danced through my mind and I turned away from the men to look at the large, abstract painting that hung over the fireplace.

Not that *kind of time alone,* I scolded myself. *Boy, I've sure come a long way from that frightened girl, haven't I?*

"Come," Max said and led us into a more traditionally decorated room.

It appeared to be a spare bedroom. There were no identifying articles. It boasted a California king-sized bed, a large, dark-walnut armoire, dresser and vanity set. Two overstuffed chairs sat in front of another huge fireplace.

Max walked over to the armoire and opened the doors. He pulled a medium size hand-carved box from an inside drawer and turned to us.

"My mother made this for my handfasting." He grinned. "But I don't mind sharing it. And," He slapped Gabriel on the back. "I know she'd be tickled to know you're going to use it too."

He set the box down on the polished walnut dresser and lifted the lid. The scent of frankincense and cedar permeated the room. He turned to us, his manner suddenly somber.

"You both must recite the ritual vows. Are you ready?"

I nodded, unable to find my voice.

Gabriel tangled his fingers with mine and squeezed, reinforcing my nerve.

Max pulled a sheet of rolled parchment from the box, removed the ribbon and unrolled it. He placed one small, white candle at each corner on the top and one small, metal disc at each corner at the bottom to weight the page.

Pulling a small white-handled knife from the box, he extended his arm, waiting for me to place my hand in his.

"Your full name?"

"Alicia Marie Chalmers."

Max's gaze darted from me to Gabriel then back again before he spoke. "Alicia Marie Chalmers, you have made your choice?"

He paused, obviously waiting for an answer.

I cleared my throat and nodded, swiping my tongue over my dry lips. "Yes. I have chosen."

Max's eyes bored into mine as Gabriel wrapped his arm around me for support.

"Now that you have made your choice, you must recite the vows of The Chosen."

I nodded, finding my voice. "I will."

"You must repeat these words exactly as I say them."

His fingers tightened around mine as he bent my fingers backward to stretch my palm smooth.

"My blood to your blood. With the gift of my blood, I offer my life into your safekeeping. By taking your blood, I accept the offer of your life. Our blood blends, mixes and changes us. It creates one life in the place of two. We shall become one new, complete being with one heart and one soul. Together we are one. I have chosen Gabriel Lucian LeBlanc."

Fear gripped me with the same strength that Max and Gabriel held me with as he positioned the sharp blade over the exposed palm of my hand. My body tensed when I realized what he was about to do.

Alicia.

I looked up into Gabriel's eyes at his mental nudge. Somehow, my fear was gone. I stood mesmerized by those silver eyes staring into mine. He compelled me then, I know he did. Suddenly my fear was gone. He filled me with the knowledge that what we were doing was right.

I grinned up at him, my trepidation wiped from my mind and I repeated the ritual as Max said it to me.

"My blood to your blood. With the gift of my blood, I offer my life into your safekeeping."

I felt Max slide the knife across my skin as I mimicked his words. There was no pain and I glanced up to Gabriel and knew he blocked the pain for me somehow. He looked down at me and winked as I continued.

"By taking your blood, I accept the offer of your life. Our blood blends, mixes and changes us. It creates one life in the place of two. We shall become one new, complete being with one heart and one soul. Together we are one. I have chosen Gabriel Lucian LeBlanc."

Max released my hand, turned to Gabriel and raised his brow. Gabriel extended his arm without hesitation, turned his large hand palm up and began to recite the ritual words.

"My blood to your blood. With the gift of my blood, I offer my life into your safekeeping," repeated his friend's words as Max dragged the knife blade across the palm of his hand.

Max took our hands and pressed the wounds together then bound them tightly with a beautiful, gold trimmed emerald cloth.

"By taking your blood, I accept the offer of your life. Our blood blends, mixes and changes us. It creates one life in the place of two. We shall become one new, complete being with one heart and one soul. Together we are one. I have chosen Alicia Marie Chalmers."

My eyes glazed over as his blood mixed with mine. Something happened when his blood flowed into my body. I tensed when I thought about how revenants became the way they were.

Never fear, my heart. You will not become my servant. A revenant consumes the blood of the vampire. The change is not the same for them. They drank vampire blood as humans. You will not consume my blood as a human.

He gazed into my eyes with such love that it brought tears to my eyes. I stared down at our hands, tied together with the green silken scarf and whimpered when a strange burning sensation traveled up my arm. His blood felt like lava flowing through my veins. I looked up at him and giggled drunkenly just as my legs turned to mush.

Gabriel lifted me easily with one arm. "Wrap your legs around my waist, Alicia. I do not want to drop you."

I giggled again. "You wouldn't dare drop me, you goon." I wrapped my free arm around his neck and my legs around his waist, then blew a raspberry against his neck. "When do I get to open doors with a look?" I asked, trying to give him the same completely serious look he always had when he did his tricks.

"You're going to have a time with her," Max said with a laugh and turned to leave the room. He gave Gabriel a meaningful glance. "I shall be gone all evening, old friend. My house is your house."

"I thank you." Gabriel smiled in his direction before turning his attention back to me. "What am I going to do with you?" He leaned down to kiss my neck.

Little slivers of desire shot through my blood, mixing with the potent addition of Gabriel's life force flowing through me.

My nether parts pulsed with need as he turned his attention solely on me.

"I love you, Alicia. Have I told you that today?"

I shook my head, still high from the mixture of his blood with mine. His blood was like an amphetamine to my system, giving me boundless energy. I practically glowed with his power.

"Your power now, my love. It is your power. You will have to come to terms with it, learn to control it. Otherwise it will control you."

I blinked down at our bound hands. "Hey! Why did he tie us together? Lemmie go." My words began to slur as the heady effects of our handfasting began to take effect.

"I cannot untie the cloth. It will remove itself once the ritual is complete."

I pulled back to look into his eyes and was mesmerized by his rapt attention. I licked my lips, suddenly nervous when I realized my precarious position.

My nether parts rubbed against his hard shaft and I ground myself against him, seeking relief. I lowered my head to his, pressed our lips together and moaned.

"God, you taste good," I panted against his cheek, then laved his ear.

"I could say the same of you," he growled. He turned his head and captured my mouth, suckling my tongue when I opened for him.

My desire for him had reached new heights. I couldn't wait to have him naked and on top of me. The picture of us writhing naked on the bed flashed through my mind and suddenly we were there. His hard cock pressed against my stomach as he lay between my spread thighs.

"No fair using vampire magic on me."

"No fair teasing my imagination with such thoughts," he said in retaliation. "Your wish is my command, my lady."

"I didn't wish for nothin'," I denied.

"Perhaps not, but you wanted this. You cannot deny it."

My breath came in short gasps as he rubbed his body against mine like a cat. I gulped air as his hands slowly caressed my breasts. He dipped his head, laving the hardened tips with the rough velvet rasp of his tongue.

The fingers of my free hand tunneled through his hair. I pulled his head to me, reveling in the sensation of his lips on my skin and the silk of his hair on my body.

Lacing the fingers of our bound hands, he grasped my hand tight, assuring our bond. Our blood flowed freely between us and suddenly, I knew everything there was to know of my husband.

He hadn't lied to me about his age. He was present at the crusades. Memories of an obscure King named Arthur flooded my mind. In Arthur's fabled castle, Gabriel passed a highly polished silver plate hanging on the wall. He turned, looked at himself with a tortured expression. His distorted reflection showed wealth and stature, yet he still walked alone.

Opening my eyes, I gazed up into his eyes. He pulled away to look at me. I pushed the hair from his face and smiled softly.

"I'm sorry you had to spend so much time alone." I searched his gaze. He didn't blame me, though he should.

He kissed me again, his teeth gently nibbling at my lips. His tongue swept into my mouth, the faint mint flavor that always seemed to be on his lips was intoxicating.

My tongue brushed against his, invited him deeper within the recesses of my mouth. He groaned against my lips and I reveled in the fact that I had such an effect of him.

He moved his lips lower, to my neck and nipped at the sensitive skin there. His hand skimmed over my shoulder, trailed down my back and slid around under my breast.

I arched into him with a moan, encouraging him to pay homage to the diamond hard nipple perched atop the swollen flesh. He stepped back, looked into my eyes and threaded his fingers through my hair. His fingers tightened in my hair. He tipped my head back and trailed his lips over the sensitive flesh of my neck, where he had bitten me. The spot tingled and burned, causing my nipples to tighten to the point of pain.

My womb clenched and I waited for the pain that would give way to a pleasure-pain I would be barely able to stand.

"Please," I whimpered as he tortured my needy flesh. My heart slammed in my chest and my breath came in short gasps.

"I would worship you," he breathed against my breast. His tongue lapped my nipple and I squirmed beneath his ministrations.

"Finally," I groaned. My free hand fisted in his hair, held him to my breast as he suckled like a babe.

His cock pressed impatiently against my lower abdomen, the sensation of his muscular thighs between my legs made my nether parts weep with need. I'd never been so turned on in my life.

"Gabriel," my cry, a mixture of overwhelming need and desperation must have finally broken through the sensual fog I sensed in his mind.

He lifted his head to gaze down into my eyes. His bright aura surrounded us, a veritable rainbow of color filled with sparkling starbursts. His eyes were aglow with that same strange iridescent orange-red that I had come to recognize as an indication of the physical or sexual hunger of his kind.

Our kind now, my love, he growled into my mind.

Shifting his hips, he thrust himself deep inside me and I screamed my nearly instant climax to the heavens.

He moved slowly, his cock gliding in and out of my moist channel as he gazed into my eyes. I raised my hips to meet his, in an attempt to get him to move faster.

He watched me, his eyes glowing with a feral light that both frightened and exhilarated me. His face, a tight mask of need, told me exactly how hard won his iron control really was.

Another, more intense, orgasm built inside me. My muscles tightened involuntarily as I reached for the ultimate pleasure.

My whole body clenched as I waited for those few precious seconds of paradise.

I heard my own piercing scream as Gabriel buried his teeth in my breast. He finally gave in to the urge to pound into me with abandon. I didn't want this orgasm to ever end.

When my incisors lengthened, I gasped and covered my mouth with my hand. The change that went through my body made me suddenly aware of the rapid beat of Gabriel's heart and the blood that rushed through his veins.

He swiped his tongue across the tiny wound on my breast and lifted his head to look into my eyes.

"You have no idea how long I've waited. How many times I've dreamt of seeing that wonderful glow in your eyes, my love."

Gabriel lowered his head to press his mouth against mine. I could still taste my blood upon his lips. The flavor was unlike anything I ever tasted before in my life. I expected it to taste metallic, abhorrent. I never dreamed it would be so spicy, so addicting. I licked my lips when he lifted his head and wondered what he tasted like and my whole body clenched with a new need.

Hunger.

He pulled away, his free hand cupped the back of my head and pressed my face into the crook of his neck.

"Bite me," he whispered into my ear, his mind touched mine and added a slight compulsion. He wanted to be sure that I would feed. Please, Alicia."

I opened my mouth, kissed his neck and slowly laved a trail down over his chest. Finding his pulse, I lapped at his spectacular pecs and flicked his flat nipple with my tongue. My tongue swirled over his pulse and I felt him grow larger within me.

"Now, Alicia. Please. Before I die." He rammed inside me, his entire body tense with the need to climax.

Finally, I gave in to both our needs and sank my teeth deep into the flesh of his chest, just over his heart. Blood flowed into my mouth. I hate to admit it, but it was delicious. It was the most wonderfully addicting thing I ever tasted. Impossibly, Gabriel grew even thicker within me. His engorged member stroked me in places I never knew existed.

"Wrap your legs around my waist," he groaned into my hair.

After I did as he instructed, he slammed himself inside me as he came. His semen sprayed into me in hot jets as the sound of his guttural groan filled the room.

My vagina tightened around him, my own climax milking his shaft as he collapsed over me, holding his weight on his elbows.

I reached up, cupped his cheek and noticed that our hands were free.

"That...that was amazing." I squirmed beneath him as his cock began to grow again and pressed against my nether parts.

He smiled down into my eyes and for the first time, looked truly happy. The lines that had formed around his mouth and eyes began to ease.

Tentatively, I touched his mind and was surprised to find that he had never been so happy, relaxed or sated in his life.

He dipped his head to kiss me. "We must go. We cannot stay here indefinitely."

"I — I don't think I *can* go anywhere yet," I said as a debilitating lethargy stole over me. My eyelids grew heavy and my hand fell from his cheek to lay limp on the bed at my side.

"I'm just so tired..." I'm not sure, but I think my words slurred as I drifted off to sleep.

I woke to the comforting sound of my husband's steady heartbeat beneath my cheek, four hours after our handfasting.

He squeezed me and kissed me on the top of my head. "We must leave this place. I do not wish to draw these people to Max's home."

I started to sit up. "I don't either," I said, chewing on my lower lip. Tears burned my eyes as I wondered if those monsters would ever leave me alone.

Gabriel drew me into his arms. "They will soon learn that you are now under my protection and will remain so, despite their efforts."

His hands traced soothing circles on my back as he held me close. I snuggled into his embrace, uncaring that he had peered into my mind again. I could do that to him now and I would at the first opportunity. Sometimes it was confusing, trying to figure out whose thoughts were dancing around inside my head.

He pulled away and gave me a smile. It amazed me, how I could still go weak at the knees just by watching the man grin.

"Time for lesson one, my love."

"Huh?"

"Your first lesson will be dressing yourself." His knowledge poured into my mind and I suddenly understood how to dress myself in the way of his people.

"Our people," he whispered in my ear. "You are one of us now."

"Yes, I suppose I am." I clothed myself with a thought, conjuring up something I had seen in a magazine but could never afford. Then as practice, I clothed him. Well, sort of.

He looked down, then back up at me, his eyebrows almost reaching his hairline.

"I'm a grown man, Alicia. What are you thinking, dressing me in children's underwear?"

CHAPTER TWENTY-THREE

H E DID A DOUBLE TAKE.

"I stand corrected, a thong with an elephant's face." He frowned, reached down and grabbed the limp material of the trunk, looked at me then raised his brow.

"I like it," I replied, circling around him to get a better look at his wonderfully muscled ass and imagined his cock filling out that extra bit of material.

Giving in to temptation, I ran the palms of my hands over his perfectly shaped cheeks and squeezed, raking my nails lightly over his flesh.

He sucked a breath between his teeth with an audible hiss.

"Why an elephant?" He looked down at himself then blushed. "Do you think me a child?"

"Of course not," I grinned. "I just wanted to watch the trunk grow." I looked down and watched with a wide grin as the trunk began to rise and his cock filled out that extra bit of material.

"I hate to be the one to bring this up, but we cannot stay here and play," Gabriel said, clothing himself with a growl.

"So," I said, flicking my gaze to his crotch. "Did you ditch the underwear or are you still wearing them?"

He gave me an enigmatic smile and winked.

"Maybe."

"Maybe, what? Maybe you're wearing them or maybe you've ditched them?" I gave him a little smack on his arm, just because I could, and stuck my tongue out at him. "You're a tease. You know that don't you?"

He chuckled, pulled me to him and gave me a quick kiss.

"We really must go. I'm beginning to get a bad feeling about remaining here."

I sighed. "Me, too. One of these days we will be able to settle down and have a normal life, won't we?"

He took my hand in his and kissed it. He led me out of Max's penthouse apartment, leading me to the roof of the building and then pulled me into his arms. Lifting my chin, he searched my eyes.

"We must leave here in a manner that may be disturbing to you. Do you wish me to compel you?"

I opened my eyes wide and stared at him. "Why didn't you compel me the other day when you turned into that giant, slimy, scale covered puke-green dragon, lizard boy?"

Did that mean that he could have saved me all that fear and anxiety I felt the other night? I didn't know whether to be pissed or laugh that he didn't automatically think of me as some shrinking violet that needed protection from the world.

"Lizard boy?" he asked, cocking that damnable eyebrow at me again. I know he knows I think it's unbearably sexy, the jerk.

"Yeah," I snapped. "Lizard boy." I fisted my hands and rested them on my hips. "Wanna make something of it?"

He took a deep breath and exhaled slowly through his nose. I'm not sure, but I think he counted to ten.

"You never cease to amaze me, woman," he replied, shaking his head. "I didn't compel you the other day because I was too weak to do so. Remember my excessive blood loss from that bullet wound?"

My gaze darted to his chest, and my fingers itched to examine the place of his wound again, just to be sure it had thoroughly healed.

"Of course I remember it. It scared the living hell out of me."

It had. He looked so weak, so pale...and gray.

"Wait a minute." I stepped away from him, shaking my head. "You don't expect me to turn into a—a dragon, do you?"

I almost collapsed with relief when he shook his head. Of course he didn't. How could I do such an unbelievable thing?

"For now you are correct. You cannot change into a dragon. Yet. Becoming a dragon is much too advanced for a neophyte such as yourself. Today, we will try a simple mist. Changing one's shape requires that you alter your molecular structure by breaking it down to its most basic composition and reassembling it almost simultaneously."

"Huh?"

He laughed and merged his mind with mine to help me break down my molecular structure to mist.

This is so weird. I projected the words because I no longer had a mouth or vocal chords.

Gabriel's soothing presence in my mind kept me calm. I took the time to look around. It was strange. I had no eyes, yet I could 'see' everything around me.

Are you ready?

As ready as I'll ever be, I guess. I glanced to my left, where Gabriel had stood only moments before. A patch of fog hovered three or four feet off the roof of the building.

Visualize yourself moving forward and you shall.

He merged his mind fully with mine to help me propel myself forward.

My gaze darted nervously downward.

I won't—

I tried to lick my lips. They felt horribly dry. I giggled a bit hysterically when I realized I couldn't because I had no lips in this form.

I won't fall out of the sky to go crashing to my death if I lose my concentration, will I?

I felt my husband's arms slide around me. His cheek pressed against mine. It was a strange sensation, considering the fact that I had no body.

You needn't worry, Alicia. The worst that will happen if you lose concentration is you will no longer continue to move forward. You will simply drift gently through the air until you regain control of your thoughts.

Well, that was a relief, sort of. I didn't want to drift aimlessly through the air either.

You need not worry, little one. I would never allow that.

You have *seen Cassie and me together, haven't you? She's the little one, not me. I'm huge, compared to her.*

He chuckled. *You are still small compared to me. You will always be my little one.*

I rolled my nonexistent eyes. *Puhleeze!* I used one of Tasha's favorite sayings. *A football player would be small compared to you, Goliath.*

You just like calling me that because of the size of my—

Hey!

My first instinct was to give him a good smack on the arm, but with no corporeal being, all I could do was sputter ineffectually.

Creep.

That does not keep you from loving me.

341

I didn't answer that. Besides, he knew I did. *Where are we going?*

I hope some place safe.

He held the visualization of our forward movement in my mind and we traveled west over the lake toward Chicago.

I was exhausted by the time we reached the other side. That insidious thirst began to eat at me halfway across the lake. He grew worried for me. I knew he did. I caught a glimmer of something in his mind about my being stuck like this until I starved to death if he didn't feed me soon, but the thought was gone, almost as soon as I'd discovered it and I wasn't sure if it was my imagination or if I'd actually sensed his concern.

I would have collapsed when we finally reached our destination. Gabriel shifted back into human form, his mind still fully merged with mine. He looked at me, somehow knowing exactly where to look to give the illusion of staring into my eyes.

"This is Micah's sister's place," he said, indicating the door behind him. "Now, visualize yourself human again, Alicia. I shall help you."

I put every bit of my lagging energy into changing back to my corporeal state. The mist around me swirled and contorted, changing into weird shapes as I put forth the effort to regain my old self.

When I finally succeeded in reclaiming my body, I collapsed into my husband's arms.

"You must feed."

His words reminded me of that terrible craving, the horrible hunger that crawled through my body, demanding blood.

Suddenly, I was aware of the steady beat of his heart, the blood rushing through his veins and the agonizing fire that scorched my insides. My whole body burned with the need to feed, to sink my teeth into his neck and drink until there was nothing left.

I pushed away from him and covered my mouth with my hand.

"My God, Gabriel, I can't control this. How can I live, with you, with anyone if I can't control myself?" I looked up at him horrified. "Changing me has turned me into some ravening beast, just waiting to suck the life from you!" My hand muffled my words and tears streaked down my face. I dashed them away and turned away from him, away from temptation. He smelled so good. His blood called to me. The strong, steady beat of his heart promised me nourishment.

Grabbing me by the arm, he turned me to him and pushed his fingers through my hair. He fisted his hand at the nape of my neck and tipped my head back to look into my eyes.

"You will feed, Alicia."

His compulsion was too strong for me to resist. I felt myself leaning forward, my mouth opened and I sank my teeth into his neck. Thick, rich blood flowed into my mouth and I swallowed it greedily. My mind, horrified at what I did, tried to make my body reject it. I wanted to stop, to spit it out but my starved body would not allow it.

Soon, the debilitating hunger subsided and Gabriel released me from his compulsion. I felt him growing weaker as I fed, and found the strength to pull away before I killed him.

"You could never hurt me, my love," he said as I closed the small wound in his neck and wiped my hands over my mouth disgusted.

"As a *Cartuotey*, I have trained those changed, like you, to feed without killing their prey." *You are but a child compared to me. Do not worry that you could ever hurt me.*

"Prey," I almost stuttered the word. "Is that what every human is to me now? Are they nothing more than prey to be fed on, used for blood and—and sex?"

He growled low and his eyes started to glow. "You will never use a human for sex."

I pushed my hands through my hair. Of course, I wouldn't. He should know that. What the hell was wrong with him?

"Look, I certainly don't need to deal with your jealousies now," I said, trying to ignore the fact that the hunger, the need, that had been so all-encompassing just a few minutes ago was just a dull ache in my middle. I wasn't starving any more, but I still wasn't at full strength and neither was he.

"You need to feed, you're gray."

"There will be blood inside."

He indicated the building behind him again and I gave it a glance.

I felt my eyes widen as I finally noticed the building. A large sign over the door proclaimed that we stood in front of the Blue Moon Café. The huge building, an ancient three story colonial was painted dark gray.

I was surprised I could tell that in the weak light from the streetlamp. The light blue moon mural painted on the front of the building glowed bright in the dark, surrounded by small glowing dots that must be stars. I stared at it for a while, rapt.

"The artist was certainly talented, wasn't he?"

A man's face grinned happily from the center of the moon. It wasn't easily visible, one had to study the mural to see it.

"Welcome to the Blue Moon, where everyone with good in their hearts is welcome." I turned to Gabriel. "What does that mean?"

"It is a message to our kind. We may enter without invitation during these hours—" he pointed to another sign below the one I read. "—as long as we have no intention of harming anyone."

"Are you saying a vampire really can't enter someone's home without an invitation?"

"Yes. That is one of only a few of the old wife's tales that is accurate." He lifted the corner of his mouth. "Amazingly accurate as it turns out. That is why so many Rogues have revenants to do their dirty work. They have similar strength and longevity, but do not have to abide by many of the rules."

"Mmmmm..." What was I supposed to say, *yippee*? It's not as though I'm a match for even a revenant. They proved that at the mall.

"You are more than a match for them now, my love. You are no longer human. *Cartuotey* blood runs through your veins. You would be surprised to find just how strong you have become."

He reached past me and rang the bell for the upper stories. I didn't see the little button there, until he pressed it.

"Yes?"

The disembodied male voice came from the speaker beneath the doorbell.

"Damien? It's Gabriel."

"Gabriel LeBlanc? Wait a minute, I'll be right down."

He wrapped his arms around me and drew me close. I snuggled within his embrace, glad for the warmth that seeped into my body from his. I pressed my nose to his chest and inhaled deeply. He always smelled so good.

The door opened behind me and Gabriel pushed me to the side, ever mindful of my safety. For some reason, he didn't want me facing the person who answered this door.

"Old friend." The man bowed his head and grasped my husband's forearms in some sort of ritual fashion. "Please, come in."

I stared at the interior in rapt fascination as we entered the small restaurant. The tables and chairs sat arranged in arcs. They resembled half moons. Several round tables, which I'm sure, were supposed to represent full moons sat in the corners of the large room. A dark blue ceiling held fiber-optic stars that, even now, twinkled merrily.

I glanced at the clock. It was three in the morning. I know I would be royally pissed if someone woke me up that early but the man just stood grinning at us as I literally gawked at the whimsically decorated café.

A woman stepped up beside the man whom I assumed was Richard. She was tall. I would guess, at least six feet. She wrapped her arm around the man's waist with a smile.

"No matter how many times it happens, I never tire of seeing a person's first reaction to the Blue Moon." She smiled and offered me her hand. "I'm Elisabeth. Welcome to our home."

I stared at the beautiful woman. Her ebony hair fell around her shoulders in long waves, the ends brushing her waist. Large sky blue eyes dominated her heart-shaped face and naturally red lips framed perfectly shaped white teeth.

"Thank you," I said, barely able to keep myself from stuttering.

The woman's beauty and bearing made me think I must be in the presence of some sort of royalty. Vampire royalty. Was there even such a thing?

"Elisabeth, Richard, I would have you meet my wife, Alicia."

The woman smiled easily and stared deep into my eyes for a moment. "I see you have already chosen." She turned to Gabriel. "I was sure I would be asked to perform the ritual for you as I did for my brother."

"Alicia's safety was at risk. Besides," he said with a smile. "I did keep it in the family. Max bound us together."

"Max? He's back from Europe and didn't call me?" Her eyes narrowed and she thinned her lips. "I'm going to have to have a talk with that man."

Gabriel gave her an enigmatic look. "I think he may need some space right now. I have a feeling he'll be searching you or Micah out soon enough." He looked puzzled for a moment as if he were searching for the right words. "His scent is different lately. I wonder if he's found his mate."

Elisabeth jumped up and down excitedly and clapped her hands.

"Oh, I hope so. He's been searching for so long. He hasn't found his mate once, you know. It'll kill him if she turns him down."

She turned and led us further into the building. "Why don't we carry on with this conversation upstairs where I can get you some nourishment?"

Richard began to close the door behind us when a loud crash rent the door in two and it burst inward. Wood flew everywhere, splinters embedded in my arms and my husband growled, promising retribution to the source of my pain.

The force of another blast threw him back into one of the beautiful round tables and it shattered beneath him. Four men rushed through the door. Two of them headed straight for Richard and Gabriel, the other two set their sights on Elisabeth and me.

"Take my hand!" Elisabeth screamed over the horrible grumbling of the revenants that followed the rogues through the door.

I did as she asked, following her as she pulled me back to an open elevator and closed the doors. She pushed the down button and we descended to the basement where we would be closer to the earth.

"We must open a portal and get help."

I agreed. Yet I was hesitant to do so. The last time I opened a portal under duress it tore a ragged hole between our dimension and the next. It almost killed Tasha and me to close it.

Something upstairs crashed and a revenant screamed out his frustration at the locked elevator door.

"It won't take them long to find the stairs," Elisabeth said as she led me through the surprisingly organized basement into a dark little room. She moved a bookcase aside and a door appeared behind it. We hurried through, closing the door behind us.

We stood huddled together in an even smaller room. It was empty, except for a table, two chairs and one small cot.

She took my hands in hers. "Visualize the portal opening right here, in this room. Don't think about those beasts out there," She said, nodding toward the hidden door. "Think about daisies, black-eyed Susans, roses any flower you can think of."

"Red and white roses they were Grandmother and Aunt Mag's favorites." Since I saw and smelled them every week for the last several months, those would be the easiest to visualize.

She smiled softly. "And your favorite?"

"The peach colored rose, commonly referred to as peace." Well, those and daisies, but the roses would be easier to visualize as they were the last flowers I'd gotten.

"Wonderful choices." She pulled me away from the door. "Now take my hands and think of those flowers. Visualize a door opening in the ground, right here beside us. It will be a door in the wall, over there." She pointed to my right. "It's filled with your favorite flowers. Do you think you can do it?"

"Yes." I nodded and closed my eyes. I would trust her, after all, her husband was upstairs taking a beating, too.

I cleared my mind of all its clutter and visualized the portal opening, filled with all of my favorite blooms.

Suddenly, a large, hole appeared in the wall and a giant of a man jumped out of the portal. Not just any man. Power seeped from his pores. His skin actually glowed with the energy stored within him. Soon, another appeared and another until four tall, muscular men, good-looking enough to die for, stood in Elisabeth's basement.

Chapter Twenty-four

THEIR AURAS AMAZED ME. THEY WERE MUCH LIKE THE AURA OF A
Cartuotey, but it was more. Kind of like a *Cartuotey* on steroids. Energy
snapped and cracked around their tall, muscular forms. Starbursts erupted
into small explosions and fizzled like children's sparklers around them.

Wide eyed, they looked at each other, then bent forward, took deep
breaths and grinned before they knelt before us. "We come to do your
bidding, mistresses."

I'm not even going to go there.

See that you do not, Gabriel grumbled into my mind.

I blew him a mental raspberry. *You should know better than that.*

He was immediately contrite, but the emotion cost him dearly. By
distracting him, I had given his enemy the opportunity to strike him.

I cut him off from my mind and turned to the group of men before me.
They were dressed in some sort of strange armor and all held strange-looking
weapons, some sort of laser swords that reminded me of the movies.

"We need your protection," Elisabeth said, indicating the door the
revenants were attempting to open. "Our mates are out there protecting us.
They are only two against many. That is how you will know them."

They nodded, stood and formed a column to file through the door when
Elisabeth opened it. She stopped with her hand on the door and turned to
them.

"Please be careful." She glanced at me. "We do not want any of you to lose
your lives. Our greatest wish is that you all return to your families safely."

They looked back at us, their faces blank.

"We have no families, mistress. You are the first women that we have seen
in a thousand years."

"How have you survived so long with no women?"

He paused. "We have...synthesized everything for our needs. Our world is
otherwise bountiful."

"What a shame," Elisabeth mumbled, shaking her head. "Looking like that, no women, no sex. What a waste."

With that said, the inter-dimensional soldiers burst through the door and cut down the revenants standing there. The monsters squealed in pain as they died. A part of me felt sorry for them. Another part felt they got what they deserved. The revenants were men who wanted to be vampires for the power it would give them.

In my opinion, they deserved everything they got.

I turned to Elisabeth. She stood near the portal watching it suspiciously.

"What's the matter?"

"We must stand guard over the open portal. Do not think that because we found decent soldiers that we are safe. We must stop other entities from gaining access to this world." She gave me a solemn look. "They were fighting something on their world."

"Oh, my God. You're right. I didn't think about that." I cast a quick glance back to the door. "And the kind of weapons they had..." I looked up at her, scared. "Maybe we should just close the portal."

She shook her head. "It wouldn't be fair to them, Alicia. We couldn't be sure that we would send them back where they belong. You could reopen the portal on a totally different dimension."

Damn! I knew the woman was right, but that didn't mean I had to like it.

"You're a Guide. Why don't you put an energy gate over it? A gate that would remain open on this side, but locked on the other."

"What's an energy gate?"

She sighed and shook her head. "How long have you known you were a Guide, sweetheart?"

"All of my life, but Grandma and Aunt Maggie would never allow me to learn to use my powers. They thought if I didn't know how to open a portal, I couldn't get myself into trouble with it."

She nodded. "I see." She glanced back at the hole in the wall of the basement regularly, as if waiting for something. "Who taught you to open a portal?"

"No one. Tasha was teaching me to close them, but no one has ever taught me how to open a gate. I don't think Tasha even knows how."

"You do." She looked meaningfully at the entrance to another dimension in her basement wall.

I shook my head. "I didn't do that. You did."

She gave me a wan smile, wrapped her arm around my shoulder and spoke to me as if I were a slow child.

"I can't open a gate, Alicia. I was born a *Cartuotey*, like my brother." She shrugged. "I know a bit about it. Shay, one of our good friends, told me how she finds help when she needs it. That is the only reason I told you to visualize your favorite flower."

She glanced back toward the opening that led to the main section of the basement.

"Though, I must tell you, your soldiers are much larger and much better looking than hers. They almost look like..." She shook her head. "Let's just hope they are at least as effective as the one's Shay conjures up." She smiled. "It makes me wonder what type of flowers are her favorites."

I took a deep breath. "Dammit! I refuse to hide down here while Gabriel and Richard fight for their lives upstairs. I'm going up there."

Besides, I had a moral obligation to the soldiers I brought over from the other side as well. They didn't ask to come here. They were compelled to follow my orders since I'm the one who opened the gate.

I visualized a sparkling field of pure energy settling itself over the hole in the wall. Energy from the other side popped and cracked as I fitted it over the portal.

Elisabeth reached out and put her hand against it, testing it.

"It looks good."

"Yeah, well it's the best I can do." I turned for the entrance to the small room. "I'm outta here. I'm going back upstairs to watch my husband's back."

"Richard is doing that. You needn't worry."

I turned to her with a frown. "Can you say you're not worried?"

She shook her head. "No, I'm afraid I cannot."

Elisabeth followed me back up the stairs and gasped when we entered the kitchen. It looked like a tornado hit it. Pots and pans lay smashed on the floor. Two dead rogues bled copious amounts of blood all over the expensive Italian tile. One of the huge refrigerators stood opened, the door ripped from its hinges. Food was everywhere.

We followed a trail of blood through the kitchen and out through the hall to find a wounded soldier on his back just outside the dining area.

"Go, I'm dying anyway." He waved us away.

A loud crash had us rushing up the stairs to the second floor to see how our husbands fared through this battle.

We found our borrowed warriors on the second floor, the rogues outnumbered them two to one, yet they fought as though it was nothing.

"Where are Gabriel and Richard?" Elisabeth called over the clash of armor and the sizzling sounds their weapons made.

One of the rogues zigged when he should have zagged and a glowing weapon cut him in two. I gagged. The rancid smell of burning flesh and rotted meat filled the room.

Elisabeth made a face. "Man, they stink!"

"One down, five to go," I breathed disgusted. I grasped Elisabeth by the arm.

"I'm sorry they're tearing your home and restaurant apart."

"Why are you apologizing? It's not your fault."

I nodded. "Yes, it is. They followed us here. They've been trying to kidnap me."

"That is a choice the rogues make. It is a choice the men who become revenants make. They choose to be what they are, regardless of the consequences. We just bring them justice."

We tiptoed up another flight of stairs to the third floor. We still hadn't found our husbands. I reached out with my senses, trying to find Gabriel through our mind link. He blocked me.

"Dammit! He's blocking me. He won't let me find him through our link."

"Of course he won't. He doesn't want you in any danger, just as Richard doesn't want me in danger."

At the top of the stairs, she continued down the hall.

"I don't think they're up here."

"Me either," I said with a frown. "The only other place I can think of is—"

"The parking lot," Elisabeth said with a gasp as she stared through a window, a horrified look on her face.

I joined her at the window and stared through the glass at our husbands facing down three rogues and an incomprehensible amount of revenants.

"Shit. How many do you think they're up against?"

"I can't count them, they're moving around too much. I see at least twelve or thirteen."

Gabriel, using his vampire talents, zipped up behind a rogue who jumped on Richard's back. He drove his fist forward, ripping its heart out just before the creature sank its teeth into the other man's neck.

It fell to the ground, writhing and bucking, its body in the throes of death as Gabriel grimaced and threw the shriveling heart on the ground.

He turned to a rogue, bared his teeth and snarled. His eyes grew red, glowing from within as he inhaled, gathered energy about him and sent a huge glowing ball of blue light into the head of the nearest rogue.

I felt my eyes widen and my mouth fall open as we watched our husbands work together.

Facing each other, they placed their hands together. Their combined energy built a ball of pure white light that surrounded them like a circle. The ball grew larger, encompassing their enemies. The rogues and revenants fell to the ground as their bodies jerked and twitched.

The light grew incredibly bright and several small explosions caused starbursts near the rogues.

No. Not near the rogues. Dust fell from the colorful explosions leaving the two touching *Cartuotey* behind. The explosions weren't near the rogues and revenants. They *were* the rogues and revenants.

Gabriel and Richard were the only two left in the circle. There was absolutely nothing left of their enemies.

I stared into Elisabeth's wide eyes.

"Did you know they could do that?"

She shook her head. "I was just about to ask you the same thing. Richard never once mentioned that he could do anything like that."

I swallowed thickly. The power our husbands possessed was immense.

"It's a good thing they're the good guys, huh?"

She nodded, obviously still stunned.

I looked down at the floor, and then my gaze tracked over the room. "Your house..."

She shrugged. "It's just a house. We have others."

"But your beautiful restaurant, it's destroyed."

Again, she shrugged, a tear tracking down her face.

"It was time for us to move on anyway." She looked into my eyes. "That is only one of our curses." She continued at my questioning look. "We cannot stay in one place too long. People have the most horrible manners. They begin to notice you don't age."

She smiled wanly, picked up a broken picture frame up off the floor. It was Elisabeth and Richard, only the picture was old, very old. Taken in the late eighteenth or early nineteenth century, the manner of dress and the cobblestone streets behind them gave them away.

"Who is the woman beside you?"

"She was my best friend. Her name was Mathilda." Her tears ran freely as she wiped debris from the face of her friend, heedless of the broken glass. "She was a Guide, but she never found her mate. She died at the hands of a rogue."

She turned to me, her eyes reflecting her pain. "So, you see, there is still the pain of loss."

"Yes, there is." I placed my hand on her arm. "I'll never forget Aunt Mags or Grandmother. They saved my life at the cost of theirs. I will always grieve for them, just as you will grieve for her."

Suddenly, somehow the circumstances of Mathilda's death surged into my mind. Normally, I'm not psychic, yet I *knew* beyond any doubt how her death came about. For once, I was in a position to give comfort instead of take it.

"It was her choice you know."

"What?" Elisabeth asked absently as her thumb stroked lovingly over the sepia toned photograph.

"She chose to give her life in exchange for yours. It wasn't your fault."

"How—how did you..."

I shrugged. "Hell, I don't know how I know half the things I do nowadays. Maybe I'm becoming psychic or something."

It beats the shit out of seeing auras. I still have that useless talent, but since I'm getting used to it, I don't notice it so much anymore.

"Just take my word for it. She knew what she was doing. Just as my aunt and grandma knew what they were doing. They loved us and made the ultimate sacrifice for us. What we do with that gift is a reflection of our love for them."

Where in the hell was this coming from?

A golden light glowed softly over her left shoulder. I couldn't see anyone there, but if I had to guess, I would guess it was Elisabeth's best friend.

Tell her I love her. Tell her I would die for her again.

The light grew closer surrounded Elisabeth in a soft glow.

She does not know the babe she carries has no soul. It is dying. I can save it. Tell her I love her.

I got the impression of a soft smile. As the light shrank, and hovered over Elisabeth's flat stomach.

One other thing, tell her not *to name me Mathilda.* She said the rest with a laugh as the light disappeared into Elisabeth's middle.

Warmth surrounded me as Gabriel's mind touched mine. He shared my experience with Richard who in turned shared it with his mate.

Elisabeth collapsed to the floor, holding the photo of her friend over her heart. Tears streamed over her beautiful face, dropping onto the sepia toned photo in her hands.

"That was her voice. You couldn't know I was pregnant and you couldn't know her voice. She actually spoke through you," she sobbed.

"And she still loves you, my love. Enough to die for you, and it seems, enough to live for you once again."

Richard and Gabriel strode through the debris and gathered us into their arms.

"Your work is not yet done, mate," Gabriel breathed into my ear. "You still have a gate to close and a few friends to send home."

"You're right. I do." I frowned and pushed shaking fingers through my hair. "What about the wounded one?"

"He cannot go home. Those who are wounded so badly in battle would not survive the trip."

"Umm...what do we do with him? We can't just leave him to die."

"No we cannot. Someone who can help is already on the way. I got word of it while you were sleeping. However, we must send the others home and close the portal."

I gazed up into his eyes and threaded my fingers through his hair.

"You look gray. You need to feed."

"As do you. Perhaps your friends would oblige."

I felt bad asking them after all they had done, but we did all need to feed. We had expended a copious amount of energy fighting those monsters and I would need more before I could send the men back to where they belonged.

I let him lead me back down the stairs and we asked the three remaining men if they would mind donating a little blood.

It was strange watching Gabriel take a long deep breath around them. He wanted to make sure their blood wouldn't harm us. He nodded and I turned to them to make our request.

"We need to feed. Would you object to our taking of your blood? Just a small amount, I assure you," I added when their eyes widened.

"If it pleases you, mistress."

Our husbands stepped forward, each of them grasping a warrior by the upper arms. Then, obviously thinking better of what they were about to do, they each brought a thick wrist to their mouths and pierced the men's skin.

Gabriel looked strange when he closed the wound and lifted his head.

"What are you?"

"We are the Sun Warriors of *Cartuotain,* those who still search for the birthplace of our mates. Are you the missing tribe?"

Gabriel answered the man's formal bow with one of his own before they shook hands in that strange way all *Cartuotey* did.

"I do believe we are."

Elisabeth stepped through the rubble that was once her home and approached her husband.

"Come on, we need to get these men back through that portal so Alicia can close it."

She started toward the basement, and then turned to look at each of us in turn before her gaze rested on the three Sun Warriors.

"Aren't you coming?"

The three men looked at each other.

"No," they said in unison.

One of them stepped forward, his black eyes glowing with intensity.

"We refuse. You cannot force us to return to that existence."

He turned and spoke to the other two men in his own language and they all nodded. "We are all in agreement. We need the softness and caring of a real woman, not the unfeeling sex of the *salimons*."

"*Salimons*?" I asked, curious. I looked from Gabriel to Richard who had suddenly become conspicuously silent.

"A *salimon*, as I recall is a...machine designed specifically for sex."

"A—a machine?"

Elisabeth nodded. "I don't remember them well, I was too young when we left to have been involved in the conversations about them, but from what I've gathered, they were invented for the men to slake their lust when the women became few."

"It's a wonder there are any of you alive. It seems like you would have died off with no way to breed."

"Longevity is our curse as well as our blessing. We can live for tens of thousands of years. But with no love, no children, what is there to live for?"

"How many of you are left?" Gabriel said as he wrapped his arm around me. *Knowing this makes me even more grateful that I have found you.*

I love you, too.

I smiled into his mind. I didn't want to flaunt our relationship in front of the others as Gabriel seemed to want to do. I realized he felt the need to stake his claim, but these men had been nothing but respectful to Elisabeth and me.

They already know we are mates.

Perhaps, but one cannot be too protective of one's mate.

I rolled my eyes at his possessiveness, even as the warmth of his love comforted me.

"So what now?" I asked. "How can they stay? They have no identity here."

"That is easily fixed," Richard said with a shrug. "I know some people in Washington who can help us with that."

"How many people do you guys have on your payroll?" I held up my hand. "Never mind. The less I know the better off I'll be."

No wonder Tasha kept saying they were going to drive her nuts. At first blush, these guys looked like normal everyday men. Well, very tall, very good looking men.

Okay, so maybe that's not very normal at all, but at least they don't have the appearance of someone who is going to have you questioning your sanity on a daily basis.

I sighed. "Either way, I have to close that portal and I may need some help. Where can we find another Guide?"

"You opened *another* portal, Alicia? Geeze. I can't leave you alone for a second, can I?"

I squealed at the sound of that familiar voice. Turning, I pulled from my husband's embrace and ran to Tasha.

"What are you doing here? I didn't expect you back so soon."

"I was told that you handfasted without me," she said with a pout. "So of course I had to hurry back here so I could read you the riot act over that." She gave me a squeeze. "But I hear that you did it for your own safety, so I guess I forgive you."

She turned, looking around at everyone in the room. "I've been told you have an injured man here. Where is he?"

Elisabeth stepped forward, gave Tasha a quick hug and said, "Follow me."

She led us back to the kitchen where the man lay so close to death. He looked up, touched my hand and smiled through his pain and weakness.

"You are real." He coughed and blood trickled from the corner of his mouth. "I am glad I came here. It is worth dying to know that a world with females still exists."

"You're not dying. Not if I have anything to say about it." Tasha reached out and placed her hand on his arm.

"Nothing can stop it now. I am too far gone. Even blood will not help me."

She snorted. "Don't you know? I am supposed to be your savior or some such nonsense. You know, the woman who has insurmountable power who is supposed to deliver our kind from evil." She made a face at the pronouncement and I put my hand over my mouth to stifle a giggle.

The others filed into the room behind us, watching as she placed both hands on the man's head and closed her eyes.

"Project to me, everyone. I don't have the power to do this on my own. He is weak. I need some help to bring him back at least far enough that he can heal himself."

I felt Gabriel push his power into me as I shared mine with her. The other newcomers stared in awe as their friend injures disappeared, healing at an accelerated rate, even for their kind.

Our kind, Gabriel whispered into my mind.

Yeah, yeah. Let me get used to it, will ya?

Micah pushed past me and took Tasha in his arms when she began to sway with weakness.

"You must feed if you are to help Alicia close the portal."

Gabriel pulled me up beside him and into his arms. "You must feed as well."

The invitation in his voice made my stomach clench with anticipation. I squirmed in his arms.

"I can't," I whispered. "Not in front of everyone."

Heat seared my cheeks as I thought about how carried away we both get when I feed.

"You must." He stared into my eyes. "Let me help you."

I nodded my assent and let him compel me.

My teeth sank deep into his neck and I drew his blood into my mouth. He tasted different somehow and I chalked it up from his feeding from the others who just came through the portal.

Thankfully, his compulsion kept my usually horny impulses at bay and I was able to feed without embarrassing myself. I closed the wound with a flick of my tongue and stepped back when he released me from his compulsion.

"We need to close that portal now," he said before brushing a kiss across my forehead.

I nodded then cleared my throat. "Yes, we do."

Epilogue

"**H**OW DID THEY TAKE THEIR SEPARATION?"

Gabriel shrugged. "It's not as though they have much choice. They know they need to learn about their new home. If they stay together, the learning will be more difficult. They know this."

"That's good." I wrapped my arms around Gabriel's waist and rested my head on his chest. "What about us? There is that little matter of the Satanists. Why won't they leave me alone?"

"They think you are the key to separating their master from his prison."

"Ha! I'm the key to separating their balls from their bodies. That's about all the key I am to them."

I loved the newfound sense of independence and power being one of The Chosen gave me. I would never feel vulnerable or weak again.

"I know you hate to leave this house. It's one of your favorites, isn't it?"

He took a deep breath and kissed the top of my head before bending slightly to rest his cheek against mine.

"It is, but never as important as you or your safety." He turned his head to kiss me.

My toes curled as his hand roamed over my back and rear. Lifting me easily in his arms, he squeezed my ass as I wrapped my legs around his waist.

Smiling, I wished our clothes away and reveled in the sensation of his hard shaft pressing against the heat of my sex.

Do it.

You are not ready.

I'm so ready, I'm about to explode, I whispered feverishly into his mind.

I didn't care about the rest. Not now. My whole life with him was foreplay. His heated looks, the soft caresses, how he held me as though I were spun glass. He pressed his lips against mine, driving his tongue into my mouth as he drove his thick erection deep into my already wet sex.

I whimpered against him knowing this was right. He was mine, just as surely as I belonged to him. I keened softly as the sensation of his mouth on my nipples drove me over the edge and I came onto him, my juices covering his hard shaft as he pistoned within my clasping vaginal walls. His cock drove deep inside me, covered with the slick evidence of my desire.

Turning, he rested my shoulders against the wall, giving himself better leverage and more control to drive even deeper inside me, and the world shattered as I came again.

"Please," I panted, leaning forward to lave his ear.

"Please what?" He rasped, his breath coming in short gasps as a line of perspiration dotted his face. His cock grew inside me, rubbing that elusive spot and I felt the beginnings of another orgasm gripping me.

He reached down to stroke my sex, his finger circling the small nubbin of nerves as it began to throb when my climax grew nearer.

"Harder," I said, droaning against his neck.

"God, you feel so good," He panted in my ear, his tongue doing magical things to my insides. Goose bumps rose on my flesh and delightful little tingles tripped up my spine as my climax overtook me.

I sank my teeth deep in the flesh just above his heart as he dropped his head to my neck, his teeth piercing my throat, just below my ear.

It was heady, like having a few drinks, energizing.

He pulsed inside me, warmth shot into my clasping channel as my muscles clenched around him. My climaxing body grew tired, boneless as he held me against the wall.

"I don't know how you do that." I kissed his chest and dropped my legs from around his waist so he could set me on my feet.

"Do what?"

"Stay standing while you're coming, like that." I stumbled a bit when he set me on my feet. "See what I mean?"

"Practice," he said with a chuckle.

"Hey! I don't want to hear that." Hell, he didn't have to know I was secretly thankful of his many talents.

"Too late. But it is good to know that you appreciate me."

I couldn't help but get that strange funny flip-flop in my stomach when he grinned at me like that.

"Oh, shut up." I stuck my tongue out at him, tempted to give him a good swat.

"We must be going. I have lived here far too long and one of our neighbors has just asked a tactless question about our age differences."

I scowled. "That's none of his business!"

He waved a hand and dressed me.

"Even so. When questions such as those arise, it is time to move on. Time to make new friends and hope we can stay put for a while. Besides, the Rogues know we live here. If we leave, it may take time for them to find us. Perhaps they will set their sights on some other poor unsuspecting victim."

"You don't really want that, do you?" I asked, aghast.

He shook his head. "No I do not, but we cannot stay here."

He gazed around the study we had holed ourselves up in, his eyes sad as he took in the homey interior.

I would miss sitting in here with him, curled up with a good book in the overstuffed chair as he worked at his desk. The fire that usually burned merrily in the fireplace was cold now, the hearth dark. Only our memories warmed the room now.

Would we ever be able to return to this house, our first home?

"Perhaps one day," he said with a nod. He held his hand out to me, palm up. "Come, it is time we moved on."

About the Author

Tianna Xander is an eclectic author of numerous paranormal, sci-fi, time travel, romance erotica books. Gaining inspiration for her characters and dialogue through her family and her addiction to the internet, she never fails to amaze readers with each new book she creates. As a reading junkie herself, Tianna has no problem reading whatever is available at the moment; from romance novels, murder mysteries and encyclopedias to books on solar energy.

Tianna's life wouldn't be complete without a "happily ever after" of her very own. She resides in Michigan with her husband, two children, three cats, two dogs and an intimidating bunny. Never one to fail to give credit where it's due, she commends her family for their constant support. After writing many books and receiving rave reviews, her family is just as proud of her. Always full of ideas, Tianna rarely puts the pen down, so readers can look forward to many more exciting stories in the future.

Tianna's web sit is located at:
http://www.tiannaxander.com

Visit www.extasybooks.com for more of Tianna's books.

The Sex Me series books 1 through 6

Children of the Triad, books 1 through 6

A Stranger in Paradise

Afraid to Dream

Edge of Ecstasy

In a Stranger's Arms

Lhampyre Yule

Seducing the Vamp

Sexy Santa Dreams

Sharing Tavia

Thor's Hammer

What to do with a Naked Leprechaun

eXtasy
books.com
explicitly exciting